JERICHO'S BOYS

PALADIN

ONLEY JAMES

PALADIN
JERICHO'S BOYS BOOK ONE

Copyright © 2023 Onley James
WWW.ONLEYJAMES.COM

Cover and Interior Design by We Got You Covered Book Design
WWW.WEGOTYOUCOVEREDBOOKDESIGN.COM

ISBN: 979-8-88992-088-5

TRIGGER WARNING

This book contains graphic descriptions of past physical and sexual abuse as well as gratuitous violence against bad people who totally deserve it.

ONE

ARSEN

ARSEN LEBEDEV SAT ON THE stoop of an abandoned building, watching the windows of the small home across the street. They'd been dark for a while, but he was in no hurry. He sat, playing a game on his phone, swearing as he made a fatal error that sent his character spiraling out of existence for the sixth time.

He sighed, shoving his phone back in his pocket, and nodded to a couple walking their dog. It was three in the morning, but time seemed irrelevant on this side of town. There were day people and night people. Sometimes, Arsen was both.

On nights like this—when he had to kill someone—he was a night person. Murder was just easier in the dark. And it didn't have anything to do with anonymity. Arsen made no attempt to hide his identity. He was well known in the neighborhood, from his turquoise hair to his distinct video game tattoos. Hell, even his good looks.

People knew who he was. He was one of Jericho's boys. That made him untouchable, even to the police. Not that they bothered with that side of town. People there took care of their own, and when they couldn't, they called Jericho and Jericho dispatched one of his "kids" to handle things. Tonight, Arsen was that kid, and he would've been lying if he said he wasn't looking forward to taking out this particular trash.

He rose and stretched as a man on a bike passed. He had a case of beer and Oreos strapped to the back. Arsen smiled. Oreos and warm beer didn't sound in any way appealing, but who was he to yuck someone else's yum? He ate his eggs with ketchup…and syrup.

There was no accounting for taste.

He stifled a yawn. The faster he got this done, the faster he could go home and lie in his own bed. He had an early morning at the garage, finishing the two late-day oil changes he hadn't gotten to. He could have stayed and gotten them done to get a couple more hours of sleep in the morning, but sleep wasn't really in the cards for him. His nightmares ensured he never slept more than a handful of hours at most.

He crossed the street, glancing at the dark, late-model BMW in the target's driveway. He liked the sleek lines of the car and the engine was most capable. But the parts were too expensive to replace. His target didn't worry too much about money, though nobody could really figure out where it came from. Nowhere good.

Arsen sighed. Even in the poorest neighborhoods, there was a hierarchy. There were those so poor that running water and electricity were out of their reach, and some who drove fancy cars back to their one-bedroom walk-ups where they watched cable on their wall-sized televisions. Not rich enough to survive in an upper middle-class area, but not as poor as the rest of them.

Arsen didn't know if being the richest poor person was any real flex or if it was something akin to being a prisoner doing the least amount of time. Whether you were there for murder or jaywalking, there were bars around you either way.

Well, being the richest poor person in their neighborhood wouldn't be a problem for Jennika Henniker much longer. She was about to learn that money couldn't save child abusers from karma.

A chill ran through him when he approached the door and the knob turned with ease. There was something terrifying about people who didn't lock their doors. It displayed a lack of fucks Arsen aspired to have someday. He spent a good amount of his life pretending not to care, but the truth was Arsen gave too many fucks about too many things.

His fuck bucket overflowed most days. Even now, creeping through the darkness, searching out his victim, he was thinking of the paperwork he'd left on Jericho's desk, the game he was supposed to be playing with his friends, and the letter he'd received from his father.

Yeah, way too many fucks.

He found Jennika in her bed—not surprising given the late hour. He pointed the gun at her, letting the muzzle hover about an inch from the center of her forehead. She'd never see it coming. One minute, she was a person, the next a memory. But that wasn't how Jericho wanted it. He needed them to know why they were being exiled from the planet.

She was much older than Arsen had imagined her to be. Not ancient by any means but mid-fifties. Her dark hair obscured part of her face, but the lines around her mouth gave him a rough estimate. She wasn't unattractive, but who she was as a person made her ugly.

He pressed the cold steel to her skin. She flinched, shaking her head like she was trying to bat away a gnat or fly. He pressed harder until her eyes flew open. Arsen lifted a finger to his lips. "Shh," he taunted.

To her credit, she didn't cry or scream—didn't look even remotely panicked about the intruder standing over her bed. "What are you doing in my bedroom?" she asked, her accent heavy. German maybe.

"Killing you."

Her eyes widened, then narrowed. "You're Russian?"

It was odd the things people focused on when their deaths were imminent. Arsen had killed a lot of people. She was the first to skip over the dying to discuss his accent. "*Aga*," he said.

"I have money," she said, her voice not particularly panicky.

Arsen rolled his eyes. If he had a dollar for every person who'd tried to bribe him out of their deaths, he could probably afford the new PC he'd been saving for. "I don't want your money."

She scoffed. "Everybody wants money."

Arsen smiled. "Not me. I just want you to die."

Her eyes glittered even in the darkness. She was almost… reptilian in her coldness. "Why? What could I possibly have done to you?"

"Me? Nothing. But I'm not really your target age range, am I? Unfortunately for Tenesha Copenhaver, Melody Shrier, and Zaneta King, they were."

She bristled at the mention of those names. "Who?"

"The toddlers you brought into your home under the guise of foster care and then abused so badly they took them from you. One after the other."

"Children need discipline," she said, tone bored. "I will not apologize for not coddling them."

Arsen's stomach churned. How often had his father said something like that? Every time Arsen got a beating? Every time his mother did? Every day. "You didn't discipline them. You tortured them. Broken bones. Bruises. Burns. Ligature marks. So, now, you have to die."

"Get on with it then," she said, waving a hand.

He didn't know what he'd expected but it certainly wasn't that. Such a cavalier attitude towards her own death. Perhaps she was a psychopath. He knew plenty of them. Or maybe she was just a narcissist who refused to die crying.

"I will not beg to be spared, if that's what you're waiting for."

Arsen stiffened. That was what his mom had said. *I won't beg.* She'd looked so defiant then. So strong. But this woman and his mother were nothing alike.

Before he could spiral down into the darkness of his thoughts, he heard a thud from behind the door to his right.

Was there someone else there? Another child? A boyfriend?

"Who's in there?" Arsen snapped, digging the muzzle of

5

the gun against her forehead until she hissed in pain.

"In where?" she asked, clearly enjoying playing stupid.

Arsen listened intently for another moment, never taking his eyes off the woman before him. But there was no follow-up sound. He glanced towards the door once more, able to make out a lock at the top even in the shadows.

A sick feeling slid through him. Did she have another little girl? Had they given her another child to foster? This was why Jericho had slated her to die. The system was too broken. They simply couldn't handle the amount of kids, so they just gave them to people often far worse than those they were taken from in the first place.

Arsen had gotten a taste of the foster system first hand. It wasn't for him. Truthfully, it wasn't fit for any child. Luckily, he'd been able to escape to Jericho's when things got too bad. "Who's in there?"

She sneered at him. "Go see for yourself. Careful, though. He bites."

He? An animal? A dog maybe? Who locked their dog in a closet? The same kind of woman who abused toddlers. He grabbed a pillow from the bed and forced it over her face, then pulled the trigger, using the pillow as a suppressor to muffle the sound.

That was when he heard it. A mewling sound and scratching on the closet door. She really had locked up an animal. Fuck. Arsen couldn't leave a fucking dog in there. It would starve before anybody even came looking for this woman. And there was no guarantee whoever found the woman would even check on an animal.

"Careful, though. He bites."

Arsen really didn't want to get bitten. But if he let a dog die, Noah would never forgive him. Hell, he'd never forgive himself. Animals and children were innocent. Sacred. They deserved to be protected.

As he got closer to the door, the noise stopped. Arsen's heart hammered against his ribs. *Chyort.* The lock was small, like something you'd find on a shed or storage unit. If he could have turned on the light, he would have tried to pick it, but he wasn't risking alerting anyone to his presence.

He took a deep breath and let it out, then stepped back, slamming his booted foot into the door once, then twice. It gave on the third kick, splintering the wood holding the lock in place and sending the door flying inward.

The smell hit him like a sledgehammer, sending him reeling backward, a combination of sweat and stale air. It was…sour. He expected a dog to come running from the room, but there was nothing. Uneasiness dripped along his spine like ice water. He slid his phone from his pocket and turned on the flashlight, aiming it towards the still darkness of the closet. His eyes landed on a dirty mattress, if he could even call it that. It looked like a crib mattress or a bed for a child.

If there was a little kid in there, this job was about to get a lot more complicated. He took two steps in, shining the light around. There was a bucket in the corner and a stack of books. On the wall was a round circle, like one of those battery-operated lights people put in their kitchens and bathrooms. But nothing else.

"Hello?" he said. "You can come out. I won't hurt you."

There was a faint scraping sound like someone shifting behind the door, like they'd hidden in the small space there. It was the perfect size for a child.

"Hello?" he said again, keeping his voice soft, hoping he sounded friendly enough to coax them out of hiding.

He really didn't want to have to drag them out. It would only traumatize them further. But in situations like this, time was important. While nobody would turn him in, he couldn't refute standing in a room with a dead body, gun in hand.

The door moved and a figure stepped into the light, shielding their face from his phone. Arsen dropped it slightly so it was no longer in their eyes. He squinted. It wasn't a child. Well, not a toddler anyway.

It was a boy. His short dark hair obscured his eyes, but Arsen could make out a heart-shaped face, chubby cheeks, and full lips. The boy huddled in on himself, eerily quiet, muscles tensed like he was prepared to fight if necessary.

Arsen didn't want to fight him. He was small, at least a good head shorter than Arsen's six feet. He wore a dirty white t-shirt covered in dark stains and a pair of dark-colored sweatpants. He was swimming in the fabric.

He was just so small.

"Hi," Arsen said again, having no idea what to say. "What's your name?"

The boy shook his head.

Did he not know his name or did he just not want to tell a total stranger? Both reasons were valid. Arsen opened his mouth to assure him it was okay to keep the information to himself, but before he could, the boy's gaze landed on the gun in Arsen's hand, his eyes going wide.

"No. No. No," Arsen chanted, raising his hands to show he meant no harm but the boy was already stumbling back, shoving the door closed.

Arsen caught it with his booted foot, pushing his way inside. "It's okay. I'm not going to hurt you."

The boy wasn't having it. He was fighting back with every ounce of his strength, clawing and biting at him. He hissed as blunt nails dug into his skin and twisted, then teeth latched onto his hand.

Arsen grimaced, taking him to the ground. "Ow. *Ah ti malen'kiy chertyaka.*"

The little demon had teeth, all right. It was only after he had him pinned beneath him that the boy stopped fighting. He just went completely limp, glazed eyes staring up at the ceiling. Something about the way the fight immediately left the boy stole Arsen's breath, leaving him choked up. How many times had he been held down like that?

"I'm not going to hurt you," Arsen said again. "I promise. Do you believe me?" The boy continued to stare up at the ceiling, Arsen set his phone down, flashlight up, to illuminate the small space, then placed the gun out of reach, turning the boy's face to meet his gaze. "Do you believe me?"

The boy blinked at him, his wide brown eyes wild, pupils blown. He was breathing heavily, either from the fight or adrenaline, maybe both. He just stared at Arsen for a long moment and then reached up, touching his hair, the fear replaced with a look of curiosity. Arsen wasn't sure how long they laid there, the boy's hands in his hair, his bottom lip trapped between his teeth.

Arsen knew he should put a stop to it, but the way the boy was petting him, staring at him with this sort of wonder, made him loathe to move. Every soft touch sent goosebumps rolling along his skin.

When it seemed like the boy had soothed himself, Arsen finally said, "I'm Arsen. Can you tell me your name?"

The boy hesitated, worrying his bottom lip between his teeth, then pushed on Arsen's chest, reminding him he was still holding him. He sat back, letting the boy scramble out of reach. Arsen frowned as he began to go through his stack of books, settling on what looked like a children's book of fairy tales. He flipped to the last page and showed it to him.

And they lived happily ever after.

The boy stabbed his finger over the word ever, then pointed to himself.

"Ever?" Arsen asked. "That's your name?"

The boy nodded, still guarded.

Could he not speak? It didn't matter. Arsen had to get him out of there. They'd deal with everything else later. He got to his feet, leaving Ever looking up at him from his knees. "We have to go. Come with me. I'll take you somewhere safe. Find you help."

Arsen pulled him to his feet but, almost immediately, he began to struggle again. Arsen tried to tug him towards the door, but he dug his heels in, shaking his head vehemently. What the fuck?

"I'm sorry but we have to get out of here," Arsen tried again, pulling once more.

"No!" the boy shouted, voice raw, then yelped when a snapping sound filled the room.

Arsen's blood ran cold. No fucking way. Had that bitch put a shock collar around his neck? He grabbed the boy's head and pushed it upwards. "Let me see. Let me see."

It wasn't a typical collar like they used on dogs. There was no buckle, nothing to easily remove it. What the fuck? Arsen pulled the knife from his pocket, flicking open the blade. "Hold still."

Arsen's heart twisted as Ever stopped fighting, once more limp in his arms. He worked the blade beneath the leather, then placed his fingers between Ever's skin and the sharp edge. The collar gave in to the blade, easily falling to the ground. Arsen tried not to look horrified at the scarring where the box had been, but it was hard. Ever slapped his hands over the scar.

"Now, can we go?" Arsen said, practically begging. "Please?"

Ever looked torn, like he wanted nothing more than to say yes, expression miserable as tears sprung to his eyes. He shook his head.

"Please, little one? Let me get you out of here? Please?"

"We can't," he whispered.

Was his voice permanently damaged from the abuse or had it just been that long since he'd spoken? Arsen wanted to revive the bitch so he could kill her again. Slowly, this time.

"But why?" Arsen asked. "She's not coming back. I promise. She's very dead."

Ever shook his head, then yanked his t-shirt up, turning around. Once more, Arsen had to fight the urge to recoil. There were hundreds of marks, all in various stages of healing. So many, in fact, that it took far longer than it should have for him to realize what Ever was actually trying to show him.

Arsen reached out without thought, tracing the outline of the object protruding slightly from between Ever's shoulder blades. Jesus. "Is that…is that a tracking device?"

Ever bobbed his head, panicked. "If I go, they'll find me. And you, too. Just go."

Blya. Blya. Blya. Blya.

Fuck.

"Okay, we won't leave the house just yet, but can we leave the closet?"

Ever eyed the doorway warily.

"She's gone, I promise."

Ever let Arsen tug him from the stench of the closet into the fresh air of the bedroom. He picked up the gun, ensuring the safety was on before stuffing it in the pocket of his hoodie.

Ever's gaze was glued to the bed, to the body of the woman who'd held him captive for God only knew how long. Arsen wasn't sure if the boy's complete lack of emotion was a good or bad thing.

Arsen set him with his back to the wall, hoping it would ease some of his anxiety, then grabbed his phone and made the call he most definitely didn't want to make.

Jericho answered on the first ring. "What's wrong?" he

asked, voice gruff from sleep.

"Who is it?" he heard his husband ask.

"Arsen," Jericho explained, then said again, "What's wrong?"

"Coe, I have a big problem."

There was a long moment of silence. Arsen never had problems. "How big?" he asked, voice grim.

Arsen let out a shaky breath. "I think I need Freckles. And his medical bag."

"Are you hurt?"

"Me? No. But someone else is. I can't leave him here, but we can't go until someone with some surgical training shows up. So, hurry, please."

"What the hell happened, kid?"

Arsen shook his head, locking eyes with Ever, who blinked at him with a sort of bemused expression. "I think I found you a new stray."

"Shit. We'll be there soon."

With that, he was gone. Arsen gave Ever what he hoped was a reassuring smile. The boy stared at him for so long, Arsen was afraid to blink and lose the contest. But then he crawled closer. Much closer. His fingers once more went to Arsen's hair, picking at it like he thought it might come loose in his hands, seeming almost amused when it held firm.

"Pretty," he said softly.

Arsen shivered. This close, he could see every detail of Ever's face. The chapped lips, the slight scarring at the corners of his mouth. Neither of those things took away from how beautiful he was. Small and delicate looking.

Arsen sat frozen, just staring at Ever's soft expression

as he amused himself playing with Arsen's hair. He was dissociating. Arsen recognized the symptoms and had done it a million times himself as a kid, the brain protecting itself from trauma.

What the fuck had they done to him?

TWO

EVER

ARSEN SMELLED GOOD. HE HAD a scent that made Ever want to bury his face in it. He was so colorful. His hair was blue like the sky. His eyes were, too, so light they almost seemed to glow in the dim light from the street lamp outside. Even his sweatshirt was colorful. A deep pink color like flowers or bubble gum or cotton candy.

Ever knew he was staring but he couldn't help it. Arsen was…what was the word? He was half-tempted to grab the dictionary from his closet so he could find the perfect term. Was there even a term for how looking at him made Ever feel?

Probably not.

He cycled through dozens of words in his head before he finally settled on one. Luminous. That was the word. Arsen was luminous, a beacon in Ever's world of permanent monochrome.

Did he belong to Arsen now? Did death transfer his ownership like with other property? He kept his face slack, his expression as docile as possible as he played. If he was

Arsen's, it was best to make him see he could behave. That he knew how to follow orders. Maybe he'd be nice to him. It hurt less when he didn't fight back.

Usually.

He didn't want to think about that. Arsen's hair was soft; it felt like feathers in-between Ever's fingers. When his thumbs would accidentally brush Arsen's temples, he flinched like Ever had hurt him. He wanted to apologize. But the words wouldn't come. He'd learned a long time ago that apologies didn't work, begging didn't help, and words meant nothing, especially promises.

So, why bother?

Ever let his gaze dip downward, sneaking a peek at Arsen's phone. The screen looked like a moving picture book, like a TV. The colors were as rich and saturated as Arsen himself, the sky so blue it hurt Ever's eyes to look at it. On the screen was a knight, like in Ever's fairy tales.

Arsen controlled the knight's movements as Ever's fingers kept combing through his hair. He watched as sneakily as he could, taking in the mountains in the distance, the forests and lakes. Ever had always wanted games like that. To be able to disappear into a game like he did with books and sometimes music.

Arsen carried a whole other realm in his pocket. A box popped onto the screen and Arsen muttered something under his breath, making it go dark.

Ever couldn't stop the disappointed sound that left his lips. Arsen's gaze flicked to his. For a split second, they were locked onto one another, neither moving.

He had kind eyes. Was he kind? He'd called Ever "little one" and had taken his collar off. That seemed like friend behavior. But Ever didn't have friends. Ever didn't have anything. Not even the courage to use his own voice.

There was a sound in the hallway, the heavy fall of footsteps on carpeted floors, and then two large men entered the room. Ever scurried back against the wall, his heart tripping so hard it ached. He put his hands over his face. It didn't stop the hurt, but at least he didn't see the bad things coming. Sometimes, that made it easier.

"Easy," Arsen said, tone low. "They're my friends. They're going to help. Okay?"

Ever was trembling, but he lowered his hands, looking at the two imposing figures. Friends. Arsen had friends. Most normal people did. At least, in books. Friends were normal. Friends were safe. Except, they weren't. Mother's friends were never safe.

"What's happening?" the dark-haired man asked.

Arsen gave Ever a patient smile, flashing perfect teeth. "May I show my friends your back? Please?" Ever swallowed the lump in his throat, looking back and forth between the men. Arsen caught Ever's gaze, pulling his attention back to him. "I won't let them hurt you," he said softly, "but we have to get that thing out of your back so we can get you out of here."

"Thing on his back?" the taller, red-haired man asked.

Arsen continued to look at Ever, nodding. "Please?"

Ever liked his voice. It was…soothing, melodic. He had an accent like Mother's, but not as harsh or jarring.

When she was mad, her voice was like broken glass in his ears. Mother. Revulsion shuddered through him, raising goosebumps along his skin. He gazed back over at the bed. He didn't have to call her that now. Not anymore.

He crawled away from the wall, letting Arsen pull him to his feet and gently turn him around. His face flushed hot as he lifted his dirty t-shirt and he heard one of them make a sound of disgust. "We can clean all this up back at the shop," the red-haired man said. "Why did you make us come here?"

"It's not the wounds, Atticus," Arsen said. "Look." Ever sucked in a breath as his fingertips brushed over the spot on his back. "They've…chipped him. Like a dog."

"Who did?" the other man asked.

"How would I know this?" Arsen asked, tone frustrated. "Maybe her, maybe someone else. But he won't leave until it's out. So, can you get it out or no?"

Ever stiffened. Was Arsen mad? He sounded mad. Ever sucked his bottom lip between his teeth, biting down until he tasted blood.

"It was probably her, right?" the other man said.

"Do you want to take the chance, Coe?" Arsen asked. "Can you get it out of him or not?"

Atticus sighed. "I can. I can give him something to numb the area, but he might need a couple of stitches. What are you going to do with him after that?"

"He's coming home with me," Arsen said, his tone firm.

So, he was Arsen's.

That knowledge left him feeling…untethered. He

wanted to believe things would be better if Arsen owned him. He looked nice. He felt nice. But once upon a time, she'd seemed nice, too. She'd bought him toys and let him eat ice cream for breakfast. But that hadn't lasted long.

What would Arsen want from him in exchange for his life? Did Ever care? Arsen would be a much better captor than Jennika. At least, if Ever could make him happy. He could cook and clean and run errands like he did for her. Maybe that would be enough. Maybe Arsen wouldn't need to sell him to others.

Yes, Arsen would be much better.

He hoped.

He felt a little sick as they removed his shirt. They had him sit backwards on a kitchen chair they dragged into the bathroom. It was a small room, barely big enough for Atticus and Ever, but Arsen squeezed himself between the wall and the chair, crouching down so Ever could peer down at him over the back.

"I'm going to give you a shot to numb the area," Atticus said, voice abrupt but not unkind. Like when Jennika had taken him to her doctor friends. The ones who never filed paperwork.

Once more, Arsen moved his head until he was looking Ever in the eye, then smiled. "Just look at me, okay?"

Ever nodded, wrapping his hands around the dowels that made up the chair back, gripping tightly until his knuckles were white. There were a couple of small pinches and a bit of a burn, but then nothing, really. Just a weird tugging sensation.

Arsen suddenly stuck his tongue out. Ever couldn't stop

himself from smiling, so he covered his mouth. That seemed to make Arsen sad. Arsen's hands closed around Ever's wrists, gently tugging his hands away from his mouth. When Ever stopped smiling, Arsen's expression went from encouraging to…something else. Disappointment.

Ever's heart plummeted to his feet. He was already upsetting him. His brain cycled through a million scenarios he'd used to try to placate Jennika in the past, none of which seemed the right one, so he did the only thing he could think of. He stuck his tongue out at him, too, mirroring the gesture. The relief that spread across Arsen's face mirrored the relief spreading through Ever like the numbing medicine in his back, dulling the panic. Crisis averted.

This was exhausting. Reading new people was hard. He was so tired. Still, when Arsen smiled, he smiled back. When he stuck his tongue out, he returned the motion. That seemed to make him happy. Ever really just wanted him to stay happy.

Would Arsen be so silly if he knew Ever was nineteen and not a little kid? In the dark, it was easy to mistake him for a child. He was short, small, often wearing clothing too big for him. Jennika had liked it that way. She wanted her friends to see him as a child. It made him worth more money.

When he was clean and his clothes fit him, he looked his age. At least, he thought he did. Shame shot through him like an electric current. When had he last showered? When was he last allowed to brush his teeth? Arsen must think he was disgusting. Unhygienic. He wasn't. He liked being clean. But he'd been in that closet for a while. He didn't even know how much time had passed.

"It's out," Atticus said. "I was able to close it with some sterile glue. Just keep it covered when you shower."

Ever didn't acknowledge the other man. He wasn't sure he was allowed to. He didn't know the rules. Would Arsen explain them or would he only tell him once he'd broken one, letting his punishment seal it into his memory?

"Leave the chip here," the other man—the one Arsen called Coe—told them. "If someone is monitoring it, it will be a while before anybody knows he's missing."

Arsen stood. "Thanks."

When they were gone, Arsen removed the gun from his pocket, slipping it into the waistband of his jeans. He then grabbed the hem of his pink hoodie, yanking it over his head. Ever stared at the strip of tan skin that appeared before his eyes over the waistband of Arsen's jeans, following the trail of hair that disappeared below. He blinked as the t-shirt Arsen wore underneath slipped down to cover him once more.

Ever's startled gaze locked on Arsen, his stomach curdling like old milk. Why was he taking his clothes off? Already? When he looked like this? Smelled like this? He needed time to prepare himself. He wasn't ready.

But then, Arsen was holding the hoodie out to Ever, once more giving him that soft, patient smile. "Put this on. Your t-shirt has blood on it. People might notice."

Ever hesitated, then took it, pulling it over his head. It was big on him, but it was still warm from Arsen's skin. Ever grabbed the fabric, pressing it to his face and inhaling deeply. It smelled like him. Sort of like spice but also like flowers.

Ever's eyes flew open when Arsen laughed. He must look crazy. His face flushed, and he felt hot to the tips of his ears. He dropped the sweatshirt, averting his eyes.

"Come on, little one. Let's get you home."

Home smelled like gasoline and motor oil and a little like dirt. Arsen lived in a mechanic's shop. Well, not in it, but on top of it. The yellow lights from a small office allowed Ever to see the shadow of cars and a bank of glass windows at the top of a set of metal stairs.

That was where Arsen led him. Up the stairs to a small room with a couch, a TV, and a small kitchen.

"I know it's small," Arsen said, "but it's clean and it's safe. Okay?"

Ever nodded, turning in a circle. Unlike Jennika's house, there were no lace doilies or tchotchkes everywhere. It also lacked the cloying scent of her perfume and the menthol cigarettes she smoked.

Ever much preferred the smell of Arsen's shirt and even the garage.

"I need to run an errand for two minutes, okay?" Arsen said, holding up two fingers. "I'll just be right over there." He pointed to a door in the wall of the garage below. "Two minutes. Stay right here."

He didn't wait for Ever's answer, just took off running, taking the stairs two at a time before crossing the shop and flinging open the door. Ever caught a glimpse of what looked like another kitchen. Did he own a restaurant?

Ever stayed just as he was, fingers twisted together inside the pocket of the hoodie. Time seemed to drip by until Arsen appeared again holding a pile of clothing. When he was standing back before him, he grinned, holding out the pile to Ever.

"These should fit. Do you want to take a shower?"

Ever bobbed his head hard enough to make him dizzy. He wanted a shower so badly. He felt so dirty his skin hurt. Arsen led him to the bathroom and turned on the light. Ever flinched away from it, blinking rapidly. It was so bright.

"*Blya*," Arsen said in a rush, reaching for one of the four bulbs that made up the light fixture, swearing and flinching as he twisted the bulb until it went out. "Hot," he said sheepishly.

Ever trapped his lip between his teeth, this time to keep from laughing as Arsen repeated the process with a second bulb. Once that light was extinguished, Ever felt better.

Arsen turned the water on then flashed another smile his way. "There's a toothbrush here, too. And toothpaste. You can use my soap. It's there." He pointed to a bottle on the shelf. "But don't use the green stuff. That's what takes the dirt and oil off my hands." He held up his hands. They were rough and calloused, the nails bitten to the quick, the skin surrounding them looking like it was permanently stained black. For some reason, it made Ever feel better.

"Are you hungry?"

Ever nodded. He couldn't remember his last meal.

"Okay, you shower and I'll make you something. It won't be fancy. I am terrible cook. I know how to make three things. Sandwiches. Ramen. Hot pockets."

Ever didn't know what two of those things were, but he was willing to eat food from the trash at this point. He flushed as his stomach growled loudly.

Arsen laughed. "You can take as long as you want, but the hot water only lasts about fifteen minutes. The water pressure is very nice, though."

With that, he was gone, leaving Ever alone in the room. He peeled his clothes off and stepped beneath the water, turning it to scalding, not even caring about the wounds on his back. Being clean was worth the pain. He scrubbed every part of himself he could reach until his fingers ached, then just stood under the water until it went cold.

He stepped from the shower, wrapping the towel around his waist, then set about scrubbing his mouth and teeth with the same force he had his body. When he was satisfied, he did his best to get the excess water from his hair before he reached for the clothes piled on the toilet.

They were soft and clean. He pulled on the joggers, noting the cream color, hoping he didn't spill his food on it. There was also another hoodie, this one butter yellow. And socks.

He pulled the hoodie over his head, huffing the fabric like a drug, disappointed when all he smelled was detergent. Arsen's hoodie smelled better.

When he left the bathroom, he found Arsen sitting on the sofa, two bowls in front of him on the small coffee table. When he looked up and saw Ever standing there, he just stared. Ever stopped short, trapped in his gaze.

Arsen studied him for so long, he reached for his face, wondering if there was something he'd missed. That was when Arsen seemed to come back to himself. He gestured for Ever to come to him. Ever did as he was told, standing on the other side of the table until Arsen told him what he expected of him.

"Sit. Eat."

Ever relaxed. That was easy. He moved around the table, sitting on the floor, the scent of whatever was in the bowl hitting him like a brick. It was a soup of some kind with long, thin noodles piled high in the middle. He grabbed the fork and dug in, moaning when the food hit his tongue. He tried not to rush it. He really did. But it tasted so good and the broth felt nice on his throat.

When his bowl was empty, he glanced up to find Arsen watching him, a sort of half-smile on his lips. Ever flushed. Arsen pushed his bowl towards him. "Here."

Ever frowned and shook his head, pointing at Arsen.

Arsen pushed the bowl again. "I'm not hungry. This is for you. Eat it. You'll sleep better." Ever frowned, hesitating. "Eat," Arsen said again, this time with more force.

Ever took the bowl, devouring it with the same vigor he had the first, only looking up once he'd done what he was told.

Arsen smiled. "Good boy."

Ever blinked at him, something quivering deep inside at the praise.

Arsen stood, holding out his hand. Ever stared at it until

he opened and shut it, indicating that he expected him to take it. Ever complied. Was he taking him to his bed?

His heart started to hammer until he was light-headed. He'd do it if that was what Arsen wanted. But he was so tired.

Arsen led him down a short hallway to two doors, pointing to the one on the left. "This is my room. If you need me, come get me. Okay?"

Ever shifted his weight on the balls of his feet, then nodded. Arsen opened the door to the right and gently nudged Ever inside. He stopped short, looking around.

It was brightly colored just like Arsen. Even though there were no lamps, the room was illuminated. There were neon pink lights that surrounded the perimeter of the ceiling and blue lights that trailed along the baseboards. On a desk were three screens, each with pictures made up of the same pink and blue neon and a tower and keyboard that emanated the same pulsing colors.

"I can turn the lights out," Arsen said.

Ever shook his head. "Pretty,' he said before he could stop himself.

Arsen smiled, looking almost proud, then pointed to a large bed in the corner, something far bigger than Ever had ever slept on before. "You can sleep here, okay? You can sleep as long as you want." Ever waited for the catch, waited for whatever it was Arsen would demand in return, but he just gave him a little wave. "I'm right here if you need me."

Then Ever was alone.

He was used to being alone. He'd been that way most of his life, trapped alone in confined spaces. But when Arsen closed the door, Ever's heart dropped, like he'd taken all the light with him. Which was stupid, because the whole room was filled with light. He sat on the bed, bouncing on the mattress a bit. It was soft. But more importantly, it was clean.

He threw back the blankets and dove into the pillows, burying his face in them and inhaling deeply, his exhaustion bleeding from every pore of his body. Reading three people had been exhausting, especially new people. He hadn't learned their tells, hadn't learned how to discern whether they were there to harm him or help him.

He closed his eyes, waiting for sleep to overtake him. But it didn't. As the minutes ticked by, an uneasiness grew within him. The room was too big. Even though he could see every corner, he still couldn't shake the feeling he was being watched. He tried to pull the covers over his head, but that somehow just made it worse. He felt...exposed. He tried to hide his face, even contemplating sliding under the bed.

But there was no room.

He bit his lower lip, his panic ratcheting higher with each second until he was on his feet without much rational thought, then he was standing outside Arsen's door. He raised his hand to knock, but then hesitated. What if he woke him up?

He didn't know how long he stood there, hand raised, worrying about what was worse—being alone or making Arsen angry enough to punish him. At least he knew what punishments felt like. He was willing to risk it if it meant this panic clawing inside him would release its hold on his lungs.

He turned the knob instead, peeking inside when the

door opened. Ever's lips parted at the sight before him. Arsen was sprawled across his bed in a pair of black pants that sat low on his hips and nothing else. He had one hand behind his head and the other flung to the side, his expression peaceful.

Ever snuck closer, watching as Arsen's chest rose and fell steadily. He was…pretty. Colorful. Luminous. He had several tattoos that Ever didn't understand, but the one he couldn't stop staring at was the print circling his nipple. It said PRESS START.

He didn't know what that meant either, but Ever itched to press it anyway. Just to know. Arsen's large body took up most of the bed, but there was a tiny sliver of space between him and the wall. Ever hesitated for only a second before climbing onto the bed as carefully as possible, then working himself into the tight space, keeping his body turned towards Arsen…just in case.

He half-expected Arsen to wake immediately, but he didn't. Instead, he rolled onto his side until he and Ever were almost nose to nose. It was so much easier to see how pretty he was up close. He had long lashes that cast shadows on his cheeks. He had a mole on his left ear. A lock of blue hair fell over one thick, dark brow.

Ever reached up and pushed it back, smiling when it fell defiantly back over his eye. He did it again, watching it rebound once more. Then again.

He was so engrossed in his little game, he didn't even notice the change in Arsen's breathing, not until he opened his eyes and looked at Ever sleepily.

"Hi," he said, voice sleep-soaked.

"Hi," Ever whispered, swallowing the lump of sand in his throat.

Arsen frowned. "Are you okay?"

Ever licked his lower lip. "The room is too big."

"What?"

Frustration leached into Ever. He hated talking. "The room is too big."

"Oh," Arsen said, giving him a soft smile that did things to Ever's stomach. "Is it better here? With me?"

Ever hesitated. What if he rejected him? What if he wanted more than sleep? Ever would give it to him if it meant not having to go back to that big empty bed in that big empty room. He nodded.

Arsen lifted a hand and cupped Ever's cheek. The skin there was rough, like sandpaper. "You're older than I thought. You're just small. How old are you, little one?"

Once more, Ever licked his lower lip, leaning close until his forehead all but touched Arsen's. "Nineteen. I'm old enough."

Arsen frowned. "Old enough?"

Ever's blood rushed in his ears. In all the times he'd been with someone, he'd never initiated it. He might as well get it over with. It wouldn't be so bad with him. Arsen smelled good and he was pretty and warm. He lifted a hand and placed it on Arsen's bare chest, feeling the shuddering breath he took when their skin connected. He made eye contact, sliding his palm down towards Arsen's belly button.

He was almost to that trail of hair when Arsen snagged his wrist, yanking him back to reality. "Hey. You...you don't have to do that."

Ever flushed, then gave him a smile. "I don't mind."

Arsen frowned, then sighed. He looked…sad. Disappointed even. "I don't…I don't *want* you to do that."

Heat flooded Ever's face, tears springing to his eyes. "Oh."

He started to scramble off the bed, but Arsen still held his wrist. "Stop."

Ever froze.

"Just lie down and go to sleep. Okay? You need to rest. You just need some sleep. You have to be exhausted."

He was. He was so tired. He was tired in his bones, in his soul. But he couldn't look at him. Ever turned to face the wall, close enough to smell the paint had it been fresh, hot tears sliding down his cheeks.

He hated this. He hated not knowing the rules. He was so stupid. It had never even occurred to him that Arsen didn't want him. Of course, he didn't. He met him covered in blood and dirt and smelling like a sewer. He was lucky he was even letting Ever lie there next to him.

He sucked in a breath as Arsen's heavy arm settled over him, then his body curled around him, his chest against Ever's back, his hips pressing to Ever's ass, his knees pressed to the back of Ever's. The warmth of his skin bled through the fabric of Ever's hoodie and he could feel his breath against his neck and ear.

Arsen's large hand settled on Ever's belly over the fabric. "Just…sleep. Okay?"

Ever closed his eyes, testing the weight of Arsen's arm, the feel of him around him. Was it too much? Not enough? It must have been just right somehow because he was fading into unconsciousness before he could formulate any kind of decision on the matter.

THREE

ARSEN

ARSEN LAY AWAKE LONG AFTER Ever's breathing had evened out. He should have released him then. It was the right thing to do. But Arsen couldn't bring himself to let go. Ever was warm and smelled like Arsen's soap and he made the cutest sounds while he slept. Besides, he had wanted Arsen to hold him.

Ever—who had absolutely no reason to trust Arsen—had come to him for comfort, had come to him because he was afraid. Arsen knew what it was like to be afraid. He'd spent many nights listening to his father rage. Bottles crashing, glasses breaking, his mother's screaming. It had been years but it was still all fresh in his mind. His mother smiling with blood on her face while she told him it was all okay.

"Go to sleep, zaichik. It's just a bad dream."

Arsen swallowed the lump in his throat. The violence was never forgotten, never far from his memories. His age had only protected him for so long, then his father had turned the violence towards him. To make him stronger. Tougher. A real man. Real men didn't cry. Real men didn't whine. Real men took their beatings in silence. Crying only prolonged the inevitable.

Arsen squeezed Ever a little tighter. Maybe he was the one who needed Ever. He'd told himself a million times he could never be comfortable with someone sleeping in his bed, but Ever was right there, taking up space in a way Arsen swore he'd hate. But he didn't. Why?

Maybe because Ever had trusted him? Arsen wanted to be the one to protect him, comfort him. He'd found him. Shouldn't he take responsibility? Wasn't that the right thing to do? How could Arsen be sure someone else wouldn't take advantage of Ever? He'd come to Arsen looking for comfort, but he'd been prepared to trade that comfort for sex. What if someone else said yes?

Ever had assumed Arsen would say yes and was heartbroken when he'd refused him. Why? Was Arsen simply the lesser of two evils in his eyes? That thought made Arsen's heart ache. Had Ever known any kind of affection that wasn't transactional? Had he been forced to give a piece of his soul away every time someone showed him any kindness? Had anybody even bothered to try?

He looked down at the boy, currently sleeping with his cheek smooshed against Arsen's bicep, full lips parted as he softly snored like a puppy. Ever was sweet-faced—that was the only way Arsen could describe him. In the dim lighting, his hair looked almost black, but in the light, it was a dark chocolate brown, just like his wide doe eyes. He had a heart-shaped face and high cheekbones but enough baby fat to make him seem vulnerable.

But Ever wasn't just cute, he was attractive. Arsen had been shocked when he'd seen him standing barefoot in his apartment, damp hair hanging in his eyes and a canary yellow sweatshirt making his golden skin glow. He'd been everything Arsen hadn't known he'd wanted. But he had wanted.

That was why he was still thinking about the way Ever looked up at him from beneath his lashes and the way his fingertips had trailed over his bare skin an hour later. Arsen never would have taken advantage like that, but he'd known Ever three hours and he was already tempting his resolve, his morals. He was a good person, damn it.

Ever was dangerous.

Ever squirmed a little closer, as if he could hear Arsen's internal struggle and wanted to make it just a little more difficult. How could Arsen ignore how well Ever fit? How he seemed to be the perfect small spoon to Arsen's bigger one? How his head tucked perfectly under Arsen's chin? How his ass pressed directly against Arsen's crotch...

Fuck.

Levi would call Ever pocket-sized, might even joke about hobbits or elves. But Ever was a fairy, something small and dainty and tempting, like in his game, *Paladin*. Arsen had fallen for the game the moment he'd played it. Knights and magic and round tables. Kings and wizards and mythological creatures. Maybe Ever was one of those creatures. Not a domovoi—they were ugly, and there was nothing ugly about Ever. Another tiny creature maybe? *Mal'chik-s-pal'chik* maybe. He was tiny like that.

"You are about the size of my finger," he murmured.

Ever rolled in his arms, a deep sigh escaping his chest. Arsen just stared. How could anybody hurt someone so sweet? So fragile? Arsen's father had beat the hell out of him and his mother, but Arsen had been sturdy, strong. He had to be. His father never allowed for weakness. Even now. Even from behind bars.

No crying. No begging. Arsen had learned to mask his pain. But Ever…he looked at people like a dog who'd been kicked too many times. Suspicious but…hopeful. Like he just wanted one person to not let him down.

Arsen closed his eyes. Maybe he was just projecting. It was clear he wasn't going to sleep. Not now. He might as well get up and get dressed. But he didn't move. Minutes ticked by, but still he lay there, listening to Ever breathe, feeling his breath against his skin.

What if Arsen got up and it woke him? He needed sleep. Those wounds needed rest to heal properly. What if Ever woke up alone and panicked again? He hadn't lasted long alone in Arsen's old bedroom. Even with the lights on.

"The room is too big."

That was what he'd said. But size was relative. When the room had been Arsen's—when he'd shared the apartment with Jericho's brother, Felix—Arsen had been grateful for a room with a door, but it had felt claustrophobic at times. There was barely enough room for his computer and the desk, which worked well when he was online with his friends, but not so much when he just wanted to hang out.

When the room belonged to Felix and Jericho had the master, Felix had often complained about it being 'the size of a shoebox,' which seemed like a major exaggeration to Arsen, but that was just Felix. Dramatic, over-the-top, excessive. That was why he was famous now. That was why everybody loved him and wanted to be his friend. Felix would love Ever.

Arsen stared down at Ever, the ache to touch him coming on so strongly and so quickly he didn't even have time to fight it. He lightly ran his finger up the bridge of his pert nose, once then twice, then caressed the spot between his perfectly straight brows. His skin was soft, his bunny teeth just a little too big for his mouth, leaving them settled lightly on his full lower lip.

Ever's eyelids fluttered, then opened, slowly blinking himself awake. Shit. Ever's hand—trapped between their bodies—curled against Arsen's bare chest, making him shiver, his cock taking notice of the barely-there touch. He needed to calm down before he scared him.

But his body just wasn't getting the memo that Ever was friend, not food. Because even with chapped lips and puffy eyes, Ever looked good enough to eat. And for the first time in a long time, Arsen was starving.

Almost like he could read his thoughts, Ever raised his hand and brushed his fingertips over Arsen's hair that hung in his eyes. He closed his eyes, praying for some modicum of self-control. Maybe if he just didn't look at him…

Ever's index finger ran along the bridge of Arsen's nose, mimicking Arsen's earlier movements. No. No. This was definitely not better. It was somehow much worse. He needed to get out of bed and put some distance between them before one of them did something they couldn't take back.

They were strangers. Ever only touched him for comfort, as a way to anchor himself, not because he wanted anything physical. Arsen couldn't ruin that trust.

"I have to go downstairs to the garage. Can you stay here and rest?" Ever's face morphed from fear to confusion to something akin to a sulk, which did nothing to strengthen Arsen's resolve to leave the warmth of his bed. "Don't give me that look, little one. I'll be right downstairs. You can come find me when you wake up and then I'll get you some food."

Ever's scowl disappeared immediately, replaced with that same placid look from last night. That one that told Arsen he was either dissociating or masking his true feelings for Arsen's benefit. Shit. He needed to choose his words carefully. Ever had spent most of his life following orders. He was clearly still trying to do so.

How long had he lived like that? How long had that woman tortured him? The scars on his back and throat indicated months. The children's book he'd shown Arsen indicated years. Had she been the only one to…own him? The idea of multiple people abusing Ever over the years left Arsen with a rage brewing deep within. It made him want to hurt something, hurt someone. Once more, he wished he could revive that woman and kill her again. She deserved something far worse than a simple bullet in the head.

But none of that would help Ever. And Arsen wasn't qualified to help this level of trauma. He needed an adult. A real adult. An adultier adult. One who understood taxes and feelings. But he didn't have one of those handy right now. All he could do was follow Jericho's advice.

Adapt. Improvise. Overcome.

He gave Ever his brightest smile. "I change my mind. You can look at me however you want. If you're mad, be mad. If you're sad, be sad. If you're happy, be happy. Okay?" He made the okay symbol with his fingers.

Ever studied his face and then his hand, like he wasn't sure if he was in trouble or not.

"I'll be right downstairs," he said again, this time extracting himself from Ever's limbs, heart tripping as he stared up at Arsen with those big Bambi eyes. "Sleep."

Ever immediately complied, closing his eyes and rolling onto his belly, burying his face in Arsen's pillow. Damn it, another order. He vowed to get better. But it was difficult to go against his nature. He spent most of his day herding a bunch of twenty-somethings high on caffeine and short on attention. That required being direct. And loud. And giving concise instructions. The boys were efficient, but they were also absent-minded and stubborn.

Ever inhaled deeply then seemed to relax. Still, Arsen watched until his breathing evened out again. If following Arsen's order got Ever more sleep, then in this one particular instance, it was okay. Until Arsen found that adult he needed.

Arsen finally forced himself to move, throwing on some clothes and his coveralls before heading downstairs to get the bay doors open on time. People had to work, so Jericho had a drop box for keys. By the time he made it to the shop, there were already four sets in addition to the jobs left over from yesterday. It was clearly going to be a busy day.

He walked to the back of the garage. There used to be a huge sofa and television as well as a gaming console there. Arsen and his friends had spent hours in the back of the shop, hiding from bullies, hiding from their own families. But now, that had all moved next door.

When Jericho had married Atticus, they'd pooled their money to buy the building next to the garage so Jericho's "strays" had a safe place to sleep at night and Jericho had a place to work where he didn't have to worry about someone accidentally lopping off a finger or losing a foot to an engine block.

The core group had never changed, but other stray kids ebbed and flowed out of the place depending on necessity. And sadly, in their neighborhood—in every neighborhood, really—there was always a need.

Arsen had considered putting Ever over there last night. He would have been safe. But a bunch of twenty-year-old sometimes killers with a penchant for caffeine, sugar, and gaming marathons wasn't really the place for Ever. At least, not yet. He needed Arsen.

Well, that was what Arsen told himself.

He popped his headphones in and started working, losing himself in the mundane tasks of oil changes and brake jobs. When he wheeled himself out from under a ten-year-old Chevy, he stopped short, heart pounding. Ever stood there in last night's clothes, fidgeting with the drawstring on his hoodie, nothing but socks on his feet. He scanned the place rapidly, eyes wide, like he was prepared to run if he had to.

Arsen quickly crossed to him, wiping his hands off on the

rag hanging from his pocket. "You're awake."

Ever trapped his bottom lip between his teeth then nodded.

Arsen did his best to give him a reassuring smile. "Did you sleep okay?"

Ever shrugged, then nodded again, risking a glance upward like he was worried his answer might upset Arsen.

"Don't feel like talking?" he asked, trying to keep his voice judgment-free.

Ever shook his head.

"Okay," Arsen said. "Do you want me to take you back upstairs? You can watch TV?"

Ever shook his head.

"Are you hungry?"

Ever shook his head.

"Do you want to stay down here with me?"

Ever nodded.

Warmth bled through Arsen's whole body. Ever just wanted to be near him. He trusted Arsen to keep him safe. That shouldn't have been the high it was. Arsen shouldn't feel drugged from it. But he did.

"Don't move, okay?"

Ever began to gnaw on his bottom lip but nodded. Arsen took the small victory. He grabbed a stool from the counter and placed it where Ever would be safe but could still see Arsen. "Sit. I don't want you stepping on anything sharp. It is very dangerous to be down here without shoes on."

Ever flushed to the tips of his ears. Did that sound harsh? Was it too mean? It was hard enough thinking in Russian and speaking in English without this emotional minefield. But he would figure it out. He'd get it right. Somehow.

Ever sat on the stool, then pulled his legs to his chest, his heels resting on the stool's edge. Arsen could never have sat that way, but Ever did it with ease, perched like the world's cutest gargoyle, chin resting on his knees, watching Arsen as if waiting for his next instructions.

"Are you hungry?"

Ever shook his head.

"Are you thirsty?"

Ever shook his head.

Arsen grinned. "Okay. I'm going to get back to work but you tell me if you need anything. Okay?"

Ever nodded then made the okay symbol.

Arsen's heart skipped like he'd been shocked. Fuck, Ever was cute.

He finished the oil change he was working on, but when he went to do a quick tire change, he noticed Ever was not okay. Every time Arsen fired the impact wrench, Ever would flinch, then jump, slapping his hands over his ears. Shit. He set the drill down, racking his brain. Ever wouldn't go back upstairs without Arsen, but he had to keep working, at least until Jericho got there.

He snapped his fingers, then ran to the office, fishing through the box they kept next to Jericho's sofa. It was called the lost and found box, but it was more a shit-people-left-in-cars-they-never-picked-up box. And Arsen had noticed something there a few weeks ago that might work for Ever.

He gave a small shout when he realized what he sought

was still there. A pink pair of kid's headphones with light-up cat ears. That would work. He grabbed his phone and synced them to his device, grateful when it showed there was still a sixty percent battery life.

He brought them to Ever and gently placed them over his ears. He then brought up Spotify. He clicked on a channel that played lo-fi music, unsure what Ever would even like. As soon as it turned on, his eyes went wide and he slapped his hands over the headphones, pressing them harder into his ears.

Arsen handed him his phone, quickly showing him how to look for music, then returning back to work. This time, when he discharged the impact wrench, Ever didn't even notice, engrossed in his music and whatever it was he did on Arsen's phone. Had he ever let another soul hold his cell phone? Even for a moment? No. Definitely not.

Arsen and Ever existed in the space comfortably for another hour or so, Arsen sometimes forgetting himself when he would glance at Ever. Usually, his eyes were closed and he was swaying to some song, but every once in a while, Arsen would find him attempting a new song, a new genre, a new playlist, and his facial expressions ran the gamut from confused to horrified. Arsen could spend a day just watching Ever play music.

It was almost noon when Levi walked in, stealing Ever's attention from Arsen's phone. He studied Levi suspiciously, his gaze tracking back to Arsen like he wanted to make sure he was close by.

Arsen didn't blame Ever for his trepidation. Levi looked

like the bad boy in a movie for teens who make poor life choices. His inky black hair was a permanent mess, he had tattoos from his jaw to his fingertips and everywhere in-between. He had several piercings along both ears, as well as a ring through his lip and another through his right brow. He wore ripped jeans, a black t-shirt, and a permanent scowl on his way-too-pretty face.

He frowned when he saw Ever. "Who's that?"

"That's Ever."

Levi tilted his head. "What's Ever?"

Arsen rolled his eyes, pointing to the boy and his cat ears. "That is. He is," Arsen corrected.

Levi snickered. "That's his name? Ever?"

"Yes, that's why I said, 'That's Ever,'" Arsen said, shaking his head.

Sometimes, it was hard to believe he was the one who didn't grow up speaking English.

Levi rolled his eyes like he could hear Arsen's irritation. "Where did Ever come from?"

Arsen looked Ever over thoroughly, head tilted. "Hard to say. He speaks perfect English but has features that are present through many different ethnic groups from Eastern Asia to Central America."

Levi sighed. "Not where is he from geographically, dude. Like, where did you two meet?"

Oh. "A job."

"A job?" Levi parroted.

"Mm," Arsen said. "The abuser with the fancy car. She had him."

"Had him?"

Arsen made a noise of frustration. "Why do you keep repeating everything I say? Am I not speaking English?"

Levi smirked. "Debatable. But I'm repeating everything you say because you're not making any sense. You found a boy at a target's house and you just…kept him?"

That wasn't exactly what happened. Was it? "He doesn't have any place to go."

"Um, foster care?" Levi asked, snapping gum that must have been in his mouth the whole time.

"Don't let the pink cat ears fool you. He's nineteen," Arsen said, feeling a tad defensive.

Levi nodded. "Okay, but you can't just…keep him. He's not a cat you found in the bushes. Even if he kind of looks like one," he mumbled, then said, "That's, like, kidnapping."

Arsen did his best to keep his tone level. "He's an adult. And he wants to be here. He likes me. I'm relaxing. Like that drug."

"Weed?"

"Ativan," Arsen said.

It was a lie. At least, at present. Levi and Arsen were doing nothing to relieve the stress growing on Ever's face. The more the two spoke, the more his anxiety spiked, until he put his hands over his headphones, pushing them against his ears once more, and closed his eyes.

Levi shook his head. "You've definitely been hanging out with the Mulvaney clan for too long."

"Jericho said I could keep him," Arsen said. It was

technically a lie but he hoped if he said it with enough conviction, Levi would just believe him.

"Then he's been hanging too long with the Mulvaney clan, too," Levi muttered.

"Technically, Coe is a Mulvaney," Arsen reminded him.

"You know you can't keep him," Levi said.

"Keep who?"

They both looked up as Jericho arrived, pizza boxes in hand.

"Keep him," Levi said, pointing to Ever, who currently looked like the see no evil monkey.

"Coe, tell him you said he could stay here," Arsen begged.

Jericho looked at Levi. "I said he can stay here. For now." He then walked up to Ever and gently plucked the headphones from his ears. "Let's eat, *gatito.*"

Ever looked at Arsen, only sliding from the stool when he nodded.

Please let me keep him.

FOUR

EVER

JERICHO FELT…GOOD. EVER DIDN'T know how else to explain it. Whenever he was around someone like Jennika and her friends, there was a heaviness to them. A weight that just sat on Ever's chest, stealing his breath. It didn't feel that way with Arsen. It didn't feel that way with Jericho, either.

When he called Ever *gatito* and smiled, it didn't feel fake or like he wanted something from him. He'd been gentle when he'd talked to Ever last night. Or was it this morning? Ever wasn't even sure anymore. Everything sort of blurred together. Maybe it was because Arsen trusted Jericho and Ever trusted Arsen. Arsen also felt good. His energy was happy and light and bright. It was like nothing Ever had ever felt before. And he just wanted to be near it.

Whatever the reason, when Jericho beckoned him to his office for pizza, Ever started to follow without thought, placing a foot on the ground.

"No!"

Even with his headphones on, Arsen's panicked shout startled him, making him flinch hard enough to almost fall off the stool. His heart hammered against his chest, and he closed his eyes, slamming his fingers over his ears.

Rough palms covered his hands, tugging them away gently, and Arsen's voice carried over the headphones. "Sorry. Sorry. I don't mean to scare you. But you can't walk barefoot. You'll hurt yourself. Hold on. One moment. Okay?"

Ever opened his eyes but remained frozen, afraid to move, watching as Arsen darted across the shop, disappearing behind the same magical door he had last night, this time returning with black sandals with white stripes across the top.

He kneeled before the stool and slipped them on Ever's sock-clad feet, then grinned at him. "Okay, there you go."

Ever looked down at the slightly too big sandals and then at the hand Arsen held out to him once he was on his feet again. He didn't take it but looked over at Jericho, who stood in the open office door watching the two of them carefully. He stood with the other boy, the loud one who asked too many questions and looked at Ever like he couldn't be trusted.

Finally, he took Arsen's hand. The way the tension bled from Arsen's face made Ever's insides feel hot and squishy. He wanted Arsen to be who he appeared to be. He wanted to make Arsen happy. Especially if he belonged to him now. If Ever was nice, maybe Arsen would keep him? Then Ever wouldn't have to learn anyone else's rules ever again.

Learning Jennika's rules cost him a lot. His dignity. His flesh. He could do it one more time for Arsen, but he didn't know if he could handle it a third time. The not knowing was the worst part. The second-guessing every single thought. It was exhausting. Like…standing in quicksand, afraid every movement might be the one that sank him deeper, trapped him further.

What was it that would make Arsen angry? Would he be angry enough to hit? To kick? To punch? Would he whip him? Withhold food? Sell him to others? Ever could handle anything but that. It was too hard to fake liking it. Not that they cared if he liked it. Mostly they seemed to want him to hate it, hate them.

Ever studied Arsen. He didn't seem quick to anger. He'd shot Jennika, though—he'd said she deserved it for what she'd done to those little girls. Ever shook his head. He didn't want to think about that…about those girls. They were so small, so helpless. He'd tried to protect them, but he was rarely allowed out of that room.

Arsen couldn't be that bad. He felt safe. He felt warm. It made Ever long to be closer to him in a way he'd never even imagined. He didn't like to be touched, but he'd wanted Arsen to touch him, had wanted to roll around in his scent. He'd slept so deeply in his arms and when Arsen told him to go back to sleep, he'd gotten to bury his face in his pillow that smelled like him.

Ever let Arsen guide him to the sofa in the office. When he handed him a paper plate with a piece of pizza on it, he took it, setting it in his lap. He watched as the loud one and Jericho ate, scarfing down the food like they hadn't eaten in weeks. He looked down at his plate, chewing on his lower lip. He'd never had pizza before.

It smelled good.

Really good.

But it looked kind of…drippy.

He watched from beneath his lashes as Arsen took a slice and folded it in half, eating most of it in one bite. When he realized they were all watching him, he picked up the pizza, folded it in half and took as big a bite as he could stomach. The flavors exploded on his tongue and he couldn't help but moan at the taste. When was the last time he'd had something that wasn't just soup or bread?

He was used to only eating once a day, sometimes not even that much, but never food like this. It was definitely going to give him a stomach ache if he ate the whole piece but he couldn't stop. When it was gone, he made a sad noise, then blushed when he realized they were smiling at him.

Jericho slapped another slice on his plate. He just stared at it, forlorn, then looked to Arsen, askance.

Arsen tilted his head, his pizza halfway to his mouth. "Are you not hungry, little one?"

He opened his mouth to answer then stopped. He didn't want to answer wrong. He didn't want to answer out loud. He hated his voice. He didn't like the way it sounded when it left his mouth. Jennika said he sounded like a girl. That his voice was too high. Too breathy.

Besides, he didn't know the right answer. What if he wasn't supposed to want it. What if he wasn't supposed to refuse it, either. He wanted to close his eyes and cover his ears and just make it all stop.

"I'll take it."

Ever watched as the loud boy's hand crossed in front of

him, grabbing his pizza. Ever didn't mean to do it, didn't even remember grabbing his hand, wasn't aware of what he was doing until he felt his teeth digging into the fleshy part of the boy's palm just beneath his thumb.

"Ow!" he yelped, pulling his skin from between Ever's teeth and rubbing the spot. "What the fuck, dude? The little shit bit me."

When Arsen crossed to him, Ever recoiled. But he just sat beside him and cupped his face. "Are you okay? Did he scare you?"

Levi gaped at them. "Is *he* okay? What about me? I'm the one who just got bit. I think he broke the skin."

Ever nodded, watching the other boy warily.

Arsen glared at the loud one. "You cannot just grab at him like that, Levi. He has trauma."

Levi rolled his eyes. "We all have trauma. I just wanted pizza, too."

"Don't touch other people's food," Jericho said.

Arsen grinned at Ever, petting his cheek in a way that made Ever want to close his eyes and lean into the caress. "He's food aggressive. I don't blame him," he threw over his shoulder. Then, to Ever, he said, "He scared you, huh?"

Ever nodded.

"Food aggressive. He's a person, Arsen, not a dog," Jericho said around a laugh.

Levi flung his arms in the air. "That is not a person. That is a feral little gremlin in a human suit."

"Levi," Jericho said sharply.

Arsen took the pizza from Ever's plate and folded it,

holding it up. "Can you say sorry to Levi, *besenok*?"

Ever chewed on his lip, glowering at Levi. Finally, he said, "Sorry."

They all looked at him, appearing surprised.

Ever flushed, looking away.

"Bite," Arsen said.

Ever complied without thought, letting Arsen feed him the pizza.

"What the fuck. You're babying him, dude. He's going to think if you bite people, you get rewarded," Levi said, sulking.

Arsen booped Ever's nose. "Good boy."

Once more, warmth bled through him at Arsen's purred compliment.

Levi made a disgusted sound. "You're all fucking weird. I'm out of here."

"Don't forget you have a job tonight," Jericho called.

"Yeah, yeah. Just keep the gremlin on a leash."

Ever spent the next few hours watching Arsen work. Whenever he was doing something that didn't make noise, he would talk to Ever, just keeping up a running commentary about whatever was on his mind. He talked about where he was from—Moscow, which was apparently in Russia. He talked about how he came there when he was a kid. He talked about his friends, about Jericho, how Jericho was married to Atticus and how they were thinking about fostering kids. How Atticus had five brothers. How

Arsen was an only child.

Ever didn't know any of them, but he enjoyed Arsen's voice. His accent and smooth tone soothed something within him. He didn't tell Arsen that, though. He didn't say anything at all. He kept his headphones on but without the music, just listening to Arsen talk as he moved around the shop.

Jericho was still there but he stayed inside on his computer, popping out periodically to ask Arsen questions about the cars he worked on. When he opened the door the final time, he looked at Arsen and said, "Knock off for the day, kid. It's getting late. I'll handle anything left before I go. Take Ever upstairs so he can shower and eat."

Arsen nodded, going to the sink to scrub his hands until they were red, then he crossed to take Ever's hand, pulling him from the bench and leading him upstairs. Ever felt shaky, unsure what he was supposed to do next.

"You hungry, *besenok*?"

Ever didn't know what that meant but it made him blush when Arsen called him that. It wasn't said with any unkindness, so he hoped it was something nice. Arsen seemed to enjoy calling Ever that. So, if it made him happy, that was okay with him.

Ever wasn't hungry, though. He wasn't sure he could eat again for another day or so. He'd had two whole pieces of pizza and they sat like a rock in his stomach. He shook his head.

"You should take a shower first. I'll use up all the hot water trying to get myself clean."

Ever shook his head violently. There was no way he was

using all of Arsen's hot water. He could take cold showers. He was used to it. Just taking a shower at all was a luxury to him. Jennika had made him use the hose outside. He'd scrub in the sink if Arsen asked him to.

"No arguments, *besenok*. Just do it."

Ever flushed so hot he thought he might start sweating. He followed Arsen to his bedroom, unsure what else to do, standing in the doorway as Arsen rifled through his drawers. This time, he gave him a pair of gym shorts and a pale yellow t-shirt from his own dresser.

When he turned his back, Ever brought the fabric to his nose, inhaling deeply. It still smelled like Arsen. Or maybe Arsen smelled like the clothes. Either way, Ever wanted to be wrapped in that smell again. He'd take a shower because Arsen asked, but he'd make it really quick so he didn't use all the hot water.

Ever did his best to scrub himself quickly, washing his face and hair and body with as much efficiency as he could, keeping the temperature lukewarm at best.

Still, when he emerged—dressed but hair still dripping— Arsen was clean, hair also slightly damp, wearing a pair of black joggers and another oversized hoodie, this one a blinding neon green. How many sweatshirts did he own? Had he showered in the sink?

Ever must have looked confused because Arsen gave him a smile. "I just ran and showered next door. There are communal showers over there. I figured it would be easier. That way we both got hot water."

Ever flushed. He'd made Arsen shower with other people

just so he could get clean. Shame pooled in his stomach like acid. He was making a burden of himself.

"Your hair's all wet," Arsen said. "You're going to catch a cold."

Ever's eyes went wide, his gaze darting to the bathroom then back to Arsen, his pulse starting to thud hard in his ears. Was he supposed to dry his hair before he left the bathroom?

Arsen took his hand and led him to the sofa, pushing on his shoulders until he sat. Before he could even guess what Arsen intended to do, he was sliding into the space behind Ever, his whole body surrounding him just like last night, his thighs warm as they pressed against Ever's hips.

"Is this okay?" Arsen asked softly.

Ever chewed on his lower lip, goosebumps erupting along his skin. Was it? Being this close to Arsen felt…nice but it also made him feel shivery inside in a way he'd never really felt before. The more Arsen touched him, the more he wanted him to continue and he didn't know what to do about that. Was that normal? Was anything about this normal?

Finally, he nodded. What else could he do?

Arsen took the small towel from Ever's shoulders and began to rub it on his hair. Ever closed his eyes, enjoying the heat of his body and gentle friction of the towel against his scalp. He didn't know how long he sat there, but, suddenly, Arsen's gentle touch became slightly more aggressive until Ever realized he was no longer drying his hair but just messing with him.

Ever snatched the towel from his head without thought, turning to glare at Arsen before realizing what he did. Fear spiked through him, but Arsen just laughed, looking down at him, then picking at the pieces of his hair.

"You look like angry baby chicken." Ever glowered at him, lips forming a pout. "Very cute baby chicken," Arsen clarified.

Ever didn't know why that distinction mollified him a bit, but it did. He faced forward once more, afraid to look at Arsen's face for too long. He let him finger-comb his hair until it parted down the middle. When he dropped his hands, Ever stayed where he was, unsure if he was allowed to leave but also not really sure he wanted to.

When Arsen didn't ask him to move or leave, he found himself relaxing against him just a bit. He gnawed at the inside of his cheek, waiting for…something. Instructions. An order. Some clue as to what he was supposed to do next.

"Are you okay?" Arsen asked after a few moments.

Ever jolted. Had he wanted him to move? He tried to get to his feet, but Arsen's hands appeared at his hips, holding him in place.

"Don't run away. I wasn't trying to scare you off. But you can sit next to me if you're uncomfortable. If I'm making you uncomfortable."

Was he uncomfortable like this? No. He liked it there. But he wasn't sure he was supposed to. He stayed as he was, stiff in Arsen's arms, as he tried to figure out what Arsen was saying.

Did he want him to sit next to him or was that the

compromise to him not staying in his lap? Did he want him to move? If so, why had he stopped him? Tears formed in his eyes, but he blinked them away. He was such a big baby. He just wanted to be normal. What did normal people do in this situation? Was this even a normal situation? Did people sit in other people's laps? Adult people?

"You're okay," Arsen said again, his hand soothing over Ever's hair. "You can do whatever you want, *besenok*. You know that, right? You don't…belong to me. You don't have to follow my orders."

Ever whipped his head around, turning his body just enough to study Arsen's face, trying to decipher his words. What did that mean? If he didn't belong to Arsen, who did he belong to? Was there someone else? Was there someone else coming for him? The tears brimming just moments ago broke free, spilling hot down his cheeks as he shook his head. "No." Arsen frowned, but Ever just shook his head harder. "No," he said again with more force.

Once more, Arsen's hands were on him, this time on his cheeks. They were big and rough and still smelled faintly of motor oil. Ever wanted to bury his nose in that scent, but he didn't know why. He didn't know anything. He was overwhelmed. He hated this. He hated this so much.

"No, what?" Arsen said, his face a mask of confusion. "Don't cry. What's wrong?"

"I don't want to belong to someone else," Ever said, panic welling within him. "Can't I just stay with you? I'll do whatever you want. I can cook. I can clean. I can run errands. I always come back." Ever's mind raced. What else could he do? " I-I can do…other things…" He trailed off, hoping Arsen understood what other things he was willing to do to not go anywhere else.

Arsen's confusion turned to…something else. Disgust maybe. Did Ever disgust him? That somehow just made him cry harder.

"Shh, don't cry," Arsen soothed, his thumbs swiping at Ever's cheeks. "You don't belong to anybody. You're never going to belong to anybody again. You don't have to do anything you don't want to. You decide what you want to do. Do you understand?"

Ever shook his head. He didn't understand. How was he supposed to survive on his own? He could read, he could sort of write. But he had never gone to school, never learned things like math or science. He didn't have a real name or a place to live. How was he supposed to survive alone?

"You don't want me?" Ever said, hating the way his voice cracked.

To his horror, Arsen's eyes filled with tears. "What? No. I—" He shook his head. "It has nothing to do with that. You can stay here…with me. I am not making you leave. But you don't have to do anything to stay. You don't have to cook or clean or be my…servant. You can just…be."

"Be what?" Ever wailed.

"Be yourself. Whatever you want to do, you can do it."

Ever shook his head. His chest felt like it was being crushed. How was he supposed to do that? "I don't know what you want from me," he finally said.

Arsen tilted Ever's head up to meet his gaze. "Nothing.

57

Nothing you don't want to give me of your own free will. You don't have to do what you're told anymore. You can just do what you want. Do the things you like."

"I don't know what I want or what I like. I just want to do what you want me to do," Ever admitted, frantic.

"Shh, *besenok*. We'll figure out what you like. Okay? We try everything and keep what works and get rid of the rest. Okay?"

Ever's brows knitted together. Everything? How could they try everything? There was so much everything in the world. The world was just so big. Even this space felt too big. If he could have chosen to live just as he was, cradled between Arsen's thighs, his big warm hands on his face, he would. It felt safe there. *He* felt safe there.

"I don't want to leave," Ever whimpered.

"Then stay," Arsen said as if it was the simplest thing in the world. "Just stay here. With me. But only because you want to. Not because you think I want you to."

Arsen released his face and Ever mourned the loss, turning to face forward again. Could he really do whatever he wanted? He decided to test his theory. He sagged back against Arsen, some of the tension leaving him when he didn't protest. He reached for his hands, which were on his thighs, taking them and wrapping his arms around his waist, waiting to see if he would pull away. Praying he didn't.

Instead, Arsen tightened his grip just the tiniest bit, hugging Ever from behind like it was something he wanted, too, his uneven breaths puffing against Ever's hair.

"Tighter," Ever said.

Arsen complied. "Like this?" he asked, voice raw.

Ever nodded. He didn't know why the tight band around him was easing the tension inside but it was. It was soothing the panic trying to well back up inside him. They sat like that for a long while, not speaking. Not doing anything but breathing in each other's space.

"I like your voice," Arsen said, dipping his head to speak the words directly against Ever's ear.

Ever turned his face into the sound without thought, shivering when Arsen's lips brushed against his skin.

Ever settled his head against Arsen's chest, his head tucking just under his chin. "I like your voice, too."

FIVE

ARSEN

ARSEN HELD EVER ON THE couch for a long time. It should have been weird. Everything about their situation would be weird to an outsider. Sleeping wrapped around a stranger was weird. Not wanting that stranger out of your sight was weird. Worrying about a stranger's every discomfort was weird.

But holding Ever didn't feel weird. It felt like not nearly enough. Arsen wanted to pull him into the bedroom and fold around him again. He wanted to feel his body molded to Ever's, wanted to hear him snore softly like a kitten and feel his finger's curl around Arsen's.

But he couldn't. For a million reasons. Not the least of which was having to get online soon. He had an audience waiting for him. Streaming his gameplay on Twitch didn't make him millions, but it did supplement his income. He wasn't a celebrity, but he'd amassed a loyal following—mostly of girls—who noticed when he didn't sign on two nights in a row.

He got to his feet, taking Ever with him. "I have to go online in the computer room for a while. Do you want to lie in my bed and listen to your music or stay in there with me?" It was clear from their conversation a few moments ago that Ever didn't know how to make choices for himself, but Arsen didn't feel comfortable ordering him around. Offering choices seemed like the lesser of two evils.

Once more, Ever caught his lip between his teeth. It was clearly a nervous habit but his lips were already chapped and bruised. If he kept it up, they might bleed and Arsen didn't want that. He'd been hurt enough.

He gently tugged the skin from beneath Ever's bunny teeth. "You're going to hurt yourself."

If he was being honest, that wasn't the only reason Arsen needed Ever to stop doing that. Whenever he chewed on that lower lip, it made Arsen want to do the same. He couldn't help it. Ever was beautiful. Not handsome. Not attractive. Beautiful. Shockingly so now that he was clean and in the light.

His hair parted down the center in soft waves and fell into big brown eyes that changed color from coffee to brandy depending on the light. He had perfect bone structure and wide eyes with long dark lashes. Even his ears were pretty.

That wasn't just Arsen's opinion. Nobody would ever say different. When it came to genetics, Ever had been blessed, at least in appearance. Arsen wanted to know where Ever's parents were. How could they have let this happen to him? He shook the thought away. This wasn't about that. It was about Arsen's inability to control his growing obsession.

Arsen could handle pretty boys, but Ever wasn't just pretty. He was painfully shy, impossibly sweet, excruciatingly

broken, and when he pouted—like he was just then—
Arsen was literally helpless. He'd give him anything. Not
that Ever would believe that.

Ever was Arsen's fucking kryptonite, custom-made in a
lab to test his resolve. As if to prove Arsen's point, he puffed
out his cheeks then made fish lips, like he couldn't decide
what to do to distract himself if he couldn't chew on that
perfectly plump lower lip. Just looking at him was making
Arsen uncomfortably hard and his pants were far too loose
for that. Luckily, his hoodie covered the worst of it. He
needed to get online and distract himself.

Quickly.

"My game is a little loud, but you can bring your
headphones and sit on the bed in there or you can go watch
TV in my room." Ever shook his head. "No, none of that.
Talk to me. Tell me what you want." When Ever looked
uncomfortable, Arsen decided to do some pleading of his
own. "Please? I love hearing your voice."

Ever's eyes went wide and Arsen got to watch a blush run
from his neck to the tips of his ears. "I want to stay with
you," he said softly.

Arsen's heart did somersaults. The guys were never going
to let him hear the end of this. He was already fucking gone
over Ever. Completely overtaken. "Okay. But let's bring
your headphones just in case. Okay?"

Ever gave a hesitant nod then followed Arsen into the
spare room, sitting cross-legged on the bed. Arsen placed
the pink cat ear headphones over Ever's ears, then handed
over his phone once more. He matched the neon lights of

the room perfectly, like he was another accessory.

Arsen watched, curious, as Ever selected the green Spotify app and then began to push random buttons, almost like he knew what he was doing. Did he know how to use a cell phone? It seemed like a stupid question. Everybody in this day and age knew how to use a cell phone, right? But did he? Arsen didn't know how long Ever had been held prisoner in that room, by that woman. He didn't know if she'd taught him the basics of how to survive.

She'd clearly sent him on errands and knew he'd come back because he was chipped. Like a dog. And beaten like a dog. And caged like a dog. Just thinking of it had Arsen's blood running hot. He should have killed that bitch slowly.

He dropped into his chair and put on his headphones, pulling his mic into place. He hit a series of buttons, bringing up his screens and signing into his account. His left screen allowed him to see what his audience saw, namely him. His middle screen was for gameplay. His right screen allowed him to read the rapid-fire chat as he played the game.

He made sure he remembered to hit record. He'd put it up on YouTube later after he edited their gameplay. Almost immediately, his screen began to fill with messages. Some handles familiar, many not. He didn't pay them much mind, just kept up a running commentary with both the audience and his friends, who signed on one at a time in rapid succession. Seven first, then Felix, Nico, and finally, Levi. Arsen wasn't sure if he was going to show or if he was still sulking over a tiny bite.

Most of the chat had no linear flow. There were men

and women alike telling Arsen all manner of contradictory stuff. He was hot. He was ugly. His accent was cute. His accent was grating. He took the bad with the good. For every one negative comment, there were twenty positives and his regulars tipped well.

Knowing Ever was three feet away made it all but impossible to concentrate on the game, but he did his best. At least Ever was safe where he could see him.

Once the others signed online he relaxed, forcing himself to focus. He didn't want to be the reason they lost this battle.

Arsen didn't have to worry about Ever. Twenty minutes in, it became apparent that Felix was going to be the reason they lost the battle.

"What are you doing?" he shouted into the mic.

Felix had gone completely rogue. He wasn't listening to the others. This always happened. Arsen was almost positive it was Felix's husband's fault. He was also a huge distraction.

"We're fucking getting creamed here, bro. What the fuck?" Seven said. "Are you blind? The bad guys are over there."

Arsen was jabbing his finger down on the button hard enough to bruise it, hoping to make up for Felix's sudden defection.

"*Blayablayablayablay.*"

"Are you having a stroke?" Nico yelled.

Arsen assumed that was directed at Felix as well.

"Fuck you," Felix shot back. "My hand slipped."

Arsen shook his head. "Your hand slipped? Is it still slipping? Why are you facing the other way? Are you trying to lose? Tell Avi to fuck off."

Avi was Felix's husband and was a bit of a psychopath but he wasn't allowed to kill nice people and nobody was nicer than Arsen. At least, not in their inner circle so he felt safe enough to speak his truth. And that truth was that Felix's horny husband was going to cost them some much needed fucking leverage.

"You need me way more than I need you," Felix said.

Arsen rolled his eyes. Usually, that was true but he was playing like it was his first day. "Go left. Your other left. Sometimes, I swear English is *your* second language, not mine."

Felix scoffed. "English isn't my second language, dick. It's my third. I speak Spanish and Cantonese, too."

Oh yeah. Their neighborhood really was a melting pot of millions of different backgrounds and ethnicities. Felix's mom was Chinese but his father had been Mexican. Seven's mother was from Egypt while his dad was Polish. Levi and Nico just called themselves mutts, which Arsen assumed meant they were just varying degrees of white.

They won the battle, thanks to Seven's magic skills, but Arsen was mentally worn out. He encouraged the others to do a side mission so he could focus on those who watched. This was supposed to be fun.

They were only midway through the main gameplay arc, and he was in no particular hurry to finish the game and defeat the enemy. Arsen had played *Paladin* alone and with friends hundreds of times, but this was the sequel so there was a whole brand new shiny world and Arsen wanted to savor every new land and storyline.

He liked *Paladin* for its hyperrealistic world-building. The makers of the game had recreated King Arthur's court with painstaking detail and it was easy to get immersed in the game, even when just doing walk-throughs. So immersed he literally jumped when Ever touched his shoulder.

When he glanced up, he noted Ever wasn't looking at him but the screen, eyes wide as he leaned in closer to get a better look, his fingers tracing the figure before him in armor. Arsen's player.

"You want to watch, *besenok*?"

Ever nodded. Arsen patted the ottoman between his legs. Ever dropped onto the surface, looking back at Arsen, uncertain. Arsen gripped the ottoman and tugged it back so that Ever was tucked against him, his head just under Arsen's chin so he could still have full range of motion. Ever was actually the perfect size.

The moment Ever's face appeared on camera, the chat went crazy.

Who's that?

Is that your boyfriend?

Oh, my God. He's so hot.

He's so cute.

Look at his cat ear headphones.

OMG.

Are you gay, bro?

I didn't know you liked dudes.

Gross

Sick

That's hot

WTF?

Are you all gay?

Is that your boyfriend?

He's cute.

You're so cute together.

"Is that him?" Felix asked, amused. "Is that the stray who bit Levi?"

"Don't call him that," Arsen muttered.

Aw, he's so protective.

I would be, too.

I'd never let him out of the house again. He's so fine.

I can't believe he's gay

Maybe that's why he left Russia

"Oh, someone's already got a crush," Seven said. "Not even twenty-four hours in. Damn. I always knew he'd fall fast and hard."

Arsen didn't bother denying it. What was he going to say? He didn't have a crush on Ever? That would be a lie. And Arsen was many things but he wasn't a liar.

"I told you he picked him over me," Levi sulked.

Arsen rolled his eyes. "You scared him and tried to take his pizza."

"See!" Levi said.

Arsen was grateful Ever couldn't hear the back and forth over the headphones like the audience could. But he could see that he and Arsen were on camera, something that he only noticed about five minutes after he sat down.

He turned, caught sight of them both, then leaned in, squinting at the tinier version of themselves before looking at Arsen in confusion.

"We're on camera. People can see you," Arsen said. "Say hi."

"People?" he whispered.

Arsen nodded. "They come on and watch me play my game with friends. They're all nice. They think you're very cute."

Ever's eyes went wide and he looked back at the screen,

leaning in to look at the chat once more, this time reading the comments. Arsen didn't know how much Ever could read but he knew he did. And there was no missing the stir his appearance was creating among the audience, especially the girls.

Ever flushed to the tips of his ears. Before Arsen could even guess his intention, he grabbed the bottom of Arsen's hoodie and pulled it over his head, hiding his face from the camera.

Arsen found himself staring down at cat ears popping out from his collar, shocked.

"You two seem…cozy," Felix teased.

"I've heard of someone trying to get into your pants but never your hoodie," Seven crowed.

Arsen did his best to smile and play along, but inside he was dying. Ever hiding in Arsen's shirt was adorable, and clearly the audience loved it. The sound of people tipping him filled his headphones again and again, but now, Ever's cheek was pressed to Arsen's bare chest, his breath puffing against his nipple.

Chyort.

Arsen grabbed his zipper, slowly pulling it down until Ever's face popped into view. "What are you doing, *besenok*? Are you shy?"

Ever slapped his hand away from the zipper, pulling it back up once more. Arsen gave a small laugh. What was he supposed to do with that?

He's so cute

You two are so cute together

What's his name?

We want to see his face

Is he your boyfriend?

Is he

Is he

Answer us

"His name is Ever and he's shy so he's going to stay where he is," Arsen said.

The chat continued to fire off thousands of comments, but he ignored it all, pulling Ever's headphones off and adjusting him so Arsen could get his hands back to the keyboard. He continued to play that way, Ever's body half-turned, his cheek resting against his chest, his fingers dancing along Arsen's ribcage, then lower to the waistband of his sweatpants, then back up again.

It was like trying to play a game with a kitten in his jacket, adorable but painfully distracting, especially with his friends making fun of him.

"Your new boyfriend is popular," Seven teased.

"And feral," Levi muttered.

"I've told you a million times not to steal food off people's plates. It was bound to happen eventually," Felix chastised.

"Whose side are you on?" Levi asked, sulking.

"Usually not yours," Felix reminded him.

"It's true," Nico said. "You should learn to keep your hands to yourself."

Arsen was glad Ever couldn't see the stir he was creating online. It would have been way too much for him. It was starting to feel like too much for Arsen, too. Every time another tip came in, the computer chimed. Arsen was starting to get a headache.

People gave money hoping to get his attention, hoping to get Ever's attention. But the only thing that had Ever's attention was the drawstring on Arsen's sweatpants, which meant Ever now had Arsen's undivided attention and the hard-on to prove it. There was no way Ever didn't feel that.

"That's all for tonight, guys," Arsen said abruptly. "I'm going to bed."

What?

Now?

That was quick

With him?

Is he your boyfriend?

Is he?

71

OMG. So cute.

Bring him on again tomorrow.

It was only ten o'clock but Arsen signed off, waiting to unzip his hoodie until they were off camera. As soon as he did, Ever looked up in surprise, the tiniest bit of guilt on his face. Had he been trying to tease Arsen? No. Of course not. He was just bored and shy. "Are you ready for bed, *besenok?*"

Ever stared up at him with wide eyes, full lips parted. The urge to lean down and kiss him was damn near impossible to ignore. Like gravity or magnets. Ever's tongue shot out to lick over his lower lip and Arsen almost cracked.

But he didn't.

Ever didn't need that. He didn't want it. They were strangers. Fuck.

"Come on. Let's brush our teeth."

Arsen led him into the bathroom where he put toothpaste on both of their toothbrushes and then handed Ever's to him. Ever stared at Arsen in the mirror the whole time they brushed their teeth, spitting when he did, rinsing when he did.

When they were done, Arsen clipped his hair back and washed his face. Ever sat on the toilet, watching intently. "Felix makes me do this," Arsen said by way of explanation. "He says skincare is very important. Because I don't want to listen to him lecture me, I just do it. It is easier that way. He is hammer and everybody else is nail. You'll see."

When Arsen finished washing his face and putting on his moisturizer, he dried his hands. Ever stood and pushed his own hair back, tipping his face up at Arsen. It took him a solid thirty seconds to realize he was waiting for Arsen to wash his face and not kiss it. It felt like someone kicked him in the heart.

This boy was going to be the end of him.

He gently wet Ever's skin and then foamed the soap between his fingers before rubbing it over his cheeks, his chin, his forehead, paying special attention to his nose just because it was so cute and small. When he could no longer justify touching his face, he told him to rinse in the sink, patting his face dry before he applied the moisturizer to his skin just as he had his own.

When he finished, Ever gave him the tiniest smile. "Thank you."

Arsen blinked at him.

He was fucked. He was *so* fucked they would have to think of a new word for fucked. Destroyed. Ruined. Done for. He would fight armies for Ever. He would let him kick him in the face. He would fight a bear for him, burn down villages, start a war. Whatever it took to make Ever smile at him like that every day.

Not even a day had passed and Ever had stolen Arsen's whole heart.

"Who knew something so small could be such trouble?" Arsen mused to himself. Ever tilted his head, looking at him like a confused puppy. "Forget it. Let's go to bed. Do you want to sleep in the computer room?"

Ever shook his head.

"Use your words, *besenok*," Arsen teased.

Ever caught his lip with his teeth but quickly released it. "I want to sleep with you."

Arsen was glad his hoodie was hiding his dick since it was starting to take notice again. He was going to have to make sure their sleeping position was different from last night's or Ever was going to run screaming, thinking Arsen was the worst kind of person.

Maybe he was. He tried not to be, but it was all so much. His body wanted what it wanted, but that didn't mean he was entitled to it. He just didn't know how to get the message to the right department in his brain because Ever smelled like him and felt so good and was so cuddly.

Before they left the bathroom, Arsen took the Vaseline from the counter and opened it, dabbing some on Ever's abused mouth. He needed to take better care of him. He needed a doctor. Several maybe. He'd talk to Coe tomorrow. He'd know how to help him.

Once they were back in his room, Arsen pulled back the covers for Ever, watching as he climbed in and scooted himself against the wall. Arsen tugged off his hoodie and laid beside him. He usually slept in his underwear or less, but not tonight. Tonight it was imperative to keep as many layers between them as possible.

He stayed on his back a respectful distance away, staring up at the ceiling like the answers to the universe were written there. He could do this. He could totally do this. Ever was a good foot away, facing away from him. It would all be fine.

As if Ever could read his mind, he rolled over, then inch-wormed his way to Arsen slowly, watching his face the whole time, checking to see if he was going to be chastised or turned away. As if Arsen could ever do that. Finally, Ever curled against his side, resting his head on Arsen's shoulder, his hand on his bare stomach.

He held very still, but Arsen could feel him trembling. When he looked down at him, Ever looked up, his trepidation obvious, like he thought Arsen would yell at him or tell him to move.

As if that were ever a possibility.

Instead, he pulled the covers up around them, then dropped his arm to Ever's shoulders, threading his fingers in his hair, combing through it like he had earlier. He continued stroking his hair until Ever's breathing evened out. What the hell was he doing? What was happening here?

One day.

One day and Ever owned him, body and soul.

Arsen would never hear the end of this.

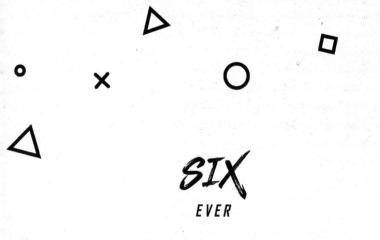

SIX

EVER

EVER WOKE TO THE SOUND of whimpering. He covered his mouth to not wake up Arsen with his crying. But it wasn't him. Beside him, Arsen's face was contorted, eyes closed, head moving restlessly on the pillow.

"Net. Tol'ko ne eto."

"Ya ne stany."

Ever knew all about nightmares. Used to have them all the time when he was little before he gave up hope that life would get better. When waking hours were the nightmare, sleep for him felt like a reprieve, but what happened when life got better? Would Ever have nightmares again, horrible flashbacks to what he'd endured before Arsen saved him? Would sleep become the place he went to relive the worst of it?

What was Arsen reliving?

Ever thought about waking him. He didn't want him to be sad. And he was sad. There were tears on his cheeks. Or maybe it was sweat. Ever put his hand to his chest. The rest of him didn't feel hot, at least not any hotter than his skin usually was beneath Ever's hands.

Usually.

They'd slept in the same bed twice. That wasn't enough time for Ever to know Arsen's "usual" but still… Arsen had been only good to him so far. He didn't want him to suffer. Arsen was lying on his side facing him, crying, whimpering, sometimes sounding like he was choking. Ever didn't know what to do.

He scooted closer, wrapping himself around Arsen tightly, locking him in his embrace. Arsen was so much bigger than him that hugging him required Ever to press his face under Arsen's chin. He couldn't stop himself from inhaling his scent. There was just something so familiar and comforting to it.

Arsen's cries ceased, but he continued to mutter words Ever couldn't understand, some garbled, some in his native tongue. All Ever could do was hold him until he settled into sleep once more. Holding Arsen didn't feel like a chore. Part of Ever thought maybe it was wrong. Not just because Jennika said boys couldn't love other boys, but because Arsen touched him so carefully. Looked at him in a way that made Ever feel hot and shivery.

But Arsen always looked sorry for it, and Ever didn't know why. He was too embarrassed to ask. He should know these things. Normal people his age knew these things. He'd read books about people who grew up and got married and had kids. He knew how things between boys and girls were supposed to go, but Arsen wasn't a girl and Ever was barely a person.

Ever listened to the blood pounding in his ears, the sound deafening. What was Arsen even thinking about? What could scare someone like him? Ever didn't know much, but he knew Arsen had killed Jennika without a thought. He knew Jericho and Atticus knew it, too.

There was talk about jobs with knowing looks and pointed stares. Ever wasn't stupid. What they did in the daylight hid what it was they were doing at night—killing people. Ever should feel bad about that. Right? Killing was wrong. But Ever had met a lot of bad, wrong people since Jennika bought him and Arsen didn't feel bad about what he did to her. None of them felt bad. Even if they did bad things.

But was it really bad? Killing Jennika had saved him.

Arsen had referred to her as a horrible person. And she was. The worst kind of person. So, what was the real sin? Allowing an evil person to keep hurting innocents or wiping out the evil to protect others? To Ever, the answer was clear. But maybe that was because he was a bad person too deep down?

Before he could think too much more about it, Arsen rolled, the solid weight of him trapping Ever beneath him, his lips nuzzling against Ever's ear like he was nestling into his favorite pillow.

Ever tried to free himself. But Arsen was so much bigger than him. His arms had fallen over Ever's, holding them captive against his sides. It was only then, only once he realized he couldn't move, couldn't escape, couldn't breath—that was when the panic set in. His heart was beating so hard, his brain yanking him back into a memory he'd never wanted to think about again.

Their laughing. His crying. Hands holding his wrists so tightly, it felt like his bones might actually shatter. The burning pain. The sour smell of his breath. The smell of cigarettes and sweat. He was going to puke.

All he had to do was cry out or scream or even just say Arsen's name but the words stuck in his throat. Just like then. His head swam, his vision going fuzzy. Was this what it was like to faint?

Ever didn't think, just raked his nails across Arsen's side and lower back, the only place he could reach. Arsen reared back, a shout of pain on his lips. He sat on his knees between Ever's legs, looking around in confusion, his hands going for his shredded skin.

Ever watched him come back to himself, saw him blink the cobwebs of his nightmares from his thoughts. That was when it happened, when his look of confusion morphed into one of horror as he realized he'd been on top of Ever.

"I—Are you alright?" he asked, voice hoarse from sleep. "Did I..." His eyes went wide and he blinked in confusion. "Did I try to hurt you?"

Ever shook his head. He didn't answer out loud. There was no way he could find his words until his heart rate slowed. And that wasn't happening anytime soon. Arsen's hands were on him, running from his shoulders to his fingertips, then over his chest and belly, not in any sexual way but like he was checking him for any injury he might have caused.

"I'm fine," he finally said, his voice equally raw, but not

from sleep. "You didn't do anything. I—You rolled over on me and I panicked. It's my fault."

Arsen stared down at him. "How is that your fault, *besenok*?" Arsen asked, shaking his head. "It's all on me. I knew I should not let you sleep here. I have nightmares. Violent ones. It's dangerous."

The nightmares didn't seem violent. He'd fallen on top of Ever but not with the intention of hurting him. "I have them, too, sometimes," Ever said. "It's okay."

Arsen's hand touched his cheek, and Ever's lids fluttered closed. He just wanted to focus on the rough feel of his hand on his cheek, even if only for a second. "I didn't mean to scare you."

Ever opened his eyes, gazing at Arsen's earnest face. "I… usually like your arms around me. But when you fell on me, I couldn't move. I just got scared."

Arsen went to move his palm but Ever snatched his wrist, holding it there, before realizing what he'd done and letting go quickly. What was wrong with him?

"I'm sorry," Arsen said again, firmer this time. "Do you want to go sleep in the computer room?"

Ever shook his head violently. That was the last thing he wanted. That room was too big, too empty, too quiet. Too much like the closet. It made his skin crawl to be in there alone. "I wanna stay here with you."

Arsen studied his face in the shadows for a long moment then collapsed beside him back on his side of the bed. "Yeah, okay."

They laid there in silence for a long time before Ever

finally said, "What are your nightmares about?"

Arsen turned his head to look at him. For a second, Ever thought he wasn't going to answer, but then he said, "My mother."

Had Arsen's mother been a monster, too? "Was she bad like Jennika?"

Arsen gave a grim smile. "No. She was very good person. Very scary when she was angry, but she was never angry with me."

The use of past tense didn't escape Ever, leaving him with a hollow feeling low in his stomach. "What happened to her?"

"She died."

Ever wasn't sure he should be asking his next question but he did anyway. "How?"

Arsen caught Ever's gaze, his expression grim. "My father shot her. In front of me."

Ever sucked in a sharp breath. "Why?" It was a weird question. Why? Did people need a why to be evil? Not in Ever's experience. "Sorry," he said quickly, face in flames.

"Don't be sorry," Arsen said, giving him that gentle smile he seemed to only save for him. Ever didn't know what to think of it. "He's a violent man. He liked hurting people. Still does."

Ever wanted to do something, to say something to make Arsen feel better, but he didn't know what. He didn't know how to make someone feel better about a dead parent or a bad one. So, he just took Arsen's hand and held it.

Arsen looked down at their threaded fingers, then at Ever. "It's not a nice story. But I'll tell you if you want to know."

Ever chewed on his bottom lip before remembering Arsen didn't like it. "I want to know."

Arsen nodded then flopped his head back on the pillow, staring up at the ceiling. "He used to beat me and my mom all the time. I never fought back, but she did. I think she did it to keep him away from me. To take the focus off of me and put it on her so my punishments were less severe. They fought more than they didn't, always about something different, but really all the same. Then, one day, there was a fight that didn't end like the others. She ended up dead and he ended up in prison."

Ever thought about all the times Jennika had beat him, had brought him to the brink where he'd hoped she would finally just kill him. But she had been too cruel for that. She had relished in his suffering. Still, there was always the chance she would go too far.

But she was dead.

"What made that fight different?" Ever asked.

Arsen looked at him thoughtfully. "Nothing. It started like most of their fights, over nothing important. Over my report card."

Ever had heard the term, seen it in books, but was not entirely certain what that was. "What's a report card?"

Arsen gave him a sad look that made his stomach dip. "It's what they send to parents to tell them how their kids are doing in school."

"Did you get a bad grade?"

Arsen's laugh was bitter. "No. All As. He didn't like that. He said I was trying to embarrass him. Make him look stupid. He said my mother and I were laughing at him for his lack of education."

Ever knew what that was like. The trepidation. The walking on eggshells. It was like sharing space with a hungry tiger. You never knew where or when they would strike, but eventually, the urge to hunt would overwhelm them and you were always prey. It was that gnawing anxiety that was the worst. Almost more than the punishment itself.

"How old were you?" he asked.

Arsen sighed. "Eleven."

Ever squeezed the hand he held. "Was your mom defending you?"

Arsen nodded. "Always. But he killed my mother to prove a point," he said, voice dull. "Or maybe it was an accident."

"An accident?"

Arsen let out another big breath.

"You don't have to tell me," Ever said.

Arsen shook his head. "Maybe it was a lesson that went too far. His gun was on the table where it always was. He took it and made me stand up, put it in my hand, tried to make me put my finger on the trigger and point it at her."

Ever's eyes widened. He couldn't imagine pointing a gun at someone he loved. Not that he'd ever had someone to love, but he understood the notion of love.

"He told me to kill her or he'd kill me. But I couldn't do it. I just…fought him, fought back, got out of his grip. That was what pissed him off. That I'd gotten away. My mother ran at him…and he shot her. And she was just…gone."

"Gone…" Ever said.

Arsen nodded, still staring straight ahead. "During the day, I'm fine, but at night, my brain won't let me forget. That is why people don't sleep in my bed."

"You let me sleep in your bed," Ever said, frowning.

"I do. Yeah," Arsen said, giving him a small smile.

Ever didn't know what to do with that information, so he ignored it, inching closer to Arsen then wrapping his arms around Arsen's much larger one, pressing his cheek to his shoulder. "I'm sorry about your mom."

Arsen looked down at him. "I'm sorry I scared you."

Ever thought about it. Really thought about it. "It was because my arms were trapped. I don't think I'd mind if I could just move my arms. It just made me think of something bad. I didn't mind you on top of…me," he finished in a whisper, his face hot.

"Something bad?" Arsen asked, pointedly ignoring Ever's confession.

Ever nodded. "The last time Jennika sold me."

Arsen was quiet for a long moment, and when he spoke again, his voice was much…harder. "The last time? She'd done it before?"

Ever nodded, trying to use the same distant tone Arsen had used. Maybe it was easier to say the hard stuff that way. "Not a lot. Only when she needed something from someone who had certain interests in people who look like me."

"Look like you?" Arsen asked.

Ever couldn't look at Arsen when he said, "She would tell them I was a little kid."

"Jesus," Arsen muttered.

Ever flushed. Was he mad at him? Should he have kept this to himself? "It wasn't a lie the first few times, technically. I was a kid, just not as small as they hoped."

"You don't have to tell me if you don't want to."

Ever shrugged. "She never let them do what they really wanted to do. She said that was a sin. That sex between two boys was wrong. So, she only let them use my hand...or my mouth. Most of them just wanted pictures." Ever shivered. "Until the last time. She said he'd paid for the privilege and that it would only be one time."

There was a low rumble from Arsen that sent goosebumps rippling along Ever's skin.

"I'm sorry," he said instinctively.

Arsen frowned at him. "Why are you sorry?"

Ever didn't know why he was sorry, just that he was supposed to be. Why was everything so confusing? "I wasn't trying to upset you."

Arsen flopped onto his side until they were almost nose to nose. "You didn't upset me, *besenok*. She upset me. She had no right to do that to you. No wonder you got scared tonight. *I'm* sorry."

It felt wrong for Arsen to apologize. He'd rescued Ever, saved him from a life in that tiny closet. There was nothing that would ever repay that. Even if he didn't know what to do now that he was out of it. "Do you think I'm screwed up?"

"Screwed up?" Arsen echoed.

Ever nodded. "Jericho said I have trauma. Like it's a disease. But Levi said you all have trauma, too. Does that make all of us screwed up?"

Arsen sighed. "I don't know. Most days, I feel like other people. But what happened to me happened a long time ago. Same with Levi and the others. The stuff that happened to you was two days ago. You're bound to be feeling it more than we do."

Ever's voice dropped to a whisper. "I don't, though."

"You don't what?"

Ever's gaze flicked to his then away again. "Feel it. I feel scared. Anxious. Everything feels really big and loud. I am scared, deep down, you're a bad person, too. Or that I'm not going to be what you need and you'll send me away. I'm scared that I don't know anything or anyone. I'm scared that I don't know how to do normal things. But when I think about the things that happened, that she did to me, what he did to me, I feel...nothing."

It was true. Jennika had done horrible, disgusting things to him. She'd beaten him, berated him, used him, sold him, had abused him in ways he'd never utter out loud to anybody because they were humiliating. But there was no...feeling there. It was like he had stepped out of his body and just watched from a distance.

"Does that make me more normal or less?" Ever asked.

"I don't know," Arsen said. "But normal is overrated."

Normal sounded nice to Ever. Even though the only normal he'd ever known was in fairy tales and the books Jennika let him get from the collection box at the church sometimes. Did people like them get normal? Jericho and Atticus seemed normal.

"Are Jericho and Atticus boyfriends?" Ever blurted.

"They're married."

"Boys can do that?" Ever said.

Arsen nodded. "Sure. Anybody can marry anybody."

"Do *they* have trauma?"

Arsen gave a soft laugh. "I think everybody has trauma to some degree. Bad things happen to everybody, but the degree of suffering is relative to the life experiences of the person it happens to. A dog that has never been beaten might think having its paw stepped on is traumatic. A dog that only gets beaten might think getting hit by a car is no different than any of its other suffering and continue to run not knowing how injured it is."

Ever thought about it. He knew which dog he was in that scenario. "How do people do it?"

"Do what?"

"How do they go through life pretending the bad stuff never happened?"

"Some forget with time, some stuff it down with drinking or drugs or sex or food. Some develop weird kinks and coping mechanisms. There is no one way to deal with trauma."

"Kinks? What's a kink?"

Arsen thought about it for a long minute. "People whose sexual preferences are considered outside of societal norms."

Ever chewed on that. "Like what?"

"That seems like a conversation for another time."

Ever frowned. "Why?"

"Because you were held hostage for most of your life by a person who hurt you and forced you to do things against your will."

"I can't talk about kinks because I have trauma?" Ever asked.

Arsen shook his head. "Not exactly."

"You said people with trauma sometimes turn to kinks, so why can't I know about it?"

"I also said they turn to food. Do you want to ask me about that instead? Between kink and food, ice cream seems like the lesser of two evils."

"So, what do you use to cope?" Ever asked. "Not kinks, I guess."

"I don't know, honestly. I guess I'm one of the ones who stuffs it down."

"Do you not like sex?"

"What? No. I love sex."

"But not kinky sex?"

"Ever!"

Ever's eyes went wide and he recoiled, heart slamming against his ribs. "Never mind," he mumbled, then flopped over, facing the wall, tears welling in his eyes.

Then Arsen was behind him, plastered against his back, arm around his waist. "Don't be like that. Don't pout. I… just didn't think sex would be something you'd want to talk about."

"Why?"

"Because you said she sold you to people for sexual purposes."

Ever bit down on the inside of his cheek, his face so hot it felt like flames were licking his skin. He didn't understand. He didn't know much about sex. He read about it in books, mostly in perfunctory terms because Jennika was very strict about what he could read. But what they'd done to him and what sex sounded like in novels didn't really seem like the same thing.

"And because of that, I shouldn't want to know about sex?"

"I didn't mean it like that."

"Do people like me just not have sex? Normal sex? I don't even know what that means."

Ever could feel Arsen's breath ruffling his hair. "You've been in a horrible situation for years. I just think it's better to concentrate on other things...for now."

"Like what?" he asked dully.

"Like just being out in the world."

Ever let tears slide down his cheeks, doing his best to not let Arsen see he was upset. "Okay."

He hadn't been asking Arsen for sex. He'd just wanted to know. Was that wrong? Should he not want to know? If people with trauma sometimes used sex and kinks to cope, why was he in trouble for asking about it? Arsen had made it clear he didn't want that with Ever. But he hadn't said he couldn't ask questions.

He hated feeling like he was wrong all the time. He hated feeling like an alien who'd crash landed on another planet where he didn't know the rules or the laws or the language. Where he didn't know what he was allowed to ask or want or care about. He'd only been asking.

He sniffled softly, wiping at his face as discreetly as possible.

The weight of Arsen's arm across his hip had made him

feel safe yesterday. Now, it just made him feel stupid. Almost like he sensed Ever's distress, Arsen shifted. Ever could swear he felt his lips against the top of his head for a fleeting moment. But then it was gone.

Then *he* was gone, rolling away from Ever. "Get some sleep, *besenok*."

Yeah, right.

SEVEN

ARSEN

ARSEN DIDN'T GO BACK TO sleep. He was sixty percent sure Ever didn't either. He'd stopped crying, but that didn't make Arsen feel any less shitty for making him sad in the first place. There was a stiffness to the way he was lying, his breathing erratic, like he was trying to fake sleep for Arsen's benefit.

Arsen was fucking everything up so badly. Should he have answered Ever's questions? What did Arsen know about kink? What did he really even know about sex? He had it, he enjoyed it, but it wasn't about *feelings*, just feeling... something. Sex hadn't ever meant anything to Arsen. How could he be expected to explain it to Ever? But Ever did deserve some kind of explanation, just maybe not from him.

Arsen crawled out of bed, pulling the covers up around Ever before throwing on a t-shirt, grabbing his cell phone and heading downstairs where he was out of earshot. He looked at the time. It was seven in the morning.

Felix would probably be up already. He owned his own company but got up early to ride to work with his husband. Besides, Felix wouldn't be mad if Arsen called with a crisis, especially this kind of crisis. He lived for drama of any sort.

Arsen hit the call button.

Felix answered on the third ring, sounding confused. "Hello?"

"I need you," Arsen said in lieu of a greeting.

Felix snorted, his tone shifting to one of boredom. "Sorry, I'm happily married. You should have said something sooner."

Arsen rolled his eyes. It was hard to believe he and Jericho were brothers sometimes. They were polar opposites. Jericho was a killer but, deep down, he was a softie. Felix on the other hand... His husband, Avi, called him an alley cat in a rhinestone collar and the description suited him.

Felix looked like a rich man's sugar baby, but he was lethal in every sense of the word. Not even a career designing for A-list celebrities could quell his love of violence.

"Something happened with Ever," Arsen said.

There was a long pause then Felix said, "That was quick. I'm gonna be honest, I didn't think you had it in you to defile the little darling. But I get it. He's pretty adorable."

Defile? Why was everyone suddenly so obsessed with sex?

But then wasn't that why Arsen had called Felix in the first place?

"I didn't defi—have sex with him," Arsen said, feeling guilty even thinking the word *defile* in relation to Ever. He deserved better than that.

"Wow, Jericho's right. You are down bad," Felix said, his amusement obvious.

It didn't surprise Arsen that Jericho was talking to his brother about him. His friends were gossips to the core and—despite his constant lecturing about staying out of other people's business—Jericho was somehow the biggest gossip of them all, sharing their secrets with his husband and their cat.

Arsen had no doubt his friends—Levi, Seven, Noah, Arlo, Zane, Lake, Cree, and Nico—had created a group chat without him so they could talk about him and Ever at length. That was what Arsen would have done if it was any of them. That was just how their crew worked.

"Are you going to help me or not?" Arsen said, his frustration growing with each passing moment.

"Help you what, babes? You still haven't told me what the problem is. Since you apparently haven't devirginized the little gumdrop."

Arsen didn't know what a gumdrop was. He shook his head, trying to focus with the word *virgin* still ringing in his ears. "I fucked up."

"Tell me everything," Felix said, breathless with excitement.

Arsen spent the next several minutes explaining the conversation with as much detail as possible, trying to pinpoint exactly where he went wrong, knowing full well Felix was about to tell him. Felix was great at exposing people's flaws in great detail, with literally no thought for their feelings.

At all.

"So, he asked you innocently about sex and kinks— topics you brought up, BTW—and you shamed him for it and yelled at him?" Felix said. "Wow. That's...a choice."

"I didn't *shame* him or yell at him," Arsen said in a heated whisper. "I…panicked."

"Panicked?" Felix echoed, then asked, "And why are you whispering?"

"Because I can't yell," Arsen said. "And yes. Panicked. Have you seen Ever?"

"What does that have to do with anything?"

Was Felix blind? Crazy? Stupid? Arsen's hand flailed as he tried to voice his thoughts in a language he found perplexing. "He's so beautiful that he doesn't seem real. Do you know what it's like to hear words like *kink* and *sex* coming out of that perfect face? Especially when that perfect face is so close to my face that I can still smell his toothpaste which is also my toothpaste?"

There was a long pause before Felix said, "What?"

Arsen shook his head. "We are not even three days in and he's in my clothes, in my bed, smelling like me and looking at me like I'm way more important than I am. I am already losing. I was not prepared to talk about sex things while cuddling him in sweatpants. They hide nothing."

"He lets you cuddle him?" Felix asked. "Interesting."

"Is it?" Arsen snapped. "*Is* it interesting?"

"You don't have to be snippy," Felix said. "And yes, it is interesting. It seems like you want him to be more traumatized than he is."

Arsen froze. "What? No, I don't."

"Are you sure?" Felix pushed.

Arsen made a noise of frustration. "Focus."

Felix sighed. "Okay, so, you're in lust. I get it. But you could have literally said a hundred other things." He gave a heavy sigh. "Oh, well. It's too late for that now, though." Almost as an aside, he asked, "Why are you calling me about kink anyway? I'm hardly the resident expert."

Now that Arsen had been shamed for accidentally shaming Ever, he was asking himself the same thing. "You have a sex dungeon in your house."

There was a sound like a laugh or an exhale. "Okay, yeah, but it's not *my* sex dungeon. It's Asa's. And it's technically a sex attic."

Asa was Felix's brother-in-law, and Arsen certainly wasn't calling *him* to talk about sex or kink. He liked to chew on his husband. For fun. "You use the sex attic."

"Of course, we *use* the sex dungeon. Who wouldn't use a perfectly good sex attic?"

Arsen felt like he was losing his mind. "So, you use sex attic but you know nothing about kink?"

Felix gave a delicate sniff like he was offended. "Do you assume everyone who's ever used a kitchen is a chef? There are layers, dude. You need someone who knows more about this than me."

Arsen's eyes went wide. "Zane?"

Zane was Asa's chew toy. Er, husband.

Felix snickered. "Too far. That's like asking for cooking advice from Hannibal Lector instead of Gordon Ramsey. Maybe we back it up a little."

What was with Felix and his cooking metaphors? "There's very much room between Gordon Ramsey and Hannibal Lector. Who are you talking about?"

"Noah, obviously. Nobody knows more about kink and

trauma than him. He's practically a therapist at this point. He'd be a good start."

"Oh. Right."

Noah was also Felix's brother-in-law. All told, he had nine brother-in-laws. No, that wasn't right. Brothers-in-law. Was that how they said it in America? American grammar was stupid and confusing and often gave Arsen a headache even after fifteen years.

"But be careful."

Arsen frowned. "Careful? Why?"

Felix's tone was smug. "He's going to adopt Ever into the feelings faction and turn that sweet baby-faced dumpling into a mouthy, feral monster. Next thing you know, he'll use phrases like 'blanket burritos' and 'emotional support vodka.'"

The feelings faction. That was what Felix's in-laws called the non-psychopaths of the family. They liked nicknames. They even had a name for Jericho's crew. The murder muppets.

"Hello?" Felix said impatiently.

"You think I should ask Noah to come over and talk to Ever about kink? Isn't that weird? Ever has been in a literal closet, maybe for years. Now, I'm going to have him sit down with a stranger to answer his sex questions?"

"You're the one who brought it up in the first place," Felix reminded him.

Arsen paced, winding through the cars still in the shop, inhaling the smell of motor oil and rubber tires. The smell soothed him somehow. It was familiar. It was home to him. "Should he even have sex questions after what he's been through?"

"You said he's nineteen, right?"

Arsen nodded even though Felix couldn't see him. "Yes."

"Didn't you have sex questions at nineteen? Even if you were having them answered by every twink in a four-mile radius?"

Felix was exaggerating. There was a time when Arsen had been a bit...free with his experimentation, but that was years ago. Now, he took care of himself more often than not. It was just easier. No matter how many times the guy he went home with said they weren't looking for a relationship, they always seemed upset when Arsen left without a word.

"I wasn't two days out of a kidnapping."

"Curiosity about sex is normal for everyone. Just because people have hurt him doesn't mean he isn't a nineteen-year-old with the same thoughts and feelings as others. Stop infantilizing him. He's not some walking trauma response. Besides, you're the one who brought it up in the first place and then you shut him down when he asked some pretty innocent and logical questions. You should apologize."

Arsen looked up the stairs to the darkened glass. Was Ever still pretending to sleep or was he just upstairs avoiding Arsen? Maybe both. Who could blame him? Fuck. "How do I tell him he can talk to Noah?"

"Maybe don't. Maybe just introduce him to Noah and let him guide the conversation. You suck at this."

"I know!" Arsen cried then winced, glancing up once more. "I know," he said more quietly. "I just want him to be okay. I don't want to keep making him cry."

There was another long pause and then Felix said, "Wow. You're already so whipped. This is going to be fun."

"You know I hate you, right?"

"Mm, it keeps me up at night. Oh, and Noah's out of town until Friday, so good luck."

"What? Friday? What do I do until then?"

"The kid has been trapped in a literal closet for years. Show him what he's missed."

"Missed?"

"Yeah. He looks at video games like they're witchcraft. He acted like pizza was Wagyu beef. He's clearly lacking in life experience. Buy him ice cream or sour gummy worms. Oh, chocolate chip cookies! Or bubble wrap or a sunset or buy him a puppy. You can show him a million firsts that have nothing to do with sex."

"Oh."

Felix snorted. "Yeah, oh. Gotta run. Good luck. Tootles."

"You can show him a million firsts that have nothing to do with sex."

Arsen sat behind the counter, making a list of things Ever may have never experienced, waiting for Jericho to arrive for his shift. Like most days, he arrived promptly at eight, giving him a wave before heading into his office to drop his stuff on his overcrowded desk.

Despite being married to a wealthy man, Jericho

maintained a solid forty-hour work week—sometimes more—not only because he loved cars but because he loved the neighborhood, considered it *his* neighborhood. Everyone knew if they were in trouble, Jericho was the one who could help. And Jericho needed to help people almost as much as the people needed help.

Arsen didn't know what sins Jericho was trying to atone for, but he took it seriously. Jericho had saved him—saved all of them—and Arsen would spend his life making sure that Jericho didn't regret wasting his time with someone like him. To most people, a six-hundred-square-foot apartment over a noisy garage might have seemed like a punishment, but to Arsen, it was everything he'd ever wanted. Freedom. Safety. A home.

Arsen knocked on Jericho's office door. "Can we talk?"

Jericho tilted his head, frowning, "Sure. What's up, kid?"

Arsen flopped into the chair across from Jericho. "Can I have the day off?"

Jericho arched a brow. "I don't think you've ever asked for a day off in your whole life. Everything okay?"

Arsen contemplated lying to Jericho, but that never ended well. "I screwed up with Ever, and I want to make it up to him."

Jericho scrutinized him closely. "Screwed up how?"

"I don't know exactly. I already told Felix. I'm sure it's all over the group chat by now." Jericho opened his mouth, but Arsen raised his hand. "Please, don't make me tell the story again. I already feel terrible. I-I hurt his feelings. That's all. So, now, I want to do something nice for him."

"Like…?" Jericho prompted.

Arsen stopped short. He hadn't expected a follow-up question. He probably should have. "Well, Felix pointed out that there's a lot of stuff Ever's never gotten to do. So, I thought I could take him to do some of them."

Jericho gave him a barely-there smile. "What did you have in mind?"

Arsen shrugged. "I thought I'd start with the library—he seems to like books—then maybe take him to the bodega to buy candy?" When Jericho opened his mouth, Arsen hurried to say, "I know it's not much, but when I have more money, I can take him to do better things like the zoo or a museum or—I don't know—a concert or a trip?"

Arsen's insides withered as he realized that his lack of funds was going to be a barrier to some of the things Ever had never experienced. But those were things that Arsen had also never experienced. Most of his money went to a savings account he couldn't touch until he turned thirty. A way to force himself to save money.

Jericho studied him in a way that made Arsen feel like he was in trouble. Finally, he reached into his back pocket and pulled out his wallet, peeling off several hundred dollars before offering them to Arsen.

Arsen stared at the wad of cash. "What is this?"

Jericho smiled. "Consider it my and Atticus's contribution to Ever's fun fund."

Arsen pushed the money back at Jericho. "That is too much."

Jericho shook his head, shaking the money in his hand in

Arsen's face. "It's really not. You know Atticus spends more than this on socks. Besides, if he were here, he'd probably try to buy Ever a house or a pony or something. He doesn't emote much, but he definitely likes to throw money at things."

Arsen's chest felt tight. What Jericho said was true. Atticus thought nothing of spending money. He'd purchased the spot next to the garage to turn it into a safe space for Jericho's kids. He bought an animal shelter when he learned they were about to become a kill shelter. Atticus had been clinically diagnosed as a psychopath but he had a soft spot for animals and children, which made him okay in Arsen's book.

"Are you sure?" Arsen finally said. Who was he to turn down money on Ever's behalf anyway?

Jericho nodded. "Take him to the bookstore. Let him buy whatever he wants. He should know what it's like to have things that are just his."

"Okay."

Jericho snapped his fingers. "And get him some clothes. Let him pick them out himself. Other essentials, too, like shampoo, soap, stuff like that. Things we take for granted. You remember what it was like in foster care. They throw all your shit in a garbage bag. Nothing ever feels like yours. I imagine what that bitch did to him was far worse."

Arsen nodded, wordlessly taking the money. Arsen had only spent a few months in foster care before he'd run away, but it had been hell on earth. While not every foster home was terrible, there were a lot of people who used it as a way to make money, pocketing the stipend they were given and treating the children in their care like animals.

His former foster family had been abusive, even more so than his own father. When he'd run away, they'd never even reported him missing. Arsen bet they'd still taken those checks. His case worker had never once shown up to check on him. They just didn't have the numbers to do so, and some foster parents counted on their absence to run their schemes.

"Oh, take him to Hollister's for breakfast. Let him order whatever he wants. Remember how much you loved that place the first time we took you?"

"Yeah," Arsen said, a faint smile forming. Jericho had taken a group of them in the middle of the night. They'd barely been thirteen. They'd run amok. The only thing that had kept them from being booted out that first night was Jericho's reputation and the money they'd dropped in there.

Arsen stood. "Thanks."

He was almost to the door when Jericho said, "Bring his headphones. If he gets overwhelmed, he's going to need them."

Jericho always thought of everything. The world outside the garage was far noisier than the garage itself. Noises that Arsen took for granted—police sirens, construction work, preachers on the corner with bullhorns screaming about eternal damnation—would be too much stimulation for Ever.

The city was never not busy.

But Ever had been out in the world before. He said he'd run errands for Jennika but always came back. Not that he'd had much choice with the chip under his skin. But still, how had he managed to find his way around? What experiences had he had? Had he experienced any joy in his life up until then?

Arsen felt a bit bad about ditching work and Jericho for Ever, but not bad enough to stay. Besides, if it got too busy, he could call Nico to come help him. He was good with cars; he just didn't like to get dirty unless he had to.

Arsen stopped next door, waving to the few people in the main room as he walked to the back where they kept clean clothes and gently worn shoes in all shapes and sizes. He grabbed what he thought would fit Ever then jogged back up the stairs to the apartment, giving Jericho a little wave as he passed.

Arsen tried to stay quiet so he didn't sneak up on a sleeping Ever and scare him, but he found him sitting on Arsen's bed just…staring. For a moment, he thought he was sleeping with his eyes open, but his head snapped to Arsen as soon as he sensed his presence.

Ever pulled his legs to his chest and wrapped his arms around them, dropping his chin to his knees, puffing out his cheeks in the world's most devastating pout. He was still upset.

Arsen approached him slowly, sitting on the corner of the mattress. "I'm sorry about last night. I…shouldn't have raised my voice. I didn't mean to scare you."

Ever gave him another quick glance that was over before it began. Ever's sulking face didn't change. He just turned his head so Arsen could no longer see his expression.

It was a good sign that Ever wasn't trying to placate Arsen, right? If he truly feared him, he would be doing everything he could to keep Arsen from punishing him. It seemed like the world's shittiest victory, but it sent Arsen's heart cartwheeling in his chest. Ever wasn't afraid of him.

He reached out and grabbed one of Ever's hands, not missing the sharp inhalation when their skin met. Ever's hands were just as small and delicate as he was. Arsen forced himself to concentrate.

"I mean it. I'm sorry I upset you. You didn't do anything wrong. It was all me. Okay?" Ever continued to ignore him, body stiff. "Please, *besenok*?"

For a moment, Arsen thought he might have to save their outing for another time, but then Ever was turning to look at him, his cheek pressed to his knees, hair falling over his pretty brown eyes. "Okay."

Arsen couldn't stop the grin that spread across his face. "Okay? You forgive me?"

Ever didn't smile back but he nodded, uncurling himself from his impossible position. "Yes."

Arsen fought back the excitement churning inside. "Can I take you somewhere?"

Ever's guarded expression returned, the tiniest hint of panic creeping into his voice as he asked, "Where?"

"It's a surprise. But a good one. I think you'll like it. Will you come?"

Ever eyed him warily. "But you'll bring me back, right? You're not…leaving me there, right?"

Arsen blinked at him. Bring him back? Why wouldn't he… The answer dawned on him then, and his heart felt like it had been put through a shredder. Ever thought he was trying to get rid of him.

Arsen caught Ever's gaze, looking him in the eyes. "I'll always bring you back. As long as that's what you want."

Ever caught his bottom lip between his bunny teeth, worrying the already abused skin until it was raw. Arsen fought the urge to free it.

Finally, Ever nodded. "Okay."

Arsen let out the breath he'd been holding. "Okay, good. Do you want to shower and get changed? I brought you some clothes to wear." It wasn't much. Just jeans and a hooded sweatshirt. It wasn't freezing outside but there was a bite to the air. "Then we'll go get breakfast."

Ever's brows went up as he said, "Breakfast?"

Arsen nodded. "It's still kind of early. But if you don't like breakfast food, the diner is open twenty-four hours a day, so their menu has many other things."

If Ever wanted a burger at eight in the morning, Arsen would give it to him. Hell, if he wanted to order the entire right side of the menu, he'd give it to him. He was almost giddy at the idea of being all of Ever's firsts. His brain short-circuited at some of the other firsts he could be for him.

No. That was a slippery slope.

"...*devirginized the little gumdrop...*"

Fucking Felix. He was putting thoughts in Arsen's head. Thoughts that he'd been trying to stomp on for hours.

"I've never had breakfast," Ever said, scooting to the edge of the bed and standing, then taking the clothes from Arsen.

Who had never *not* had breakfast? "No?"

Ever shook his head. "Jennika said food was earned."

Jesus. Arsen really had killed her too quickly. "Well, she's not here anymore. Food is a necessity and you can have whatever you want whenever you want."

Ever's gaze floated to a spot over Arsen's shoulder, the wariness returning. "She said I needed to look small, helpless. They liked me better like that."

Something cold and slimy felt like it slithered in Arsen's belly at that statement. *They*. He didn't ask who they were. Ever hadn't explicitly stated what Jennika had done to him—let others do—but it didn't take a genius to know she'd been selling Ever's body, likely to pedophiles.

"You don't have to worry about that anymore. You can eat as much as you want whenever you want. I promise. Whatever makes you happy."

Ever watched him from beneath sooty lashes for a long moment before asking, "Whatever makes me happy?"

Arsen nodded, earnest. He needed Ever to believe him, to trust him. "Whatever you want."

"Okay," Ever said.

Before Arsen could even guess his intention, Ever was coming up on tiptoe and smacking his lips against Arsen's cheek. He didn't even have time to react before Ever was scurrying out of the room to the bathroom, leaving Arsen holding his face like he'd slapped him.

What the hell was going on in Ever's head?

EIGHT

EVER

EVER WAS OVERWHELMED. HE DIDN'T want to be. He sat in the corner booth, his eyes scanning the restaurant for any potential threats. But there weren't any. It was just a bunch of regular looking people who didn't pay him or Arsen any mind, at least not until Ever slipped his headphones on. Then he drew some looks, but more curious than unkind.

He didn't want to wear them. Or he didn't want to need them. He knew how it made him look. But the noise was too much. Dishes clattering in the open kitchen, the cooks laughing and shouting at each other, the sound of utensils on china, even the low hum of dozens of voices making small talk had his skin crawling.

He didn't ask Arsen to turn the music on. That had to count for something, right? He just needed a way to block out the ambient noise but not Arsen.

A young girl with bright red hair in a ponytail, dozens of freckles, and a smattering of hearts tattooed next to her right eye approached the table in a powder blue uniform.

She gave Arsen a huge smile that made Ever want to bite

her harder than he ever had Levi. "Hey, sexy. Who's your little friend?"

Sexy? Was she Arsen's girlfriend? Ever glowered at her without saying a word. She arched a brow at him like she was waiting for a response. When she didn't get one, she turned her attention back to Arsen.

"This is Ever," Arsen said. "Ever, this is Magnolia." Arsen gave Magnolia a smile that made Ever contemplate stabbing her with his butter knife. Why did he have to smile at her like that? "He's shy."

"Oh," she said as if that made perfect sense. "Whatcha having?"

They hadn't even touched the menu, but that didn't seem to matter. Arsen just started listing off food. "Eggs, scrambled and over easy. French toast. Pancakes. Waffle with butter and powdered sugar. Bacon. Sausage. Hash browns. I think that's it. To start."

Magnolia blinked at him. "Are you expecting others? 'Cause this booth only holds four max and I'm not having Henry yell at me again."

Arsen shook his head, giving Ever that look he seemed to save just for him. The one that made him feel like a rescue dog. "It's just for us. Ever here has never had breakfast food before."

Magnolia stared at him blankly. "What?"

"He's never had breakfast," Arsen repeated, but louder as if that was the problem, not his statement. His voice carried to the people sitting at the counter.

"Who's never had breakfast?" an old man at the counter

asked.

"Ever here," Magnolia called, pointing to him. Ever shrank back against the corner of the booth.

The middle-aged woman reading a paper at the counter gave him a shrewd look. "Never ever?"

Ever shook his head.

"Well, damn," another old man said. "He needs to try the biscuits and gravy."

"Or the eggs Benedict," another server called.

"Or the crispy French fritter things from New Orleans," another said.

"Beignets, you heathen," a dark-haired woman said without looking up from her novel. Ever wondered what she was reading.

Fifteen minutes later, plates started arriving and didn't stop. Ever felt a little like he was under a microscope as dozens of curious patrons watched him take bite after bite, waiting for his opinion on each of their recommendations. When he liked something, they cheered, but when he didn't, they would all make a sad sound in tandem. He tried to pretend to like things even if he didn't, but he didn't have a really good poker face.

"You don't have to fake it, little one. They're all adults. This is your breakfast, not theirs," Arsen reminded.

Ever nodded but still continued to try to please everyone. Life was just easier when people were happy with him.

After about an hour of eating, Ever tapped out. "I can't eat anymore," he whispered. "Please?"

Arsen's face grew stormy and he leaned over the table,

grabbing Ever's chin and forcing it upwards. "Are you sick? Was it too much? You didn't have to eat it just because they brought it."

"I'm sorry," Ever said, chest tight.

The concern faded into the sad puppy look again. "Don't be sorry. You didn't do anything wrong."

"Sorry," Ever said again then flushed.

Arsen asked for the bill, but Magnolia just shook her head. "It's already been covered by your fan club," she said, pointing to the group at the counter.

Ever felt tears spring to his eyes and, for a split second, feared he might cry. They didn't even know him. Why would they buy him food? But Arsen hadn't known him either and he'd still rescued him, still gave him food and clothing and shelter. Still let him sleep beside him.

Ever didn't know how to repay him or any of them. What could he ever do to make up for eating so much food? Maybe they would let him work it off in the kitchen. He should try to get a job so he could let Arsen be.

His gaze darted to Arsen, hoping he would speak up and tell them that they could pay. But Arsen just said, "Are you sure?"

They all nodded. "Bring him back for round two next week. We made a list of stuff we missed."

"Yes, okay. We can come back next week," Arsen said.

They could? Ever would still be with Arsen next week? That quelled some of the unease brewing inside. Arsen stood, holding out his hand to Ever, who took it eagerly, threading their fingers together and clutching tight enough for Arsen to squeeze back like he was trying to reassure Ever.

Just touching him made things better. Arsen made everything better.

Ever kept his headphones on as they walked the block to the bus stop, waiting only a few minutes before it pulled to a stop before them, the brakes hissing like some kind of mythical creature from one of his novels or from Arsen's game.

Arsen didn't let go of Ever's hand, not even to pay the fare. Once that was handled, he led him to the back, gesturing for him to sit in one of the two seats that allowed a direct view down the aisle.

"Now you can see everything," he told him with a smile.

Once more, Ever fought back tears. Arsen thought of everything.

They rode the bus for about twenty minutes before they were deposited outside a large strip mall with fancy columns and several department stores. It was far nicer than anything in their neighborhood. Ever looked at Arsen, confused, but he just gave him another reassuring smile and then removed his headphones, settling them around his neck.

"You won't need those here. I promise."

Arsen guided him towards a two-story building with a wall of windows. There were books displayed everywhere. Ever's heart galloped. A bookstore. It was a bookstore. He looked at Arsen, unable to contain his excitement. As soon as Arsen opened the door for him, he rushed inside, stopping short and inhaling deeply. It smelled different than the library.

It smelled like ink and coffee, it smelled like paper. Ever

grabbed a book and fanned the pages, sniffing again, the scent like a drug to him. There were so many books. Two stories of books. He'd never been to a book store before. Jennika had taken him to the library twice, both times to make up for something horrible. But this was different.

There were books on tables and books on the walls. They were on shelves and in alcoves, and in the corner was an entire section for children with little chairs and games. Ever spun in a circle. He didn't even know what to look at first.

When he turned to Arsen, he found him watching him with an amused look. Heat crawled up his neck to the tips of his ears. "Sorry."

"For what, *besenok*?"

"I don't know," he wailed, bewildered.

This was all so confusing and overwhelming. He needed to get it together. He needed to act like he wasn't too damaged to function in society. People were watching them. He shrank against Arsen, wrapping himself around his arm and resting his head on his bicep.

"I brought you here to find some books to read. I know you're bored watching me work."

"I don't have any money."

"Well, today, you have a benefactor," Arsen said.

Ever frowned. "A what?"

"A benefactor. Someone is covering the bill for all of this. You don't have to worry about anything," Arsen promised, leaning down enough for Ever to feel his breath ruffle his hair.

Yeah, right. "What do I have to do for this money?"

Arsen sighed. "Nothing, *besenok*. Jericho and Atticus want you to have things of your own. They want you to enjoy your day. They'll never ask you for anything, I promise. This isn't reciprocal."

There was nothing Ever wanted more than to believe Arsen was who he said he was. He'd never done anything to prove otherwise. But they had known each other less than a week and he was showering him with gifts and attention. All the things Jennika had done in the beginning. But Arsen didn't feel like Jennika had. Even as a child, Ever had sensed there was something…off about her. She smiled too wide, her words were too sweet, too…sharp. Like the big bad wolf posing as Red's grandmother. A small voice had whispered that she couldn't be trusted. He never heard that voice with Arsen.

Arsen put his arms on Ever's shoulders, walking him deeper into the store. "Let us spoil you today. Please? It will make me so happy to see you happy."

Ever was having a hard time concentrating with the warmth of Arsen's body pressing against his back. "Okay," he managed.

Ever lost track of time. They could have been in there an hour or seven days. He moved from aisle to aisle, a sense of urgency hurrying his steps. There were so many options. He couldn't settle for anything less than looking at them all but it was impossible.

Arsen trailed behind him. Each time Ever would say a book sounded interesting, he'd set it back on the shelf only to see Arsen retrieve it and add it to a basket he held. He wanted to protest, but he'd promised he'd let them spoil him.

Arsen insisted they get coffee at the cafe in the center of the store. Ever didn't know what to order so he asked Arsen to surprise him.

"Is there anything you don't like?"

"Olives," Ever said, then blushed when Arsen gave him that puppy look.

"Have you ever had coffee?" Arsen asked.

Ever shook his head. "Jennika said caffeine gives people cancer."

"Jennika was a liar," Arsen said with a shake of his head.

While Arsen stood in line, Ever couldn't resist going through his finds, looking at each book lovingly before returning it to the stack on the table. He'd found a book about vampires and one about faeries. He also found a murder mystery and something listed as a thriller.

He blushed when he looked at the two romance books he found, one between a man and a woman, the other between two men, both featuring muscled half-naked men on the covers. Arsen had assured him there was nothing wrong with reading romance novels.

Ever had taken the ones he'd wanted but had also quickly exited to the young adult section where he'd found a few more titles. He wanted to hurry home and start reading.

Arsen returned with a drink topped with whipped cream and drizzled with chocolate and a cookie the size of a small plate. Literally the same size as the plate. Ever took a sip of the drink, eyes widening at the sweetness on his tongue. He couldn't help the way he began to suck it down, stopping only when a knife of pain split his skull, causing him to wince.

Arsen chuckled. "Brain freeze. Do this."

Ever watched as Arsen pressed his thumb to the roof of his mouth. At first, Ever thought he was joking, but did it anyway, willing to be a joke if that was what Arsen wanted. But it wasn't a joke; it really did help. When he looked at him, relieved, Arsen placed his large hand over Ever's smaller one.

"Drink a little slower and it won't happen again."

Ever gave a stilted nod as Arsen's skin seemed to sear into him. He gave his drink a break, instead picking at the warm chocolate chip cookie, his eyes rolling in pleasure at the taste. It tasted almost as good as touching Arsen felt. That was dangerous.

Ever knew he would be sick from all the food later but he couldn't bring himself to care. It was all too yummy.

Once they finished and Arsen paid for Ever's books, he assumed they'd head home, but that wasn't the case. Instead, they walked a few stores down to the shop with a giant bullseye on the top. Target. Ever quickly returned his headphones to his ears.

"Why are we here?" he asked warily, uneasy with the number of people in the vast space. It smelled different there. Not bad but…chemical. And there were far more people there than at the bookstore. People pushing carts filled with groceries and children and plants and even a television.

"You need clothes, shoes, underwear."

"Clothes?" Ever looked down at his borrowed outfit. "Oh."

"Yeah, you don't want to keep having to wear mine, do

you?"

Yes. Arsen's hoodie smelled like him. It smelled like his spicy soap, motor oil, and the sharp woodsy scent of his cologne. Wearing Arsen's hoodie was like being wrapped in a permanent hug and he was already mourning the loss.

"Okay," Ever said, dejected.

Arsen studied him closely—so close Ever made himself small, crossing his arms over his chest.

"You can still wear my t-shirts and my hoodies," Arsen said softly. "If that's what's worrying you."

Ever's gaze slid to the floor. "Okay."

Arsen put a hand on his back. "I just want you to have things that are just yours. Just in case."

Those three words stabbed at Ever's heart. In case of what? In case he sent Ever away? In case he had to leave? In case someone took him away? But he didn't say any of that. He was being ungrateful.

Instead, he did as Arsen asked, picking shirts and jeans and a few hoodies as well as socks and underwear, pajamas and soap. Arsen wouldn't let him see the total of their purchases and insisted on carrying all the bags, not only to the bus but several blocks back to the apartment.

It wasn't quite dark when they returned, but it was dinner time. Ever refused to eat. He couldn't. His stomach was already churning. Arsen said it was fine but insisted that he take another shower with his own things and then put on his new comfortable clothes.

As always, Ever did as he was told. His clothes were comfy. The pants were soft and thin with navy and white stripes, the shirt just a plain white tee but one he wasn't swimming in. Even so, he took a seat on Arsen's bed, picking up his zippered hoodie from the night before and slipping it on, bringing it to his nose and inhaling deeply.

He grabbed one of his books from the bag sitting on the edge of the bed—the romance novel—and curled up in the corner where he usually slept, opening the book and reading the first paragraph.

He didn't remember falling asleep but he must have, because when he woke, the room was cast in shadow, the only light coming from the street light outside. Ever's pulse shot up, leaving him a little breathless. He wasn't afraid of the dark necessarily, but he didn't want to be in it alone. He quickly exited the room, his heart rate slowing as he entered the family room where the lights burned bright.

No Arsen.

He didn't have to search. He could hear him shouting and laughing from the other room, could hear him pounding on the keys of his keyboard then cackling as he did something Ever couldn't see.

When he entered the computer room, Arsen didn't notice at first, but as he crept closer, he must have caught sight of him. He grinned, waving him closer, then tugged him until he was sitting on the stool between his knees, Arsen's arms bracketing him on either side as he resumed his gameplay.

Ever glanced at the chat, seeing his name appear again and again, but the lines moved too fast for him to read and comprehend. It didn't matter. He didn't want to read, he just wanted to enjoy the feel of Arsen's chest pressed against his back and the feel of his chin brushing his hair and bumping his head every time he spoke or shouted something to his teammates.

On the desk in front of Ever was a bag of candy. Every few minutes, Arsen would stop and shovel some into his mouth. When he noticed Ever watching, he took a handful and held them in front of him. In retrospect, he probably meant for Ever to take them from his hand—which he did. But not with his hand, with his mouth, eating like he was a baby bird or a zoo animal, his lips brushing Arsen's palm briefly as he took the candy.

He started to chew before he fully comprehended what he'd just done. Once he swallowed, he looked up at Arsen, who was no longer looking at the game but staring at Ever with a look in his eyes that made his belly feel warm and shivery. He wanted to look away, but he couldn't. He just stared up at him, held captive by the heat in his gaze.

He wasn't sure who moved first, but Arsen's lips were suddenly brushing his, leaving a shocky buzzing sensation in their wake. It wasn't a kiss like in his romance novel. There was no tongue or mouths crashing together. It was barely-there, whisper soft, and the single most erotic thing Ever had ever experienced.

Before he could even react, Arsen was pulling back, dazed. Ever's heart squeezed, a jolt of awareness spiking through him, when it seemed Arsen might dip his head once more—might kiss him again. Ever sat frozen, holding his breath, his body responding in ways it never had before.

A chime rang out from the computer, jarring Ever from

his paralysis. He jumped to his feet, retreating to Arsen's bedroom and leaping onto the bed, pulling the covers up to his chin.

This time, he didn't mind the shadowy room. It felt almost safe. Safe enough to trace his lips, his fingertips not feeling nearly as good as Arsen's lips had.

They still tingled.

Or maybe it was all in his head. Either way, Ever was shaken. His first kiss. He bit down on his lip until he tasted blood, his emotions swinging wildly like a pendulum between confusion and elation.

What did it mean? Did it mean anything? Arsen had said he didn't want sex from Ever. Had he changed his mind? Kissing wasn't sex. Was there a line Ever didn't know about? Something somewhere between kissing and sex?

Ever flopped onto his belly and buried his face in the pillow, groaning at the way Arsen's scent stirred him, made his skin hot and his pants uncomfortably tight.

He just needed to go back to sleep. Life was less confusing when he was unconscious.

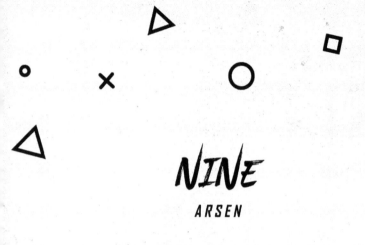

NINE

ARSEN

IT TOOK APPROXIMATELY THIRTY SECONDS for Arsen's actions to go from his lips to his brain, but by then his mouth was already on Ever's. It wasn't Arsen's fault. Right? How was he supposed to resist when Ever was literally eating out of the palm of his hand, then looking up at him with those wide innocent eyes? Arsen was only human.

A human with no self-control.

As soon as he pulled back, he watched, transfixed as Ever's tongue swept across his bottom lip, like he was trying to taste whatever trace of himself Arsen had left behind. He wanted more. Did Ever? He dipped his head, hoping one of them had the sense to stop it from happening again.

The tip notification blared through the speakers. Ever sucked in a startled breath then shot to his feet, mumbling something as he hurried off, leaving Arsen staring at the space Ever had occupied just seconds before. The notifications started to chime again and again, but Arsen couldn't think and definitely had no interest in the people watching or the game paused on the home screen.

Someone cleared his throat in Arsen's headset.

"Um...you realize we're all still here, right? You're on camera, dude," Seven said, sounding both amused and shocked.

Nico cackled. "That was...awesome."

"That was hot," Felix said. "Like, the polar opposite of what I told you to do but hot nonetheless."

Arsen glanced at the screen where comments from viewers were coming in fast and furious.

I told you that was his boyfriend

Gay!

Is this what this channel is now because ew

Is this what this channel is now because HOT!

I need more Ever content. He's so cute.

You guys are so hot together. Give us more of that!

I can't believe they're all gay. What? How is that even possible?

Will he be on tomorrow night?

Yes, bring back Ever

Ever's so cute. We stan. Like a little woodland creature

Ever!!!

Ever!!!

Ever's so cute.

My sweet baby angel.

I just want to squish him.

Protect Ever at all costs.

Can we get a better kiss? That was pretty G rated.

I'd pay to see you two with an OF

"I'm signing off," Arsen said, distracted.

He ended the session, tearing off his headset and jumping to his feet before stopping short. What was he going to do? What was the plan? Was he going to go confront Ever? Apologize? Say it wouldn't happen again? Did Ever think Arsen expected something in return now for the day they'd spent together, even though none of it had been his money?

He scraped his fingers through his hair with a snarl then dropped onto the spare bed. What the fuck had he just done? He dug his palms into his eye sockets like if he just rubbed hard enough he might get some fucking clarity. But there was none, there was just Ever, wide-eyed, lips parted, tongue peeking out beneath his adorable bunny teeth.

Fuck! It was taking every ounce of willpower Arsen had not to go crawl into bed with Ever and apologize. Or kiss him again. Or both. Or maybe more. Arsen definitely wanted more. He wanted Ever naked beneath him, staring up at him with that same shocky, innocent look. Did that make Arsen a bad person? Did wanting to bury himself inside Ever make him a bad person?

When their lips met, Ever had made just the faintest—barely audible—whimper and it had made Arsen so hard so fast he'd grown dizzy. He was still very much hard. And there was clearly very little blood flow left for his brain.

Arsen was sure nobody had heard the sound but him, which was good because Arsen didn't want anybody getting that part of Ever but him. Just him.

No.

What?

This wasn't right. It wasn't normal or rational. A week ago, Arsen hadn't even known Ever existed, and now, he wasn't sure he could exist without Ever. That was fucked up. It was all kinds of toxic. But Arsen wanted it, anyway. He wanted Ever, anyway. Wanted Ever to want him back in the same fucked-up, toxic, cant-live-without-you way Arsen felt about him.

Or maybe he was just horny? Maybe he just needed to go jerk off in the shower and get himself together before he did something to Ever he couldn't take back. Not that he would

ever force himself on him, but Ever was delicate, fragile…
He was so new to all of this. Even forcing that kiss on him
could upset the delicate trust Arsen had just barely created.

His phone dinged, and he stood, snagging it from the
charger on the desk, stomach churning as he turned it over
to see a text from the group chat.

Arlo: What was that?

Dimitri: Who was that?

**Noah: Who was who? I'm lost. I'm out of town.
What'd I miss?**

**Felix: Arsen just kissed his pocket-sized, closet-
candy in front of the whole world.**

Noah: The rescue?

Cree: He's not a puppy

**Zane: Too bad, Noah would just adopt him and he
could live in luxury like his other dogs.**

Seven: Is Ever okay?

**Levi: You all really have such a hard-on for this kid.
Like just because he looks like a bush baby doesn't
mean you have to dote on him like one.**

Arsen: What is bush baby?

Arsen blinked as a picture of a bug-eyed but adorable fuzzy creature popped up on his screen. It kind of looked like it was smiling. Ever was probably not smiling. He was probably crying or scared or confused. And Arsen was in there watching his stupid friends mock him from the comfort of their own homes.

Nico: Sorry I was in the shower. What'd I miss? Has A already gotten sweet little Ever into bed? Jericho is gonna be pissed, bro

Arsen: Arsen didn't do anything. I wouldn't do that.

Arlo: But it looked like you could if you wanted.

Dimitri: Do you? Want it?

Arsen flopped back onto the bed, staring at the text. Of course, he fucking wanted it. Who was he kidding? Clearly, not his friends.

Arsen: It doesn't matter what I want.

Felix: Don't be such a martyr.

Noah: What's happening?

Felix: Arsen here thinks sweet little Ever is off the menu because of his tragic backstory. Apparently you can't want sex if you've been traumatized.

Noah: Tell me you didn't say that.

Arsen rolled his eyes before typing: That's NOT what I said.

Zane: You sort of did, though.

Arsen: You weren't even there.

Cree: You guys all seem so sure Arsen is trying to fuck this kid. Didn't he, like, just rescue him from life in a literal closet? It's been like three days. Not fucking him seems like any easy ask. You guys are perverts.

Lake: Wait who is not fucking who? I'm too lazy to scroll back up. What did I miss? Wait. Is this about Arsen kissing Ever in front of all of Beyonce's internet?

Levi: Why is everybody acting like this kid is so innocent. He might look like a Walt Disney creation but he is a feral little demon. I still have the mark where he bit me.

Dimitri: Let it go, Elsa.

Levi: Said the psychopath. Didn't you murder Arlo's ex?

Dimitri: Technically Arlo did that.

Arlo: He just helped me hide the body.

Noah: I know this is an encrypted app but dude ixnay the urdermey chat.

Arsen sighed. Their chats were always like this. It started as one thing and then morphed into something wildly off topic. They were all killers. There wasn't a single one of them who hadn't killed someone. Even sweet little Arlo. Up until Ever, Arlo had been the shyest, most quiet person Arsen had ever met. But he'd still beaten his ex to death with a brick.

Felix: Ever just doesn't like you, Levi. That's not a character flaw. It's good instincts.

Arlo: Arsen, don't let Ever's past be the reason you do or don't do something. That's not fair to him. I speak from experience.

Noah: Arlo's right. It's not Ever's fault he was put into that situation. He's still a person.

Arsen stared at his screen. How was he the bad guy here?

Lake: You guys act like this shit went down years ago. Homie was living in a closet last week. Like shouldn't getting laid not be the top priority? Why are you all so horny all the time?

Noah: We're not telling Arsen to fuck Ever. We're telling him to stop treating Ever like he's too damaged to know his own mind and body. You can have a fucked-up relationship with abuse and still want to have sex

Arlo: Nobody's saying that

Arsen: I never said any of that

Zane: Can I just be the voice of reason here for two seconds and suggest we get Ever a therapist?

Felix: You think my brother isn't already working on finding one that will keep his mouth shut?

Noah: Also, not to be unkind but if he was assaulted like Arsen thinks, he needs more than just a therapist. He's gonna need a doctor's appointment, blood tests... He could have picked something up from one of these creeps. He might need medicine.

Noah's gentle reminder felt like a baseball bat to the back of his head. Arsen didn't know exactly what had been done to Ever, but it was clear he'd had some level of assault forced on him. He did need all of the things Noah suggested, but Arsen worried taking him somewhere to be poked and prodded would just re-traumatize him.

Not that Ever seemed all that traumatized in the first place. Was Arsen trying to force Ever into the role of victim like Felix said? His stomach churned at the thought. He just didn't want to hurt him, and it seemed impossible that someone who had suffered the abuse Ever had could just be...fine. But...who was Arsen to say he wasn't? This was all too much.

Arsen: I'm going to bed

He powered off his phone so he wouldn't be tempted to dive back into the conversation to defend himself. None of it helped. Well, a therapist for Ever would probably help. And a doctor. Hopefully. But neither of those things helped Arsen feel less like a predator. He stared at the door across the hall. Was Ever in there waiting for him? Was he dreading his arrival? Was he even still awake?

Arsen closed his eyes. He would just give Ever some space. They could figure it out in the morning.

"You can't be weak. The world breaks weak men."

Arsen blinked back tears. His muscles ached and burned. How long had they been standing there like this? It felt like hours. He was somehow both hot and cold, his organs shaking within him, his teeth clacking together like it was the dead of winter, even as salt stung his eyes and beads of perspiration rolled down his skin.

The room itself felt too small, like he couldn't breathe, but that was because his father's large body was wrapped around him, looming over him, his paw-like hands covering Arsen's, squeezing until the metal of the gun dug into his skin. Even with his father's hands on his, the gun was slippery in Arsen's damp palms. He just wanted to drop it and run, but there was no escaping. His father was a big man and he always got what he wanted.

Was Arsen crying? He couldn't even tell. He didn't know. His whole body was malfunctioning at once.

Logically, Arsen knew he was dreaming. A part of him recognized that there were differences between this dream interpretation of his mother's death and what really happened that day but it didn't matter. It didn't *feel* any different.

The dreams weren't always like this—so vivid. Sometimes, they were hazy, like his brain was wrapped in cotton. Other times, they were sharp enough for Arsen to smell his mother's blood as she bled out on the kitchen floor.

Sometimes, like tonight, he was right back in it. His father's hands on his, trying to force him to pull the trigger. Other times, he was standing to the side, an observer watching as his father berates them, intimidates them, beats them with his fists, until it finally culminates in this one… last…stand.

Just like most dreams, there wasn't a linear timeline. It didn't run from start to finish like a movie. It jumped around. Things changed—minute details. No nightmare was ever quite the same.

It had been a good night. He'd thought his father would be pleased. But, as usual, he was wrong. His report card started it, but it could have been anything. Whatever he could use as an excuse.

Arsen was no longer holding the gun. There was no gun. He was back at the beginning of his memory. His dream. His nightmare. Whatever it was.

His father was furious. "You think you're better than me?" he asked in Russian. "You think you'll get a big fancy job and a fancy car and leave this place?"

Goosebumps erupted all over, not just at his father's tone but at the sound of his father speaking Russian, breaking his own rule. Only English was spoken in the house. He'd said it was to help Arsen and his mother better acclimate, but it was really just another form of humiliation. A way to mock them for not speaking English as clearly as he did.

Arsen blinked in confusion. "What?"

His father sneered at him. "Oh, now, you don't speak your native tongue?"

There was no right answer, Arsen knew it. His mother knew it, too. His father lived for these games, for these traps. Arsen was too American, not American enough. Too Russian. Not Russian enough. He spoke too much or too little. He didn't try hard enough or he tried so hard he must be mocking his father's lack of education. Arsen wasn't going to win this.

That was when his mother stepped in. "Ilya," she said sweetly, stroking his face. "Why don't we skip dinner and go out? We can go to the club and—"

That was as far as she got before his father backhanded her, driving her to the floor. His father was so big and she was so small. Or maybe she just seemed so in comparison to his father. She never acted small. She was so tough. And yet, that was where she stayed, on the floor, her skirt hiked up high on her thighs, her face swelling rapidly.

How had it devolved so far so fast?

It was just a normal fight.

Until it wasn't.

Arsen was back in his father's arms. He was trying to force his finger over the trigger. But it was impossible. Arsen's hands just weren't big enough. He was only eleven. And it was a big gun. Heavy. His mother often rolled her eyes behind his father's back as he waved it around, and when he wasn't there, she would tell her friend, Anya, next door that he was overcompensating. That it made him feel like a big man when he flashed it at people. They would laugh.

His dad always needed to feel like a man. It was in the way he talked, carried himself, and interacted with his friends— these wannabe mobsters with their weak ties to powerful families. Lackeys, his mother would call them.

These lackeys constantly joked about Arsen being too small, too thin, too frail…too feminine. Arsen didn't think there was much that was feminine about him, not compared to other boys in his school—like Felix. Felix loved lace and flowers and skirts. That was why Arsen never invited him over.

That was the real reason Arsen's father hated him. Because he was gay. Arsen still didn't know what it was that had given him away, how his father had known his orientation long before even Arsen himself. But it didn't matter now.

"Zhmi na kurok," his father growled in his ear.

Pull the trigger.

"No," Arsen whispered, shaking his head.

"You're a man. Men have to do hard things."

Arsen wasn't a man. He wasn't. He wasn't even a teenager. He didn't want to do hard things. His whole life was hard. This wasn't fair. Other kids got to play outside and go to school and live normal lives.

Arsen's mom sat up a little straighter, righting her skirt and turning her frigid stare from his father to him. She gave him a warm smile, tears rolling down her cheeks. "It's alright, zaichik." She turned to look at his father. "I'm not afraid to die."

Arsen's father sneered. "Bitch."

"Arsen!"

Arsen bolted upright, fighting the sudden weight on top of him, his hands wrapping around thin arms as he tried to shake off his dream. Ever. It was Ever on top of him. Ever holding him down. No. That wasn't right.

Arsen scanned the room, disoriented. Why was he in the computer room? Why was Ever there? What time was it? Was he still dreaming? Ever gazed down at him, eyes wide.

Arsen blinked, eyes stinging. When he realized he was still gripping Ever's arms, he released him abruptly, causing him to fall forward.

Arsen caught him, righting him, flushing before muttering,

"Sorry."

Ever frowned. "You were having another nightmare."

Right. That.

Arsen sucked in heavy breaths, trying to get his heart rate back to normal, but it seemed useless. Though he was awake, the nightmare still had its hooks in him. He tried to distract himself, asking, "Did you hear me all the way in the other room?"

Ever hesitated then shook his head. "When I woke up, you weren't in bed, so I came to look for you. You were… crying."

Arsen's hands went to his face, and he realized Ever was right. He wasn't just covered with sweat but with tears. "Oh." He looked up at Ever's face, painted with neon pink and blue from the LED lights surrounding them. "I'm sorry if I scared you."

Ever frowned. "You didn't."

Arsen fell back onto the pillows, Ever still sitting on his hips. He didn't make any attempt to move and Arsen truly didn't want to move him. He just stared up at him, letting his presence sooth the jagged edges of his memories.

Arsen's crew had so many names for Ever. Angel. Dumpling. Bush baby. Gremlin. But none of those things described him with any accuracy. "You can lie down," he offered.

Ever shrugged. "Okay."

He didn't move to the side as Arsen expected he would but instead blanketed himself over Arsen's body, his head on his chest, his arms sort of starfished to the sides. Ever was so literal.

After a minute, he said, "Your heart's beating really fast. Mine does too after nightmares."

Arsen smiled. It wasn't the nightmare. It was having Ever's body on his. But he wouldn't tell him that. He didn't want to spook him. He brought his arms up around him, locking his fingers in the center of Ever's back, just wanting to hold him. "Is this okay?"

Ever hummed, the sound vibrating from his chest straight into Arsen's, then he wiggled a bit like he was settling in. "Uh-huh."

He sounded sleepy. Arsen was tired, too, but the dream was still too fresh in his head to attempt to sleep again. It would suck him right back down into it.

Still, he closed his eyes, enjoying the heat and the weight of Ever pressing into him. But he needed to address what had happened earlier. What had sent Ever running from the room. "I'm sorry...about earlier."

"Earlier?" Ever echoed.

Arsen nodded even though Ever wasn't looking at him. "The kiss..."

Ever lifted his head, folding his palms under his chin as he looked up at Arsen.

"You are? Why?"

That brought Arsen up short. What did he mean, why? *Because I don't want to be another person who victimizes you and takes away your choices.* "Because...I should have asked for permission."

"Oh. Is that a thing?" Ever asked.

Arsen blinked at Ever. "It's supposed to be, yeah."

"Oh," Ever said again, thoughtfully. "They never ask in my books. It's always guys taking what they want. They never say they're sorry."

That was disconcerting. "There's a difference between fiction and reality, *besenok*. Your body is your own."

Silence stretched between them like a line pulled tighter and tighter, the tension only snapping when Ever whispered, "You can have it."

Arsen's breath punched from his lungs in a gasp as he willed himself to calm down.

Ever didn't just say that. He couldn't have. There was no way he'd just casually offered up his body to Arsen. "What?"

Ever tipped his head, doe eyes looking at him curiously. "My permission. To kiss me. Whenever you want. You have it."

There was no universe in which Arsen would ever be worthy of someone like Ever. He was truly the sweetest boy in the world. "I—"

Ever shook his head, eyes closing, his voice filled with disappointment. "I'm probably not that good at it. But I could learn."

Chert. There was nothing Arsen wanted more than to teach Ever anything he wanted to learn about kissing or sex or anything else. But this wasn't the time or place. Cree was right. They were all perverts.

Maybe Arsen was misunderstanding. "What do you mean?"

Ever dropped his cheek to the hands resting on Arsen's

chest, hiding his face. "That was my first."

"First?" Arsen echoed.

"First kiss."

"Ever?" Arsen blurted.

Ever's head popped up, looking at him in confusion, like he wasn't sure if he was calling his name or asking for clarification. "Yes?"

Arsen wanted to kick himself. Of course, it had been Ever's first kiss. Who would Ever have been kissing? Nobody good. Nobody who would be gentle or take care of him or make sure he was safe. That flicker of rage sparked in Arsen's chest. He hoped that woman was burning in hell.

"I didn't know," he said for lack of anything else to say.

"Was I supposed to tell you?" Ever asked. "I didn't know you were going to kiss me. Or I was going to kiss you. I'm not sure who kissed who," he admitted, seemingly distracted by his own train of thought. "But...I've done other things. Not things I wanted to do. At least, not with the people who did them."

Arsen found himself squeezing Ever tighter. "None of that counts," he promised.

Ever frowned at him. "It doesn't?"

Was it dismissive to say his experiences didn't count, like they didn't matter? That wasn't really what he was saying. But how did he say the things other people had done to him were valid but weren't the same thing as sex between two willing people?

Arsen tried to remember how Jericho had explained it to them all those years ago, when they'd gotten the first of many sex talks.

"Sex without consent isn't sex, it's assault. Jericho's been drilling that into our heads since we were old enough to even truly care about sex." Arsen listed off Jericho's rules on his fingers. "Always wear a condom. Always get tested. Always get consent."

Ever nodded like he was committing this information to memory. For some reason, it bothered Arsen. Ever didn't need to worry about sex with other people. Arsen couldn't stomach the thought. He mentally shook himself. This wasn't the time.

He focused on recalling the rest of Jericho's talk. "If they say no, it's assault. If they're drunk, it's assault. If they're unconscious, it's assault. Sex is about pleasure between two people. Assault is about power over another person."

Ever seemed to chew on that for a while, once more resting his head on Arsen's chest. "Then I've really never done any kind of sex."

Arsen found himself kissing the top of Ever's hair, something unknotting in his chest. "There's nothing wrong with that."

"But I want to," Ever said, his voice barely above a whisper.

Arsen's heart clenched. "There's plenty of time for that."

Ever waited a beat before asking, "With you?"

Arsen's brain turned to mush, all rational thought grinding to a halt. He opened and closed his mouth several times as he tried to think of any other reply than *yes, please.* Finally, he said, "I—"

Ever cut him off. "Never mind. Good night," he continued

in a rush, wiggling free of Arsen's arms and rolling to face the wall like he always did. At least, he wasn't crying this time. And he didn't run away. Probably because he didn't like being alone. But Arsen would take it. He'd take anything that meant Ever was beside him, toxic or not.

He rolled onto his side then, after hesitating for only a moment, he folded himself around Ever, putting his arm around him and pulling him close. He breathed easier when Ever burrowed deeper against him, even if it meant his cute little ass was rubbing against Arsen's crotch.

Fuck.

He pressed his face against Ever's neck, inhaling deeply, recognizing the scent as one of the soaps he'd bought just hours ago. "Good night, Ever."

"Good night."

TEN

EVER

THINGS BETWEEN EVER AND ARSEN were…awkward.

That was the only word Ever could think of to describe the last few days. On the surface, it didn't seem like anything had changed between them. Each day, Ever would sit on the couch in the loft overlooking the garage while Arsen worked down below. He would read his book and covertly watch him work, and watch him laugh and joke with Jericho and the customers.

At lunch, Arsen or Jericho would make sure Ever had something to eat. Arsen would sit upstairs with him, watching intently as Ever tried whatever new food he'd brought for him. One day, it had been Indian food—Arsen's personal favorite. Another, it had been Korean barbecue. Today, there were subs from the place down the street.

Everything had been delicious.

At least once a day, Arsen would take Ever out into the world. He seemed determined that he try one or two new things each day. The activities varied greatly. Blowing bubbles. Trying hot chocolate. Sitting on the roof and stargazing. Eating ice cream. Even a bubble bath. Sadly, Arsen had left Ever to that particular task alone.

It was all fun—everything Ever never even dared dream of, really—but nothing distracted him from the memory of their kiss and his pathetic attempt at flirting with Arsen after, or the weird tension that existed between them since.

At night, Arsen played his video games and entertained his adoring fans. Ever curled up in the corner of the bed and watched from afar, reading his book—casting him and Arsen as the main characters in his head—wishing more than anything he could go back to his seat between Arsen's knees. He liked being boxed in by him. It felt safe.

And Ever rarely felt safe. Not that he worried about Arsen or Jericho, but every customer felt like a potential threat. Every trip outside the garage felt like it could be his last. It hadn't been that way at first. When Arsen had liberated him, he'd been scared and confused, but elated to finally be free of Jennika.

But with each passing day, his unease grew. Maybe it was the tension between him and Arsen getting jumbled in his head. Or maybe this was the trauma that Arsen had warned him about. The trauma that seemed to make him untouchable in Arsen's eyes.

Or maybe Arsen just didn't want him. Not that Ever could blame him. Arsen had a life. He had a job and an apartment and friends. He had hobbies and fans. Ever didn't even have a last name. He was a ghost, forced to rely on Arsen and Jericho for everything.

He wanted to help, but Arsen knew the loud noises of

the garage scared him. No matter how much Ever tried to hide his discomfort, he jumped at every sound, and it was only getting worse. But he had no other options. He had no birth certificate, no birthday, no social security card. All things Jericho insisted he needed if he wanted a life in the outside world.

Did Ever want a life outside? Not really. Every day, his anxiety grew, this weird sense of dread that weighed on him, growing heavier with each moment. Jennika was dead. He knew that. He'd seen what was left of her body. His injuries were almost healed. But the scars remained. And they were ugly inside and out. *He* was ugly.

Ever shoved the thought away, glancing at the clock. Unease filled him like an icy finger down his spine. It wouldn't be long until his doctor's appointment. When Arsen had first told him about it, he'd just nodded blankly, but now that it was growing close to the time when he would have to go, he was having a hard time quelling the panic clawing up his throat.

Jericho had made the appointment—said the doctor was a friend of the family. Jennika had called her doctor friend that, too. He'd looked like a doctor. Had degrees on his wall, had all the things he needed to bandage Ever's burns, suture up his cuts, set his broken bones. But it was Ever who'd paid the bill. Did all doctors expect to get paid in sexual favors from children? Had Ever finally aged out?

He wanted to pace. He wanted to tear at his skin or pick at his nails—something, *anything*, to drive away the fear. He knew it wasn't rational. He did. He really did. But he couldn't seem to get his body to understand. He hugged himself for a solid minute until something moving below caught his attention.

Arsen. He was talking to a boy his age with shaggy brown hair. The panic inside Ever was now replaced by something else at the sight of them. Jealousy. Ever folded his hands on the back of the sofa and placed his chin on them as he watched the two.

Watching Arsen was one of Ever's favorite pastimes. Every morning, Arsen would start off in navy blue coveralls and clunky oil-stained work boots, a headband pushing the hair out of his crystal-blue eyes. But by noon, he'd stripped off the top half, tying the sleeves around his waist, leaving him in nothing but a tight tank top—today, it was black—that showed off well-muscled arms and tattoos just as colorful as his hair.

Arsen was really handsome. No, that wasn't the right word. Arsen was...hot. With his aqua hair and aqua eyes and that square jaw that always had just the barest hint of scruff on it at all times. His nose was just the slightest bit crooked, like it had once been broken, and his rough, calloused hands were permanently stained around his nails, but that did nothing to detract from how much Ever wanted him.

But, unfortunately, he wasn't the only one.

There was a parade of girls—and guys—who seemed to stop by the garage for the sole purpose of flirting with Arsen. The girls would wiggle and squirm and put their half-naked bodies in his way as much as possible. The men were even more forward, asking for his number or hinting they'd be interested in…something more.

It grated Ever's nerves. People complimented Arsen on his long lashes, his full lips, even his perfect teeth. To his credit, Arsen took it all in stride, smiling politely but always brushing them off. If he even noticed them at all.

But Ever noticed. He couldn't not notice. They were so bold, far bolder than Ever could ever dream of being. And he did dream. Dreamed of more than just barely-there kisses and being held all night while he slept. Not that he didn't like being held at night. He loved it. Too much. He was starting to think he'd never be able to sleep again without the weight of Arsen's body pressing against him, his arms snug around him.

But that was all it was. Sleep. So, Ever just watched from the loft, like Rapunzel in her tower, letting his eyes linger on the way Arsen's muscles flexed with every movement, wanting to know how they would feel flexing beneath his fingers.

There was nothing wrong with looking, right?

Ever flopped back onto the couch with a huff. He wanted to do more than look. He itched to touch Arsen like he wanted to. To trace his tattoos with his fingers, to know what his skin tasted like, to know what that scruff felt like scratching its way across his body.

Ever wanted to try the things he'd only read about in books, wanted to try them the way they were supposed to happen. Sex, not assault. He wanted to know what those things felt like with someone he wanted, with someone who wanted him in a way that didn't hurt. But after the way Arsen had reacted to their kiss, Ever was pretty sure that would never happen.

Ever was too broken, too damaged. Arsen deserved better than a boy who couldn't leave the house without a chaperone.

Ever's pulse raced as the door to the apartment opened. He expected to hear Arsen's voice telling him it was time to leave, but when he looked up, it wasn't Arsen standing there but the guy who had been talking to Arsen just moments ago.

"Hi, I'm Noah. You're Ever, right?"

Ever frowned at him but nodded, then pulled himself into an upright position. "Yeah," he managed.

Noah gave a little wave and a warm smile. Ever couldn't help but notice his freckles. He seemed friendly. But Ever knew looks could be deceiving. "I'm one of Arsen's friends." Ever must have looked skeptical because Noah continued, "Jericho is married to my husband's brother. I thought I'd come say hi."

Ever pulled his knees to his chest. "Hi."

"Can I sit with you for a few minutes?" Noah asked, pointing to the opposite end of the couch.

Ever nodded but still kept a close eye on him.

Noah sat, giving him another reassuring smile. "Arsen tells me you're seeing Dr. Charon today?"

Ever gave a lop-sided shrug, unwilling to give away any information until he knew what Noah wanted from him.

Again, Noah gave him that encouraging smile. Like Ever was a child. They all treated him like that. He might as well be.

He forced himself to focus on Noah as he said, "She's

really nice."

Ever's eyes went wide. "She?"

Noah nodded. "Yeah. She's a friend of my father-in-law. She takes care of all of us when we need non-emergent care. She's kind of like our family physician."

Ever frowned. Why did they need an outsider? "Don't you have an actual family physician? Isn't Atticus a doctor?"

Noah gave a little laugh. Ever liked the way it sounded. Almost like music. "Yeah, he is. But he likes to spend his time in the lab looking at slides under a microscope more than he likes giving yearly physicals or running labs and doling out prescriptions. He'll do it, but he'll complain about it. And nobody wants to listen to Atticus complain. Well, except Jericho. He loves it. Dr. Charon likes what she does and she's willing to keep our secrets and keep her questions to a minimum."

"Secrets?" Ever echoed.

Was Noah threatening him? Letting him know that if he told the doctor what he knew about them killing people, she wouldn't do anything about it? Ever would never tell. They saved him. The least he could do was keep that secret for them. Besides, he didn't really understand how any of it worked, but Jericho said they only killed bad people and he believed Jericho to be good. He believed that in his soul.

"Mm," Noah said. "Secrets like how you got here. How you have no name, no insurance. She understands the true meaning of patient confidentiality. You're safe with her."

Safe? Noah was trying to make him feel better, not threaten him. "Oh."

Noah gave him a sad smile, like he knew his tragic backstory. "It's okay if you don't believe me."

Ever studied Noah. *Did* he believe him? He had no reason not to. Arsen clearly trusted him. Jericho, too. But trusting people had never really worked out in his favor before. Trust was earned and he'd only met Noah five minutes ago. "I don't know you."

Noah nodded. "Then let me tell you something about myself."

Ever sat forward the tiniest bit. "Okay."

Noah took a deep breath. "When I was a kid, I was kidnapped by a really bad man who convinced me that he was my father, even while he did horrible things to me. Things no father should do. Things nobody should do. He let other people do those things to me, too."

Ever's tongue darted out to wet his suddenly dry lower lip. Was he telling the truth? It didn't feel like a lie. But why would he just tell Ever all of these things unprompted? Ever flushed as it dawned on him that Noah knew what Jennika had done to him. What she'd let others do to him. Of course, he did. They all did.

Noah's gaze left him to look at the wall over Ever's shoulder. "It was so bad that I buried those memories deep down until something triggered them and they all came rushing back."

"Why are you telling me this?" Ever asked, genuinely confused.

"Because I'm hoping it will help you believe that we all just want to help you. That we can be trusted. That Arsen can be trusted. Nobody in our circle will ever do anything to hurt you. You're safe with us."

"Levi tried to steal my food," Ever heard himself say.

Heat bloomed on his face. Why had he said that?

Noah laughed once more. "Levi has no manners. I heard you bit him."

"Not hard," Ever mumbled.

Noah waved a hand. "It's good for him. Maybe, next time, he'll keep his hands to himself."

Ever's gaze strayed to the platinum band on Noah's left hand. "You're married?"

"Yeah. We got married a few months ago. Finally. We've been together for a while, but I had to work through my shit and deal with my past before I could officially commit myself to Adam forever. I didn't want to bring my old life into my new one, you know?"

Ever sucked his bottom lip between his teeth, chewing thoughtfully. Noah had trauma and a husband. "Did Adam know about your past?"

"Yes. Adam's the one who triggered my memories," Noah admitted.

Ever's gaze went wide. "And you...married him?"

"It wasn't intentional. Well, it was. But he gave me the chance to walk away. I didn't take it."

Ever floundered, wanting to ask a million questions but having no idea what questions were out of line. "Did what happened to you change the way he treated you?"

Noah snorted. "No. But you have to understand, my husband...he doesn't have the same feelings other people do."

"What does that mean?"

"My husband is a psychopath. He doesn't feel guilt or remorse. He has no real empathy."

Ever's pulse whooshed in his ears. "What does that matter?"

"When people know about your past, sometimes, they tend to try to insulate you. They want to put you in this victim box and they expect you to behave accordingly. You're supposed to have flashbacks or triggers. You're supposed to fear certain people or hate certain smells. They treat you with kid gloves. Adam never did that. He couldn't. He wasn't capable."

"So, after your memories came back, you were just... fine?" Ever asked, hating how much he envied Noah.

This time, Noah's laugh was bitter. "No, I was definitely not fine. I'm still not. Certain smells do trigger my memories. I will never have kids because I am too afraid that someone will hurt them like they hurt me. Sometimes, when my past comes crashing in, I drink too much and Adam has to wrap me in a blanket burrito and watch hours of cartoons with me until I can pull it together again."

"A blanket burrito?"

"It's a thing. Being wrapped tight in a blanket. It has a calming effect. It helps." Ever nodded but still didn't quite understand. "Are you having any...triggers?"

Ever brought his thumbnail to his lips, gnawing it between his teeth for a moment. "I... Not really? I...I'm scared. A lot. I hate loud noises. Mostly, I just feel stupid."

Noah blinked at him. "Stupid?"

"I feel like I don't know anything. People look at me like

I'm a freak because I've never had pancakes or my own shampoo or because I'd never heard of Spotify or Netflix. I feel like an alien. I feel…stupid."

Noah scooted closer without thought then stopped short, like he didn't want to startle Ever. "You're not stupid," he said sternly. "None of this is your fault. Nothing that happened to you is your fault."

"That doesn't make me any less stupid," Ever said. "I never went to school. I don't know my real name. I don't even know where I came from. I don't remember if I had a mom and dad. If I did, where are they? Are they still looking for me? I don't even know math."

Noah waved a hand. "Nobody knows math. It might as well be witchcraft."

Ever giggled then slapped a hand over his mouth.

Noah smiled. "I can see why Arsen thinks you're cute."

"What?" Ever asked.

Noah shook his head. "Nothing."

Nothing? "Arsen thinks I'm cute?"

Noah shifted in his seat, peering down into the bay below. Ever did the same, looking just in time to see Arsen quickly turn back to the car in front of him, like he hadn't been staring up at them.

Once Arsen went back to his task, Noah leaned in, his tone almost conspiratorial. "Between you and me? Arsen thinks you're adorable."

Ever's heart sank. "Like a kitten?"

Noah's look was lecherous. "No. Definitely not."

"I don't know what you mean," Ever said, frustration

leaching into his voice. "He treats me like I'm a kid."

Noah once more glanced down at Arsen, like he worried he was eavesdropping somehow. Once he seemed assured, he said, "He would kill me if I told you this, but when it comes to him, *you* have all the power. It's been a week and he would kill for you. He's…so into you."

"Into me?" Ever repeated.

Noah nodded emphatically. "Mm, beyond. He's just freaking out over the kiss."

Ever could feel himself growing hot all over. "You know about the kiss?"

Noah winced. "He was live streaming, remember? About five hundred people witnessed that kiss."

"Oh, my God."

Noah waved his hand. "It's no big deal. Trust me, there are entire accounts that live stream way dirtier stuff than that—You know what? Forget I said that." Almost as an afterthought, he said, "But, if it's any consolation, you do have quite a few fans of your own now."

"I do?" Ever asked, bewildered.

"My point is, Arsen doesn't want you to think that you owe him sexual favors in exchange for food or clothing or shelter. He doesn't want you to feel obligated to…'earn your keep.' He just really likes you. And from what I know about Arsen, he doesn't really ever like anyone in that way."

"That way…"

"Like a boyfriend way. Like a dating way. Arsen's never had a serious boyfriend, but I definitely think he wants that with you."

Ever shook his head. Arsen liked him? Arsen would kill or die…for Ever? Arsen liked him in a boyfriend way? That made no sense. Arsen didn't even know him, couldn't know how completely unworthy he was. He probably just felt sorry for Ever.

He said as much to Noah.

Noah gave him this soft look. "He is sorry for what happened to you. That's true. We all are. But Arsen is the polar opposite of my husband. Arsen feels everything. He wants nothing more than to make the world safer for people like you and me. He will never stop worrying about you or your feelings. Not because he pities you but because he wants you to be safe. That's just who he is as a person. Don't you want the same for him?"

Ever blinked at Noah. Would he be crazy for saying yes? They'd literally known each other a week. "We barely know each other."

Noah shrugged. "You two are bound together by this completely bizarre shared experience—this crazy, fucked-up thing that happened to both of you. There's no getting around that. Adam and I are, too. We shared this tragic connection that shaped who we are as people. The world would definitely say that my marriage is toxic."

"They would?" Ever asked.

Noah laughed. "Yeah, definitely. Like, take right now. I bet if I took my phone from my pocket, my husband—who has the emotional intelligence of an inchworm—has probably texted me ten times and called me three because I've been away from him for an hour. Is that healthy? No.

Do I find it weirdly hot? Yeah. Because nobody ever cared about me before Adam and nobody will ever care for me like he does because nobody understands how fucked up I really am like he does, ya know?"

Ever nodded slowly. "I think so?"

"Our relationship only has to work for us. And any relationship you have with anybody else only has to work for the two of you."

Ever shook his head, unable to move past Noah's monumental confession. "Arsen *likes* me?"

Noah nodded. "Very much so."

It couldn't be true. "Like...in a boyfriend way?"

"Yes."

"But he won't do anything about it because he thinks I'll feel obligated to have sex with him because I don't have a job?"

Noah seemed to bite back a smile but said, "Yes."

"So, what do I do?" Ever asked.

Noah tilted his head. "What do you want to do?"

"I-I just want him to kiss me again," Ever blurted.

Noah grinned. "Then tell him that. Directly."

Ever felt his eyes bulge. "What? Like just say it? Out loud?"

"Well, he's clearly not able to read your thoughts," Noah said.

Ever frowned. "People can do that?"

Noah laughed. "You'd be surprised."

Ever let that go. He didn't have time to wonder if the supernatural was real. Instead, he sat chewing on his lower lip, contemplating Noah's advice. "Are you sure he likes me like that?"

"I would be willing to bet a kidney, maybe even my own."

"What?" Ever said.

"Nothing," Noah answered quickly. "But, if you want something to happen between you and my bleeding heart friend down there, I'm afraid you're going to have to be the one to make the first move. He's too sensitive."

"I don't know if I can," Ever whispered.

Noah hopped to his feet, giving him two thumbs up. "I believe in you. If you need to talk, just use Arsen's phone and call me. Oh, and don't be scared of the doc. She's good people. Also, they're probably going to make you see a therapist. You'll feel like it's not helping but I promise it work—"

Noah cut himself off, looking down at his pocket. He pulled his phone free and grinned, showing it to Ever. An unnaturally beautiful man stared back at him, and above his picture was his name. Adam. Noah shook his phone at Ever and grinned. "See? He can't live without me. Bye."

Then Noah was gone, leaving Ever sitting on the sofa in a daze. Had that conversation really just happened? Could Noah be trusted? He seemed so…normal. Likable. But what if he was wrong? What if Ever asked Arsen to kiss him and he refused and made him leave?

Even as Ever thought it, his heart rejected the notion. Noah was right about one thing: Arsen *was* a bleeding heart. Even if he rejected Ever, he wouldn't kick him out. It would just get even more awkward, if that was possible.

But the rejection alone might kill him.

ELEVEN

ARSEN

"TVOYU MAT."

Arsen swore as his wrench slipped, pain shooting up his arm as he drove his finger into the filthy screw sticking out of the motor mount he worked on. He shook his hand out as if that might shoo away the throbbing ache left in its wake, then checked to see if he was bleeding.

He wasn't.

This was his second injury of the morning. He was too distracted. Distracted by Ever. Sweet, pretty Ever with his big, doe eyes and his perpetually pouty lips, and who smelled like Arsen's detergent and lavender-scented soap. Arsen shouldn't find it sexy that Ever preferred Arsen's hoodies to his own and Arsen's bed to his own...but he did. He found everything about Ever sexy, and it was driving him insane.

It wasn't Ever's fault he got cuter every day. He smiled more—revealing those adorable bunny teeth—and when he did, it did something to Arsen's heart. He was still painfully shy. When they went out, he rarely spoke, often making Arsen order for him while he hid behind him, his headphones firmly in place. Arsen would be lying if he said he didn't like being the shield between Ever and the world. He needed one.

Arsen wasn't the only one bewitched by Ever. Everywhere they went, people went out of their way to smile at him, give him things for free, try to coax a smile from him. Teen girls and boys went out of their way to flirt with him. Even Arsen's online fans seemed to prefer Ever to him, demanding in the comments section to see him. Asking if they broke up. Begging for even a glimpse. But Ever kept his distance. Arsen just didn't know if it was because of the audience…or him.

Despite that, Arsen was still doing his best to introduce Ever to new experiences. He went along without complaint, even when it was obvious he was humoring Arsen. Ever never said no, even when he wanted to. Even if it pained him. Even when Arsen gave him an out. Every time, he'd paint a smile on his face, shake his head, and take Arsen's hand, threading their fingers together like it was them against the world. And when he did, Arsen fell for him all over again.

Still, Arsen never lost sight of Ever's need to please him. He did his best to try to gauge what Ever really wanted from barely-there context clues. He was an expert at masking his feelings; years of beatings would do that, Arsen knew from experience. Even at the doctor's office, Ever had never once complained. He'd sat quietly through every test and procedure, every needle stick, a distant smile on his face.

That was how Ever got through anything unpleasant. He

just forced a smile on his face, no matter how miserable he was. Even when it was something he clearly hated. Like pickles. Or coleslaw. Both foods Arsen had added to his mental do-not-buy list, even though Ever insisted they were fine. Great, even.

But that was Ever. He would suffer for the pleasure of others. He wanted to please Arsen, even if it caused him personal distress. Even when it was clear he was upset with him. No, upset wasn't the right word. Leery? Confused? After the kiss, something had changed, and after Ever's conversation with Noah, it had changed again. Arsen couldn't keep up with their ever morphing relationship.

Ever still wanted to make Arsen happy, that much was obvious. The only silver lining Arsen could see was that Ever's need to make him happy no longer stemmed from fear but just a need to *want* to please him.

He didn't know how to tell Ever that just being near him was all he needed. Even if it sometimes felt like torture— like at night when he was tucked up under Arsen's chin, his breath puffing against his chest as he made these little half moans and whimpers in his sleep. Arsen had learned to sleep with a permanent hard-on. But his dreams were x-rated and starred Ever every time.

In his dreams, he gave in to every dirty thought he had about Ever. In his dreams, he stripped him naked, spent hours exploring his body, didn't stop kissing and licking and stroking until he was crying and begging beneath him. He shook his head. The last thing he needed was those thoughts creeping in during his work hours. He was already a mess.

Arsen glanced up into the loft, already knowing when he did, Ever would be there, peeking over the sofa or the rim of his book, watching him. Four days ago, he would have ducked out of sight like a groundhog if Arsen had risked a glance, but now, he stared back. Hard. If anyone else had looked at Arsen like that, he'd think they were plotting his murder...or maybe his seduction. Either way, Arsen would fear for his safety.

But not with Ever. No, when Ever looked at him like that, Arsen feared for Ever's safety. Because it made Arsen think those very dirty thoughts that were never far from his mind when he should be changing out the motor mount on a 2008 Toyota Camry. It made him think about what noises Ever would make the first time Arsen kissed him with intent, the first time he touched his naked body, the first time he pushed inside him.

Fuck.

Arsen was half-hard just knowing Ever watched him. He sat on the sofa, his cheek resting on his folded arms as he watched Arsen with an almost dreamy expression. What was he thinking about? Did he want Arsen, too? Did it even matter?

When they locked eyes, Ever didn't look away. He just sucked his bottom lip between his teeth and chewed thoughtfully. Arsen would be a liar if he said he didn't like knowing Ever watched him. But the intensity of his gaze made Arsen...nervous?

No, that wasn't the right word. Anxious, maybe? Not in a scary way but in the way he felt when he played survival horror games. With every level, the intensity would rise and the anticipation would grow. Waiting for the attack was half the fun. And when it came, it was cathartic. This expulsion of energy that had been building since level one.

And that was what this felt like. It felt like...foreplay. No, even that didn't seem right. There was no English word for the feeling. But in Russia, they would say it was *predvkushenie.* That anticipation that came just before you tasted something you've been craving. And he craved a taste of Ever. Did Ever want that, too?

Arsen groaned out loud even as he waved at Ever, smiling like an idiot when Ever raised his hand and wiggled his fingers in return. Yeah, he was fucked. He wanted to play with Ever in every conceivable way.

"Arsen."

Arsen's head jerked towards the sound of his name. Jericho stood in the office doorway. He cocked his head, indicating he wanted Arsen to step inside. If it had been anybody else, Arsen would have thought he was in trouble, but not with Jericho.

Arsen set down the wrench and wiped his hands uselessly on the dirty rag that hung half out of his pocket. He followed Jericho inside, sparing a glance upwards at Ever, who still watched him like a hunter stalking his prey.

The world's most adorable predator.

Arsen fought the urge to smile.

Once inside, Jericho fell heavily into his chair, fixing Arsen with a look that set his teeth on edge.

Arsen dropped onto the other chair across from him.

"What's wrong?"

Jericho's mouth formed a grim line. "When Charon took blood from Ever, I had her run a DNA test on him. We figured, if he was a missing person, maybe we could track him through familial DNA, like they did with Noah."

Arsen's stomach dipped like he was on a roller coaster. Had they found Ever's family? Were they taking him away? "And?"

Jericho shook his head. "Nothing. Not a single genetic match. No cousins, no siblings. Nobody in his family has ever had their DNA collected in the US."

"What does that mean?" Arsen asked, wiping his sweaty palms on his thighs.

Jericho sighed. "No missing persons reports from the city. No DNA matches. No fingerprint matches. Jennika wasn't the type to kidnap a kid. If she was, there would have been more. She acquired the three girls she abused through the foster system. But there's no trace of Ever there, either. I hate to say it, but he was probably trafficked into the country."

"Trafficked," Arsen echoed, not because he didn't understand but just because the word made him a little sick.

"There's a big trafficking problem here. She had him chipped like a dog. She had some very shady, known associates with ties to organized crime. She never even bothered to name him. He named himself. If she had legally adopted him, there would have been a paper trail. We'd have a name or something to trace. But there's nothing."

Arsen's chest was tight. Ever had been with Jennika so

long, he had no recollection of his parents, where he was from, when his birthday was. He only knew his age because Jennika had let it slip. How old was Ever the first time she abused him? He must have been so tiny and so scared. Arsen felt a little like throwing up.

"Why?" he heard himself ask.

Jericho frowned. "Why?"

Arsen met Jericho's gaze. "Why did she…buy him?"

Jericho shrugged. "The two most common reasons for trafficking are forced labor and sex work. The former is mostly adult women, the latter is women and children. I think Jennika wanted a domestic servant who she could abuse without interference. So, she bought one."

"She pimped him out to others," Arsen said. "She beat him and sold him to men who hurt him."

"I know," Jericho said quietly.

A sudden heat rushed through him, his fists clenching and jaw tight as he said, "And we can't even tell him who he is."

"We're going to keep looking. All we know from his DNA is that he's of southeast Asian descent. The two most trafficked regions are Thailand and Vietnam, but that's still millions of people. You might need to prepare Ever for the very real possibility that we might never know where he came from."

Arsen hurt for him. "What if his parents have been looking for him all this time?"

Jericho sat forward in his chair. "I'm not going to lie, it's possible they're the ones who sold him in the first place. It happens. More often than it should."

"What kind of parent sells a child?" Arsen said, disgusted.

"You know what kind. Desperate people. Evil people. We've seen this before. Hell, here in the U.S., there are baby brokers and people 'rehoming' kids on Facebook. We know kids are worth a lot of money to the wrong people. It looks like Ever might be one of those kids."

A sudden wave of panic welled in Arsen's chest. "What am I supposed to tell him? That he'll never know who he really is? That he might never meet his family? Is it even legal for him to stay? You can't send him back to a country he doesn't know. How does that even work? What happens to an undocumented person if they don't even know where they're from? Do they just guess? He wouldn't have any family or money or speak the language. He'd be all alone."

Jericho raised a hand to silence him. "Don't get ahead of yourself. Nobody even knows he's here."

"But he can't stay a ghost forever. What if he wants to get a job or a driver's license or go to school? He can't stay in the loft for—."

"Arsen!" Jericho cut him off sharply. When he looked at him, he said, "We're not going to let anything happen to him. You know the connections we have. If we have to, we'll buy him a whole new identity. He can be whoever he wants. There's nothing that can't be faked so that he can stay here."

Arsen looked Jericho in the eye. He needed him to really hear what he was about to say. "I won't lose him. No matter what it takes."

"I know, kid. But don't get ahead of yourself. Go get your boy and have lunch."

Arsen's shoulders sagged. Jericho wasn't his enemy. He nodded and stood then left, shutting the door behind him. He walked to the sink and scrubbed his hands before trudging up the stairs. When he got to the top, Ever smiled, poking a finger against the glass. Arsen couldn't help but press his finger against Ever's, heart tripping as he giggled.

Whatever expression Arsen was wearing must have been bad because Ever's laugh died quickly, his own expression replaced by a look of dread. Arsen entered the room and smiled, but Ever wasn't buying it.

"What's wrong?" he asked, fear creeping into his tone.

"Nothing," Arsen assured him, trying to brighten his smile before he looked away. He couldn't lie to his face.

He would tell him after they ate.

"Liar."

Arsen's head snapped back to Ever, whose face was a storm cloud. Was he...mad? "What?"

"You're lying," he said, his tone accusatory.

He was lying. But a few days ago, Ever would have never dared say so. This was progress. Arsen fought the urge to smile. He didn't want Ever to think Arsen was laughing at him when he was truly just happy he trusted him enough to stand up for himself. An angry Ever meant he knew Arsen would never hurt him. That was huge.

That was everything.

Still, Arsen shook his head. "I'm not lying—" At Ever's flat stare, he conceded, "Okay, I am, but only because I wanted to eat before we talk."

Ever's brows knitted together. Arsen could literally see the wheels in his brain turning. Finally, he said, "You're sending me away."

Arsen's eyes went wide. "What? No." He dropped down beside him on the couch, gripping Ever's face between his palms, putting his face as close to his as he dared. "Listen to me. No matter what happens, I'll never send you away. Ever. Do you believe me?"

Ever hesitated, his expression miserable. His gaze slid away from him and, like always, he worried his lower lip between his teeth. Finally, he nodded, whispering, "Yes."

Arsen dropped his hands, feeling something unknot in his stomach. "Okay, good."

But Ever wasn't done questioning him. "Then, what's wrong?"

Arsen sighed. He wasn't going to let it go. "I just talked to Jericho. When you were at the doctor, we took some of your blood, hoping it would help us track down your family, but we didn't find anything."

Ever blinked at him. "Oh. Is that all?"

Arsen frowned. "Is that all? Don't you want to know who you are?"

Ever shrugged. "I don't know. I've been thinking about it since I talked to Noah. There are only two ways I ended up with Jennika, right? I was either sold or kidnapped. I'm not entirely sure I won't hate my parents either way. I don't know how to not blame them for all the things she did to me. Does that make me a bad person?"

Arsen scoffed, grabbing Ever by the back of his neck and hauling him close, pressing his lips to his forehead.

"Nothing could make you a bad person."

When he pulled back, Ever looked flustered. "Nothing?"

Arsen shook his head. "Not to me."

"Really?" Ever asked, hesitant.

"Really, really," he promised. That seemed to quell some of his unease. Arsen decided to change the subject. "Are you hungry? What new thing do you want to try today? Italian? Ethiopian?"

Ever shook his head, jutting his chin out in a way that made Arsen's pulse jump. He was so cute, even when he was being obstinate. Now that he'd seen it, Arsen hoped he never stopped fighting.

"So, what new thing do *you* want to try?" he asked patiently, hoping this would be the day Ever made his own decision.

Ever's brown eyes found his, his voice stern. "I want you to teach me to kiss."

Arsen's breath punched from his lungs. "What?"

Ever sank back against the corner of the sofa, glowering at him. "You asked."

"I—" Arsen stopped short. "You're right. I did."

Ever sat forward, voice hopeful. "So, you'll do it?"

Arsen floundered. It wasn't like he didn't want to do it. He thought of nothing else. But kissing led to more. And Ever wasn't asking for more. Arsen didn't know if he was strong enough to not try for more.

"Do you not want to kiss me?" Ever asked, disappointment creeping into his voice.

He watched as Ever's lower lip pooched out and he

looked up at him with sad eyes through long, sooty lashes. Arsen narrowed his eyes, taking it all in. It was all so… calculated. Was he trying to manipulate Arsen into getting what he wanted?

It dawned on him then. Noah. Fucking Noah. This was his doing. It had to be. He'd taken his sweet, baby angel, Ever, and turned him into a devious little shit willing to use every weapon in his arsenal to turn Arsen into his puppet.

And worse than that, it was totally working. "Of course, I want to kiss you, *besenok*," he admitted. "I haven't thought of anything but kissing you since the day we met."

Ever's cheeks turned pink, and his lips twitched in a smile he fought to hide. "Then do it. Kiss me. For real."

"For real?" Arsen asked, a jolt of awareness going straight to his dick.

Ever flushed, looking away. "Not like the other night. But…like how they do in my romance novels."

Chert.

Arsen had no idea how they kissed in romance novels but he doubted very much it was anything chaste. Was Ever asking him to put his tongue in his mouth? Arsen wasn't going to survive this. He wasn't sure Ever would, either. What the fuck was he thinking? Fuck. Fuck. Fuck. He was grateful Ever had moved a few inches from him because he was losing all sense of rationality.

"Okay," he heard himself say.

Ever's eyes lit up. "Really?"

Arsen closed his eyes and nodded, resigned. He was never going to say no to Ever.

Ever.

And it looked like Noah had made sure Ever knew he had the upper hand. The bastard. "Yes, really," Arsen promised. "But...not right now. Tonight. I only have an hour for lunch, and if I start kissing you, I might never stop."

Arsen watched as Ever's pupils blew wide, his lips parting in a quiet gasp at Arsen's words. He found himself staring at Ever's open mouth, thinking about things far dirtier than kissing. He shifted in his seat, grateful he still wore his baggy coveralls.

"What do you want to eat for lunch?" he asked, pretending to ignore Ever's shocked expression.

"Italian," Ever whispered.

"Good."

Arsen's losing streak continued. Not only had he lost that afternoon's battle against Ever, he lost every battle in the game until his team angrily kicked him offline, telling him to come back when his head was in the game and not up his ass. But how could his head be anywhere but with Ever, who was curled up on the bed three feet away in plaid pajama pants and a long-sleeved t-shirt, pretending to read his book while he covertly watched Arsen?

The answer was he couldn't. Arsen had never been so... aware of another human being in his life. It felt like some kind of magnetic force pulling him towards him. No matter what he was doing, Ever was never far from his mind, and getting back to him was his main priority.

Ever looked up from his book as soon as Arsen signed off. He dropped his headphones and walked to the bed. Just the act of walking towards him, knowing what they were about to do, already had Arsen half-hard. This was going to be an exercise in patience like he'd never known. Some kind of hero's trial.

He sat in front of Ever, criss-crossing his legs. Ever's tongue darted out to lick over his lower lip, then he marked his page and set his book down, waiting. He looked so…vulnerable, so trusting of Arsen. He didn't want to fuck up that trust, but he was also desperate to taste him, to touch him.

So, he did.

"If you want me to kiss you, you're going to have to be closer than this," Arsen teased, his hands gently sliding under Ever's knees and dragging him until he was almost in his lap. Ever's small, delicate hands fisted the fabric at Arsen's shoulders, and he was breathing heavily like he'd run a marathon. Fuck, he was trembling and they hadn't even started yet.

"Hi," Arsen said, pressing his nose against Ever's for a second, hoping to reassure him somehow. He didn't want this to be stressful for him.

"Hi," Ever said, breathless, his minty breath puffing against Arsen's cheek.

"Are you sure you want to do this?" Arsen asked. Ever's rapid nod made him smile. "Okay, but if you don't like something—if you get scared, or if I make you uncomfortable—you have to tell me to stop. Okay?"

Ever's nod was slightly less enthusiastic. "Okay," he said quietly.

Arsen wasn't convinced. He took Ever's chin between thumb and forefinger, gently forcing him to meet his gaze. "I'm serious. I won't get mad. It won't hurt my feelings. Just say the word and it stops. I stop. Promise me."

Ever blinked rapidly then swallowed hard. "Yeah, okay. I promise."

With that out of the way, Arsen suddenly felt completely out of his element. He'd kissed more than his fair share of people, but it had never meant anything. It had never had any weight to it. It was just…perfunctory. Part of the process to get inside his partner in a far more satisfying way.

But this was important. This meant something, and gazing down at Ever's wide eyes had his heart in his throat. Arsen traced Ever's bottom lip with his thumb, his cock jumping at the tiny sound Ever made. Fuck. He couldn't wait another second. He dipped his head, capturing Ever's bottom lip between his own, sucking gently. Ever made a happy noise that made Arsen feel feral. He forced himself to pull back—to give Ever a chance to change his mind.

Ever had other ideas. He used Arsen's sweatshirt to drag him back to him, their lips colliding awkwardly. He was so perfect. Arsen took Ever's face in his hands, fixing the angle so their mouths fit better, but not daring to break the kiss, trying to ignore his already throbbing cock as Ever's mouth opened beneath his.

He was so fucking eager, so fucking hungry…for Arsen. God, it was too much power. But Arsen didn't feel powerful. He felt like Ever controlled his every thought. He was excited and nervous and desperate for more of him. Everything about Ever turned him on. The sounds he made, the way his hands spasmed into the fabric of his shirt each time their mouths surged against each other. Even the taste of his toothpaste. Arsen's toothpaste.

He was so gone.

Arsen wrapped his arms around Ever, pulling him tighter against him, making a satisfied sound as Ever wrapped his legs around his waist without hesitation, like he couldn't get close enough to satisfy either. When he swept his tongue into Ever's mouth, he met it eagerly with his own and they quickly found a rhythm to their kisses.

Arsen lost track of time, of everything but Ever in his arms, wrapped around him, whimpering and whining into his mouth. Every kiss had weight, binding them together on a soul-searing level. It was like being drugged. He'd never tried ecstasy but he imagined it was like this. Ever was addicting. He was Arsen's perfect drug.

Arsen's hands slid down to Ever's ass, dragging him higher into his lap so he could feel how hard he was. Ever gasped into his mouth, rubbing against him mindlessly. Arsen could feel he was hard, too. The only thing between them was the thin layer of Ever's pajama pants and Arsen's basketball shorts, and it wasn't nearly enough to provide any protection against what they both clearly wanted.

Arsen knew he should shut it down but, instead, he slid his hands up under Ever's shirt, his fingertips trailing along his spine then outward. Ever sucked in a breath as Arsen traced the outline of one of the scars on his back, dropping his hands to Arsen's arms like he wanted him to stop.

Arsen pulled back. "Are you okay? Did I hurt you?"

"They're ugly," Ever whispered.

Arsen studied Ever's kiss-swollen lips and his lids at half-mast, so drunk on him it took a moment for him to understand what Ever meant. "Nothing about you is ugly. Trust me."

Ever looked so pretty, so sweet, Arsen couldn't not dip his head one more time. Ever kissed back, but more hesitantly, clearly still worried about Arsen's hands on his bare skin.

Maybe they needed to talk more?

Arsen broke their kiss a second time, but before he could ask if Ever was sure he wanted to continue, Ever's face fell. "We're not done already, are we?"

Arsen cupped his face, his thumbs tracing his cheekbones. "I just don't want things to go too far."

"You don't want to fuck me," Ever said, sounding disappointed.

Arsen's mouth fell open at Ever's bold statement. Neither he nor his dick were prepared to hear that word falling from that tongue. "I've never heard you swear before," he mused. "And also that's not true at all. I do want that. All of that and so much more. I want all of the things. But I don't want to rush you."

Ever's face screwed into a look of confusion. "I've waited nineteen years. How is that rushing?"

He had a point.

Arsen shook his head. That was his dick talking, not his

brain. This was all new to Ever. "I just think tonight we should stick to…making out."

"Making out?" Ever echoed, biting his lip. His dreamy expression was driving Arsen crazy.

Ever was literally going to be the death of him. "Yes."

Ever wiggled against him, rubbing his crotch against Arsen's. "Does making out include this?"

Chert. "It can…yeah."

Ever wrapped his arms around Arsen's neck, dragging him back down for another kiss, whispering against his lips, "Let's do that, then."

"Ever…"

Ever whined, his mouth still working over Arsen's. "Please? This feels too good to stop."

Ever wasn't wrong. Arsen had never been so turned on in his whole life. His body made the decision before his brain did, and he upended Ever on the bed, hovering over him as his head hit the pillow.

Arsen caught his gaze, voice stern. "Clothes stay on."

Ever sighed, tone dripping with disappointment as he said, "Fine."

Fuck.

TWELVE
EVER

EVER HAD BEEN THROUGH HELL in his life. He'd endured by letting his thoughts float away somewhere safe—somewhere far outside of his pain. But this—this feeling—was the opposite of that.

He floated, for sure, but on this wave of euphoria he'd never experienced before. Every atom, every cell, every molecule engaged until Arsen's touch made him want to purr like a cat.

Everything felt right. The heavy weight of Arsen's body pressing him into the mattress, the spicy scent of his deodorant, the smoothness of his skin beneath Ever's fingers. He wanted to memorize it all, save it to replay at a later date when he could give it the attention it deserved.

Arsen was so careful with him, lying with only half of his body on Ever, probably worried Ever would panic beneath his full weight like last time. But Ever didn't feel trapped, he felt drunk. Every move Arsen made elicited a sensation so good Ever couldn't stop the tiny sounds spilling out of his mouth.

He would have been embarrassed if every one of those sounds didn't elicit a response from Arsen. He could hear it in his ragged breaths, in the way he seemed to bite off a growl whenever Ever made those noises.

That was the real turn on—being wanted by Arsen, and seeing how his body responded to Ever's. The way he fought for control. How every time he kissed Ever, he didn't seem to want to stop.

It was powerful. It made Ever feel powerful. Important. Wanted.

Arsen had said clothes had to stay on, but Ever couldn't stop himself from sliding his hands under Arsen's hoodie. Where Ever's skin was marred with scars, Arsen's was smooth like silk, and when he moved, his muscles flexed beneath Ever's fingers deliciously.

If making out was like this, sex had to be better. But he couldn't imagine anything better than Arsen's lips on his, the way his tongue teased its way into his mouth in a dizzying rhythm, even the way his arms caged him in. It was all perfect.

Arsen's mouth broke from his, trailing kisses along his jaw and down his throat. Ever just completely gave in, too blissed out to even worry if he was doing something right or wrong. He rode the wave of pleasure, safe with Arsen… safe under Arsen.

Ever's hands flexed, his toes curling as Arsen continued to explore. His lips were so soft, his tongue wet as he licked at the hollow of his throat and then sucked on his earlobe. Every time he moved to a new spot, the scruff on his cheeks and chin scraped Ever's skin, leaving him craving more.

Arsen spoke as he moved, murmuring things in a language Ever didn't understand, his low, smooth tone hypnotic, only sinking Ever deeper into this almost trance-like state.

The more they kissed—the more Arsen touched him— the more Ever wanted, and the more his body demanded, until kissing only left him frustrated and so hard he ached. Ever didn't really understand what he wanted, only that he did. He shifted restlessly beneath Arsen, whining with need.

"Shh," Arsen soothed, kissing Ever's forehead, his nose, his cheeks. Ever gave another helpless whimper. He needed more. "I got you."

Arsen shifted then, his thigh pressing against Ever's throbbing cock in a way that stole his breath and his sanity. He couldn't stop the moan that escaped. "Do it again… please?"

This time, Arsen did growl, this sort of low rumble right in Ever's ear. Goosebumps erupted over his whole body as Arsen did as Ever asked, moving his thigh once more. The pleasure that simple movement brought was shocking, and Ever's hips moved of their own volition, seeking more.

Ever could never have imagined anything like this sensation. It was rapturous, like a religious experience. This sort of pleasure could only be considered holy. The way Arsen moved against him was certainly worthy of worship.

Arsen captured his mouth in a kiss that was far dirtier than any other so far and started to pulse his leg against Ever's erection in a steady rhythm until he was rolling his hips up to meet him, his fingers digging into Arsen's back, spurring him on.

When Ever whined, Arsen sped up his movements. "Feel good?" he asked against his lips.

"Hnf," was the only thing Ever could manage.

Good was such an insignificant word; this was... brilliant. Spectacular. Incandescent. Addictive. Some kind of erotic torture designed to make him crazy. And he couldn't stop himself from chasing the sensation, rubbing against the thick muscle of Arsen's thigh, not even knowing the outcome but still reaching for something...more. He needed more.

He made another frustrated sound.

"What's wrong, *besenok*?" Arsen asked, tone almost teasing.

Was he enjoying Ever's misery?

"More, please," he begged, hoping Arsen would know what he needed. Arsen always knew.

Arsen gave a low chuckle that melted the last tiny bit of Ever's sanity. "More what?"

Ever floundered. How was he supposed to know? "Just... more. It hurts. Please... I need..."

Arsen's voice was growly as he asked, "Need what?"

"I don't know," Ever said, bewildered, still moving against Arsen, flushing with embarrassment.

He sucked at this.

Arsen's weight disappeared. Ever's heart sank. They couldn't be done already just because he didn't know what he wanted? But then Arsen was over him, using his thighs to widen Ever's and settling between them, keeping the weight of his upper body on his forearms now bracketing

Ever's head.

"Wrap your legs around me," Arsen demanded.

Ever did without thought, sucking in a breath as his cock aligned with Arsen's in a way that sent a shock of spine-melting ecstasy through his whole body. "Oh, fuck."

He yelped as Arsen nipped his earlobe with his teeth. "You cursing might be the sexiest thing I've ever heard."

Ever couldn't even respond. He was far too caught up. Was this what sex between two people who wanted it was like? Was it like this every time? How did people function in the real world knowing they could be doing this instead?

It was all too much, too perfect. Arsen's mouth was hot on his, his hands now threading in his hair, moving him just how he wanted him as he fucked up against him again…

…and again

…and again.

Until heat pooled in Ever's belly, his body acting of its own accord, meeting every one of Arsen's movements with a desperation he couldn't explain.

What would it be like without clothes, without any barriers between them? What would it be like to have Arsen not just on top of him but inside him? Moving inside him. His pulse pounded in his ears. His head was spinning, and he was dizzy at the thought of letting Arsen have every part of him. At *wanting* Arsen to have every part of him.

It was that thought that pushed him off the cliff—sent him free-falling into the most intense experience of his life, his release pulsing from him, taking the last remnants of his brain function with it.

Arsen didn't stop, just kept surging against him, chasing his own pleasure. That only made it hotter. Arsen using him—using his body to make himself feel good. It was all so much.

Arsen gave a harsh groan, grinding his hips against Ever's one last time, before collapsing on top of him. "Is this okay?" he asked, voice raw.

It took Ever longer than it should to know what he meant. Was he okay with Arsen on top of him? He didn't know how to tell him he'd happily suffocate under him if it meant he could feel like this forever.

"Mm," was all he managed, eyelids at half-mast.

They were both sweating. Ever's pajama pants now stuck uncomfortably to his skin, but he couldn't move. Didn't want to. His bones had turned to Jell-O, and if they never returned to normal, Ever would still think it a worthy sacrifice.

Arsen's head lay beside his on the pillow, his breath ragged in Ever's ear. He had done that. He had put that dopey expression on Arsen's face, had worn him out.

Ever already wanted to do it again.

"Are you okay?" Arsen managed.

Ever couldn't stop the small laugh that escaped. He was better than okay. He was…giddy. High. He was sure his brain had melted.

"Is that a yes?" Arsen asked, kissing his temple.

Ever tilted his head closer to Arsen. "Yes. But I'm sticky."

Arsen scoffed. "Yeah, the only downside to orgasms."

Orgasms. His first. Hopefully not his only. "Can we do it again?" he blurted.

This time, it was Arsen who laughed. "I think you'll find that there's a refractory period between performances."

Ever made a sad sound. "Can we do it again later?"

Arsen rose up on his forearms. "I've created a monster."

Before Ever could formulate a response, Arsen rolled off him and onto his back, then raised his arm so Ever could slide beneath it. He curled into his side, letting his head rest on his chest, able to hear Arsen's rapidly beating heart even through his sweatshirt.

"Can we do it without clothes next time?" Ever asked.

Arsen laughed low. "We'll see."

"Can we do other things later?" Ever asked, sliding his hand up under Arsen's shirt to splay his hands over his flat tummy.

Arsen hesitated before asking, "Like what?"

Ever chewed on his bottom lip, willing himself to be brave. Noah said he held the upper hand. That Arsen wanted to give him what he wanted. "Like, can you put your hands on me? And…your mouth? Not up here but…lower."

Arsen sucked in a breath, his belly dipping beneath Ever's fingers. "You can't just say things like that."

Something withered inside Ever. He tried to move away. "Sorry."

Arsen held tight. "No. Don't run away. You can say whatever you want. I just meant it turns me on when you say stuff like that and I'm trying so hard to be the good guy."

Ever looked up at him. "You are a good guy. You're the best guy," he promised. "You saved me. You're just like the paladin in your game."

Arsen scoffed. "I'm no knight."

Ever shrugged as best he could while curled into Arsen. "Well, I'm not a princess, but you still saved me. That makes you better than a knight."

"How so?" he asked, amused.

Ever was serious. Arsen was so much better than any fictional character from a video game. "Knights take oaths, swear allegiance, do things out of obligation. You could have left me in that closet to die, but you didn't. You could have dropped me at a police station, but you didn't. You could have just left me on a street corner…but you didn't. Because you're a good person. The best person. *That* makes you better than any knight."

When Arsen didn't say anything, Ever looked up once more to find him looking down at him with a sort of shocked expression. "Did I say something wrong again?"

Arsen squeezed him against his side until Ever thought he might crush him. "No. No, you didn't. I was just thinking about my life if I hadn't opened that door and it scared me a little. We barely know each other but the thought of my life without you in it scares me."

Ever's heart did a cartwheel in his chest. "Me too."

They fell silent after that, but Arsen kept dropping kisses on the top of Ever's head, his fingers drawing lazy patterns on his back through his t-shirt.

Just as Ever was starting to drift off, Arsen said, "Let's get cleaned up and go sleep in my bed."

Ever was loath to stand up, but he nodded. "Okay."

Arsen crawled over him to stand then grabbed his hand,

pulling him to his feet and leading him out the door. They were almost to the bathroom when a thought crashed down on Ever like an anvil. "Arsen?"

"Yeah?"

Ever's heart clenched. "What happens if they never figure out who I really am?"

Arsen didn't hesitate. "Then we create a new identity for you. You can be whatever you want to be."

"I just want to be yours," Ever blurted, immediately blushing.

Arsen tugged Ever in front of him, his arm wrapping around him from behind like a steel band, lifting him off his feet and carrying him like he weighed nothing. Ever's knees came up to his chest as he tried to wiggle free with a laugh but Arsen wasn't budging.

"I swear you're trying to kill me," Arsen said, hauling him into the bathroom like a sack of potatoes and depositing him on the edge of the sink.

They were supposed to be cleaning up, but as soon as Ever's butt hit the cold counter, he wrapped his arms and legs around Arsen once more in a full-body hug. "Thank you."

"For what?" Arsen asked, his confusion obvious.

"For not being a bad guy."

Arsen hugged him back but said, "I'm a murderer."

Ever didn't care. "Nobody's perfect."

When Arsen stepped back, he reached for the hem of Ever's t-shirt.

He snatched his wrists, panic clawing at him. "No."

Arsen frowned at him. "What's wrong?"

Ever froze. What *was* wrong? Arsen had seen Ever's back before but not the rest. Not the other scars. "It's bad."

"What's bad?" Arsen asked, brow furrowed.

Ever swallowed the lump of sand in his throat. "The… damage. The…scars. It's worse in the light."

Arsen blinked at him then kissed his forehead. "It's okay."

Ever's heart hammered in his chest. It didn't feel okay, but he nodded, releasing his wrists. Arsen peeled Ever's shirt off, dropping it to the floor, then hissed as he saw Ever's back in the mirror.

Ever looked up just in time to see Arsen's expression grow dark. He didn't know what it looked like since the last of his injuries had healed, but even before then, his back had been a road map of pain. Long tracks of scar tissue criss-crossed his shoulders and trunk where the belt buckle had torn his skin. There were random burn scars on his upper arms, a puncture wound from where Jennika had jabbed a screwdriver into his shoulder for burning dinner.

It was all so ugly. *He* was ugly.

Arsen hugged him again, hard, like he was trying to say something without words. Ever just sat there, limp in his arms. Those scars were permanent. They would never go away. He would look like that forever. It was humiliating.

Arsen stepped back and pulled his own shirt off in one fluid motion, then turned to show Ever his back. There was a strangely-shaped scar on his right shoulder—two wide marks side by side.

Ever reached out and touched them. They were smooth.

"My father shoved me into a steam pipe when I was little.

We all have scars, *besenok*."

When he turned to face him once more, Ever's hands fell on his torso, fingertips tracing the scorpion tattoo on the right side of his chest. "Why is this the only tattoo not in color?"

"We all have it. Seven, Lake, Cree, Nico, Levi, Felix, all of us. We got it for Jericho. So he'd know what he means to all of us."

"Why a scorpion?"

"'Cause he's a Scorpio," Arsen said then added, "And 'cause it looked cool and was cheap enough for all of us to afford at the time."

Ever smiled at that. It was all so sweet and normal. Except, it wasn't. Arsen was a killer and so were his friends. So was Jericho. It seemed so surreal to think that Ever lived among killers but had never felt safer.

He trailed his hand across Arsen's chest to the tattoo encircling his nipple. The words "Press Start" surrounded the areola. What did that even mean? Before he could ask, Arsen took his hands and brought them to his lips. "Shower," he said, like he was reminding himself.

He pulled Ever from the counter. Once he was on his feet, Arsen's thumbs hooked in the waistband of his pajama pants. Ever closed his eyes. He didn't want to see Arsen's reaction.

There were more jagged scars across his ass, his thighs, and a few across his hips from when the belt got away from her. He stood, trembling, eyes squeezed shut as he waited for Arsen to say something. Anything. To ask what happened. But he didn't.

Ever sucked in a breath, eyes jolting open, as Arsen's lips trailed over the scar on his hip, then one across his ribs. He was on his knees in front of Ever, looking up at him with those pool blue eyes. He reached back and gripped the counter, not at all sure what to do with his hands in this situation. He wasn't entirely sure what the situation was.

Arsen kissed Ever's belly again then his thigh, then his tongue traced the dip of his hips, hands sliding behind Ever to cup his ass, squeezing gently. Ever didn't know anything about refractory periods, but he was already half-hard again. Arsen watched his face as he placed open-mouthed kisses over Ever's belly.

Ever nodded. He didn't really know why. It just felt like Arsen was asking him something. Arsen took him in hand, tongue darting out once more to run along the underside of his cock, before his mouth closed over him, engulfing him in the most perfect heat.

Ever's knees buckled at the first pull of Arsen's lips. Arsen's hands dug into Ever's hip bones, holding him up even as he sucked him. He was so strong. It was so hot. Ever had to be dreaming. A low moan escaped, but he clamped down on his lip, trying to muffle it.

Arsen pulled off with a pop. "Don't be quiet on my account."

Ever blushed, squeezing his eyes shut once more. If he kept watching Arsen's head bobbing, he was going to come in three seconds. He was already getting that same intense heat pooling in his stomach, his spine tingling. It just felt so fucking good, each movement sending sparks over every nerve ending. The sound of Arsen sucking was obscene. And so fucking sexy.

Ever's fingers threaded through Arsen's tresses without thought, gripping tighter every time Arsen took him to the back of his throat, the muscles there convulsing around him, encasing him in the tightest, wettest heat. Soon, he was fucking into Arsen's mouth without thought, desperate to come for a second time. He was so close…he just needed a little more.

"Oh, fuck. Oh, fuck. Arsen…" He didn't know why he said his name, only that he needed to say it. Then he was coming a second time, his release spilling onto Arsen's tongue before he could even warn him.

Arsen didn't stop, though. He just kept sucking until Ever shivered from oversensitivity, pushing him back with a hiss. Arsen got to his feet, then captured Ever's lips in another kiss, letting him taste himself on his tongue.

"Now, we can shower," Arsen said, reaching over to turn on the water.

THIRTEEN

ARSEN

ARSEN DIDN'T REALIZE HOW RARE it was for all his friends to be in one place until they converged on him as a group while he stood at the counter searching for a part for a vintage Mustang. Seeing them together made him instantly uneasy, like he was about to be confronted like in those old intervention shows. Even though he eyed them warily, he continued to search for the part in the system, refusing to acknowledge out loud how weird it was to see them there midday.

In high school, they'd practically lived in the back of Jericho's shop, haunting his ratty, oversized sofa while they played video games long into the night, costing him a fortune in food. This garage had always been their safe space, their real home, but jobs, school, and family got in the way lately.

Jericho still insisted they all meet twice a month at his place for "family" dinner but, day-to-day, it was rare to find more than one or two of them together unless there was an emergency. It wasn't that they weren't still close, they just mostly kept in contact through texts and while they played games at night.

Arsen's lack of greeting did nothing to deter his friends. Nico hopped up on the counter, leaning over and sticking his head in front of Arsen like he wanted to see his screen.

"What are you doing?" Arsen asked, irritated.

Nico grinned, blond curls bouncing. It was hard to believe someone who looked so angelic could be such an asshole. "You were staring at that screen so hard I was sure it was porn."

"Oh, Arsen wouldn't do that. He's in lurvveee," Seven cooed, swooning dramatically against Nico's dangling legs. Seven had recently cut his hair down to almost nothing, breaking hearts everywhere, but despite that, his tawny skin and sea glass eyes still were enough to pull any guy he wanted. Not that Seven cared about that stuff. He was too busy with school.

Arsen rolled his eyes at their teasing but didn't say anything. It was pointless. They would have their fun regardless. He couldn't even be mad. They all knew he would have done the same. Hell, he *had* done the same when Jericho had come home madly in love with Atticus after one hook-up in the murder cabin. Or when Felix had fallen for his husband even while they were hate-fucking.

This was just what family did.

"Where is your angel-faced boo? I'm dying to meet him in person," Felix asked, looking behind Arsen like Ever might be hiding back there.

Felix was dressed down for a change. Normally, his outfits were handmade and wild, as expected for an up and coming designer, but whenever he came to the neighborhood, he toned it down. Well, toned down for Felix. He wore baggy jeans and a crop top with his mom's falling-apart cardigan hanging off one shoulder like he was Ariana Grande, his long, wavy chestnut hair pulled into a ponytail.

Arsen glanced behind him to the apartment. "Upstairs. Sleeping. He was up late."

Lake and Seven exchanged knowing glances.

"Was he now?" Lake asked, a smirk on his face.

Lake looked like a douche with the hood of his Gucci hoodie pulled up, his light brown hair barely visible. The sweatshirt was a hand-me-down from Felix but with his bone structure and perfect features, Felix said he was just destined to look like a frat boy forever.

Lake batted his lashes. "Doing what?"

"Doing who?" Seven corrected, arching a brow.

Cree was the only one not teasing him. But that was just Cree. He never spoke unless he had something important to say. He just stood, tall and silent, hair pulled into a knot on the top of his head, watching silently. He would text in their threads, but even while gaming, they rarely heard his voice. Ever might actually talk more than Cree. He had always been more of a thinker than a talker. But given how he grew up, he probably hadn't really been given much chance to voice his personal opinions.

"Why are you all here?" Arsen asked warily.

It was Levi who spoke, holding up a plastic shopping bag. "We brought stuff."

"What kind of stuff?" Arsen asked, instantly suspicious.

"Stuff for Ever," Levi mumbled, refusing to look at Arsen.

Arsen's heart tripped in his chest, and he looked at each of his friends in turn. "I swear, if there are condoms or lube in that bag, I will toss every one of you in the car crusher at the edge of town. Nobody will look for you."

Seven snorted. "Like we would ever do that."

"You did do that. To me. On my fifteenth birthday. In front of Jericho," Arsen reminded them.

"Yeah, but that was different. You were determined to get laid," Felix reminded. "It was hardly a secret. We were just helping make your birthday wishes come true."

"Yeah, so that your first hook-up wouldn't leave you with a birthday gift that kept on giving, you know?" Nico said.

"Yeah, we wouldn't do that to Ever," Lake said. "He's too…cute and squishy."

He mimed squishing Ever's face. Arsen hated the jealousy that instantly shot through him. If any of them tried to squeeze any part of Ever, Arsen would remove their hands with a rusty saw.

"Yeah, like one of those silly little stuffed animals Noah has," Nico agreed.

"A Squishmallow!" Levi said, snapping his fingers. "That's what Ever looks like. A Squishmallow." Then he looked at his hand. "Even if he bites like a hellhound."

Arsen rolled his eyes. "Now that you've told me what isn't in the bag, maybe tell me what is?"

"That's for Ever to know and you to find out," Seven said. Before Arsen could stop him, he cupped his hands in front of his mouth. "Ever! Ever? Wherefore art thou?" he shouted dramatically.

Felix slapped his arm. "You're going to scare him, dick. He's really shy."

"How do you know?" Levi asked. "I'm the only one who's met him."

"I just… I just do," Felix said, waving a hand like he refused to justify his answer.

Arsen was about to tell them to leave when Ever popped his head out of the door at the top of the stairs, eyes sleepy and hair standing on end. He was wearing Arsen's hoodie, which went almost to his knees, and a pair of pajama pants with fish all over them. As soon as he saw the amount of people gathered downstairs, his guard went up. His stiffening shoulders only relaxed when he realized Arsen stood with them.

"The guys brought you some…stuff, *besenok*," Arsen said just loud enough to be heard. "But you don't have to come down if you don't want to."

Ever hesitated then disappeared. For a second, Arsen thought that was the end of it. The disappointed looks on his friends' faces let him know they did, too. Just as they started to hand the bag over, Ever returned, wearing the ugly black flip-flops Arsen had given him his first day there.

He slowly made his way downstairs, studying them all as he made his way to Arsen. He crowded against his back, hiding from them.

"Shit," Lake said, sort of wondrously. "He's even cuter in person."

"What do you have for him?" Arsen asked. "Show me first."

"Bro, what do you think we have in here? A live cobra?" Nico asked. "Calm down."

Felix chuckled, seemingly amused by Arsen's overprotectiveness. "Yeah, we were talking about how Ever has never gotten to try certain things so we bought stuff for him to try. Some of our favorite things."

Arsen blinked at them. "Things?"

Ever peeked his head out from behind Arsen. "Like what?"

"Candy," Seven said, voice saccharine sweet. "So much candy you'll have a sugar rush for a week."

"Could you attempt to sound less like you're trying to coax him into a white van?" Nico asked. "Creeper."

Ever moved to stand in front of Arsen, standing on his tiptoes to peer over the counter at the generic white plastic bag. "Is a sugar rush a good thing?"

"It's the best thing," Lake promised.

Ever looked at Arsen, who nodded. "Up to you."

He wasn't going to deny Ever the chance to continue trying new things. When Nico hopped off the counter, Arsen took Ever by the hips and plopped him down in the empty space. He crossed his legs in front of him, looking over all of them, now more curious than scared.

"What should he try first?" Felix asked.

"Pop rocks. Definitely pop rocks," Seven declared, then looked at Ever, voice smug. "I picked that."

Ever nodded, taking the pink package Seven offered. He kept one for himself. He tore it open, showing Ever what to do. Arsen tried not to smile as Ever followed suit. Seven put the candy in his mouth then waited for Ever to do the same.

They all watched him keenly. Ever shrank a bit under their scrutiny but finally dumped some of the candy into his mouth. Arsen didn't know what pop rocks were. He only knew that Seven loved them. Arsen had never been someone who ate candy—not because he didn't like it but because it reminded him of his father. He used to bring it home whenever he was sorry for the previous night's beating.

Arsen shook the thought away. This was about Ever. As soon as the candy hit his tongue, Ever's eyes went wide. For a moment, he looked horrified, like he was contemplating spitting it out. Seven dumped more into his mouth then opened it wide for Ever to see. A weird sound escaped. The closest thing Arsen could think to compare it to was the sound the jumper cables made when they touched the connectors on a car battery. A...crackling sound?

Ever parted his lips, his face lighting up as his mouth also made the same noise. The others laughed, easily falling under his spell. Even Levi looked...fond. Seven closed his mouth, loudly crunching the candy so Ever did, too. Baby see, baby do.

When the packet was empty, he looked sad.

Nico snatched the bag. "Mine next. Mine next."

He pulled a large bag free then tore it open, taking one and eating it before he offered the bag to Ever. It occurred to Arsen then—they were each trying the candy they offered to prove to Ever they weren't trying to trick him or give him something dangerous.

Arsen's chest felt tight. He made eye contact with Cree, who smiled and nodded, like he knew what Arsen was thinking. Maybe he did. There was something almost magical about Cree. There always had been since the day they'd met.

Ever took the candy—a sugar-coated worm—then popped it into his mouth. It took about thirty seconds before his whole face contorted, like he'd sucked on a lemon, his body shivering.

Ever blushed as the others laughed.

"Sour gummy worms," Nico said. "They're the best."

Arsen smiled as Ever continued to chew thoughtfully. "Do you like it?"

Ever nodded and reached for another, popping it in his mouth then repeating the shiver that came once he started to chew, smiling the whole time. Arsen felt himself smiling, too. Just seeing Ever happy made Arsen happy.

Was that love?

The taste test continued for almost an hour. Cree brought Reese's Pieces and Milk Duds. Felix brought Starburst. Ever liked the pink ones the best. Lake brought Skittles and Life Savers. The only thing Ever didn't like was the Milk Duds, but he hid it well. Only Arsen knew he was faking it. He always did.

Just when it seemed like the taste test was winding down, Levi stepped forward, a sulky look on his face. He didn't say anything but thrust the large plastic bag at Ever. "Here."

Ever took the bag, a guarded look on his face. He peered inside, then pulled the last items out one by one. Jolly Ranchers, Gummy Bears, and two Pixy Stix. Ever tried the gummy bears first, popping two in his mouth and chewing, then going back in for more.

Arsen gently plucked the bag from his hand. "You're going to make yourself sick. Here." He handed him one of the sugar-filled straws. "Try this and one of the Jolly Ranchers and then maybe we take the rest of the day off from sugar, yes?"

He wasn't trying to parent Ever, but he had a hard time getting Ever to eat three times a day as it was, much less feed him his body weight in candy. Arsen didn't want Ever making himself sick attempting to appease his friends. Even now, Ever made a show of upending the sugar-filled straw into his mouth, nodding at the others to let them know he liked it.

Disaster nearly struck when Ever attempted to bite the Jolly Rancher and almost broke his teeth, but soon, he figured it out, tucking it into his cheek like a chipmunk.

The guys stayed a few more minutes, each of them making small talk before they disbanded, giving various excuses from school to work.

As soon as they were alone, Arsen stepped between Ever's open knees, hands finding his waist to help him down. Ever wrapped his arms around Arsen's neck, gazing at him, lips puckered, clearly expecting a kiss. Arsen smiled, then plopped a kiss on his perfect mouth. When he didn't deepen the kiss, Ever made a disappointed sound.

Arsen was also disappointed. There was nothing he wanted more than to take Ever upstairs and eat *him* for lunch, but he had to focus on work and then stream for a couple of hours. Then he would spend the rest of the night making Ever beg, cry, and scream in whatever way he could.

He pressed another kiss to his mouth, then said, "I have to finish my shift. Jericho isn't coming in today. Later. After I finish my game. Okay?"

Ever's full lower lip jutted out in an exaggerated pout, but Arsen wasn't buying it. The little shit was learning all too quickly how to get what he wanted from Arsen. If he didn't set some kind of boundary, they'd have no place to live because Arsen would give up all his responsibilities just to have Ever naked and willing underneath him twenty-four hours a day.

"Don't you make that face at me," Arsen murmured, even as he leaned in and gave him a kiss that lingered, giving in to the urge to slide his tongue between Ever's slightly open lips. He tasted as sweet as he looked. "Go read your book, okay?"

Ever sighed, then nodded.

"Good boy."

Ever's lips fell open, a hazy look crossing his face. Arsen had no idea how to decipher what had just happened, so he just ignored it…for now. "Do you want me to order you lunch?"

Ever shook his head, putting his hand on his stomach. "I think I'll throw up if I try to eat lunch."

"Yeah, you might just want to sleep it off," Arsen said, helping him from the counter.

Ever stood on tiptoe, threading his fingers behind Arsen's neck and forcing his head low enough for him to kiss him again. Arsen allowed it, even as he walked him backwards towards the steps, only breaking the kiss when they reached the bottom tread. "Upstairs, now, *besenok*. Let me know if you get hungry."

Ever sighed, glowering at him. "Fine."

Arsen watched him go with a smile.

He really had created a monster.

They were finally raiding the church. This wasn't the last level, but it was where they would finally find the last chest containing the piece they would need to assemble the puzzle, allowing them to fight the final boss. It was going to take all of them to get past the guards. Lake was in charge of the mission, even though Arsen was currently in charge of the stream. They tried to take turns on who got credit for the views.

"Pay attention, Arsen. On your six," Lake shouted into the mic.

Arsen turned, running the enemy through, blood flying as the body crumbled to the ground. Arsen crouched beside the body, stealing the pouch full of gold and healing potions, then took off at a run to join the rest of the team.

Arsen shot a look at the time. It was already ten o'clock. Was Ever already sleeping? "After the raid, I'm out."

Seven snickered. "You're so whipped, bro."

"You're so jealous," Arsen countered.

"I'm jealous, if anybody's interested," Nico offered. "Ever

is so fucking cute, dude. He's, like, pocket-sized, like those little sugar gliders. I want to carry him around in my pocket all day and feed him."

Felix made an irritated sound just as his character beheaded a woman who looked like someone's *babushka*. "He's not a purse dog."

"Dude, did you just take out Grandma?" Cree asked, disgusted.

"That outfit was hideous," Felix said. "She had it coming."

"Focus, guys. We just have to get into the church and get the chest and then we're golden," Lake said.

Arsen didn't hear Ever enter the room—didn't even know he was there until he stood beside him. He pushed Arsen's hand off the keyboard so he could step between his arms, plopping into his lap, then wiggled forward, his legs sliding easily beneath the arms of the chair so he could cling to Arsen, laying his head on his shoulder.

Arsen didn't have time to ask what he was doing. Lake kicked in the door to the church, revealing twenty plus guards with swords and crossbows. Arsen slid the chair closer to the desk, hands returning to the keyboard, but it was hard to concentrate. Ever smelled so fucking good and his lips were pressed against Arsen's throat, his breath puffing against his skin in a way that was getting Arsen hard.

The shouting in his headset was deafening as Lake screamed orders at them. In the end, they won but just barely. Ever snuggled against Arsen the entire battle, not at all fazed by his jerky movements or his shouting in Russian. Arsen would have thought he was asleep if it weren't for Ever's fingertips under his shirt, making patterns on his back.

Arsen ended the game but not the feed. He removed his headphones, leaning forward to read the comments.

Ever!

Told you it was his boyfriend.

Thanks for making all of us feel really single.

I want an Ever.

I want an Arsen.

I want them both together...where I can watch.

Arsen rolled his eyes.

Ever sat up. "Are you done?"

Arsen nodded. "Yeah, I still have to—"

Ever's lips were on his, his mouth opening against Arsen's, tongue running along the seam. The stream was still running, but he couldn't refuse something Ever offered so eagerly. He slid his tongue inside for just the briefest moment then pulled back.

"We're on camera, *besenok*," Arsen reminded.

Ever was undeterred, unzipping Arsen's hoodie and sliding his hands across his bare chest, his lips finding Arsen's neck.

"So turn it off," Ever said, dipping to kiss Arsen's

collarbone. "You said we could play after your game. You said you're done. Let's play."

Bozhe Moi.

Even with his headphones sitting on the keyboard, he could hear his friends whistling and cheering. The chat on the side was flying far too fast for Arsen to read it, but he was sure it was borderline pornographic. He didn't even care. His hands were sliding under Ever's ass, his fingers teasing under his shorts. Fuck it. Arsen gripped him tight and stood, Ever clinging to him like a koala. Arsen didn't get far. He dropped to the edge of the bed, Ever still in his lap. The camera couldn't see them, and the mic likely couldn't pick them up, either. But, honestly, Arsen didn't care. Ever clearly didn't, either.

He was already pushing Arsen's hoodie off his shoulders, his palms splaying over his chest. As he let his hands roam, his tongue darted out, licking over his lower lip.

He traced the tattoo around Arsen's nipple. "What does 'Press Start' mean?"

"Press the button and find out," he teased.

Ever's eyes were all pupil as he looked at him then back down to Arsen's chest. His fingers dragged over Arsen's nipples. He groaned, bucking up against Ever so he could feel how hard he already was.

The way Ever's eyes lit up was everything. He bit his lip, concentrating as he ran his thumbs over the tight peaks, making Arsen shiver.

"Fuck, you're killing me," Arsen managed.

Ever smiled, then leaned his weight against him, like he

was asking for something. He wanted Arsen to lie down. He complied without thought, liking the way Ever looked on top of him.

Ever hovered over him, then placed an open-mouthed kiss right in the center of his chest, his tongue darting out to lick at the skin there. Arsen gave a shuddery breath but held still, letting Ever do what he wanted.

His hands slid down to Arsen's ribs, but his mouth closed over one nipple, licking over it like a cat, before he scraped over it with his teeth. Arsen hissed, his hands squeezing Ever's ass and grinding his hips against him. "Where did you learn that?"

Ever looked up, face serious as he said, "Romance novels."

Then his head dipped once more, and he was sucking, then licking, then tugging at Arsen's nipples with his teeth until it was Arsen who was coming unglued.

"Is this okay?" Ever asked quietly.

"Whatever you want is okay," Arsen answered, meaning every word.

When Ever slid off the bed to the floor, Arsen instantly regretted giving Ever free reign. Was he pushing him too far too fast? Felix and Noah both said Ever was an adult and capable of making his own decisions. This was his decision, right? Who was Arsen to refuse?

When Ever's hands caught in the waistband of his shorts, Arsen lifted up, letting him slide them off, pushing up on his elbows to look down. Big mistake. The sight of Ever looking up at him with those wide eyes and that perfect face was too much.

Ever came up on his knees, his hands gripping Arsen's thigh as he rubbed his face against his cock, then licked a broad stripe along the vein that ran along the underside. Fuck, maybe Ever was part *kot*. He certainly enjoyed using his tongue.

Arsen gripped the sheets as Ever explored, not taking him in his mouth but kissing his inner thighs, the crease of his leg, running his nose along the dip just above his hip bone. It was fucking maddening.

He closed his eyes, enjoying the sensation even as he cursed it. It took him by surprise when Ever's mouth closed around him, causing his whole body to tense. There was no hesitation, no timidity.

Ever gripped the base with his hand, bringing his lips down to meet it, sucking hard enough to make Arsen moan. "Did you learn that from romance novels, too?" he asked, breathless.

"Mm," Ever hummed, sending the most delicious vibration along Arsen's dick.

As Ever worked him over, Arsen decided he would write the biggest thank you note to Barnes & Noble, maybe even to every author in the romance section. *Chert*. It should be illegal for someone to look so sweet while doing something so goddamn dirty.

Arsen's fingers threaded through Ever's hair, but then he stopped. He didn't want him to feel forced or rushed, didn't want to inadvertently bring up any bad memories. He dropped his hand to his thigh. Ever took his wrist and put his hand back on his head without missing a beat.

Fuck.

Still, Arsen tried not to grip him too tight or work himself too deeply into Ever's mouth, but it was impossible. Ever was even better than he could have imagined. Even though Ever blamed the novels, part of Arsen feared the real reason Ever had gotten so good at this. And it wasn't from anything good.

But Arsen didn't want to think about that. It wasn't the time. Others might have forced Ever, but he wanted this. He'd initiated this. He wanted to make Arsen feel good, and fuck, if he wasn't doing a perfect job. He'd imagined this scenario too many times during too many cold showers.

Ever was better than any fantasy. He ran his tongue along the crown of Arsen's cock, then licked over the slit.

Arsen's eyes rolled behind closed lids. "Oh, fuck. You're so good. *Da, vot tak. Zdes. Zdes.* That feels so fucking good."

Dirty talk wasn't really Arsen's strong suit in any language, but as soon as he said it, Ever pulled off, lips spit-slick and parted, chest rising and falling rapidly, that same dazed expression from earlier on his face. "Say it again."

"That feels so good," he repeated.

Ever shook his head. "The other part."

The other part? "You're doing so well?"

Ever blushed then looked down, nodding. Did Ever want him to…praise him? Oh, fuck. That was why he'd gone all gooey when Arsen had said "good boy" earlier. Arsen's aching cock was now throbbing. There was nothing Arsen wanted more than to spend the rest of his life telling Ever how amazing he was.

He ran his thumb along his cheek. "You are. You're perfect. Perfect and so fucking pretty."

Ever made a tiny sound, then slid his mouth back over Arsen, once more enclosing him in the wet suction of his mouth. He wasn't sure he could take much more. He sat up, his hands fisting in Ever's hair, rolling his hips just enough to get the rhythm he needed.

"Oh fuck. That's it. God, you're so good. Your mouth feels so fucking good. Just looking at you on your knees for me is gonna make me come. *Vot tak. Vot tak.*"

Ever whined around his cock, his gaze flicking up to meet Arsen's. That was it. Two more thrusts and he was coming hard, spilling onto Ever's tongue, groaning as he swallowed it all. When he was finished, Ever sat back on his knees, looking up at Arsen expectantly.

"Come here, my good boy," Arsen said, pulling Ever back into his lap. "It's my turn."

He peeled Ever's shirt off, dropping it onto the floor, then buried his face against his neck, kissing the skin there, licking a stripe to his earlobe. "Kiss me. I want to taste myself on your tongue."

Ever did as Arsen asked, making another high-pitched whine when Arsen sucked. He slid his hand into Ever's shorts, swiping his thumb over the tip. He was already leaking. He used the pre-cum to smooth the slide of his hand on him, but that wasn't enough. He licked his palm then returned it. He really needed to start keeping lube in every room in the house.

That didn't seem to matter. Ever was already fucking into

Arsen's fist, his face buried in his neck. "Don't hide. I want to watch you." Ever hesitated, but then sat back. "You don't have to be shy," Arsen said.

Ever didn't look convinced, but a couple more strokes of Arsen's hand and Ever forgot all about being watched. He seemed to forget about everything but chasing his own pleasure. He tipped his head back, lips parted, eyes closed. He was so fucking beautiful. Arsen could watch him like this forever, could study the way he was falling apart. The way his breaths increased…

The half-bitten sounds falling from his lips…

And then, he started swearing, "Oh. Oh, fuck. Don't stop. Please. I'm almost… I'm so close… Oh, fuck. Oh, fuck."

Arsen had to bite back a smile. Hearing *fuck* fall from that innocent face was his new favorite drug. Ever's blunt nails dug at Arsen's shoulders, leaving tiny half-moon indents in his skin. Would he scratch at Arsen's back when he was inside him, when he was driving into the tight heat of his body? Fuck, if he could have gotten hard again he would have.

Ever cried out, then he was spilling over Arsen's fist, pitching forward and sinking his teeth into Arsen's shoulder. Arsen couldn't stop the growl that escaped. He'd been too hasty with Ever. He should have taken his time, should have given him more attention than a handjob.

"Will you fuck me next time?" Ever breathed into Arsen's ear.

Jesus. "Is… Is that what you want?" Ever didn't look at Arsen, just nodded against his throat. "Then yeah. I will."

"Good," Ever said, then tacked on, "I'm hungry."

Maybe he'd finally found a way to get Ever to eat. "Do you want to order food or go to the diner?"

Ever leaned back. "Can we order food from the diner? I'm too tired to move. I feel like my brain melted."

Arsen reached for his phone to place the order but realized quickly it was in his room. Which was down the hall. Which meant passing in front of the camera, which was still on. He gently set Ever on the bed and pulled his clothes back on, not bothering to zip his hoodie.

He went to the computer to make sure there was nobody on the stream, eyes going wide as he realized they were all still there. Chatting. About him and Ever and what they were doing off-camera. Arsen rolled his eyes, disconnecting, before he went back to Ever.

"Let's go, *besenok*. You'll have to look at the menu."

Ever shook his head, then gave him wide eyes and that over-exaggerated pout. "I can't walk."

Arsen snorted. "I'm onto you," he said, even as he picked him up bridal-style, carrying him into their room and tossing him onto the bed. "You won't be able to get your way just because you pout at me."

Ever looked disappointed. "I won't?"

Arsen shook his head. He fell on top of Ever, snagging his wrists and holding them hostage. "Of course, you will. Just try to use your powers for good instead of evil."

Ever giggled. "Okay. Now, feed me."

FOURTEEN

EVER

EVER LOOKED FOR HIS BOOK everywhere. Under every pillow, every couch cushion. Even in the bathroom, just in case. Everywhere. But it was gone. There was a chance Arsen had moved it while he was cleaning earlier, but he wasn't there to ask. He had walked down the street to grab their food from the deli.

Ever had tried—again—to get Arsen to let him cook—he knew how—but Arsen refused, saying he wanted Ever to focus on getting comfortable in his new space before taking on any domestic chores.

Ever smiled. That was just how Arsen was. He only cared about Ever and Ever's feelings. Still, he felt bad. Arsen wasn't made of money, and what he did get, he spent sparingly. When Ever had called him out on spending money on take-out, he said it was him cutting into his gaming fund, not bill money, and if he wanted to spoil Ever, he could.

It seemed like a dream. Ever had dreamed of escaping Jennika a million times over the years, had even thought about finding a way to end it all himself. But he just couldn't do it. The promise of something more, someday, had always been too alluring. And now, he had it. Sometimes, he worried he had died and this was heaven. Did heaven smell like diesel fuel and motor oil? Maybe so.

Ever sucked in a breath. The garage.

That was where he had left his book. He'd sat on the counter after lunch and pretended to read while he covertly watched Arsen bending over the engine of the vintage car he wouldn't stop gushing about. Ever hadn't cared about the car, but staring at Arsen's butt while he talked with passion about something that excited him was addicting. Especially, with his low, sexy voice and that sometimes heavy accent.

He was so…manly.

"Good boy."

The way he'd purred that right in Ever's ear… It was like he'd figured out the cheat code to Ever's secret desires, and whenever he said it, it melted something low in his belly. They still hadn't had sex. Arsen had been called to Jericho's condo to take care of something and Ever had fallen asleep waiting.

He'd woken just enough to feel the bed dip as Arsen curled around him, and he'd fallen back to sleep almost immediately. When he'd woken up, Arsen was already in the garage. Ever had gotten dressed and joined him.

That was how he'd forgotten his book. Ever had pouted about not getting what Arsen had promised, and Arsen had given him the dirtiest kiss and told him to be a good boy, and Ever had immediately melted into a puddle.

It was okay, though. Arsen would never use his powers for evil. Ever wasn't so generous. Now that he'd figured out how easily Arsen gave in when Ever pouted, it was hard not to employ the device any time he wanted to get his way. Not that Arsen really ever refused him. But, sometimes, real life got in the way of Ever's playtime.

Ever slid his feet into the oversized sandals he used just for tromping around in the garage and headed down the stairs. It was loud. Jericho had left this enormous industrial-size fan blowing, facing the open back door. He'd said it was to help get rid of some of the excess fumes from a piece of equipment he'd fixed for a friend. Ever thought Jericho only fixed cars, but Arsen said he'd fix anything that needed fixing if he knew how. Apparently, that included street sweepers. Ever knew the fumes were bad for them. Even the boys next door complained, but Ever was starting to associate some of these smells with home.

Relief spread through Ever as his gaze fell to the counter. His book was exactly where he hoped it would be, on the counter, face down, and open to the page he'd left off on. He picked it up and checked, letting his eyes scan the first paragraph, then marked it with one of the business cards sitting on the counter. If he started reading right then and there, he'd probably still be reading in the same spot when Arsen returned.

Before he could turn to go back upstairs, the hairs on his arms stood on end like there was a ghost in the room. He froze. Something was wrong. He had lived in a constant state of fight or flight his whole life. He was so hyper-aware of every microscopic shift in his environment—not because it could save him but because he could at least mentally prepare himself for whatever came next.

He didn't want to turn around. His heart was pounding hard enough to make his mouth go dry and his head swim a little. He swallowed down the heavy sense of dread choking him, turning at a near glacial pace, already knowing things were about to get worse.

A man stood behind him, head tilted to the side, eyes cold. Ever took in a black t-shirt, black jeans, and black boots, his gaze stuttering when they fell to the badge hanging from his neck and the gun on his belt.

A police officer.

Ever let out a shuddery breath, relieved. Until he really, really looked at his face. The dark hair, the brown eyes, the slightly overlapping front teeth. Ever started to shake. He couldn't help it. The man was close enough for Ever to smell the sour sweat and the stench of drugstore cologne.

That was what did it. The smell. That was what threw him right back into the memory. *"It's okay if you scream. I like when you fight back."*

That was what he'd said when he'd held Ever down the first time. He wasn't the only one, but he'd been the first. Bile clawed its way up his throat. Would the man still hurt him if he threw up again? That hadn't stopped him last time.

Where was Arsen? He must be almost home by now. He just had to wait him out. Then Arsen would be there. Arsen would save him. He just had to—

The man moved so fast, Ever didn't have time to react.

There was nowhere to go, trapped behind the counter. Maybe if he could have willed his feet to move, he could have locked himself in Jericho's office, but his legs were cement. And he didn't even know if the office had a lock.

When Ever's feet did finally decide to move, he did the only thing he could think of, running at the man full speed, driving his shoulder into his chest. He just needed to stun him. To get past him. He could hide upstairs. There were locks upstairs.

When they collided, the hit jolted through him like he'd hit a wall. The man wasn't big but he was stocky. Ever tried to get past, but he easily snatched him from behind, slapping a hand over his mouth and dragging him farther into the shop.

Ever tried to scream but there was no hearing it over the fan. The man laughed, lifting him off his feet. Ever tried kicking, biting, scratching, but it was useless. Everything went fuzzy, pain exploding in the side of his face. The man had hit him. It had to have been his fist, but it felt like a brick, making him see stars like in a cartoon.

The man slammed him into the wall, his hand around his throat, and Ever was too disoriented to even try to fight back.

The man shoved against him like he was still fighting, even though he was simply hanging there, his knees ready to give out. "Ever. Ever. Ever. You need to relax," he hissed. "Or I'll wait until your little gamer boyfriend comes back and let you watch while I paint his brains all over these bricks."

Panic knifed through Ever at his words. He tried to speak but the man's hand still covered his mouth. He blinked back tears.

"There's no need for the hysterics," the man said. "I just want to talk to you. If I move my hand, will you behave?" Ever's stomach churned, but he nodded. "Good."

The man removed his hand but still leaned against him. His breath smelled like nicotine and coffee as he panted in Ever's face, sounding winded. "Now, I don't know what that bitch told you about our arrangement, but I encourage you to keep your fucking mouth shut. You see how easily we found you, even without your little chip?"

Ever's teeth chattered. Was he cold? He felt numb. "I don't kn-know anything. Sh-She didn't tell m-me anything."

The man smiled. "See. Then there's nothing to worry about." Ever's stomach churned as the man's look went from menacing to…something else, that look men got right before they touched you like they had a claim. Something shriveled inside him as the man ran a finger over Ever's lips. "Were you this pretty when you were on your knees for me? It was dark in that closet. You certainly smell better."

Ever wanted to scream, wanted to cry or fight or run, but that wasn't an option. Instead, he screwed up every ounce of courage he had and spit in the man's face. "F-Fuck you," he ground out through clenched teeth.

The hand around his neck squeezed, then slammed him hard into the bricks once more. "I'd cut out your tongue but you were so good at using it." He sneered.

Ever turned his face away, squeezing his eyes shut.

"I was trying to be nice, but a pretty little piece like you… my boss could find a lot of uses for you. We could probably even auction you off to another private bidder. Though, the next one probably won't be looking for a servant…but a slave. One who knows how to use their tongue." He slid his hand down over Ever's shorts, fingers dipping below his waistband. "But I can think of other parts that are less necessary."

Ever squirmed in his grip. "Don't fucking touch me."

"Are you actually trying to fight me?" The man laughed in his face. "You weren't this foul-mouthed the last time we met."

Ever went limp, closing his eyes. The man was right. He was taller, stronger, bigger. It was less painful when he didn't fight. He squeezed his eyes shut and just thought of Arsen. Would he be mad? Would he hate him for letting this happen?

He stood there, dancing on a knife edge, waiting for an attack that never came. Instead, there was a nauseating crunch and a sickening wet sound Ever could only hear because the man was so close. Close enough for Ever to feel the spray of saliva when the man made a gurgling sound like he was drowning.

Ever's eyes flew open.

The man was staring, wide-eyed, his mouth contorted in some sort of horror movie grimace. Arsen was behind him, his eyes narrowed, his mouth twisted into a hard line. Ever could feel his rage, and he watched as Arsen's hand twisted, grunting with the effort of whatever he did.

Something inside Ever died. Arsen was furious. Arsen would hate him now. His happy life was over in an instant, once again thanks to Jennika. Some people really didn't get happy endings. Real life wasn't like the movies.

The man slumped, then crumpled to the floor in a heap. Ever blinked, trying to take in what was happening as he convulsed on the ground, fluid still bubbling from his mouth as a pool of liquid formed behind his head.

"Ever!"

Ever heard his name, but it sounded a million miles away. He wanted to look at Arsen, but he couldn't seem to tear his gaze away from the…twitching. What could make somebody do that? His eyes were still open but…vacant. Had he just suddenly had a seizure? Could the universe have granted Ever that gift?

Arsen's hands were on his shoulders, shaking him. "Ever? Ever? Ever, baby, *malysh*, talk to me. Did he hurt you? Did he touch you? Are you okay?"

The jarring motion shook Ever from his stupor, but it still felt like he talked to Arsen through a thick pane of glass. "I'm sorry."

Arsen's brows knitted together, and he gathered Ever into his arms, hugging him until he thought his ribs might break. "Sorry? For what? Why are you sorry?" He pushed him back enough to look him over. "Are you okay? Did he hurt you?"

Ever opened his mouth to say he was fine. That was when he saw it: the screwdriver in Arsen's hand, covered in blood and…hair? He looked down at the body on the ground. And it was just a body. The man was dead. There was no shaking or twitching anymore, just stillness and a cold, vacant stare, like the fish Ever used to buy at the market.

A giggle bubbled from his lips, just like the fluid had bubbled from the man's. He'd kind of looked like a fish. He pressed the palm of his hand to his mouth, worried if he didn't he'd start laughing and never stop.

"Ever?"

Arsen had killed him. Arsen had somehow used that screwdriver to kill him. To protect Ever.

"I-Is he dead?" he asked, already knowing the answer but needing to hear it out loud.

Arsen nodded. "I saw him on you, scaring you, *touching* you, and…"

Ever's gaze found his. "And?" he asked dully.

Arsen stepped into Ever's space. "And nobody hurts what's mine."

"I'm…yours?"

Arsen looked at him like it was silly of him to even ask. "Of course, you are. Didn't you say that's what you wanted?" Ever just stared, willing his brain to just…comprehend something. But it felt like every word, every action, was just bouncing off some impenetrable shield.

When Arsen looked at Ever's face, he took a step back, dropping the screwdriver. "I understand if you don't want to be with me after this. Knowing I kill people and watching me kill people aren't the—"

Ever threw himself at him, a sob escaping. Arsen's arms closed around him again. Once the floodgates opened, Ever couldn't stop the torrent of tears, the low, keening sounds that fell from his lips, the shudders that wracked his body.

It was humiliating, but it was completely out of his control.

Arsen just held him, whispering words Ever didn't understand until he had no more tears. By the time they stopped, Ever's nose was stuffy, and his head hurt, his ears felt full and his eyes burned. He was exhausted in a bone-deep way he couldn't explain. He opened his mouth to say so but all that came out was, "I'm hungry."

Arsen stared at him for a moment then chuckled. "I got you."

He led Ever to the counter, picking up the bag he'd dropped on the way. He sat him on the counter and handed him his sandwich and the bottle of soda from the bag. "Eat."

Ever wasn't sure why he'd said he was hungry. He wasn't. But it had seemed like something…normal to say. Something to break the tension of sobbing over the dead body of the asshole who'd just threatened to rape and sell him. He watched as Arsen returned to the body, grimacing down at it. He kicked at his badge with his sneakered foot. "*Pizdets.*"

Ever took a bite of the turkey sub, chewing and swallowing without tasting it.

Arsen pulled his phone free and dialed a number. "Coe. I got a big problem—Yes, bigger than that—Dead police officer in your shop big—He attacked Ever—No, I know—What was I supposed to do?—Yeah, yeah. Okay. Bye."

"Is Jericho mad at me?" Ever asked.

Arsen gave him a soft look. "Of course not."

Ever nodded, though he wasn't sure he believed that. He took another bite of his sandwich as Arsen walked to the back door and looked up and down the alley before closing and locking it behind him. When he walked back to Ever, he ran a hand over his bare thigh, then squeezed. "I need you to tell me exactly what happened."

Ever swallowed the bite in his mouth without chewing, wincing as it scraped its way down his esophagus. "I-I don't know what happened."

Arsen leaned forward, brushing his lips against Ever's shoulder. "I need you to try to remember. Did you know him?"

Ever might have cried if there was even one ounce of moisture left in his body, but there wasn't. He just gave a stilted nod, his gaze pulling back to the body like he couldn't help it. "He was one of the ones who…"

Arsen's head snapped around, and he looked at the man's dead body like he was contemplating killing him again. It thawed some of the ice in Ever's veins. Arsen wasn't mad at him. Arsen still cared.

"He's a cop," Arsen said. "Did you know that back then?"

Ever shook his head. "He said something about his friends wanting me to keep my mouth shut. Said he didn't know what Jennika had told me about their…operation."

"Operation?"

No, that wasn't it. Ever shook his head. "Arrangement. He said he didn't know what she'd told me about their arrangement." Ever balled his hands into fists. "I told him I didn't know anything. That's when he—"

Arsen went still. "When he what?" he asked, voice frigid.

Ever shuddered. "Started touching me. Telling me that he

remembered...things. That he—" Ever couldn't stop the way his body shook. "I spit on him. That was when he got mad."

Arsen's hands closed around Ever's cheeks, his thumb brushing against his left eye socket. "Is that when he hit you?"

Ever shook his head. "That was before."

Ever couldn't even feel any pain, just the distant knowledge that his face felt swollen. He'd learned a long time ago how to remove himself from the physical damage by focusing on something else, like the dead body on the ground.

Ever's voice sounded dull even to his own ears. "He threatened to cut out my tongue, then said he was going to sell me for sex to the highest bidder."

"*Kusok der'ma,*" Arsen muttered. "I kill these people too slowly."

Ever suddenly remembered the phone call. "Are you in trouble?"

Arsen frowned. "What?"

"Is Jericho mad at you?"

Arsen gave him a reassuring smile. "No, *besenok*. He's not mad. Nobody's mad. We just have to clean up the mess. Sometimes, that involves calling in some friends."

"Friends?"

Arsen nodded. "Mm." He gestured to the sandwich. "Eat something."

Ever took another bite, chewing dutifully. He jumped when the side door—the one connected to the apartments next door—popped open, Nico and Levi entering before shutting it and pushing a big lock into place, barring anyone else from doing the same.

They looked at the body on the floor.

"Shit," Levi muttered. "Jericho said you iced a cop, but I didn't believe it. How'd you do it?"

Arsen shrugged. "I grabbed a screwdriver and jabbed it into the base of his skull."

Ever's turkey sandwich threatened to make another appearance as his stomach sloshed. Was that what that sound had been?

Nico walked over and hunkered down beside the body. "This guy isn't one of ours."

"One of ours?" Ever echoed.

"Our cops. I know every cop in our neighborhood, even the narcs. He's not one of them." He shoved the man onto his side and pulled his wallet free, flipping it open and showing it to them, even though there was no way for them to read from that distance. "Jamesville. Detective Soderberg with the violent crimes unit."

"He had some kind of arrangement with Jennika," Arsen said. "It makes sense how she kept slipping through the cracks if she had an inside man."

Ever remembered something then. "He has a boss."

Arsen frowned. "What?"

Nico tossed the wallet onto the body, then floated closer with Levi. "A boss?"

Ever gave a stilted nod. "When he was threatening to sell me—"

"Sell you?" Nico said, sounding furious.

Ever nodded, a feeling like bubbles in his chest. "He said

his boss could find a lot of uses for me."

"Like his literal boss?" Levi asked, but not like he expected Ever to have an answer.

"I fucking hate dirty cops, man," Levi muttered. "If they sent him here to threaten Ever, then there's going to be more of them."

Ever's heart tripped. More of them? What if, next time, they hurt Arsen? Or Jericho or Nico? Even Levi? "I should leave."

Arsen looked at Ever like he'd kicked him. "What?"

"It's not safe for you if I stay here."

Arsen stared at him for a full thirty seconds, then squished his face between his palms and kissed him hard on the mouth. "You're not going anywhere. We can handle ourselves. There's safety in numbers, and I promise you, if it comes down to us or the Jamesville police force, we still have the numbers on our side."

Nico nodded. "You haven't even seen how deep the rabbit hole goes, gumdrop."

"Gumdrop?" Ever echoed, confused.

Levi nodded. "Gumdrop."

As far as nicknames went, he supposed it could be worse. Arsen called him *besenok* and he didn't even know what that meant. A shock of adrenaline shot through his veins as something else occurred to him. "He called me Ever."

They all looked at him. "What?"

"He called me Ever. He called me Ever," he said, voice rising in panic.

That wasn't possible. How? How would he know that?

"Isn't that your name?" Nico asked.

Ever shook his head harder. "No."

Levi frowned. "Ever isn't your name?"

He felt like he'd been punched in the diaphragm. "No," he wailed, hating the sound of his own voice.

Nico looked at Arsen then Levi before asking, "What is your name?"

"I didn't have one," Ever said quietly.

"Didn't have one?" Nico said. "Like, at all?"

Ever shook his head, the heat of his embarrassment thawing some of the ice in his veins.

"Everybody has a name, right?" Levi asked, looking back and forth between Arsen and Nico.

Ever shrugged, voice dull. "She just called me 'boy.' She said I didn't need a name. She said it would be like naming the dishwasher or garbage disposal. Even pets had names, but not me. I wasn't even human to her."

They all stood quietly for a moment or two before Arsen took his hand, squeezing it. "Are you sure he called you Ever?"

Ever nodded. "He definitely did."

Levi shook his head. "How would he know that?"

"I mean, it's hardly a secret," Nico said. At their confused looks, he shook his head like they were all dumb. "Ever is all over Arsen's live streams. They've been all over town. Wherever they go, people fall all over themselves talking about how adorable and sweet he is. Someone is bound to be talking about the boy who seemed to have dropped from the sky never having eaten a Snickers or scrambled eggs. Jamesville is literally the city next door. Isn't that where you took him to the bookstore?"

Arsen nodded gravely.

"I should leave," Ever said again, fear ratcheting up with each passing moment—not for himself but for them. He couldn't live with himself if anything happened to them because of him. He wasn't worth all this.

Arsen gripped his chin hard, turning him to look him in the eye, his face as stern as Ever had ever seen it. "You're not leaving. That's never happening. Not to protect me or them or anybody but you. Got it?"

Ever blinked at him. "Okay," he said, breathless.

"Good."

FIFTEEN

ARSEN

ARSEN KNEW THAT WHENEVER THERE was a crisis of this magnitude, Jericho had no choice but to call in reinforcements. Reinforcements like his in-laws, the Mulvaneys. He knew Jericho would bring Atticus. He'd also known the drama of stabbing someone in the shop would bring Felix and his husband, Avi. However, he hadn't expected to get Avi's twin brother, Asa, or his husband, Zane.

Arsen was just grateful the whole Mulvaney clan hadn't shown up. Ever wasn't quite ready for that level of chaos. He sat on the counter, legs crossed, bottom lip trapped beneath bunny teeth, watching Asa and Avi with interest and maybe a little trepidation. The two weren't incredibly tall, but they were broad and muscular, and so identical they could be bookends. Mirror twins, opposite in every way.

Nico and Levi hovered close to Ever, like self-appointed bodyguards, placing a physical barrier between Ever and the corpse on the ground. Knowing his friends wanted to protect Ever made Arsen's heart trip a little. He was lucky to have all these people in his life. Ever slipped his headphones onto his ears, but there was no music playing in them. It was just one more barrier between him and the world.

Avi ran a hand through his deep brown hair, then crossed tattooed arms over his chest, whistling low. "A screwdriver to the brainstem. Gnarly."

"Mm," Asa agreed. "I didn't think you had it in you, firestarter."

Arsen rolled his eyes at the nickname. No matter how many times he told them Arsen was short for Arseny and not a nickname given for a felony, they ignored him. He'd just stopped trying. "He was going to…hurt…Ever."

Arsen tamped down the bile trying to claw its way up his esophagus. What would have happened if he hadn't gotten there in time? Gruesome images flooded his brain, but he pushed them away even as his pulse thudded hard in his ears. He never should have left him alone, not even for a minute.

"Hey," Avi said, dragging him from his thoughts. "We get it. I'd kill anyone who even looked at Felix sideways." When Felix didn't react, Avi nudged him. "Hey, I'm being romantic here."

Felix rolled his eyes. "Two days ago, you threatened to rip a guy's heart out because he forgot your queso. Forgive me if I'm not swooning." Almost as an afterthought, he said, "Besides, I can take care of myself."

It was true. Felix might look like a pampered trophy wife, but he had claws. Literally. Silver-tipped claws gifted to him by his husband—claws Arsen had witnessed him use first-hand to geld a pedophile. If Arsen had to put money on who would win in a fight between Avi and Felix, he'd back

Felix every time. And not just because Avi was obsessed with him.

Zane, however, wasn't a fighter. He was all brain, no brawn. He was a reporter and a true crime writer, which came in handy when the people closest to you were largely responsible for the exceedingly high number of unsolved murder cases in the city.

Zane crowded closer to Felix, who absently lifted his hand to Zane's springy dark curls, fingers winding through them without thought, like he was petting him. Felix and Zane were…close. Arsen pretended it was just because they all lived together and did his best not to ponder how close the four of them truly were.

"What did he want?" Zane asked.

Arsen spit on the body. "He was warning Ever to keep his mouth shut about his and Jennika's 'arrangement.'"

"She had a partner?" Felix murmured.

"And a boss," Ever said quietly, flushing when they all looked at him.

"A boss?" Jericho asked. "What do you mean?"

Ever wrapped his arms around himself, and Nico and Levi stepped closer instinctively. "He said his boss could think of a lot of things to do with someone like me. He didn't specify what, but"—Ever shuddered—"I can guess."

Atticus's lip curled in disgust. "We all can."

"So, they're running a human trafficking ring," Asa said.

"In my fucking neighborhood," Jericho muttered. "That shit pisses me off."

"He's a Jamesville cop," Nico said.

"It's not our territory," Levi reminded him. "Besides, we usually wait until someone asks us to get involved."

"If we didn't, we'd never stop working," Nico said.

Jericho shook his head, his mouth a grim line. "Jennika lived in our neighborhood. Ever lived in our neighborhood. He was ours to look after."

Asa sighed, sounding more put out than disturbed. "If there's a trafficking ring and the cops are involved, it's our job to take out the trash."

Asa didn't say that due to any sense of responsibility. He didn't have the ability to feel guilt or remorse or empathy. Right now, Arsen envied that about him. He was swimming in guilt. Not about killing that piece of shit, but because he almost didn't get there in time.

"Yeah, Dad will insist on it," Zane said.

"If he came here to deliver a message, they're going to notice pretty quickly when he doesn't come back," Asa pointed out. "Killing a cop is...problematic."

Heat rushed through Arsen's veins at Asa's words. So what if it was problematic? He was hot all over, his blood whooshing in his ears, drowning out everything but his sudden rage. Every time he thought about Ever and that asshole touching him, it made him crazy. It made him want to revive the man and torture him slowly. It made him want to hear him scream.

"I wasn't going to let him rape Ever," Arsen snarled. "He had his hands all over him."

"Whoa. Easy, killer. Nobody is saying you did anything wrong," Jericho said. "We're on your side."

Felix gave a low "Mm," then glowered at the corpse. "I fucking hate rapists," he said, placing the heel of his boot on the man's nose. It gave with a sickening, wet crunch.

"Gross," Zane muttered.

"We can get rid of the body and we can clean up the evidence, but they're going to know this was the last place he came and they're going to come knocking," Asa said.

"Good," Atticus scoffed, drawing their attention.

"Good?" Avi echoed, giving his brother a curious look.

Atticus wasn't a fan of the wet work. Everyone in that room knew he preferred to leave the murder to his husband.

"Yeah, good," Atticus repeated. "They'll come straight to us. If other cops come sniffing around, we'll know exactly how deep this cover-up goes. If it's just low-level thugs, we'll know it was a gang paying off a cop. One is infinitely easier to clean up than the other."

"You just want me to wait around and see who tries to hurt Ever again?" Arsen snapped. "That's your plan?"

Arsen jumped when arms wrapped around him from behind. "They're just trying to help," Ever said quietly against his back, his warm breath puffing between Arsen's shoulder blades.

Arsen's hands covered Ever's, all but engulfing them. He gave them a squeeze, hoping Ever knew that he didn't think any of this was his fault. After a moment, he pulled Ever to stand before him, needing to wrap his arms around him, needing to feel the heat of his body and smell the shampoo in his hair. He needed to reassure himself that Ever was alive and well.

Asa and Avi took Ever in, almost like it was the first time they'd noticed him. With those two, it was possible.

Asa snickered. "He really is adorable. Like a kitten…or a teletubby."

"Teletubby?" Ever echoed.

Zane glared at his husband. "They're these creepy little alien-like creatures who babble in gibberish that my husband is eerily obsessed with. You do *not* look like a teletubby."

Asa rolled his eyes. "I didn't say he looked like a teletubby. I said he was as adorable as one."

Avi shook his head. "You don't look like a teletubby," he assured him.

"He's more like Toothless from *How to Train your Dragon*," Zane said.

"Oh, or that super cute animated spider from that short with the fuzzy legs and big eyes," Felix added. "Or Totoro or Eevee from Pokémon. So squishable."

Arsen rolled his eyes, dropping his chin onto Ever's head right between his cat ears. "He's not a teletubby or a Pokémon or Totoro. He's just Ever. And Ever is cuter than all of them."

"Someone is in love," Felix said under his breath in a sing-song voice.

Arsen didn't care. He was in love. He'd tell Ever that to his face. He'd tell all of them. He'd skywrite it if he had to. He just needed Ever to know he meant it. He was the only thing that mattered to Arsen.

"Alright, enough fucking around," Jericho said. "Let's get

to work. August is bringing the van to the alley in…" He looked at his cell phone. "Forty-five minutes."

"What is he going to do with it?" Ever asked, glancing at the body.

"Disarticulate it and dissolve it in lye most likely," Avi said, like he was discussing the weather.

"Sometimes, he just dumps it in a bucket of acid until it's soup," Asa added. "Either way, we need to tarp it up so we can bleach the floors."

"Won't that be a dead giveaway if the cops are stupid enough to tell someone this is the last known whereabouts of the detective? I mean, bleach lights up under luminol, too. It's going to look like a crime scene," Nico said, frowning.

"It is a crime scene, but there's a big difference between suspecting someone was murdered because of bleach stains and knowing someone was murdered because their DNA is still detectable everywhere," Zane said.

"Yeah, one is circumstantial evidence," Atticus said. "The other is a death sentence after a long stay in a federal prison."

"Besides, the cops on this side of town are on our side," Jericho said.

"But these aren't our cops," Levi reminded. "They're Jamesville. We have no control over Jamesville PD."

"This conversation is irrelevant," Felix said. "If this guy was working for a human trafficking ring, they'll never send the cops here to look for him, and if the cops are running the trafficking ring, they're not going to show their hand by accusing us of a crime when they have no body. Let's just clean up and go home. I'm tired and I do not miss the smell of diesel."

Jericho nodded, then looked from Ever to Arsen. "Why don't you take Ever upstairs and shower. We'll be out of here before you know it."

"I should help," Arsen said. "This is my mess to clean up."

Jericho shook his head. "You did your part by keeping Ever alive. We'll take care of the rest." He pointed to the stairs. "Go."

Arsen knew better than to argue with Jericho, so he sighed and pushed Ever towards the stairs. Ever seemed as reluctant to leave as he was but allowed himself to be led out of the garage. Once in the apartment, Arsen told Ever to take a shower, then watched the others below as they worked.

If there was one thing the Mulvaneys and Jericho's boys had in common, it was crime scene clean-up.

They were practically experts by now.

When Arsen exited the shower, Ever was waiting for him on the bed, perched on his knees in nothing but a pair of barely-there striped sleep shorts and Arsen's slit-side black tank top that left little to the imagination. Arsen's dick took notice immediately.

Ever sat back, tilting his head. Arsen once more had the feeling he was being stalked…by a kitten. "What are you up to, *malen'kiy hischnik*?" he asked suspiciously.

Ever looked him up and down, then bit his lip and

pouted, his gaze locking onto the towel around Arsen's waist. "You promised."

Was Ever expecting Arsen to be able to think of what he'd promised him while looking at him like that? He could barely remember his own name with Ever's soft, smooth legs on full display and his torso peeking out from his shirt. There was too much skin and Arsen's blood was flowing in the wrong direction for higher thought processes.

Ever's hand shot out, curling into his towel and dragging him closer. He was deceptively fast for someone so little. Arsen wanted to remind Ever that more than a half dozen people were downstairs and could—technically—arrive any moment to interrupt...whatever this was.

That was what he wanted to do.

It was the logical, adult thing to do.

But then Ever placed an open-mouthed kiss just below Arsen's belly button—his hands not removing the towel but sliding up underneath it to grab his bare ass—making a satisfied sound when Arsen's erection started tenting the towel.

Arsen groaned, his hands falling to pet Ever's dark hair. He was being seduced...well.

Ever bit Arsen's hip, dragging his teeth along the skin there, before moving to give the other the same treatment. If Ever had learned this from a romance novel, too, Arsen was going to get him the biggest bookstore gift card he could afford.

Ever rose up to let his tongue trace the tattoo around Arsen's nipple before closing his mouth over it, sucking in a way that made Arsen light-headed. Ever had figured out how to get Arsen going far too quickly. *Chert.* His soft, wet tongue swirled, then sucked then bit until Arsen was throbbing.

A library card.

He was going to get him one of those, too.

Chert.

But no matter how much he was enjoying the attention—how much he wanted Ever to play out this little seduction—he still had to ask, "Are you sure you want to do this tonight? After what just happened?"

Ever sat back on his knees, eyes bleak. "Do you think I want his hands to be the last thing that touched me?"

Why hadn't Arsen thought of that? He didn't want that, either. He didn't want anybody touching Ever but him. Ever.

"Well, when you put it like that…" he murmured, gently toppling Ever onto the mattress and climbing over him. He loosely pinned his wrists to the mattress, studying Ever's face, looking for any fear or trepidation, but there wasn't any. There was just heat and anticipation.

"If you start to panic, you tell me. Promise?" he asked, more for his peace of mind than Ever's. He didn't want to feel like he was taking advantage of a situation.

Ever nodded, curling up to smack a kiss on Arsen's parted lips. "I promise. Can we do it now?"

Arsen snickered but then dipped his head to kiss Ever's forehead, his nose, then finally his mouth, tangling their tongues briefly before pulling back. "This is your first time, though, so it's all about you. You have to just lie back and let me do the rest."

Ever's lip pooched adorably and he leveled puppy eyes at him. "It's my first time, so shouldn't *I* get to decide how we do it?"

Once more, Arsen felt like he'd been put in checkmate by an amateur player. How did he keep falling into his traps? "I just want you to be happy."

"Being with you does make me happy," Ever said, like Arsen was stupid. "But having you inside me will make me happier."

Arsen's cock jerked at his words, and he was grateful for the resilience of the towel still knotted at his hips, creating a small barrier between his painfully hard dick and Ever.

"You're trying to kill me, aren't you?" Arsen said. He released Ever's wrists. "Then what do you want to do, *besenok*?" He trailed a finger along Ever's side, watching in fascination as the muscles jumped beneath his hand. "What do you want *me* to do to *you*?"

Ever stared up at him, pupils blown, lips parted, his hand rising to stroke his thumb along Arsen's lower lip. "Kiss me?" he asked, breathless.

"As if you could stop me," Arsen teased, leaning down and slanting their mouths together. Ever tasted like spearmint and he smelled like flowers, and kissing him created this euphoric effect that made Arsen feel almost high.

That was Ever, though—kissing him was drug-inducing. The more their lips met, the harder it was for Arsen to pull back, to give space. The more Ever's tongue darted out to tease his own, the more Arsen wanted. Each kiss grew longer, hotter, more intense until Ever was writhing beneath him, whining into his mouth, his blunt nails digging into Arsen's back.

"Please," he whispered.

Arsen sucked Ever's bottom lip before reluctantly pulling back. "Please, what? What do you want?" he asked, nosing his way under his chin to suck a bruise onto his neck, then his collarbone, his fingers teasing over his ribcage.

"I want—Oh, fuck—I want your mouth on me," Ever managed, canting his hips up so Arsen could feel how hard he was.

Arsen bit back a groan. Nothing turned him on like drawing swear words out of that innocent mouth. Ever wanted Arsen's mouth on his cock. Arsen wanted that, too. But not yet. He wanted to drag this out as long as he could. He wanted Ever delirious by the time Arsen pushed inside him.

He bit at Ever's chin, his jaw, sucked at his earlobe. "Like this?" he taunted.

"No," Ever whined.

Arsen smiled against his skin, moving lower, to push Ever's shirt to the side, nipping at his ribs, then running the flat of his tongue over one nipple, then the other. "Like this?"

Ever released a shaky breath, grinding against Arsen, another frustrated sound escaping. "No."

Arsen still gave his other nipple the same treatment. "Then where, *besenok*?"

Ever laughed quietly, catching on to Arsen's teasing. He tangled his hands in Arsen's hair, pushing his head down with a steady pressure. "You know…" he panted. "Stop playing."

Arsen smiled. "I'll never stop playing with you."

Still, he moved lower, placing open-mouthed kisses wherever his lips fell. Ever's hip, his belly button. Anywhere. He loved the taste of Ever's skin.

By the time his mouth hovered over where Ever wanted him, he was almost off the bed, so he slid to the floor then hooked his thumb in the waistband of Ever's shorts, snaking them down and off.

Ever moaned like Arsen had already put his mouth on him. He was so fucking responsive. His noises were addictive. Arsen lifted Ever's leg, kissing the inside of his knee, his thigh. Then he slid his hands under Ever's ass and dragged him until his hips hovered at the edge of the mattress.

He splayed Ever's legs wide, nosing at his cock. "Here? You want my mouth here?"

"Yes," Ever whispered like a prayer. "But don't make me come," he added hastily.

Arsen bit back a smile, moving to the crook of Ever's leg, breathing in the scent of him. At the rate they were going, they were both going to get off before the finale. "That's a big ask."

Ever sat up on his forearms, fixing him with a heavy stare. "I want to come with you inside me."

Arsen was gut-punched, his cock so heavy it ached. *Chert.* He closed his eyes, willing himself to stay the course. *Ne konchai, ne konchai.* "You keep talking like that and this is going to be over before it starts."

Ever flopped back on the bed again. "Fine," he said dramatically.

Arsen shook his head, amused, then swallowed him down. Ever rewarded him with a porn-star worthy moan that shot lightning through his blood. He was so fucking sexy.

Arsen wanted so badly to just say fuck it and climb on top of Ever and fuck him until he was a drooling, sobbing mess, but he didn't want to be another bad thing that happened to him. He wanted to make it so good for him. He deserved that. So, he vowed to take his time. To take him apart slowly.

SIXTEEN

EVER

THE MOMENT ARSEN'S MOUTH WAS on him, Ever forgot all about not coming. It was so hot and wet, the suction so perfect, he could barely stand it. He knotted his hands in Arsen's hair, telling himself to push him away, but his body wasn't getting the memo, his hips curling, working him between spit-slick lips again and again.

When Arsen pulled off, Ever couldn't stop the irritated whine that escaped, once more rising up on his forearms to give Arsen a stern look. Arsen gave him a dirty smile, kissing his belly.

"Relax, sweet boy. I'm not done with you yet," he promised, putting Ever's legs over his shoulders.

Before Ever could even guess what he would do, he was spreading him open, his nimble tongue spearing against his hole. "Oh, my God," he heard himself say. That shouldn't feel so good, right? Why did that feel so fucking good? Ever felt like he couldn't breathe.

Arsen gently bit the inside of each ass cheek, the scruff on his chin abrading the flesh there in direct opposition with the soft, slick silk of his tongue probing him. "What?" Arsen murmured against him. "Didn't read this in your romance novels?"

Ever shook his head, knowing Arsen couldn't see him. But he couldn't speak. It didn't matter, though. Arsen was busy anyway, swirling his tongue in a way that made Ever dizzy. Did people do this? Lick and suck at each other's most intimate parts?

If not, they should.

Fuck.

It felt so… Good wasn't the right word, but it was all that came to mind. He couldn't think; what little brain power he had disappeared with every swipe of Arsen's tongue. Ever whimpered, moaned, writhed as Arsen took his time, licking and sucking and nibbling at him. He could come just from this, he was sure of it, and he found himself trying to test the theory by bearing down on Arsen's tongue, wanting it inside him.

"Please," he managed, voice as raw as his nerves, his heels working against Arsen's shoulders, fingers so tight in Arsen's hair, he worried he might start pulling it out at the root.

Arsen's mouth disappeared, then the rest of him, leaving Ever's feet to flop onto the cold floor. He laid there, too stunned to move, barely hearing the sound of the side table open and close over his heart beating in his ears.

Then Arsen kneeled between his legs once more. He trembled, dancing on a knife's edge as he waited to see what Arsen would do next. He had only a moment to register Arsen's finger at his entrance before it was pressing in just as

Arsen's mouth closed around his cock.

Maybe it was the shock—the sudden invasion—but the perfect suction of Arsen's mouth wasn't enough to cancel out the burn of his entrance. Panic flooded Ever, his mouth going dry. He couldn't stop the whimper that escaped.

Arsen stopped immediately but left his finger where it was, barely inside. "Are you okay?"

Hearing Arsen's voice quelled the sudden panic. Ever forced himself to take a couple of deep breaths and looked around, remembering he was there, in Arsen's bed, with Arsen. Not some monster. "Yeah. I-I'm fine. I just…freaked out for a second."

Arsen kissed his thigh so softly Ever wanted to cry. "Do you want to stop?" he asked gently.

"No," Ever cried, then winced. "No," he said again, softer this time. "I just…needed a second. Is that okay?"

Arsen kissed his leg once more. "It's all okay. Whatever you want to do is okay."

Ever's heart felt too big for his chest. He was so fucking in love with Arsen, he ached from it. It was on the tip of his tongue to say so but he didn't want to freak him out.

"I'm…I'm good. I'm ready."

When Arsen eyed him warily, Ever lifted his hips, sliding his finger deeper. The burn was gone, replaced by an unfamiliar pressure and a feeling of fullness. He tried again, rocking his hips, once then twice, until Arsen's knuckle dragged over a spot inside him that had him moaning.

What the fuck was that? Ever glanced down as if he might find the answer there, but instead, he found Arsen watching him ride his finger.

"Oh, fuck," he whispered.

Ever's curse seemed to break Arsen from his spell, his finger curling over that spot inside with far more deliberation than before. Ever couldn't stop his cry of surprise, his cock leaking onto his stomach. Arsen did it again. And again. "Oh, my God," he said, voice full of wonder.

Arsen smiled. "Yeah?"

"Do it some more," Ever begged, cheeks flushing.

He heard Arsen's muffled laugh but was too gone to care. He was too busy chasing that sensation, that zing that made his brain numb. Each time Arsen did it, Ever's body bowed like he was possessed until he was moaning. "More. I need more."

Arsen's finger disappeared, but before Ever could mourn the loss, he pushed back in with two. The stretch and burn was still there, but it disappeared much quicker this time, only pleasure trailing in its wake as Arsen fucked into him.

Ever wanted to come with Arsen's dick inside him, but the more he moved, the harder it was to hold back. It just felt so good. "Fuck. Fuck."

"You want to come?" Arsen asked, nuzzling his cock. "We have all night. Let me make you feel good."

Ever considered it, but then shook his head. "No. I still want you inside me first."

It felt important.

Arsen's fingers slid free, leaving an empty, aching feeling. The bed dipped, and then Arsen was over him, his towel now gone, his cock slotted against Ever's. "How do you want it, *besenok*?"

Ever chewed on his lower lip for a long moment. "Can… can we do it like this? So I can see your face? I-I need to see your face."

Arsen's eyes went wide. "Yes. The answer is always yes."

Arsen sat up, bringing Ever with him, wrestling his shirt over his head before gently pushing him back into the mattress.

Ever could feel himself trembling, but he couldn't help it. He was nervous, but he was also excited, his nervous system firing on a hundred different levels. He wanted it to be good for both of them, not just him.

Arsen pressed a chaste kiss on his lips. "You're in control. We can stop anytime you want. Okay?"

Ever nodded. "Kiss me."

Arsen found his lips again, but it was slower this time, unhurried, his hips rolling against Ever's in a way he found distracting.

"Condom," Arsen muttered suddenly.

Ever froze. "What?"

He pulled back slightly. "Condom? I need to get one."

Ever frowned. "Why?"

Arsen studied him, frowning. "Well… I mean, I'm negative for anything and you are, too, so I guess we don't have to use one, but some people say it makes it easier the first time."

Ever chewed on his lower lip. Was it weird to say he didn't want anything between them? Was it stupid or childish or gross? He glanced up at Arsen's face. His look was so earnest it made Ever's chest hurt.

Finally, he said, "Can we just not use one?" He looked away, afraid Arsen might see how desperately he wanted him to say yes.

Arsen's lips brushed his forehead. "When are you going to get that I would amputate a limb if you asked me to? It's all okay. Whatever you want, whenever you want it, it's yours. *I'm* yours. *Navsegda*."

Ever stared at him, shocked. "Oh."

Arsen shifted, widening Ever's legs. He closed his eyes, focusing instead on the sounds. The lube cap opening, the heavy sounds of their breathing, the way the bed shifted and squeaked with each movement. Then Arsen was back, his weight a comforting pressure, blunting out the fear. Ever's breath hitched as the head of Arsen's cock pressed against his entrance.

"Just breathe, okay?"

Ever nodded, wrapping his arms around Arsen's neck, the air punching from his lungs as Arsen breached him. The burn was intense, his body instantly rejecting the invasion. He was big—far bigger than he looked and he looked pretty intimidating. Or maybe Ever was just too small.

His nails dug into Arsen's skin, half-panicked whining sounds falling from his lips, but, this time, Arsen didn't stop—he knew Ever didn't want him to stop. He just slowly sank deeper into him until their bodies were flush against each other.

Arsen was so deep inside him. The thought made his whole body hot and cold. Arsen was inside him. Did Arsen like it? He wasn't moving, just sucking in panting breaths in-between kisses to whatever skin he could reach. Ever's neck, his jaw, his ear.

"Are you okay?" he finally murmured.

Was he? Ever shifted experimentally. The burn was gone, replaced only by that feeling of fullness. "Yeah," he managed. "You can move."

Ever was no longer hard, the pain and the anxiety taking its toll, but when Arsen rolled his hips, his eyes widened at the sensation.

Arsen groaned. "You're so fucking tight. Fuck."

Heat shot through him. He didn't know if that was good or bad. Was he making Arsen feel good? He wanted to do that for him. His dick twitched at that thought. Arsen wasn't thrusting, just sort of rocking into him. Ever tried to catalog everything. The weight of Arsen on top of him, his sweat-soaked skin beneath his palms, the way his back muscles moved and flexed. The way his breathing sped up with his movements until he was working into him.

"Does it feel good?" Ever heard himself ask.

"*Da, da,* you feel so good," Arsen promised, his voice like gravel.

Ever slid his hands into his hair, pulling him down to slant their mouths together. Arsen's kiss was greedy, his tongue aggressive. He was driving into Ever now, pulling almost all the way out and slamming home, the head of his cock hitting that same spot inside with each motion.

Ever felt dizzy. "Am I doing good?" he asked against Arsen's lips.

Arsen's hips stuttered at the question. He nipped Ever's lower lip, then his mouth was back at his ear. "You're doing so well. So fucking good. My good boy. So fucking perfect."

Heat pooled in Ever's belly, his cock hardening at Arsen's praise. "Promise?"

Arsen kissed him once more. It was sloppy and messy and absent, like he was too caught up in his own bliss to focus on hitting his mark. "I promise," he whispered. "Do you feel good?"

He did. But he didn't know how to verbalize why. He liked making Arsen feel good. He liked the feeling of their bodies joining, liked the way Arsen said his name like a prayer and used his body like he just couldn't stop himself. "Yes."

Arsen sat up between Ever's open legs, dragging him until his hips were on Arsen's thighs, his legs splayed wide. His thrusts slowed as he grabbed the lube, pouring it into his palm, then wrapped his fingers around Ever's flushed cock.

"I think we can do better than that," he said, squeezing until Ever moaned. "That's better."

Then he was moving once more, fisting Ever in time with his thrusts until Ever's mouth went dry and he couldn't stop the *uh-uh-uh* sounds that escaped each time Arsen drove into him.

Ever couldn't stop looking, couldn't stop watching as Arsen fucked him, jerked him off, and looked at him like he was the only thing in the world. That was what did it. The half-drunk look on Arsen's face and the lust in his eyes when he watched Ever.

Heat pooled in his belly and he thrust up into Arsen's

fist, no longer able to control his movements. "Oh, fuck. Oh, fuck."

"Yeah?" Arsen asked, voice wrecked. "You gonna come for me?" Ever whined. He was so close. So close. "Do it. Come for me, my good boy. Let me see it."

Ever sucked in a startled breath as his orgasm punched from him, sparks erupting behind his eyelids as he came hard, coating Arsen's fingers and his stomach.

"Oh, fuck. You're so good," Arsen muttered. "I can feel you spasming around me. Fuck. Fuck."

Before Ever could catch his breath, Arsen was leaning forward, Ever's knees over his arms, practically folding him in half so he could kiss him as he drove into him, far deeper than Ever even dreamed possible.

"I want to feel it," Ever said against his lips. "I want to feel you come inside me. Please?"

Arsen made a sound that was almost a snarl, his hips slamming home again and again until he groaned low in his throat, grinding against Ever as he came. Ever could feel it, could feel the way his cock pulsed inside him, filling him up. It was a heady feeling.

He'd done that.

He couldn't stop the giggle that escaped. Arsen collapsed on top of him, gulping in heavy breaths. "What's so funny?" he asked, digging his fingers into Ever's ribs just hard enough to make him squirm.

Ever laughed, batting his hands away. "Nothing. I just feel...happy."

Arsen lifted himself up onto his forearms. "Yeah?"

Ever nodded, pushing Arsen's hair back off his forehead, giving him a smile. "Yeah."

"Good. That's good," he said again, dropping his head onto the pillow beside Ever's but making no move to get off him.

A week ago, that would have terrified Ever, but now, it made him feel safe. Arsen would kill for him. Arsen *had* killed for him. He'd die for him, too, Ever was certain of it. He would always put himself between Ever and any danger that came for him.

"I love you," Ever said, the words tumbling out before he could stop them.

Heat flooded his face, and he contemplated trying to shove Arsen off him and then running away, but he was trapped. He could only lie there, waiting to see if he'd just ruined everything.

Arsen didn't miss a beat, pressing his face against Ever's neck. "I love you, too," he said, pressing a kiss to his pulse. "I love you, too."

"No, no, no, no, no," Ever cried, running from the hoard of zombies lurching towards him.

"Left-click. Left-click," Arsen said, his hand hovering over the mouse, like he was contemplating doing it for Ever.

When it came to gaming, Arsen had a hard time letting go of control, especially when it came to Ever. Because he was just so bad at it. Still, he was having fun. And the others watching the stream seemed to have fun watching him get mauled by zombie hoards again and again.

"I *am* left-clicking," Ever shouted through peals of laughter. "There are just so many of them." He gave up attacking, instead turning and running to put some distance between himself and the threat so he could recover some of his vitality.

Arsen's lips were suddenly next to his ear. "Use the big first aid kit," he coached. "And the grenade."

"But I only have one," Ever whined, partially because he didn't want to waste his hard-earned grenade and partially because Arsen's hands were riding up his inner thighs out of the camera's line of sight.

With one of Ever's hands on the controls and the other on the mouse, Arsen was free to do whatever he liked to him. He took full advantage of Ever's vulnerability, all while acting like nothing was happening.

"There's one of you and eight of them, and you only have enough ammo to take out three or four. You can't use your machete. Just…trust me."

Ever nodded but didn't leave the safety of his hiding spot just yet. He glanced over at the chat, eyes catching on the emojis first. Lots of hearts, frogs, and flowers. He didn't understand what most of them meant. For the most part, people were nice.

"Okay," Ever said, more to himself than to anybody else. He took a deep breath, sending his avatar back into the fray. As he crept behind the walls of the dilapidated house, he could hear the zombies just out of sight, knocking things over, groaning, all looking for him.

His heart slammed against his ribs, adrenaline coursing through him in a way he only felt when he played these horror games or when Arsen was inside him. There was something so exhilarating about being afraid in a controlled environment, knowing that the monsters on the screen couldn't really hurt him but feeling the anticipation all the same. It was…addicting.

Ever took a deep breath and rounded the corner, hurling the grenade. "No!" he shouted, realizing his mistake.

It was too soon. Only two of the zombies fell, leaving another six lurching towards him.

"Fuck," Arsen said, urgency creeping into his voice as he said, "Shoot them. Shoot them."

Instead, Ever just took his hands off the keys, covering his face with his hands. He couldn't watch. He was as good as dead already. He hated seeing his avatar torn limb from limb, then munched on by hungry flesh-eating creatures. It felt…demoralizing.

Arsen laughed, his arms coming around Ever, easily taking control of the game. Ever watched from between his fingers as Arsen took out the hoard with nothing but a handful of bullets and a rusty machete. Was it weird that Ever found that hot? He was just so good with his hands.

Ever flushed thinking of all the things those hands had done to him since the first time they'd had sex. Arsen had made him come on his fingers more than once, all while praising him.

"My good boy."

Ever shifted uncomfortably, his dick half-hard just thinking about it.

While Arsen continued to play to the save point, Ever checked the comments. They always came fast and furious whenever Arsen brought Ever onto a live stream. Not all of them were kind, many of them were crass, and some were just plain nonsensical.

Ever's so cute.

Premature evacuation, bro

<3 <3 <3

You should let him play Paladin.

You two are so hot together.

Kiss.

Kisssssssssssss

He sucks

That one hurt, even if it was true. In his defense, he'd spent most of his life in a closet and only started playing video games two days ago after a viewer promised Arsen a large donation if he taught Ever to play a scary game. Ever had been more than willing to do whatever helped Arsen earn money, even though Arsen insisted he made plenty from subscribers and tips.

He scanned more comments.

You need to kiss more.

Ever agreed.

You're so bad at this game. Never change. It's so cute.

Fuck you, but thanks.

You two should get married.

Ever sighed. Maybe someday.

How am I this obsessed with two gay boys?

They were, too. They were obsessed with Arsen and Ever. The majority of the comments revolved around Ever and all the things they wanted to see him do with Arsen, many of them X-rated.

<3

I love you, Ever. Ditch the Russian and be mine.

Ever snorted. Yeah, right.

When is Ever getting his own Discord?

Ever didn't really even understand what Discord was. Only that Arsen seemed to meet up in certain rooms to play with certain people. It was all very confusing for Ever. He just liked playing the games, even if he was terrible at it. And Arsen said he liked showing him off.

But his popularity wasn't the only reason he was there. Jericho had a plan. A plan Arsen hated but that they'd all admitted had merit. The only way the dead cop could have known Ever's name was if he'd heard it through the neighborhood or he was watching him online.

Maybe a combination of both. Either way, Jericho wanted Ever front and center—a way to safely use him as bait to see if that cop was all talk or if there really was a "boss" they needed to take out in order to keep Ever safe. And others.

It was the others that scared Ever. How many other boys were living like him? A domestic servant to a narcissistic lunatic? A sex slave to a monster, having their bodies traded for money? How many kids were snatched from their mothers so young they couldn't even remember them? That was why Ever didn't mind being the bait. He was free. So many others weren't.

With each passing day, Ever grew more uneasy. The silence was almost worse than the attack. It was like living every day with a sword swinging over his head. He wanted this over with. He wanted to be normal. Atticus was working on securing a new birth certificate and social security number for Ever, something that took more time and money than

Ever could even fathom.

He'd offered to pay him, but Atticus had waved him off, saying there was no benefit to being as disgustingly rich as he was if he couldn't use it to help people who needed it. It was so weird. Arsen insisted the Mulvaneys were psychopaths, vicious murderers who tortured people for their crimes. But they just seemed so...nice.

Only when the noise of the game quieted did Ever realize he'd zoned out. He quickly reached for the gummy worms in the bag in front of him and put one in his mouth, tipping his head up to show Arsen the half dangling over his chin.

Arsen looked down and smiled, dipping his head, teeth scraping against Ever's lips as he stole half of Ever's treat, smirking as he chewed it triumphantly. Ever slapped his cheek softly, glowering until Arsen reached over and took another worm, swinging it in front of Ever's mouth.

Ever took the apology worm, chewing and swallowing, then showed Arsen his empty mouth. Arsen swooped in, kissing him deeply, sucking the sour taste from his tongue until Ever moaned low, his half-hard cock now fully at attention.

Arsen continued to plunder his mouth, his hand sliding beneath his t-shirt, fingers skimming his belly in a way that made Ever's stomach swoop. He heard the chime signaling that the people watching were "paying" Arsen—a strange sort of online currency the platform converted into real money twice a month. That was what Arsen called it: a platform. He said Ever's appearances made him lots of tips because the world loved Ever.

Ever only cared that Arsen loved him. He said he loved

him, had whispered it a hundred times a day since that night. It had only been four days, but it felt like just yesterday and a hundred years ago at the same time. He loved Arsen like they'd known each other in every lifetime, comfortable with him in every way. But no matter how much time they spent together, no matter how many times he let him into his body, it just never seemed like enough.

Ever's hands slid along Arsen's jean-clad thighs. Arsen gripped his chin, holding him in place so he could taste his mouth at his leisure. They should stop. They were on camera in front of roughly six hundred people at last count. All watching Arsen tongue-fuck him with enthusiasm.

That should bother Ever, right? People watching Arsen kiss him, touch him, manhandle him. But it didn't. He wanted everyone watching to know Arsen was taken—not just the ones online but the girls who showed up at the shop, giggling and flirting. He wished they could see him, too. Maybe they could. Maybe they were watching.

Good. They needed to know Arsen was his. Just his.

And Arsen proved it every night, fucking him long into the early morning hours, then dragging himself out of bed to go to work, just to do it again the next night, sometimes even during lunch. Ever almost felt guilty about how sleep deprived Arsen was. Almost. It was hard to feel guilty after several mind-numbing orgasms. Arsen buried inside him was quickly becoming an addiction.

Arsen pulled his mouth away, but then dropped three more kisses in rapid succession onto Ever's slack mouth. He looked at the camera, a dopey grin on his face. "Stream's over. See you next time."

He signed off quickly, pushing the buttons to take them offline. Ever glanced once more at the chat log on his monitor, heart stopping at the second to last row of comments.

Ever. Ever. Ever.

I seeeeeee you…

See you soon.

He slapped Arsen's arm and pointed, the words sticking in his throat. It could be just another online creep. It wasn't the first weird thing someone had said to him. It wasn't even the first weird thing that day. Levi said the chat section was the wild west, and the only way to deal with it was by blocking, reporting, or ignoring the bad apples.

But this seemed different. Malicious. It left Ever feeling like he needed a shower. Arsen took a screenshot then turned off the monitor. "Don't worry about it. It's probably nothing."

He was lying.

And they both knew it.

SEVENTEEN

ARSEN

A MUFFLED SHRIEK CUT THROUGH the fog of Arsen's dreamless sleep, shooting his heart rate into the stratosphere before he was even fully conscious. He reached for Ever, eyes still closed, sitting bolt upright when he realized he wasn't beside him. He glanced around the darkened room, his brain trying to decide if what he'd heard was real or simply some kind of panicked hallucination. When another shrill scream came from far away, Arsen grabbed the gun on his side table and ran barefoot to the glass wall that overlooked the garage below.

Relief flooded his system as soon as his gaze landed on Ever, but the excess adrenaline pumping through his body made him light-headed. He sagged against the wall, heart still hammering, dropping the weapon to his side, taking a few deep breaths, willing himself to relax.

Below, Ever sat on the couch—the couch Jericho had dragged out of storage just for him—with Nico perched above him on the back, working one of those spider-like scalp massagers through Ever's hair. Ever shivered and squealed, seemingly delighted at the sensation. Arsen remembered the first time Levi had used one of those things on him. It left a feeling like running water that he found both pleasant and disturbing.

Felix was also there. He sat beside Ever, doing his best to hold Ever's arm still as he dragged something along his skin. Arsen couldn't even imagine what it was this time. Stickers? Temporary tattoos? It could have been anything.

Arsen's friends—the friends who always claimed they had school or work as an excuse to not hang out—seemed to have infinite time when it came to Ever. They were there every day. Every. Single. Day. Not always together but all of them, usually once a day, made an appearance. At first, Arsen thought maybe they worried he couldn't protect Ever on his own, but now, he realized they just wanted to be around him.

They seemed addicted to bringing Ever his next first experience. And there was no shortage of experiences. Boba tea. Sushi. Garlic bread. Coloring books. Lake's chunky monkey muffins. Seven's *babcia*'s pierogi recipe. A slinky. A furby. The list went on and on. Arsen tried not to be jealous. After all, Ever had let Arsen give him the ultimate first experience. But still, he was greedy with all of Ever's firsts.

But Ever had become his best friends' new favorite pet. Especially Levi's. Levi, who'd acted like Ever's very existence was a personal slight, now arrived everyday with treats for him. Only, he didn't care about Ever's firsts. Instead, he brought Ever's favorites. Peanut butter ice cream. Coke slushies. A cupcake from the shop on the corner. Flaming

Hot Cheetos. Even this one special Japanese soda that could only be found at the Asian market on the edge of town.

Some small part of Arsen worried Levi was trying to steal Ever away from him. It could happen. Arsen was hot, but Levi was thirst trap hot, girls following his stream just to stare at him hot, had been offered money for sex hot. *And* Levi and Ever had started out hating each other. Plus, Ever loved romance novels, especially those with the enemies-to-lovers trope. What if Ever decided that was his next first?

When Arsen had said as much, Nico had laughed himself sick but wouldn't say why the idea was so funny. He'd assured Arsen that Levi just felt guilty because of how mean he'd been about Ever when he'd first arrived. He was trying to make amends. Arsen should be grateful. These guys were more than his friends, they were brothers-in-arms. They literally knew where every body was buried. For them to keep the neighborhood safe, they needed to function as a unit. They couldn't do that with infighting and jealousy.

Once Arsen knew Ever was safe, he returned to the bedroom, brushing his teeth and splashing water on his face before throwing on a zip-front hoodie and shoving his feet into shoes. He took the stairs, two at a time, down to the garage. Ever turned to look at him as soon as he was on the first floor, eyes shining and a huge smile on his face.

Arsen's heart tripped over itself. Ever wore a full face of makeup. He was so fucking…pretty. Black liner accentuated his huge brown eyes, and a dusty mauve color made his already lush mouth look even more so. He had pink cheeks and inky lashes and tiny crystals glued beneath each eye.

It took Arsen a full minute to realize Ever was looking at him expectantly. "You look very"—he struggled to think of a word suitable enough—"beautiful, *besenok*."

Ever beamed at his words. "Felix did it."

"Oh, I know," Arsen said ruefully, arching a brow at the culprit.

Felix smirked. "He looks hot, right?"

"He always looks hot," Arsen said, walking to the couch and leaning down to plop a kiss on Ever's glossy, slightly sticky mouth. That was when he noticed the markers on the table and the one in Felix's hand. "What are you doing?"

"Baby wanted to match you," Felix said.

Baby? That was new. There were many terms of endearment when it came to Ever. Gizmo. Ewok. *Fragolina*—Nico said it meant "little strawberry" in Italian. Gumdrop. Little one. Ever's nicknames were as plentiful as the gifts he received every day. Arsen moved around Nico, who had yet to say a word. When he saw Felix's art project, his chest tightened. There, on Ever's arm, was a scorpion drawn in black sharpie.

Felix smirked at him, well aware of the effect the drawing was having on him. "He wanted the real thing, but I thought, if you woke up and found him missing, you'd call the National Guard."

Felix was right. Crazy or not, Arsen didn't want Ever out of his sight. Not until they figured out how deep this trafficking ring went. There hadn't been any new cryptic messages from their mysterious watcher, but that might have been because Arsen had been keeping Ever offline. If he wanted to play games, they came down to the garage so he could play on the PlayStation, something else that had made an appearance with the old sofa.

"You're not usually one for sleeping late," Nico mused. "Even on your days off, you're usually up before the sun, like some kind of psycho."

"He didn't get much sleep last night. We were up really late," Ever supplied cheerily. "Arsen was teaching me some stuff."

"I bet he was," Felix murmured, patting Ever's head like he was a dog. "Like what, babydoll?"

"Yeah, what is it Arsen's been teaching you into the wee hours of the morning?" Nico asked, tone salacious. "Tell us everything. Every scandalous detail."

"He taught me to play *Resident Evil 7*," Ever said. "Oh! And *Until Dawn*."

Arsen's lips twitched as Felix and Nico exchanged disappointed looks. Served them right.

"Oh," Felix said, clearly disappointed.

That wasn't all Arsen had been teaching Ever, but neither Nico nor Felix needed to know the intimate details of their sex life. Their very active sex life. A sex life Arsen had been hoping to resume when he woke up ten minutes ago. Hell, the more he looked at Ever's glossy lips, the more he wondered what they'd look like wrapped around his cock.

"Why are you guys even here? Don't you have school?" he asked Nico before looking at Felix. "And don't you have a whole company to run?"

"Wow, rude much?" Felix asked. "I brought Ever some

presents. And Nico brought him breakfast."

Arsen narrowed his eyes on Nico. "You brought *my* boyfriend breakfast?" he asked, tone measured.

Nico gave Arsen a sly look, sliding his hands into Ever's silky dark hair, massaging his scalp. "Mm," he said. "I brought him some new toys to play with."

He moved his hands down to Ever's shoulders, working the muscles there until Ever moaned, sending a gut-punch of lust through Arsen.

Nico's knowing smile widened, his hands sliding down Ever's arms. "I didn't want him to be bored waiting around for his workaholic boyfriend."

Arsen dropped to sit beside Nico on the couch, facing away from Ever, his voice low enough for only Nico to hear. "You can stop touching him."

Ever stared at the television, unaware of the tension between Arsen and his friends. Felix was not. His lips twitched. Arsen knew they were doing this on purpose—pushing his buttons. But it didn't stop the jealousy swimming in his belly.

"How can I do that?" Nico simpered, cupping his hand under Ever's chin and tipping his face up to show Arsen. "Look at how adorable he is. Such a cute baby. Aren't you, *fragolina?*"

Ever nodded, completely oblivious to Nico's teasing.

Arsen leaned into Nico's space, clamping a hand around the back of his neck and dragging him close enough for his springy blond curls to press against his nose as he spoke directly into his ear. "It's going to be really hard to defend yourself in this neighborhood if both your hands are missing. Stop. Touching. Him."

"Okay, okay, jeez," Nico said. "I was just kidding. Felix was playing around, too. Why don't you ever get all alpha male on him?"

"Felix is married," Arsen said. "And not currently pawing my boyfriend."

Felix nodded. "It's true. I can barely keep up with the three men I have at home."

"Three?" Ever asked, eyes going wide.

"Mm, Zane and Asa live with us, too. And even though you're the sweetest, I don't think you're quite ready for the big leagues. The sex attic requires Olympian-level experience. You're still rocking training wheels."

"Sex attic?" Ever repeated, looking to Arsen as if to confirm whether Felix did indeed have a sex attic.

Arsen didn't have any idea how to explain to Ever that the twins and their husbands had a very complex relationship that would likely require diagrams and teaching things he wasn't sure Ever was ready to know.

Luckily, the bell on the counter dinged before Ever could question him further. Arsen glanced towards the front, realizing for the first time that Jericho was nowhere to be seen.

"Where's Coe?" Arsen asked.

Felix and Nico exchanged a look, then Felix grimaced. "In his office with the blinds shut. Probably sexting his husband." He shivered. "Or worse."

"What's sexting?" Ever asked.

"I guarantee you Arsen will teach you as soon as you get your own cell phone, buttercup," Nico said.

Arsen was grateful for the length of his hoodie. It was hard to hide an erection in sweatpants, and the idea of Ever typing out all the dirty things he wanted Arsen to do to him was making him horny.

He wandered to the front of the garage, mentally rolling his eyes when he saw the girl at the counter. Not a girl. A woman. She was at least ten years Arsen's senior, not that you'd know it from the deeply scooped tank top and barely-there shorts she sported.

She had her strawberry-blonde hair swept into a braid that curled around her shoulder to hang over her cleavage like an arrow, pointing exactly where she wanted people's eyes to go. She had heavy eye makeup, overly-lined lips, and several poorly done prison tattoos that told the neighborhood all about her gang affiliation.

"Hiya, Arsen," she purred.

He plastered an overly polite smile onto his face. "Cherry. What's up?"

She leaned forward, setting her breasts on the counter, then her elbow, propping her chin on her hand, lips pouting as she said, "My car has a flat tire...again."

Arsen frowned. "Another one? That's the third one in the last two weeks. Do you live in a construction zone?"

The amount of flat tires the women in this neighborhood got seemed statistically impossible, but maybe not when Arsen considered the amount of renovations happening all over their town. Gentrification was creeping closer every day, with huge development companies coming in and buying up whole city blocks so they could hike up the rent and force people out of homes they'd lived in forever.

Cherry shrugged. "I don't know how this keeps happening to me," she said, tone whiny as she swayed her body closer. "Can you fix it?"

Before Arsen could respond, Ever stepped in front of him, leaning his back against Arsen's chest. Arsen looked down, frowning at the top of Ever's head—not unhappy to see him but surprised. Ever rarely cared about what was happening in the garage, much less about the customers.

Cherry frowned like she'd found a bug floating in her drink, giving Ever a hard once-over.

"Who are you?" Ever asked bluntly, tone hostile.

"Cherry," she said, her tone equally malevolent.

"Cherry?" Ever said. "That's your name?" He leaned harder into Arsen. "Are you dropping off or picking up?"

Her upper lip curled in a sneer. "Dropping off."

"Where's your car?" he shot back.

"Who is he?" Cherry snapped, looking at Arsen over Ever's head. "Does Jericho have *another* gay brother?" Arsen didn't speak, trying to figure out what the hell was happening. To Ever, she said, "Who are *you*?"

"I'm Ever," he said, taking Arsen's arms and wrapping them around his waist, then tilting his head.

"That's your name?" Cherry parroted meanly. "Well, *Ever,* is it? The adults are talking. Why don't you go find your brother. Maybe he can help you scrape that gunk off your face. You are a boy, right?"

Okay, that was enough. Arsen opened his mouth to tell her to be nice, but before he could say a thing, Ever hissed at her. Just opened his mouth and…hissed. Like a cat. Like a feral cat.

Cherry jumped back. "What the fuck? Is he special or something?"

Arsen grinned, tipping Ever's face up then kissing him square on his frowning mouth. "Very," Arsen murmured, unable to stop himself from kissing him again. Then once more for good measure.

Arsen heard the door open behind him, and then Jericho was leaning against the wall beside him. "What's up, Cherry? You're here a lot lately," he said, tone bored. "Let me guess. Another mysterious flat tire?"

She folded her arms under her breasts. "Yeah," she said, tone defensive. "I think I ran over a screw or something."

Jericho stared her down for a long minute. "You said that last week," he finally said. "But it looked almost like someone had slashed it. Deliberately. With a knife. Seems like someone has a grudge."

Her gaze floated away from Jericho's. "What?" she mumbled.

Felix suddenly appeared, leaning over the counter, voice obnoxiously loud. "My brother said, it sounds like someone doesn't like you. Make any enemies lately? Stick your stubby little fingers in someone else's pie?"

"What?" she said again, sweeping a nasty look over all of them. "You know what? Never mind. I'll just take my business somewhere else."

Felix cupped his face. "Oh, no. Wait. Please, don't go," he mocked, deadpan.

She gave him the finger and stormed off, Arsen assumed in the direction of her car.

When she was gone, Jericho shook his head. "Good riddance. That girl is trouble."

"She's ugly," Ever said, voice sullen. "And stupid. And I don't like her hair. And her boobs are too big."

Felix snickered, patting Ever's head. "Easy, killer. You don't have anything to worry about. Even if your man wasn't already obsessed with you, he's been strictly dickly for as long as I've known him. The closest I ever saw to him having a crush on a girl was Nala from *The Lion King*. So, unless Cherry sprouts fur, I think you're safe."

Arsen was only half listening. Ever had been jealous. Of Cherry. He'd come to stake his claim.

He spun Ever around and slanted their mouths together, his dick twitching at Ever's surprised whimper. His lips weren't just sticky, they tasted like strawberries.

"Okay, you two. Take the show upstairs or I'll have to start charging the customers extra," Jericho said around a laugh.

Arsen didn't break the kiss, just spun them, walking Ever backwards to the stairs before letting him go, smacking his butt gently to prompt him to keep moving. If Ever wanted some reassurance that Arsen only had eyes for him, he'd happily give it.

As soon as the door of the apartment closed behind them, Ever wrapped his arms around his neck and jumped, legs going around his waist like he was a koala. His lips found

Arsen's, whispering, "Fuck me."

"I—" What was Arsen going to say? No? He'd planned on spending the morning buried inside him anyway. "Yeah, okay," he said before kissing him once more.

Arsen carried him towards the bedroom, but Ever broke their kiss, shaking his head. "Not there. The other room." Arsen frowned but opened the door to the computer room. "Not the bed. The chair."

Arsen huffed a laugh against his mouth, but it quickly died as Ever's tongue slipped past his lips to tangle with his own. "We can slow down, *besenok*. We've got all day."

Ever ignored him. As soon as Arsen collapsed into the chair with Ever in his lap, his hands were unzipping Arsen's hoodie, pushing it out of the way, his head dipping to lick over his nipple. Fuck. Ever knew how quickly that got him going. Not that he wasn't already hard enough to hammer a nail through a board.

Arsen gripped Ever's ass dragging him closer to grind their cocks together with a groan. Ever made a happy sound, then moved to give Arsen's other nipple the same attention.

Arsen's hands slid up under his shirt, forcing Ever to sit up just long enough to pull it over his head. Ever moaned, rolling their hips together as he sucked a bruise onto Arsen's neck directly over his pulse. He was marking his territory. Where everybody could see it. Ever was jealous. That shouldn't have been the turn on it was. He didn't want Ever to feel insecure, but he did love how much Ever loved him.

He gave a shuddery breath, his hands sliding into Ever's pants, fingers dipping to tease over his hole. Ever hummed his approval into Arsen's ear, nibbling at the shell of his ear. "Finger me."

"Christ. When did you get so demanding?" Arsen teased, stretching to reach the lube that laid on its side behind his subwoofer.

Ever used the time to suck another mark into the skin over his collarbone. "Since some slut named Cherry shoved her boobs in your face."

Arsen didn't think this was the time to give Ever a lecture on slut-shaming. When did his sweet boy learn to be so sour? Was this his friends' doing? Felix could easily have been the culprit. He had a barbed tongue and zero filter. Or maybe Ever had always been this feisty but was just waiting to be comfortable enough to speak his mind.

He was that comfortable with Arsen.

"That's not very nice," Arsen admonished playfully, coating his fingers and sliding them between his cheeks until Ever was pushing back, trying to get them where he wanted them.

Arsen made a pained sound as he slipped a finger into the tight heat of Ever's body. He wanted it to be his throbbing cock. He was aching at the thought of burying himself in that perfect heat.

Ever's mouth found his, fucking his tongue between his lips as he worked Arsen's finger deeper. "Another," he demanded.

Arsen didn't try to dissuade him, just did as he was told. Ever was in charge—Arsen was just there to serve him. Or service him. Whatever he wanted, really.

When Arsen complied, Ever's responding hiss was one of pain but, just as quickly as the sound escaped him, he was rocking back, rolling his hips, his hand plunging into Arsen's sweatpants and wrapping around his cock, stroking it with purpose, making another pleased sound when he found him leaking. "I'm good. Fuck me."

"Ever…" Arsen said breathlessly.

Ever pulled back, giving him a pouty face, voice sullen. "Please? Haven't I been good?"

Arsen's cock twitched at Ever's pleading. He already had him wrapped around his finger. Arsen was his goddamn slave. Fuck.

Even if it was an act, a role-playing exercise, some newly discovered kink, Arsen was more than happy to give Ever the words he needed to hear. "Yes, baby. You've been so good."

"Better than her?" he asked, riding Arsen's fingers with abandon.

Arsen groaned, biting Ever's chin, his neck, his collarbone. "Better than anyone in the whole fucking world."

Ever suddenly slapped Arsen's arm. He pulled his fingers free, wiping them on his sweatpants as Ever wiggled from his lap, getting rid of his pants and underwear before cocking an expectant brow at Arsen. He stared for far too long at the naked perfection that was Ever, scars and all.

When Ever gave another impatient sound, Arsen remembered what he was supposed to be doing, hooking his thumbs in the waistband of his sweats. Ever waited just long enough for Arsen to get his pants out of the way before grabbing the lube, slicking Arsen's cock, and turning away from him.

Arsen frowned, but then Ever was holding his cock still so he could sink down on him, both of them gasping at the intrusion.

"Don't hurt yourself," Arsen begged.

"I-I'm not. It-It doesn't hurt," he managed. "Feels so… full of you. You're so…deep like this."

Arsen gripped Ever's hips hard, dragging him down even as he drove up into him. "Jesus. You really are trying to kill me."

Ever whined, rising up then dropping down once, then again, like he was testing whether he could take it or not. Arsen tried to let Ever set the pace, he did. But each time Ever rose up then dropped down, it sent these bolts of pure heat through him until he couldn't stop himself from holding Ever in place and working up into him.

For his part, Ever didn't seem to mind. He almost instantly went limp in Arsen's arms, leaning his head back against his shoulder so that Arsen could hear every breath he drove out of his lungs with each thrust.

It was addictive.

"Fuck. You're so tight. So hot and wet. You feel so fucking good. So good. You're doing so good for me."

Ever whimpered, his cock flushed and leaking, bouncing with every movement.

Arsen grabbed the lube, slicking his hand and wrapping it around Ever's hard length, jerking him in time with his movements.

"Oh, fuck. Oh, fuck," Ever chanted.

Arsen smiled. It was always so easy to know when Ever was close. His mouth got away from him and he'd start to babble curses. It was still so hot hearing those words come out of that innocent little mouth in that breathy, sweet voice.

Ever took back control then, chasing his own pleasure, fucking up into Arsen's hand, then dropping back onto his cock. Arsen had to fight to stave off the climax threatening to overtake him.

He wanted Ever to come first. "Are you close?"

"So close. Fuck. Don't stop. Don't stop. Don't stop."

Arsen didn't point out that Ever was the one moving, Ever was the one fucking himself on Arsen's cock, jerking himself with Arsen's tightened fist.

"Come on…let me hear you," Arsen murmured against his ear. "You sound so hot when you're coming on my cock. Come for me and I'll fill you up."

Ever's breath caught, and then he moaned long and low, his release spilling over Arsen's fist. He continued to milk him until Ever flinched away, oversensitive.

"My turn," Arsen said roughly.

He put Ever on his feet, bending him over the bed so he could grab his hips and slam into him again and again. He didn't think about anything but the heat building in his spine and the pleasure just out of reach. Every thrust had Ever going up on tip-toe, driving these tiny little cries from his lips that drove Arsen crazy.

Ever was so hot, so perfect. All Arsen's. "You're mine," he said. "Just mine."

His orgasm slammed into him then. He gripped Ever's

hips tight enough to bruise, working into him in tiny, aborted thrusts as he came.

As the post-orgasm high wore off, he blanketed himself over Ever to kiss his shoulder. "Are you okay?"

Ever wiggled his butt a little. "Can you just stay inside me?"

Arsen laughed, placing more kisses wherever he could reach. "I'm afraid not." Ever shivered as Arsen pulled free. He dropped down to the mattress, dragging Ever with him, snuggling him close. "But give me an hour and we can do it again."

Ever made a sad sound. "Half an hour."

"Forty-five minutes," Arsen countered.

Ever huffed out a long-suffering sigh. "Fine. Forty-five minutes."

EIGHTEEN

EVER

"I WANT TO START BY saying this is a safe space."

Ever eyed Dr. Jeremiah Jones warily. Jeremiah Jones. It seemed like a fake name, an alias hiding a much cooler identity. If this was a web comic or graphic novel, Dr. Jones would be an undercover superhero. But this wasn't a book. This was Ever's reality. And in reality, Dr. Jones was Ever's new therapist.

Ever had been there for about ten minutes now. He sat on an overstuffed but comfortable purple sofa, knees drawn to his chest. Dr. Jones sat in a tall high-back chair, legs crossed at the ankle. He had frogs on his socks. The thought stuck in Ever's head, like a song on a loop. Why frogs?

He looked…kind, Ever supposed, but his size alone was imposing. He was tall, well over six feet, and the olive green, probably cashmere cardigan he wore clung to well-muscled arms and a trim waist. He had warm, dark skin and intelligent, whiskey-brown eyes framed by gold-rimmed glasses that would have looked nerdy or awkward on anyone else.

But Jeremiah Jones was a walking contradiction. His sweater and shoes were expensive, but his jeans seemed well-worn, threadbare at the knees, not because it was trendy but because they were well loved. And despite his high and tight hair cut, his put together outfit, and this almost militant feel about him, he had tattoos on the back of both hands and deep scarring on his knuckles.

When he caught Ever staring, he smiled. "I'm a boxer. Well, I was when I was in the Air Force. Now, I'm a therapist, obviously."

"A boxer turned therapist?" Ever said. Another contradiction. How did one go from beating people half to death for sport to wanting to help them? "Okay."

Could Ever really afford to judge? His boyfriend had killed two people just in the few weeks they'd been together and his friends had killed far more, but they all treated him like a pet. Like a baby. Something that should annoy Ever—he was an adult, after all—but it didn't. He liked being babied. He liked getting presents and attention and getting away with pretty much anything. Did that make him a bad person?

Ever continued to study the doctor. He couldn't gauge the man's age. It could have been thirty, it could have been forty-five. It was hard to tell. His face was wrinkle-free, but there was a sadness to his eyes that made him seem like an old soul. Ever just wanted to know if he could trust this man. Not that age was a signifier of trustworthiness.

Jericho and Arsen said he could trust Dr. Jones. And he trusted them. So, there he was, sitting on a couch, heart in his throat, waiting to bare his soul to a stranger.

After a moment, he smiled at Ever, then offered him a bowl of candy. Ever took a black-labeled BlowPop, unwrapping it and popping in his mouth, grateful for something to do.

"What I mean to say is, you don't have to be afraid to speak plainly here. I'm a good friend of the Mulvaneys. We share...similar interests. But that doesn't mean anything you tell me will leave this room. I'm bound by law to keep your secrets."

Ever blinked at him, twirling the lollipop over his tongue. "Okay."

Dr. Jones shifted in his seat, taking a piece of chocolate and unwrapping it, chewing and swallowing before he said, "Jericho has given me a very brief description of your life up until now, but I'd like to hear it from you. Would you want to talk about it?"

"Does anybody?" Ever muttered, not really expecting an answer.

Dr. Jones smiled. "Not at first but, eventually, yes. Sometimes talking through the trauma is the only way to heal."

The man's question hung in the air between them, unanswered. Instead, Ever looked around the office as if his surroundings could offer some insight into the man across from him. It was as clean and tidy as the man himself, but a little shabby. Another contradiction.

The building itself was old, and the exposed brick was more from disrepair than an attempt at decor. The hardwood floors were marred by water stains, and the furniture all seemed second-hand, but Ever couldn't shake the feeling it was all…fake. All designed to make people think he was one of them. Whatever that meant.

"Dr. Jones—"

"Jeremiah, please."

Ever squirmed, not really comfortable using the man's first name for some reason he couldn't put his finger on.

"Jeremiah," he conceded. "What if I don't have any trauma?"

Jeremiah tapped his pen against his chin. "Do you think you don't have trauma?"

Ever shrugged. "Everything I read tells me I'm supposed to be…spiraling. That I should be having nightmares and panic attacks. That I should be afraid of the dark or going outside. That certain sounds or smells should trigger me. I don't have any of that."

Jeremiah nodded. "When you think about your time before—before you were rescued—how does it make you feel?"

Ever shrugged once more. "It doesn't."

"Can you expand on that?"

Could he? Other than the initial fear he'd felt in the spare room the night he arrived, there'd been nothing. "It feels like it happened to someone else. Or maybe a different version of me. It's not like I don't remember or that I've blocked it out. It's almost like I'm watching a movie. It just… I don't feel anything when I think about it. There's just before and after. Is that weird?"

"Have you ever heard of the term dissociation?" Jeremiah asked.

Ever shook his head, picking at a stray thread on the back of the sofa cushion.

"Sometimes, immediately after a traumatic experience, or sometimes even during years of prolonged abuse, your brain will...wall off the bad things. It's a sort of self-preservation technique."

"Okay?" Ever prompted, hoping the man would explain further.

"Did you ever feel like you were outside your own body? When you said it was like watching a movie, did you mean it was like watching bad things happen to another version of yourself?"

"Yeah," Ever mumbled.

"Do you feel numb or detached when you think about it now?"

"Yeah. I guess so."

Jeremiah nodded. "Dissociation is common, but when that dissociation disappears, *that* is when you can experience the effects of chronic PTSD. Right now, your brain is just protecting itself while you get your bearings, but it can also leave you with a sense of not knowing who you are."

Ever gave a humorless laugh. "I don't know who I am, Dr. Jo—Jeremiah. I don't even have a name."

He frowned. The first real crack in his cool facade. "Ever isn't your name?"

"It is now," Ever said, cheeks flushing.

Jeremiah twirled the pen over his knuckles. "What was

it before?"

Ever watched, transfixed as the pen moved, spinning through his fingers almost like magic. "I didn't have one."

"No?"

Ever corrected himself. "I mean, I'm sure I had one when I was born. At least, I hope I did. It would suck if my mom didn't even care enough about me to name me before she sold me or gave me up for adoption or let me get kidnapped…or whatever."

Jeremiah nodded. "And the woman who held you captive? What did she call you?"

"On a good day, Boy, mostly. On the bad days, nothing at all. It's probably easier to torture someone if you don't think of them as actual people. Even dogs and cats have names. Her other victims had names. But not me."

Jeremiah made a vague sound then asked, "Is that how you felt? Not human?"

"I felt…" Ever started, a sudden lump forming in his throat. "I don't want to talk about this."

"Okay. That's fine. We don't have to. But can you tell me why you chose Ever as your name?"

Ever trapped his bottom lip between his teeth. "I don't really remember," he lied.

Once more, Jeremiah made a sound that conveyed nothing. But Ever felt like he knew he lied. Which he had. But he was still offended Jeremiah thought he was lying, which was kind of fucked up.

But didn't he deserve to keep some secrets to himself? He knew why he called himself Ever, he just didn't want to say.

It was too embarrassing.

"Do you remember when you started calling yourself that?"

He shrugged, hugging his legs tighter. "When I learned how to read, I guess."

"How old were you then?"

"Eleven…twelve, maybe? When she needed me to be able to go out and run errands without her. At first, she would just send me with a list and her debit card, and the corner store would just take the note and pull her items, but as I got older, they became less interested in helping me. So, she taught me to read."

"What else did she teach you?"

"Only things that would benefit her. She taught me to count. She taught me basic units of measurement because I needed to know how to measure ingredients when I cooked. Everything I learned from her was on a need-to-know basis and there wasn't much she thought I needed to know."

"She never taught you to count? To add? Subtract? Nothing?" Jeremiah asked, tone neutral, like he didn't want Ever to think he was judging him.

Ever's laugh tasted like bile on his tongue. "I wouldn't say nothing. She taught me having an opinion got my mouth duct taped shut for days. She taught me burning food got me burned in return. She taught me that breaking things got my fingers broken. She taught me that being in her presence when she was in a bad mood was going to leave me needing a doctor. And she taught me that people who were supposed to help me—like those doctors—were the very same people who abused me. But no, math, history, science, that stuff I had to learn on my own."

"You seem…angry."

Was that the word for the hot, tight feeling in his chest? He shrugged, suddenly feeling like if he tried to talk, he might scream or cry instead, and he didn't want that. She didn't deserve his tears or his suffering. She'd done enough to him. "Wouldn't you be?"

"Certainly. But when we started, you said you didn't feel anything at all. Anger is a feeling."

Ever didn't want to be angry. "I just want to be happy," he said, words thick.

"And are you?" Jeremiah asked.

Tears burned Ever's eyes. "Am I…?"

"Happy?"

Ever blinked rapidly. "I—" He shook his head. "I don't really know what happiness is."

"What emotions do you know?" Jeremiah asked.

If anyone else had asked that, Ever would have thought he was mocking him, but Jeremiah was serious. "Sadness. Fear…"

"Anger."

Ever swallowed hard then nodded. "Yeah."

"Anxiety?"

Once more, he nodded.

"How about depression?"

Ever shrugged.

"What about love?"

What about love? Arsen's face immediately came to

mind. Arsen protected him and took care of him and kept him safe. Arsen loved him. He told him so every night and every morning before he went to work downstairs.

"Who are you thinking about right now?"

"What?" Ever asked, cheeks burning.

"When I said love, your face changed completely. Who were you thinking about?"

"Arsen," Ever admitted. "He loves me."

"And do you love him?"

Ever nodded. "Yeah."

"I see."

Ever's gaze flicked to Jeremiah, and that tight feeling returned to his chest. "Don't say it like that."

"Like what?" Jeremiah asked, tilting his head in a way Ever found inexplicably infuriating.

"Like it's not real. Like it's just some fake emotion or trauma response. I love him and he loves me. Even if we haven't known each other that long."

Jeremiah frowned. "I didn't think that at all. But it seems like you might."

"No."

"No?"

"No," Ever said again, faintly. "People can fall in love at first sight. People can find their soulmates. People can have their happily ever after. Just because it happened fast doesn't mean it's not real."

"Nobody's saying it isn't real, Ever. Nobody but you."

"I love him," Ever said fiercely.

"I believe you," Jeremiah assured him. "But at some

point, we're going to have to examine why you're so sure nobody else does."

Ever glared at him. "I didn't say that."

"I think this is enough for one day. No? Why don't we talk again in a few days?"

Ever nodded, miserable, feeling like he'd failed a test somehow.

"What does your name mean?"

Arsen looked up at Ever in surprise. He didn't blame Arsen. It was a strange non sequitur. They'd been lying in bed, Arsen's head on Ever's belly, talking about fairly mundane things. The part for a '65 Shelby that hadn't come in on time, the pasta they'd made off a YouTube tutorial an hour ago that had somehow tasted like rubber soaked in lemons, Felix's diatribe in the group chat about proper post-sex etiquette and the cleaning of sex toys.

They'd talked about anything and everything...except Ever's therapy appointment that afternoon.

"My name?" Arsen echoed.

Arsen hadn't pushed Ever about his session at all. He appeared perfectly content to let Ever act like the whole thing had never happened. And Ever was grateful. Arsen treated it as if it was any other night. He'd let Ever control everything, from dinner to the shower sex, which was how they'd ended up eating pizza naked in bed with damp hair and a movie playing on Arsen's laptop in the middle of the mattress.

The pizza was long gone, the movie was over. Now, they were lying there, Ever's legs twisted in the sheets, Arsen lying sideways, head heavy on Ever's slightly bloated tummy.

Ever nodded. "Mm. What does it mean?"

Arsen grinned, his cheeks turning a bit pink, then he lifted his arm and flexed, the muscles popping in a way Ever found…pleasing. "Virile. Strong," he said in an exaggerated deep voice before deflating back to normal. "My father had high expectations for me."

Arsen's father. He rarely talked about him. Not that Ever blamed him. Who wanted to talk about the man who killed your mother?

"Your father's in jail, right?" Ever asked.

Arsen nodded. "'Til he dies."

"Do you ever go visit him?"

Arsen's lip curled. "I tried. A couple of times after I turned eighteen. Jericho thought it would be a good way to give me 'closure.' Whatever that means. But…it just made me angry."

"Angry?" Ever repeated. He was hearing the word a lot.

"Yeah. My father… He's never apologized. I know that seems like a ridiculous thing to say. How does someone apologize for killing your mom? But I thought he'd be… remorseful at least. But he wasn't. Not even a little bit. If anything, he blamed me. Took every opportunity to tell me he was ashamed of me, even during our visits. It was always, 'Sit up straight, stop holding your hand like that. Why are you wearing pink? Are you trying to embarrass me?'"

"He was ashamed…of you?" Ever said, breathless.

How could anyone be ashamed of Arsen? He was perfect. Smart. Sweet. Hardworking. Funny. Sexy… Ever's hand moved by itself, his fingertips skimming over Arsen's jawline, his cheekbones, his lips.

"He couldn't handle having a gay son. He said he was embarrassed we shared a last name."

"What an asshole," Ever muttered.

Arsen chuckled, his features shifting beneath Ever's fingers. "I'll never get used to you swearing."

"Should I not?" Ever asked.

"You should do and say whatever you want. I'll always find you adorable."

Ever grew hot until the tips of his ears felt like they were on fire. He steered the subject back to Arsen. "But you kept his last name anyway?"

"Mostly for spite, partially because a name change is a really difficult process. Expensive, too. Especially for someone who's immigrated here."

"What does your last name mean?"

"Lebedev?" Arsen said. "It means swan."

Ever's lips twitched. "So, your full name means horny swan?"

"Hey!" Arsen scraped his teeth across Ever's stomach until he flinched away with a laugh. "It means…well, yeah, I guess it kind of does. My dad said it meant 'swan bringer' after a man who used to raise swans for the nobles. But my father was often full of shit."

Ever laughed, his finger tracing the bridge of Arsen's

nose. "Why do you call me *besenok*?"

Arsen grinned, reaching up to boop Ever's chin. "Because it suits you."

Ever rolled his eyes. "But what does it mean?"

"It means little demon."

Ever's mouth fell open. "You think I'm a demon?"

"You did hiss at a girl just yesterday," Arsen pointed out. "Besides, I mean it like…a term of endearment. Like baby or honey or sweetie."

Sweetie. Ever loved hearing certain words in Arsen's accent. It made them sound special, even when they were very generic. "Should I call *you* something? A term of endearment?"

"What do you want to call me?" Arsen asked gently.

Ever frowned. Nothing he thought of seemed special in any way. They were just names he heard thousands of times, in a million different romance novels. "I don't know," he said, flopping back against the pillows.

Arsen took Ever's free hand, playing with his fingers. When he finally spoke again, his voice sounded unusually shy. "Back in Russia, my friends and family called me Senya. It's not exactly a term of endearment but more like a family name. Something only the people closest to you use."

"But nobody here calls you that," Ever said. "And you think of them as your family."

"They are. True. But once we got to the States, my mom was the only one who continued to call me that. After she died, hearing anyone else say it was…painful. But now…" He kissed Ever's palm. "It would be nice to hear you say it."

"Senya," Ever repeated, noting the way Arsen's eyes went soft. "Senya," he said again, liking the way it felt dripping off his tongue. "And nobody else calls you that? Not even your dad?"

Arsen rolled onto his side, burying his face against Ever's stomach, his words muffled. "No. Here, everybody calls me Arsen. Even my father. He said it sounded tough. That it commanded respect. That it would help me toughen up."

"I'm sure other people think you're pretty scary," Ever assured him as he carded his fingers through his hair.

"Do *you* think I'm scary?" Arsen teased, rubbing his nose against Ever's skin until he squirmed before blowing a raspberry, making Ever squeal.

"No," he said around a giggle.

Arsen rolled back to look up at Ever. "Good. I don't ever want you to be afraid of me."

Ever's heart caught in his throat. He couldn't remember a time where he was afraid of Arsen. Even in the beginning, he was far more afraid he'd give him to someone else than he was of Arsen harming him personally. He was still afraid, if he was being honest, and the reason hadn't changed all that much.

"I'm not afraid of you," Ever admitted softly. "I'm afraid of being without you."

Arsen looked into his eyes. "That's not something you need to worry about."

"Mm," Ever said, noncommittal. Was that something Arsen could promise when someone had already threatened Ever twice? But he didn't say that. He didn't want to ruin their night.

"Why did you want to know about my name?"

Ever shrugged. "Something Jeremiah said today. He asked why I'd named myself Ever. It got me thinking about names."

"And…what did you tell him?" Arsen asked carefully.

"I lied," Ever admitted. "I said I didn't remember."

Arsen frowned, taking Ever's hand once more. "Why did you lie? You're not a liar."

Ever sighed. "I don't know. 'Cause it's embarrassing."

"What is?"

Ever closed his eyes. "Why I picked my name. Or how, I guess."

"Will you tell me?" Arsen asked softly.

Ever chewed on his bottom lip, his stomach churning with pizza and anxiety. "I didn't learn to read until I was old. Like, when most kids were thinking about their first year of high school, I was sounding out words like cat and hat. Up until that point, my world was really small. The size of a closet, really."

Arsen squeezed Ever's hand.

Ever just stared at the opposite wall. "Jennika kept the blinds closed, but, sometimes, when she wasn't home, I would look outside and see kids playing. Watching them play was really all I knew about the outside world. Until she started bringing home these picture books and workbooks. They were for little kids, preschoolers. But I didn't know that. Once I mastered those, I learned how big the world really was, how big the universe was."

Arsen's palm was sweaty. Or maybe it was Ever's. He didn't know. It didn't matter. "Her teaching me to read was the best and worst thing that ever happened to me. Best, because I had some kind of skill most of the world possessed, but worse, because books showed me that my life wasn't normal and that most people were living happy lives. Most kids were living happy lives…but not me."

"Ever…" Arsen said, voice raw.

Ever gave him a watery smile. "I preferred fairy tales because nobody was living those lives. There were no frog princes or children finding houses made of candy in the woods. I loved fairy tales, even the really dark ones. But my favorite book was *The Ugly Duckling*. Because his life sucked like mine. He wasn't like others and neither was I. But, eventually, he grows up and realizes that he was just in the wrong place with the wrong people. He wasn't a duck…" Ever looked down at Arsen in awe. "He was a swan. Like you."

Arsen smiled up at him. "See? You were meant to be with me the whole time."

Ever swiped at the tears on his cheek. "I sound so dumb."

"You do not. When did you choose Ever as your name?"

Ever shrugged. "Happily ever after… It was my favorite part of every fairy tale book. It implied that no matter how bad things got, afterwards they got to be happy. I would say it over and over again. If I could just get through my bad stuff, I would be happy ever after. Every beating, every attack, every time someone touched me against my will, I would just repeat it to myself. Happy ever after. Happy ever after. Until, one day, the Ever in 'happy ever after' was me. So, when you asked…that's how I answered."

"What's embarrassing about that?" Arsen managed, words thick.

Ever shrugged. "I was a nineteen-year-old, living in a closet, clinging to a baby book of fairy tales. It's stupid and lame and hopeful…and embarrassingly naive."

Arsen frowned at him then took Ever's hands, kissing each of his palms. "Hope is never stupid."

To Ever's horror, he burst into tears. Arsen jolted into a sitting position, wrapping his arms around him.

"I'm sorry," Ever sobbed.

Arsen shook his head against Ever's. "For what?"

Ever flailed. "I-I don't know. I'm just…sorry."

Arsen sighed heavily but held Ever tighter. "You don't have anything to be sorry for, but if you just want to cry… then cry."

Ever didn't want to cry, but he had no choice—the tears wouldn't stop coming no matter how much he tried to stave them off. He cried until his face was on fire and his nose was stuffy and he was sure he was puffy and swollen. He cried until he had no tears left. Again.

"I don't know why this keeps happening," he whispered against Arsen's chest an hour later.

"You don't?" Arsen asked, kissing the top of Ever's head. "If I had been through what you've been through, I might never stop crying. The fact that you wake up and smile every day is so fucking impressive. Like…you're the strongest of all of us."

Ever's eyes burned. "I'm just so...tired."

"Of course, you are," Arsen said. "Who wouldn't be? Let's just get some sleep."

Ever nodded. "Yeah, okay."

Arsen kissed the top of his head. "Good night, *besenok*."

"Good night...Senya."

NINETEEN

ARSEN

EVER WASN'T OKAY.

The change didn't start as anything overt; there was no key moment Arsen could point to and say this was the day he noticed it. It was subtle, insidious—creeping in a bit at a time, unnoticed. The more Ever went to therapy, the closer his trauma floated to the surface, and that was affecting him in a number of ways. Something Dr. Jones assured Arsen was normal, even if it did nothing to make him feel better about it.

It started with nightmares, something Arsen was all too familiar with. Some nights, Ever would whimper and whine and mumble, but remain asleep. Those nights, just holding him seemed to be enough to ward off whatever memories were tormenting him. Other nights, he would wake sweaty and screaming, fighting Arsen in his disoriented state. But whenever Arsen asked what he'd dreamed about, Ever would always just blink and smile through his tears, saying he didn't remember.

Arsen didn't fault him for the lie. He knew better than

anyone that talking about the nightmares only prolonged the space they occupied in your mind. He would provide whatever distraction Ever needed. Sometimes, that was sex. Ever would demand that Arsen fuck him—use him—until Ever was too exhausted for anything but a dreamless sleep. Other times, he'd put his headphones on and listen to music, wrapped around Arsen like he was a body pillow.

But, day after day, Ever's nightmares started bleeding into his reality. More often than not, Arsen woke not to find Ever struggling with sleep but missing from their bed entirely.

Like now.

Arsen blinked open bleary eyes, glancing at the digital clock on the side table. It was a little after three in the morning. Ever was gone…again. Arsen sighed, rubbed his lids, then rolled to his feet in one fluid movement. The first few times he'd woken to find Ever missing, the panic had almost killed him, but now, he just felt a pang of sadness as he padded barefoot and shirtless into the living room.

Ever sat on the sofa in his sleep shorts and Arsen's t-shirt, gazing down into the bay like he was keeping watch. Which he was. He grew increasingly paranoid every day, certain the people who'd taken him would come back again and make good on their threat to sell him back into slavery. Arsen wanted to assure him that wasn't the case, but until they figured out how deep the trafficking ring went, they were stuck in limbo.

The Mulvaneys' hacker, Calliope, had run down not one but two previous cases of human trafficking in Jamesville—a massage parlor, which had a handful of women being trafficked for sex, and a rich couple, who had a woman working as a domestic servant for over ten years. In those cases, the focus was on punishing the abusers, not how the victims ended up in the hands of those abusers. Which was really no help to them.

When Arsen touched Ever's shoulder, he jumped, then looked up at him, expression guilty. "Sorry."

"Why are you up so late, *besenok*?" Arsen asked, sitting beside him then tugging him into his lap.

Ever shrugged, snuggling into his arms. "I couldn't sleep. I didn't want to wake you up. It's late. You have to work soon."

Arsen's heart twisted, frustration feeling like a knot under his ribs. He wanted Ever to wake him if he was afraid. But he didn't say that. Ever would just feel worse, and Arsen couldn't handle making him feel bad. "What are you doing out here?"

Ever shrugged again, gaze floating away from him. "Nothing. Just...looking around."

Arsen grazed his lips over Ever's hair, squeezing him against him tightly. "I'm not going to let anybody hurt you. There's an alarm on the doors downstairs and on the back entrance. Nobody's getting in here without us knowing it."

Jericho wasn't a fool. He knew that protecting the neighborhood meant protecting himself. He'd always had an alarm system, but when he got married, Atticus had insisted on upgrading it. He said he didn't trust the low-budget tech Jericho had bought online.

Atticus thought that, if it was cheap, it was poorly made.

Jericho had let Atticus upgrade the system because it made him happy. And all Jericho cared about was making Atticus happy.

"I know," Ever said. "I just wanted to…see for myself," he finished quietly.

Arsen sighed, tucking Ever's head under his chin, keeping his hand pressed against his cheek, mostly so Ever couldn't see the worried look on his face. He wasn't worried for Ever's safety, just his sanity. This lack of sleep wasn't healthy. He had dark circles under his eyes. He was losing weight again. He tried hard to fake it for the others, laughing and joking, but the joy never reached his eyes anymore.

They were all worried. They wanted to run head first at the problem, kill first and ask questions later. Arsen did, too. As far as he was concerned, he had no problem going in, guns blazing, and letting everyone know that anyone who messed with Ever would be handled with extreme prejudice. But that wasn't how Jericho worked.

Jericho was a wait and see kind of guy. He wanted all the facts. For most of his life, he hadn't had the Mulvaneys' wealth or connections. If any of Jericho's boys were caught committing a crime, they would have done time for it. Even if the victim was a total shitbag.

While Jericho wasn't waiting, exactly, he was treading lightly. They knew at least one cop had been involved, but there were likely more. If they made too many inquiries too fast, they were likely to tip them off, and that could cause them to retaliate against Ever. Calliope was doing her best to follow the money to see where it led, but it was slow-going. These people, whoever they were, were good at covering their tracks.

"I'm sorry," Ever whispered suddenly, startling Arsen from his thoughts.

"What?" Arsen mumbled, even though he'd heard him.

"I don't want to be like this. I know you didn't sign on to take care of me forever," Ever said, voice soaked with tears.

Arsen felt like he was choking. Ever was breaking his heart. He didn't know how to make him see what was so obvious to everyone else. "Of course, I did," Arsen said, shaking his head. "I've been all in since the moment I saw you."

"Maybe I should stop going to therapy," Ever said suddenly. "Things just keep getting worse the more I go. I thought it was supposed to make me better. This doesn't feel better. This feels awful. I hate it. I *hate* it. It was so much easier when I felt nothing at all."

Arsen didn't know what to say. Ever wasn't wrong. The more he went to see the doctor, the worse he got. But everything Arsen read said this was common. That, in therapy, things often got worse before they got better and that Ever needed to keep feeling his feelings so he could heal. But Arsen hated watching him suffer.

"What does Dr. Jones say about your nightmares and you sitting up all night keeping watch?" Arsen asked, continuing to stroke his hair. As Ever's silence stretched, Arsen's hand stilled. "Have you not told him?"

"Was I supposed to?" Ever asked, voice meek and full of mock innocence.

Arsen snorted. "Don't play dumb with me. That cute face

only gets you so far."

Ever squirmed free of Arsen's hold so he could sit up, straddling his thighs, leveling the full force of his big puppy eyes and that full pouting mouth at him. "How far does it get me, exactly?" he asked, trapping his lower lip between his bunny teeth, rolling his hips against Arsen's.

Arsen's hands came around to grab his ass and squeeze, even as he said, "You can't distract me with sex either."

Ever's brows went up, and he raked his gaze over Arsen in a way that left a trail of fire in its wake. "No?" he asked, dipping his head, brushing his lips along Arsen's collarbone, his thumbs tracing over Arsen's nipples. "You sure?"

Arsen's eyes rolled, lids falling shut as he arched up under him without thought. Ever's touch was lethal.

Arsen settled deeper into the sofa, hands gripping Ever's hips, aligning their bodies in a way that made them both suck in a breath.

Shit.

"*Besenok*," Arsen said, his name a warning.

Ever trailed his mouth upwards to suck at the spot just behind Arsen's ear, the one that made goosebumps erupt along his skin and that made his dick hard. Well, harder. Ever had learned all of Arsen's weak spots far too quickly.

"Senya," Ever breathed into his ear.

Arsen couldn't stop the near growl that fell from his lips. "You're in so much trouble," he teased, fingers threading in Ever's hair to drag his mouth to his, nostrils flaring as Ever's lips parted so easily. He was always so good for him. So responsive. So ready.

"Promise?" Ever asked against his lips.

Arsen ran his hands up under Ever's shirt and along his back, tracing the familiar shape of his scars. Something Ever used to hate but that now made him shiver.

"You're such a little tease," Arsen murmured, between deep, drugging kisses.

Ever pulled back, locking eyes with him, pupils blown. "Who's teasing?" he asked, then peeled his shirt over his head, tossing it to the side.

Arsen sucked in a breath as Ever practically bent in half to capture one of Arsen's nipples between his lips, biting down just hard enough to make him hiss, his hips bucking once again.

Ever made an appreciative sound, his hand dropping to trace the ridge of Arsen's erection tenting his sweatpants.

He bit back a groan, his hand closing around Ever's wrist. He should stop this. This wasn't the time. Ever was using sex to try to distract him from the fact that he was keeping key information from his therapist. Ever wrenched his hand free of Arsen's grip, then slid it under his waistband, making an appreciative sound as his palm closed around the hard length of Arsen's cock.

But it was working. Fuck, it was working so well. He fucked into Ever's tightened fist, enjoying the rough catch and slide a little too much. How was he supposed to say no? Ever was so cute and sexy, and he smelled like heaven, and he was making these high-pitched sort of frenzied noises like he was desperate for Arsen, like he needed him.

"Ever…" he breathed.

Ever moaned, then trailed his tongue along the corded tendon of Arsen's neck. "I love when you say my name."

Arsen used his free hand to knot his fingers in Ever's hair, pulling him back up for another dirty kiss. "Ever," he said again, this time against his open mouth.

Ever whimpered.

"What do you want?" Arsen asked, tongue teasing over Ever's.

"You know what I want," Ever whined.

"Say it," Arsen demanded softly. "Nicely."

"Fuck me. Please," Ever begged into his mouth. "I need it. I want you inside me."

Arsen bit Ever's lower lip, then sucked at it. "Right here?"

"Hnf," was the only response Ever seemed capable of managing, working Arsen with purpose. Fuck. He wasn't going to refuse him. No matter how much of an asshole that made him.

He dumped Ever unceremoniously onto the sofa. "Don't move."

Ever blinked at him but remained where he was. Arsen went to the bedroom to grab the lube. He wasn't going to risk hurting Ever just because they were both too horny to wait. When he returned to the living room, he'd found that Ever hadn't listened to his directive at all. He was bent over the back of the sofa, his cloth-covered ass swaying enticingly.

The boy was a menace. "You are not being a very good boy," Arsen murmured.

Ever looked over his shoulder. "No?" he asked, then

hooked his thumbs into his shorts and slid them down to mid-thigh, revealing so much golden skin. The picture he made was obscene. "How about now?"

Was this really the Ever he'd met just weeks ago? Fuck. Arsen didn't even notice he was moving until he gripped Ever's ass, bending to bite the flesh there just hard enough to make him moan. He slicked two fingers, then slid them over Ever's hole, rubbing but not pushing in.

Ever keened, then made a sound of frustration when Arsen didn't comply with his unspoken demand.

Arsen laughed low. "Are you going to be good?"

"Yes," Ever hissed.

"Promise?"

"Yes," Ever whined, pushing back against Arsen's hand.

Arsen ran one hand along Ever's spine to his hair as he sank his fingers from his other hand inside him, both of them making a desperate sound. Ever was not willing to wait for Arsen to work him open slowly. He fucked himself on Arsen's fingers again and again until he gave another frustrated noise. "Hurry up," he begged.

Arsen wanted to tease him a little more, but his cock was throbbing, desperate for the tight, sucking heat of Ever's body. He pulled his fingers free, then shoved his sweatpants out of the way, kneeling between Ever's open legs on the sofa. He took a moment to add more lube before lining up, rubbing the head of his cock around Ever's hole until he pushed back against him, taking Arsen in without any help from him.

Jesus. He would never, ever get over how fucking good it

felt being inside him. Ever was rocking himself back against Arsen, just fucking himself on his dick just as he'd done with his fingers. Arsen fisted Ever's hair, pulling him back against him so he could bite at his neck. His other hand found his hip, holding him still so he could drive into him over and over until the only sounds were their panting breaths, and the slap of skin on skin, and Ever's high-pitched whines.

"Can I...?" Ever begged, his hand hovering over his own cock.

"Yeah, touch yourself," Arsen said. Ever never needed his permission, but he always wanted it. "I love watching you make yourself feel good."

And he had the perfect position, staring down over Ever's shoulder, watching him stroke his flushed and leaking cock with purpose. Jesus, he was so fucking pretty like this. Flushed and begging, too caught up in his own pleasure to be embarrassed by the sounds falling from his lips.

It was making Arsen crazy, forcing him to drive into him harder and deeper. He wasn't going to last much longer, anyway. Maybe it was the late hour, or the desperate conversation, or just Ever's clumsy but always effective seduction technique, but he could feel himself losing his resolve, hips snapping faster as he chased that shocky pleasure that drove him towards his release.

"Are you close?" Arsen breathed against his cheek.

"Yes. Yes. So...fuck...so, hnf," Ever babbled.

Two more hard thrusts and Arsen was gone, his orgasm draining the last thoughts from his mind as he spilled inside Ever, leaving him feeling brain dead and loopy even as he continued to work his way in and out of Ever's body in short, aborted thrusts.

Ever moaned, long and low, his release painting the sofa cushions before he sagged forward, folding himself over the back of the couch once more, back heaving like he was fighting for air.

Arsen was, too. He collapsed on top of him, not wanting to pull free just yet, knowing soon his body would make the choice for him. That was when something caught his eye. He froze, frowning as he tried to make sense of the white, wispy clouds rolling along the edge of the bay doors.

Arsen blinked, then shook his head, like that might help clear up his confusion. *Dym.* Smoke. It was smoke. Actual smoke. Curling upwards towards the garage's high ceilings. He sucked in a breath as flames erupted, licking their way up the inside of the wooden panels with startling quickness.

Ohrenet! Fire. There was a fire. Even as he thought it, the shrill sound of the alarm began to sound. Ever screamed, then slammed his hands over his ears, panicked.

"Ever!" he shouted, hoping to pull him from his spiral long enough to get him to safety. He yanked their clothes back into place. "We have to go. Now."

Arsen pulled Ever to his feet, his blood pounding so hard it left a metallic taste in his mouth. The alarm made it feel like his eardrums would rupture at any moment. But he had to get Ever out. The amount of flammable liquid down there was enough to turn the entire building into a bomb, one that could take out not just them but everyone living next door.

"Come on, *Bystrey. Bystrey,*" he said uselessly, not giving Ever a choice as he gripped his wrist and dragged him towards the back of the apartment where a door led to a side entrance with a set of stairs that opened to the street. He was at the bottom tread when he realized his phone was still by his bedside table. He turned back, briefly considering running back to get it, but there was a hissing sound, then the sprinklers kicked on, dousing them in frigid water. Hopefully, it would be enough to keep the garage from going up in flames.

They burst through the door to find people already there and more coming from all over to watch the spectacle. Most of the people Arsen knew, but a few he didn't recognize. The acrid smoke was thicker outside, burning his eyes and nose and causing him to tug Ever into the street where the others stood. Where it was hypothetically safer.

Arsen was relieved to see most of the boys from next door all standing there, safe. But it did nothing to relieve the lump in his throat. Silas, the guy who was the youth center's current resident advisor of sorts, stumbled out the door with a large fire extinguisher, sweeping it over the flames now crawling up the brick towards the roof.

Arsen watched, dazed, as the flames died under a flood of white foam until only the smoke remained. It was only then he felt Ever's blunt nails digging into his arm where he held onto him.

Arsen looked down to check on him only to see Ever wasn't watching the fire but something—or someone— else across the street. Arsen's gaze followed, landing on two people, who stood there smirking, not even trying to hide. A man with greasy hair and ripped jeans smoked a cigarette. Beside him, Cherry wore a smug expression and not much else, her dress barely covering enough skin to escape an indecency charge.

"Who'd Jericho piss off?"

Arsen dragged his attention from the two across the street to address Silas's question. He dabbed at his brow with his sleeve, sweating from the heat. Not Jericho. Ever. Ever, who couldn't tear his gaze from across the street. Ever, who was trembling like a leaf beside him.

"Maybe it was an accident?" Arsen said, hedging.

Silas gave him a doubtful look but said nothing. The sound of sirens filled the air. When Arsen turned back to look at the two across the street, they'd vanished. But Ever continued to stare, like he was afraid to turn his back on them.

Arsen suddenly remembered something. "Can I use your phone, man?"

Silas's eyes went wide, but he nodded, patting himself until he found his phone in his hoodie pocket, handing it to Arsen.

He dialed Jericho's number. He answered before the phone had fully rang even once. "Hello?"

Arsen could tell he was awake. It sounded like he was shutting a car door. "Coe."

"Are you guys alright? We got an alert from the alarm company. Is it real? We're on our way. What happened?"

The smoke was dissipating somewhat, leaving only the newly charred doors behind. But not even the fire could hide the message left behind, scorched deep into the wood, likely by some kind of accelerant. He could hear people on the street murmuring and pointing to the words as they were revealed.

"Someone left us a message. In fire," Arsen said dully, staring at the words.

"Shit," Jericho snapped. "We'll be there soon. Don't say shit to the cops."

Arsen rolled his eyes. "Yeah, man. I know that."

Jericho made a frustrated sound. "I know. I know. Shit. How's the damage? Is it bad?"

"I don't think so. Silas had a fire extinguisher and put it out. I think the sprinklers deployed, though, so there might be water damage."

"And you said those sprinklers were a waste of money," Arsen heard Atticus say.

Arsen gathered Ever to him. "We're definitely going to need some new doors. And maybe a few more of those giant fans."

"As long as you're both okay," Jericho said, sounding grim but also relieved.

Arsen looked down at Ever once more. "We're alive."

That was about all Arsen could commit to.

Now, Ever really wasn't okay.

TWENTY

EVER

"'YOUR DEAD,'" ATTICUS READ, DEADPAN. "Y-O-U-R? If a cop wrote this, I weep for our justice system. They couldn't even get the grammar correct?"

Ever was only half-listening. They were at Jericho's and Atticus's condo with the others. Jericho had taken pictures for the insurance company and for their own evidence collection before they'd left. Those photos were now stuck to a white board propped up on the mantle in front of their television.

The boys had gathered immediately at Jericho's place. Arsen had tried to coax Ever to go to bed in the guest room, but he wasn't going anywhere. He might be useless, but he wasn't going to miss out on whatever Jericho wanted to discuss.

Instead, he sat on their insanely soft, overstuffed sofa, a blanket around his shoulders, while Levi and Nico sat on either side of him like sentries. Ever had his head on Levi's shoulder. He wanted it to be Arsen, but he hadn't stopped moving since the fire. He was too pissed. Ever could only follow with his eyes as he continued to pace.

Seven, Lake, Zane, Cree, and Felix had all opted for the

floor. The twins sat on the other side of the couch. Jericho and Atticus stood, also keeping an eye on Arsen. Ever was worried. He'd never seen Arsen this mad before. But he was fuming. His jaw was tight, his fists clenched. Ever wanted to apologize, but he didn't want to draw attention to himself, even if this was all his fault.

The sun was up, streaming through the large floor-to-ceiling windows. By the time they'd left Jericho's garage, the smoke had cleared, but the inside was uninhabitable. The fire department and local cops had left the charred remains of the doors behind, letting Jericho know they'd be there for him if he needed clean-up.

The neighborhood really did seem to love Jericho. Even if they couldn't publicly sanction his neighborhood watch, they appeared to respect that, sometimes, he could take care of things in a way they couldn't. Ever shuddered, looking at the scorch marks on the photos once more.

The Jamesville police clearly lacked the same dedication. That message was meant for him.

"You really think it was a cop who set the fire?" Zane asked. "That seems like a bold move."

"It was that Cherry girl and some guy," Ever mumbled, then returned to chewing on his lower lip. He could feel Arsen's eyes on him but was afraid to meet his gaze directly, preferring to just track his feet as he moved.

"Ever's right. I saw them, too. They were across the street watching. They wanted us to know it was them."

Cree made a disgusted noise. "At least they did some of the hard work for us. If Cherry's involved, that means it's

4Loco. That's one mystery solved."

"I thought they just slung fentanyl now? You would have thought they'd get the message after what happened to Mercy," Levi said, twirling a blow pop in his mouth, the candy clicking against his teeth noisily. Each movement displaced Ever's head slightly, but he didn't care. The warmth of Levi's skin bled through his t-shirt to Ever's cheek and hearing his voice so close was soothing.

Still, he couldn't stop himself from asking, "Mercy?"

"Our sister," Felix said, giving Jericho a sad smile. "She got trafficked by their crew a long time ago and then sold to some creepy research facility. But by the time we figured out what happened, it was a whole new regime in the gang. They had assured us they were out of that business. Said the cargo was too risky."

"Yeah, guns and dope bring slightly less heat than humans, even if it's not as lucrative," Lake said.

Ever's heart squeezed. "So, you guys just…let them go?" Ever asked.

"We're not like Atticus and the twins. We don't have an army of lawyers at our beck and call or a Calliope to fabricate fake paper trails. We have to be really careful," Nico said. "And, like we said, we punished the ones who were involved."

"If we killed every criminal in our neighborhood, it would be a massacre. Everyone does what they have to just to survive out there," Seven added.

"What he means is, we have to pick our battles," Cree said. "The cops turn a blind eye as long as we're discreet, but I don't think they'd be so forgiving if we dropped a whole crew."

"This is my fault," Ever said, closing his eyes. "None of this would have happened if I wasn't with you. Maybe I should—"

"Don't finish that sentence," Arsen said, voice hard enough to bring Ever's gaze to his, tears pooling in his eyes. "You're not going anywhere. *Anywhere*," he said again.

Ever sniffled, tears rolling down his cheeks. Levi put his arm around him. "You don't have to yell at him."

Arsen blanched. "What? Who is yelling? I'm not yelling." He looked at Ever. "I'm not yelling. I'm not mad. Well, I'm not mad at you. But I do need to kill someone…soon. Or I won't be held responsible for what I do next."

"Damn, firestarter. I didn't know you had it in you," Avi teased.

Jericho gave Ever a soft smile. The one he seemed to save just for him and small children. "We're long past letting you go, little one," he said. "This isn't on you. We should have known they weren't going to let it go after we took out that cop. They were just biding their time. Waiting for us to let our guard down."

Nico sighed. "It's very much an eye for an eye in our neighborhood."

"Yeah, but enough is enough."

All eyes swung to Atticus who was dressed the most casual Ever had ever seen him, wearing black joggers and a threadbare too-tight t-shirt that read JHH Grad Night. Ever didn't know what that meant, but it made it hard to ignore the way Atticus's muscles bulged from beneath the sleeves. Ever hadn't ever noticed how fit he was before.

"Freckles…" Jericho said.

Atticus shook his head, his expression full of the same barely-contained anger as Arsen's. Ever had never seen Atticus or Jericho mad. They both always seemed happy and level-headed.

But Atticus was vehement. "No. I get that you're all about caution, but this is too far. They went after our kids," he said, sweeping a hand over the group. "You told me when we got married that they were my responsibility, too. I don't like people messing with what's mine. Neither do you. Why aren't you angrier? They were perfectly fine burning down the business your father built. They tried to kill Arsen and Ever. What if they hadn't woken up in time?"

Ever flushed, hoping Arsen didn't feel the need to announce how they had very much not been asleep when the fire started. Though, they had been distracted. If Ever hadn't seduced Arsen on the sofa, who knows what might have happened.

"Is it just me or is Freckles kind of hot when he's being all psychotic?" Nico stage-whispered.

A few others made an affirmative noise that earned a glare from Jericho before he said, "I know but—"

"No," Asa said. "I can't believe these words are coming out of my mouth, but I agree with Atticus. They're throwing down the gauntlet. They are trying to intimidate us."

"There is no us," Jericho said. "This is our problem."

Atticus scoffed. "Nice try. You don't get to tell me I inherited your kids, but you get to disavow my asshole brothers. For better or worse, baby."

Avi snickered. "Baby?"

"We want to play too," Asa said. "Put us in, coach. We know how to send a strong…message to the right people."

"What does that mean?" Ever asked dully, eyes burning.

"It means we need a show of force," Felix said. "They think they can intimidate us, so we need to hit back harder. Felix locked eyes with his husband. "Way harder."

Avi nodded. "I get you're all about an eye for an eye, Jericho, but the Mulvaneys…we have our own philosophy."

"And what's that?" Seven asked, amused.

Avi smirked. "You take an eye, we're gonna take your whole fucking head."

Cree's eyes went wide, but then he shrugged. "Yeah, I respect it."

"They're right. We have to make a spectacle," Zane said. They all looked at him, seemingly surprised. "What? These groups only respect violence. Look at how the cartels handle things. Their kills are always over-the-top, horror movie level brutal. To send a message. Don't fuck with us. We need to make sure the 4Loco crew knows that messing with Jericho will fuck up their whole world."

Felix looked at Zane fondly. "I love you."

Zane beamed.

Ever didn't quite understand the dynamic with those two and the twins, but he was grateful for the help. Even though he still thought it would be better—safer—if he just left.

"No," Arsen said.

"No?" Levi asked, frowning. "No, what?"

"No show of force, no sending a message. I want them

dead. All of them. From the top to the lowest level fucking runner. All of them. Dead. I don't care if I go down for it. Ever won't feel safe until everyone involved is dead."

Everyone stared at Arsen with varying levels of surprise.

"Killing an entire gang…that's like fifteen people. You bring the cops into this, that's a lot of heat. And nobody is going to believe you did it alone."

Arsen shrugged. "I don't care. I want them all dead."

Ever should be more upset, he knew that. Maybe this was just more dissociation, but he didn't care if they killed everyone. He didn't care even a little. Arsen was right; he wouldn't feel safe until he saw their bodies with his own eyes.

He just wanted this over.

All eyes swung to Jericho, who rubbed his palms over his face. "You know what you're asking for, right?"

Arsen nodded.

Asa clapped his hands once. "I don't know about you guys, but I'm excited. I'm hoping you'll allow the Mulvaneys to provide the assist? If there's one thing Avi and I are good at, it's making a spectacle of a body."

"It's practically an art form by now," Avi agreed.

"Fuck," Jericho said, looking to Atticus.

Atticus shrugged. "They're right. Ever's not going to feel safe until they've all been put down. Just like Noah. It's just going to be a very intricate operation if we're going to start dropping cops."

Avi grinned. "Yes. We haven't had a good slaughter in a long time. It's time to remind these motherfuckers who they're messing with."

Jericho rolled his eyes. "Calm down, Al Capone," he said, pointing at Asa. "We have to tread lightly. They're not just your garden variety gangbangers. If the 4Loco crew got back into the trafficking game, there's more than one cop on the payroll. Otherwise, it wouldn't be worth the risk. We need to know how far this goes. We can't kill an entire police department, and this kind of thing only works if we cut off the head of the snake, not the tail."

He settled a hand on the back of Atticus's neck like he was trying to soothe him.

Atticus took out his phone and hit a button. "Callie, remember that back burner project? The human trafficking one? Yeah, they just tried to burn down Jericho's garage. With the kids in it—Yeah. Priority one." When he noticed the others staring at him with wide eyes, he said, "She'll have something for us in a few hours."

"Also," Felix said when Atticus hung up. "I don't want to harsh anyone's murder high, but we're gonna have to clear this with Papa Mulvaney."

The twins exchanged a look then smiled at Atticus in a way that gave Ever the creeps. "Call Aiden," they said in unison.

"If Aiden asks, he won't say no," Avi said.

"Yeah, Dad gives him anything he wants," Asa finished.

"See?" Zane said. "Problem solved."

Problem solved. Those words echoed in Ever's head. It was that easy. He just had to survive until then. Maybe by that point, he'd stop feeling so guilty.

It was noon, but it might as well have been midnight. Truth be told, with the blinds and curtains drawn, it was darker than any room Ever had been in for some time. It was dark like the closet. So dark it would have scared Ever if he wasn't numb to it—if it wasn't for the reassuring thumping of Arsen's heartbeat beneath his ear.

Was it bad that Ever hoped this numb feeling would linger? Jeremiah said therapy often triggered the brain to respond to trauma, and that feeling those emotions was part of the healing process. He wanted to get better. He did. But he was so tired. Tired of having no safe haven, even in sleep. All those things that had never bothered him once he'd gotten out...now they were there in spades—so many triggers he could have marked them off on a checklist. A person's voice. The smell of someone's cologne. Slamming doors. Food sizzling in a hot pan. Sometimes, like in his sleep, it was nothing at all. Just memories and blind panic.

But now, hours after a fire had almost killed them and burned down their house, Ever felt...blissfully numb, like someone had given his brain an anesthetic. And he didn't want the bad stuff to come back, no matter how much better he'd feel eventually. He would keep going to therapy. For Arsen. He'd do anything for him, but he hated it. So much.

They were supposed to be sleeping. It was only about one in the afternoon, but after lunch, Jericho had sent the other boys home and then shooed them off to bed, reminding them they'd been up for hours and would need to be well rested for what was to come.

Arsen hadn't said much since the meeting. In the shower,

he'd washed Ever's body and hair, had allowed Ever to do the same for him. He'd even toweled him off and helped him dress, all without uttering a single word. It left Ever feeling untethered, like he was bobbing in the ocean, getting farther away from shore.

He didn't like the ambiguity of Arsen's silence. If he was mad, he'd rather he yell at Ever or something. Hell, even hitting him would be better than the silence. It was rubbing Ever's nerves raw.

It didn't seem like he was mad at him, though. When they'd gotten under the covers, Arsen had pulled him in, arranged the sheets and comforter around them. He wasn't sleeping anymore than Ever was. He could tell by his breathing and the rapid beat of his heart. But still, he remained silent until Ever couldn't take it anymore.

"Are you mad at me?" Ever finally asked, hating how small his voice sounded.

Arsen's arms tightened around him briefly. "What? No. Why would you ever think that?"

Why wouldn't he think that? He'd done nothing but cause Arsen trouble since the day he'd rescued him. There were people who wanted to kill them, kill Arsen's friends, kill the only father figure he'd ever known...because of Ever. People had tried to burn them alive, had wanted Ever dead so badly they'd set Jericho's business on fire, knowing there was a potential for it to spread to the apartments next door.

"You've been really quiet."

"I'm quiet because I'm pissed off. Not at you," he hurried to add. "At them. At this situation. At the fact that we gave them a chance to walk away and they chose to engage. So, now, we have to retaliate. We have to hit back harder. These games make me feel…"

Ever tilted his head up. He was just barely able to see Arsen's silhouette in the shadows. "Make you feel…"

Arsen didn't answer right away. Ever wasn't sure he'd answer at all. He returned his head to Arsen's chest, letting the sound of his heart lull him. When Arsen did speak, the words vibrated through his chest beneath Ever's ear. "It makes me feel like my father."

Ever sucked in a sharp breath, jerking his head up to look at Arsen again. "You're *nothing* like him. Your father was a monster. He killed your mom because he was a bad person."

"I've killed people, too."

Ever shook his head vehemently. "You killed Jennika because *she* was a bad person. That's not the same. You kill to keep people safe."

Arsen threaded his fingers in Ever's hair, blunt nails scratching over his scalp in a way that made him feel tingly and sleepy. "Logically, I know that. But sitting there, in a room full of men who kill for fun as much as for necessity— hearing them throw around words like *retaliation* and *show of force* makes me feel like I'm no better than my mob enforcer father."

Ever's heart twisted. He didn't want to be the cause of Arsen's distress. Maybe it was selfish to want his abusers dead. Maybe things would die down on their own if they just gave it a chance. He'd be okay with that if it made Arsen happy. He only wanted Arsen happy.

"You don't have to do this," Ever said, squeezing Arsen in a hug. "We could let the Mulvaneys take care of it. Or we can just…wait and see. Maybe they'll think the fire was enough to scare me into silence," he finished quietly.

"'You're dead' is a pretty straightforward threat, *besenok*. Besides, I *do* want them dead. I want *all* of them dead for what they did to you. And when they're dead, I won't feel an ounce of pity or guilt. My father never felt that way, either. Sometimes, I wonder if my father and I are just two sides of the same coin."

Arsen was nothing like his father. His father was a monster who tried to make his son do his dirty work for him then somehow turned himself into the victim. Arsen was sweet and kind and gentle and beautiful. He was bright and colorful and…perfect. He was the best thing that ever happened to Ever.

Then he remembered something he'd read in a book once. "Isn't a coin's luck good or bad based on whether it lands heads or tails? That is something real, right?" Ever asked, face growing hot.

What other nineteen-year-old didn't know the difference between what was real and what was fake? His stomach churned, hoping Arsen didn't think he was stupid for not knowing something so simple.

"It's a superstition, but many people believe it," Arsen said. "I believe it."

Ever felt something unknot within him. "Well, if you're the same coin, then you're the good side and he's the bad. That's all that matters."

Arsen squeezed him, then kissed the top of his head. "I suppose you're right."

Ever's hand slid up under Arsen's t-shirt, tracing the ridges of his muscles. He wasn't trying to start anything, just suddenly needed to be as close to him as possible and the heat of his skin was hard to resist.

They lay in silence for a long while, still not sleeping. Ever's mind began to wander, a new different panic starting to seep into his thoughts. Panic about the future. He couldn't stop himself from asking, "What happens after?"

There was a long pause, then Arsen asked, "After what?"

Ever's heart tripped. "After they're all dead. What happens to us? To me?"

Arsen's answer came much faster this time. "Nothing happens. We go back to living our lives. You're going to get a new birth certificate and a new social security number, and then you can do or be anything you want."

That sounded like a fairy tale. A story much too good to be true. "Not everyone gets happily ever after."

"Maybe so, but I'll die trying to make sure you get yours," Arsen said.

"It's not that simple. A new name isn't going to teach me math. According to Jeremiah, I have the education of a sixth grader. I definitely can't do what I want."

"Jeremiah also said your IQ was above average and that you're super smart. Just because nobody ever taught you doesn't mean you can't be taught. I'm good at math and numbers, but I'm terrible at reading and history, and I went all the way through high school, barely making a C in my core classes. All those boring facts about dead people who only seemed to make things worse. I don't care about Poland in the thirties."

Ever smiled at the disgust in his voice. As if that lesson in particular had been the final straw to kill Arsen's love of history. "I just want to know what everybody else does."

"We're all just faking it, *besenok*. You know as much as the rest of us. The math they taught us in school? I've never needed it once. You can learn addition, subtraction, multiplication, and division. Everything else was a waste. None of us knew the important things like filing taxes or creating a budget. They didn't teach us how to be adults, just how to sit quietly in a room for eight hours for little to no reward. You're not nearly as behind as you think you are. But I can and will teach you whatever you want to know... except history. I won't do it."

Ever smiled. "Okay." Something else occurred to him then. "Will I get to keep my first name when I get my new birth certificate?"

"I don't see why not?" Arsen said. "In two days, there won't be enough people left from your old life to matter. Only us."

Ever dropped a kiss on Arsen's chest. "What about my last name? Will they just pick a random one for me?"

Arsen was quiet for a bit. "It doesn't matter what your last name is."

Ever frowned. "Why?"

"Because eventually it will be mine."

TWENTY-ONE

ARSEN

ARSEN GAVE EVER ONE LONG, last look, then kissed his hair and slipped out of bed. He would be upset when he woke to find Arsen gone, but it had taken so long to get Ever to sleep that Arsen just couldn't bring himself to wake him now that he was sleeping so hard, starfished on his stomach, mouth open, drooling adorably onto Jericho's guest pillow.

Arsen shoved his legs into the sweatpants he'd left pooled on the floor and pulled on a hoodie, not bothering to zip it up. The others were already gathered, scattered around the living room, likely waiting on him. They could wait another minute. He walked to the kitchen and poured himself a black coffee, taking a sip and wincing as the bitter liquid burned its way down.

After another sip, he shuffled back to the others, not sitting on the couch but on the arm, looking out over the sea of faces. Asa and Avi sat side by side on the couch with Seven, Lake, and Cree stuffed in beside them, not looking terribly upset by the close proximity.

Felix was on the floor in a pair of flowy black pants and a

tank top, cleaning his nails with a butterfly knife. Zane lay between his legs, head on his thigh. Arsen couldn't imagine trusting anyone enough to have a blade dangling over his head like that, but Zane was unfazed.

Other than Felix, everyone else looked like they'd crawled out of bed and headed straight to Jericho's living room. Most were in sweats and t-shirts. All but Levi. He wore his uniform from the convenience store, having likely come from work. Nico sat on the floor with Levi, staring up at Jericho and Atticus expectantly.

"What's the word?" Seven finally asked. "Did you talk to Daddy?"

Arsen's lips twitched as the others laughed. It was no secret that Seven had taken a liking to the Mulvaney patriarch. The fact that the man was married really hadn't slowed his crush any.

Atticus nodded. "I did. He brought up something that hadn't occurred to me yesterday during our initial meeting, though it should have. Traffickers have victims. Victims often stashed away in places where they are totally dependent on their captors."

Arsen's stomach clenched. Why hadn't that occurred to him? He felt sick at the thought of more kids just like Ever trapped somewhere, waiting to be sent into a life of misery and servitude. "Fuck."

"He's not willing to sanction his sons' participation until he knows if there are victims and where they're located to ensure their safety."

"So, what do we do?" Arsen asked.

"We need someone on the inside to talk," Felix said, like it was obvious.

Maybe it was. Arsen hadn't been on his game since the fire. Everything had happened so fast that he was still reeling. His mind just kept coming back to what might have happened had Ever not been awake.

"It's not that easy," Lake said.

He was right. Gangs only survived by loyalty and that loyalty came from fear. The potential for retaliation from their own members usually trumped getting the shit beat out of them by strangers.

Usually.

Arsen sat forward, dropping his elbows onto his knees before scrubbing his hands over his face. "These guys are hard to break, man. They get jumped into these gangs. They're beat half to death by their own crew."

Avi smirked. "I don't know. We're pretty persuasive when we need to be."

"I mean, the last 4Loco shitbag we tortured sang like a fucking canary as soon as a blowtorch was involved," Seven reminded him.

Arsen winced. That 4Loco shitbag had shown up to kill all of them and had almost gutted Arsen in the process. They'd gotten the jump on him, but just barely, and only because there were far more of them than him and he hadn't been prepared.

"Yeah, and I still have the scar to prove it," Arsen said, hand floating to his side without thought.

"Come on, firestarter," Asa teased. "You telling me you

don't want a little payback for these fuckers trying to flambé you and your boyfie?"

It wasn't about that. Of course, he wanted revenge. He wanted all of them dead. He'd said as much yesterday. He just didn't think it would be as easy to break one of them as the others thought.

Atticus cleared his throat. "The good news is Calliope has identified the cops involved. Luckily, there are only three with a paper trail leading back to the crew."

Arsen frowned. It had been less than a day. What had changed? "I thought you said she was having a hard time following the money to the cops being paid off?"

"That's 'cause the money was flowing in the opposite direction. We thought the gang was paying off the cops to look the other way, but it's the cops who are paying the gang to do their dirty work for them. Once she realized that, she was able to run them down pretty quickly despite their countermeasures," Atticus said.

"Who are they?" Cree asked.

Cree's adoptive father was a former cop. Now, he was a drug addict, hooked on prescription pills following an injury sustained in the line of duty. He'd been a piece of shit before the drugs, but he was worse now. And his mother spent all her time praying, as if that would somehow fix the problem she refused to believe existed. That was why Cree tried to never visit home. He didn't think of them as his real parents, anyway.

"Two detectives and the police chief," Jericho said, voice grim.

"You want us to take out a police chief?" Nico said, eyes wide. "People are going to be all over three dead cops, Coe. Four if you count the guy Arsen already took out."

"You think it's an accident that we haven't heard dick about that guy? No. Even if they do suspect he's dead, they're keeping it quiet because they can't afford questions, either," Asa said. "Trust us, this isn't our first rodeo."

"One missing cop isn't the same as three dead cops. And even if they don't find the body, nobody is going to ignore a missing police chief. Especially not with three other detectives gone, too."

"That's where I come in," Zane said, waving a hand lazily from the floor. "Calliope is going to make it look like one of the detectives 'anonymously' forwarded me information due to a guilty conscience, asking me to break the story about a mysterious cartel with a local gang and even the police chief in their pocket."

Arsen frowned. A cartel? For all the crime in their neighborhood, the cartel was blissfully far removed from them. Sure, they were likely somewhere in the 4Loco supply chain, but not close enough to be local.

"Do you think that will work? Blaming it on some random cartel activity?" Levi asked. "I mean, won't the cops try to find out who killed their people even if they were dirty?"

Zane scoffed. "You would think, but that's not what will happen. We've seen it a million times before."

"Yeah, they just need all the loose ends tied up in a believable story," Asa said.

Felix nodded. "We point them towards an easily digestible boogeyman, the Keyser Soze of our story, and we make these murders look like retaliation for ratting them out to Zane. A story he can spin any way he wants."

"Won't they investigate? Look for this mysterious cartel?" Arsen asked.

"Jamesville PD?" Felix asked. "Hardly. They lack the resources, and this is a bad look for them. They're going to be under fire for having four dirty cops in one small police force. The local politicians will want to bring in new management immediately and then pretend the whole thing never happened."

Zane nodded. "An investigation drags things out. They'll want to close this case and move on as quickly and quietly as possible. That's why we're giving them the cartel. It's an easy out. Nobody blinks about cartel violence and it's also not shocking when nobody is ever punished for the crime."

"What about the feds?" Lake asked. "Won't this draw their attention?"

Avi made a face. "Debatable. But if it does…we have connections. Let's dive off that bridge when we get to it."

"Yeah, right now, we need to find someone who will spill all the intimate details of the operation," Asa said. "Leave us to handle the cover-up."

"Who has that kind of information that would be willing to talk?" Atticus asked. "Not everyone in the gang can be privy to everything in their operation, no?"

"They're not a very big crew," Seven said. "I would imagine, when moving human cargo, you need all hands on deck. Even if they're taking women and children primarily, not everyone is gonna go without a fight. There are guards, lookouts, enforcers, handlers. They can't afford to not have everyone pull their weight."

Arsen glanced at the closed bedroom door, grateful Ever was still asleep. Hearing them so casually discuss the captivity of these victims would probably only make him feel worse, and he was already swimming in unnecessary guilt. None of this was his fault. But it had taken forever to convince him of that.

"So, who's the weakest link in the organization?" Lake asked.

"Cherry," Jericho said without hesitation, his expression grim.

Arsen's eyes went wide. But before he could say anything, Levi said, "What? Wait…you want us to torture a girl?"

He didn't sound opposed to the idea, more surprised. Torture wasn't really something they had to do in their line of work. At least, when they weren't teaming up with the Mulvaneys. Usually, their jobs were like Jennika. Quick and quiet. In and out. Torture wasn't something any of them enjoyed. At least…not as far as Arsen knew.

Jericho gave him a flat stare. "No, I want you to torture a gang member who happens to be a girl."

"Not to sound like a misogynist, but isn't she just…like, one of their girlfriends? What makes you think she'd know anything?" Nico asked.

"You wouldn't know she was anyone's girlfriend the way she was all over Arsen," Felix quipped.

"Yeah, but now, we know she was probably just finding excuses to come check us out for them," Cree said.

"Male or female, Cherry is the weakest link. She's easily recognizable, and she's been running with them since she was a teenager," Jericho said. "She most likely knows where the bodies are buried, literally and metaphorically."

"Couldn't she be one of their victims?" Nico asked. "Like, maybe she was trafficked, too. Especially if she started running with them in high school. She definitely used to be a pro at one point."

Nobody asked how Nico knew that. He had intimate knowledge of the sex workers in the area and not because he liked to frequent their establishments. Nico's mom was an exotic dancer and an escort when he was a kid. He had a soft spot for the industry.

Seven sighed. "I don't know, man. Torturing a girl—especially one who potentially used to be a victim themselves? That feels wrong."

"Know what happens when those girls age out?" Felix asked. "They become recruiters. Conning people like my sister into falling into their trap so they can go on to be victims. I have no sympathy."

"If you guys don't want to do it, we will," Asa said, sounding unbothered. "My brothers and I don't give a shit what they got going on in their pants. We're equal opportunity monsters. If she wants to play with the bad guys, she gets to suffer the consequences."

Avi shrugged. "Yeah, if she helps snatch children from their homes and sells them to people like Jennika, then fuck her. She crossed the line. Every bad guy has their villain origin story. We don't really give a fuck. If they meet the rules, we get to torture and kill them. That's just how it is."

Arsen wasn't particularly excited about the prospect of torturing anyone, male or female. But if there were other victims—ones they could leave in danger by taking out an entire crew in one go—Arsen would do what he had to do. Ever was priority number one. If the only way he felt safe was them killing everyone from the pawns to the king, Arsen would clear the whole chessboard. He didn't care who he had to hurt.

"But she knows we know it was her who set the fire. It's hardly like we can give her a call and ask her if she wants to go for coffee," Atticus reminded them.

"She knows you. She doesn't know us," Avi said. "They have to have a base of operation, no?"

"That dive bar on 5th with the pool tables. The one that's open 'til five a.m. I walk past it on my way home from the night shift. They're always hanging out on the corner there," Levi said, his irritation obvious. "I'm sure they're slinging dope out of there, too. They have to maintain that cover even if they've moved onto more lucrative revenue streams."

Asa looked at Avi and grinned. "Wanna go play some pool?"

"You think these people won't know who you are?" Atticus asked.

Jericho gave Atticus a fond smile. "I didn't know who you were until Arsen hunted you down for me. Your names are far more familiar than your faces. Especially in our neighborhood. Nobody expects a Mulvaney around there."

Asa and Avi shrugged. "Great. So, we'll acquire the target, get the info, and let you know what we find."

"Uh-uh," Arsen said. "No way you're doing this without me."

"Or me," Felix said.

"Or us," Lake said, swinging his finger between the others.

"Or me."

Everyone turned to see Ever standing in the doorway of the bedroom, still looking sleep dazed. Sometimes, he looked like a lost little boy.

Arsen shook his head. No way were they compounding on Ever's trauma. "No, *besenok*. You're not coming with us for this."

Ever stared at him. "I am. You guys are doing this for me. I'm going to be there."

"You really want to watch us torture someone, gumdrop?" Felix asked.

Ever's gaze flicked to Felix, his expression the coldest Arsen had ever seen it. "Yeah. I really, really do."

Avi clapped his hands together, delighted. "Sounds like a full house. We'll be in touch when we have her and a location that will accommodate the whole family."

TWENTY-TWO

EVER

THE VENUE THEY CHOSE WAS far from the city—a large concrete monstrosity set in the middle of a large parking lot that formed an imposing silhouette in the darkness. They'd driven through a dozen desolate streets to get there.

Ever hated the place on sight. Something about it made him feel this staggering sense of dread deep in his belly. He didn't say that, though. It had been hard enough getting Arsen to agree to let him come along.

The door of the facility was heavy iron, and it made a horrible racket when Arsen and Seven pulled it open. Arsen said the whole building belonged to the Mulvaneys—one of several properties purchased behind a wall of paperwork and left empty for their personal use.

As they entered, Ever's head was on a swivel, taking in rust-colored stains on the concrete floors and walls and large, industrial machines that were as baffling as they were terrifying. There were only windows along the very top of the two-story building, leaving it feeling a little like a tomb. Large plastic sheeting separated the rooms, but provided just enough privacy to make it feel like something terrifying lurked around every corner.

"What is this place?" Ever asked, voice barely above a whisper, half afraid he might wake whatever ghosts still lingered there.

"Meat-packing plant," Arsen answered at the same time Felix said, "A slaughterhouse."

Slaughterhouse? "What's a slaughterhouse?"

"It's where they kill and butcher animals for meat," Felix said. "Only now, we use it to butcher bad guys."

Felix, Lake, and Seven had cleared their schedule when the call came in, refusing to be left behind. Levi and Nico had gotten stuck at work. Cree had opted out of the torture. Ever didn't know him well, but he liked him. He was a gentle, quiet soul.

Arsen fixed Felix with a pissy look. Felix shrugged. "What? It is. Why are you trying to coddle him? He's about to watch us torture a girl to death. I think we're past the kid gloves. No?"

Ever's stomach churned. Arsen didn't want him there, he'd made that really clear. But he'd been overruled, first by Jericho then by Atticus, who assured him that Ever was entitled to help punish his abusers and that, in the end, it would be cathartic. Ever hoped they were right. At the moment, he just didn't want to throw up. There was a weird scent in the air, like iron and rot, and it was making him sick.

Asa popped his head around a corner and waved them back through the clear flaps. Ever held back a shudder as he noticed strange dark spots on the cold plastic as they passed through it. They ended up in a large tiled room filled with stainless steel counters and a large table. Ever's eyes went to the large drain on the floor beneath it.

Cherry was on that table, eyes darting around, but otherwise, she was perfectly still. She was naked, though someone had used plastic to cover her head, chest, and hips. When Avi saw them staring, he waved a hand over her. "Like it? Very Dexter-like, no?"

Ever didn't know who Dexter was or why he strapped people to tables, but he couldn't imagine it was for anything good. He looked at the others, who loitered around the room. Jericho and Atticus stood off to the side, a large brown bag open beside them. Seven went to stand with them. Lake and Felix moved closer to Cherry on the table.

"What's happening? Where am I? Why can't I move?" Cherry asked in rapid succession.

It was only then that Ever realized she couldn't move her head. Was she just now starting to realize her predicament?

Atticus glanced up from his phone. "I've given you a paralytic. Just from the neck down, of course. We need you to be able to talk."

"And scream," Asa added, unrolling a black cloth, revealing a bunch of wicked-looking weapons that made Ever's stomach swoop.

The twins and Atticus were so…calm. Felix and Jericho, too. They looked almost…bored. Ever didn't know how to wrap his head around it. How could these people be the same people who had helped him at every turn? How could they be so composed?

"You should be thanking us," Avi said. "At least you can still blink." He hovered over her, adding, "For now. If you don't tell us what we want to know, I have these bad boys here." He held up two strangely shaped metal contraptions. "These hold your eyelids open. Do you know what happens when you can't blink?"

Ever's eyes burned like it was him on the table. He didn't know how anyone could put those things in someone's eyes and he didn't want to know. Apparently, he wasn't alone.

Seven shuddered. "Aw, man. I hate eyeball stuff."

Asa ignored Seven, clearly not done tormenting Cherry. "It only takes about four minutes of not blinking for you to be in agony. In another hour, you'd be going crazy not just from the pain but from the constant signal from your brain begging you to blink. After a few hours, things get really gruesome… Wanna hear about it? Or maybe we should just let you see for yourself."

Avi snorted, putting his face in her line of sight. "*See* for yourself…get it?"

"What the fuck is happening?" she cried, a broken sob ripping from her lips. A lump formed in Ever's throat, and he regretted his decision to attend almost immediately. "I didn't do anything. You got the wrong person."

"Who said you did anything? Guilty conscience?" Felix asked.

"Yeah, maybe we just like to torture people for fun?" Avi quipped. He picked up a scalpel and nicked her forehead, smiling when she hissed and a drop of blood beaded from the wound. "Did you ever think about that?" he tsked.

"No, 'cause you only think about yourself."

Ever's gaze followed the drop of blood down the bridge of her nose, wincing as it pooled in her left eye, making it look eerily blue. She caught Ever's gaze. "Let me go. Please? I'll do anything."

Ever caught his bottom lip between his teeth, gnawing on it. Maybe this was a bad idea. Arsen's hand caught him under the chin, pulling his focus. "Why don't you go stand with Seven?"

Ever nodded, floating closer to the taller boy.

"Please," Cherry begged again, louder this time.

"Offer declined," Atticus said drolly. "You're not getting out of this, so you can do away with the hysterics. They're not going to sway us. We don't care how much you cry. Hell, my brothers actually kind of like it."

Ever's jaw dropped as Cherry's whole demeanor changed. She immediately stopped crying, her face going from terrified to sullen fast enough to give him whiplash. "You people are fucking insane," she snapped.

"Tell us something we don't know," Asa said, waving a hand.

"How about that you guys are already dead. My crew will fuck you up when they hear about this," Cherry promised.

"Sure, Jan," Lake said, voice dripping with sarcasm.

Ever didn't know who Jan was, either. It was like he was in a play where nobody had given him the script.

"I want to play, too," Felix said. Ever's eyes went wide as Felix hopped up on the table in one graceful move, straddling Cherry's hips. "Hey, girl."

Avi handed him a small box.

She sneered at him. "What are you going to do? Give me a makeover?"

Goosebumps erupted along Ever's skin as Felix's smile widened. He opened the box. Ever's mouth went dry as he watched him pluck small objects from the box, placing each one over his fingers. They looked like...claws. Metal claws.

Felix locked eyes with her. "Funny you should say that..." He swiped two fingers across her face, quick as a snake, laughing when blood flowed down her cheeks. "Oh, look at that... You look better already."

Real fear crept into Cherry's eyes then. Not the fake hysterics from moments before, but real actual terror. "I-Is this because of the fire?" she stuttered. "We knew it wouldn't kill you. We knew there was an alarm. It was just to get your attention."

Felix leaned over her, squeezing her bloody face, the claws digging into her skin. "Mission accomplished, bitch."

"Yeah, I think it's safe to say you have our unwavering focus," Seven said from his spot beside Atticus.

Ever made a sound of frustration. When were they going to ask their questions? He'd just do it himself. When Ever stepped into her line of sight, she blinked rapidly, like she was unable to process how he was a part of this. "Are there others?" he asked point-blank.

"Other what?" she snapped, giving him that dismissive once-over she had the day they'd first met.

Except, this time, Ever had the upper hand. He ignored her nasty look, his voice calm and quiet. "Other victims.

Like me. Where are they?"

She rolled her eyes but said nothing.

"Roll your eyes at him again and I'll pluck them from your skull and give them to him as a Christmas present," Felix promised.

"You… You're not really going to hurt me," she said, her voice wavering. "If you do, my crew will kill you. All of you."

Jericho laughed, speaking for the first time. "When we're done, there won't be enough left of your crew to even realize you're missing."

"And we're most definitely going to hurt you," Avi said coldly. "How much and for how long depends entirely on you."

Asa nodded. "You have a lot of sins to atone for, Cherry." He turned, grabbing something that looked like a saw. "Don't make me start sawing off body parts. That paralytic only keeps you still. You'll still feel every agonizing cut. And I won't make it quick."

Ever's stomach lurched. If Asa cut off any part of her, he was definitely going to throw up. Probably a lot. And that would be really embarrassing after begging them to let him come. He prayed she had some sense of self-preservation.

Cherry looked like she was going to throw up, too. "Why should I talk? You're just going to kill me, anyway."

"You got us there," Atticus said, stepping forward. He pulled something from his pocket. A syringe. "But if you tell us what we want to know, I give you this injection and you just drift off to sleep and never wake up."

"Conversely," Lake said, his tone frigid, "you could die

screaming. Option A sounds better to me."

Ever tried again. "Are there other victims out there? Waiting to be…sold?"

Cherry's gaze drifted away from him to stare at the high ceiling overhead.

Asa shrugged. "Okay, we gave you a chance…" He picked up her arm, running a finger along her wrist. "I'm going to start here. Then my brother is going to use that torch over there to cauterize the wound. The pain might knock you out. But my other brother—the doctor—has this handy, dandy little med box that will allow us to wake you right back up. So, we can do this over and over and over…"

"Tick-tock, Cherry," Jericho said. "We're losing our patience."

Ever closed his eyes, willing Cherry to make the right choice. He really didn't want anyone to lose a limb.

"I'm not a snitch," she said meekly.

Ever leaned over her, forcing his voice to be as cold and unfeeling as the others' had been. "You're going to die. And so will all your friends. Soon, there won't be anybody left to care if you talked or not."

Ever could see Arsen's shocked expression in his periphery, but he forced himself to keep looking at her. He needed her to understand there was only one choice and that was to talk. "Look. I don't want them to torture you, but I won't stop them, either. Think about that."

Ever could smell the sour stench of Cherry's fear. Her face was a mask of frustration as she seemed to truly understand there was no way out of it. "I knew when we found that bitch dead that you were going to be trouble. They didn't believe me," she said. "They said you'd just disappear. But I knew better."

"Do you want a gold star?" Lake asked.

Silence stretched until it grew uncomfortable. Arsen's lip curled in disgust. He looked at Asa. "Just do it. She's clearly not going to talk."

Avi grinned then grabbed the torch on the table, showing it to them as a blue flame erupted from the tip. "I'm ready. Let's go." He leaned into Cherry's space. "I want to warn you, burning flesh smells a little like barbeque. It can be kind of disconcerting when it's your own."

With that, he nodded towards Asa, who placed the teeth of the saw against her wrist.

"Wait!" Cherry shouted. "Wait…" she said again, softer. "I'll talk. What…what do you want to know?"

"Where do they keep their cargo?" Jericho asked. "We know there are other victims."

Cherry's eyes shut slowly, and for one terrifying moment, Ever thought she was going to change her mind. Then she said, "There's a shipping container on an empty piece of property about forty minutes outside the city. We keep them there."

A shock rocked Ever's whole body. There really were more people like him. He'd known it on some level, but to hear her say it was…too much. His heart was hammering, blood rushing in his ears. *There were others. There were others.* "How many?" Ever muttered. When Cherry stayed silent, he grabbed her bloody face. "How many?" he screamed.

"How many? How many?"

"Ever…" Arsen said, pulling him away from the table, even as he tried to get back to her. He wanted to hear her say it. He needed to hear her admit there were more.

"A handful!" she shouted. "The others have already been placed. And don't ask me who because nobody tracks that shit. There are a few kids we picked up online and two girls they brought over from Vietnam."

"Picked up online?" Ever echoed. "What does that mean?"

"Kids are easy to come by," she said. "There's nobody keeping tabs on them. We buy them from re-homing sites, out the back door of immigration camps. Hell, some parents will sell them flat out for a small fee. And nobody even looks for the foster kids once they're placed. There just aren't enough employees, and half the ones there are willing to look the other way for a price. Kids are disposable."

"Is that how you got me?" Ever asked, breathless. "Someone just gave me away?"

She turned dull eyes on him. "Don't blame that on me. You were before our time. We only got involved after half of the original crew was locked up on gun running charges. Those cops hate doing their own dirty work. We didn't want the heat, either, but they reminded us that working with the cops was better than making enemies of them. Besides, they paid well."

"Where does your crew hang when they're not at that bar?"

"That house on 9th and Hoover. The pink one with the green shutters. But you won't find them there. They're at the cabin. They're making the exchange tomorrow."

"The exchange?" Jericho asked. "What exchange?"

She rolled her eyes. "The exchange, the sale. Whatever you want to call it. The cops know you took out Detective Douche. They're worried you're onto them. They're dumping the cargo off on some wannabe Hell's Angel types in exchange for fentanyl, which is much easier to hide than a bunch of whining, screaming brats and hysterical girls."

"They're going to just…pass them off to a biker gang? What will they do with them?" Arsen asked.

"The girls, they'll turn out, and the kids, they'll probably sell. Sometimes, they keep them. Just depends."

Ever wanted to scream. He wanted to grab that knife off the table and stab it into her heart. How could she say something like that? Like they didn't even matter? Like they weren't even people? "Don't you care at all?"

"You really are just a tiny baby still. Maybe she should have taken you out of that house every now and again. Even after everything she did to you, you really still think there are good people in the world? There are only two kinds of people. The victims and the victors. You just have to decide what team you're on. I got tired of being a victim so I did what I had to do to survive. I can't worry about other people. Only myself. You worry about other people and the world will eat you alive."

"Wow," Asa said. "I thought I was cynical."

"Just kill me already," she muttered. "I gave you what you wanted."

Atticus stepped forward. "Not quite yet. What happens

next is this: you're going to tell me all the painstaking details of this exchange, and then you can die. Got it?"

"Whatever," she muttered.

Ever turned to Arsen, his hands landing on his chest, voice pleading. "I want to go home now. Can we go home now?"

Arsen nodded, kissing his head. "Yeah, *besenok*. We can go home."

TWENTY-THREE

ARSEN

"WE GO IN AT DAWN," Jericho said, earning a groan from the boys.

"Aw, man. I got off work at three a.m. I'm not going to be raid ready in an hour," Levi complained.

"The exchange is being made tomorrow afternoon. We have to go before then or we run the risk of not rescuing them in time."

Atticus rolled his eyes. "And it's the only way to assure *we* don't get surprised. According to Cherry, these idiots are out there right now getting drunk and partying. That means most of them will be sleeping or unconscious at dawn, and even if there's a guard, they won't be on their game. With this many targets, we have to think logically."

Levi huffed. "I don't wanna think logically. I want to have one day where I can sleep more than an hour," he whined dramatically.

"You don't have to go," Ever said softly from where he sat smooshed between Levi and Arsen on the couch. "You can sleep. I'm sure the others can do it." Ever looked at the others with wide eyes. "Right?"

They all smirked as Levi's face fell. "What? No. No, it's cool. I was…I was just saying. It's all fine. I'm good," he finished in a barely-there mumble.

Ever gave him a huge smile, then hugged Levi's arm. Arsen watched as his grumpy, tatted friend flushed red to the tips of his ears, staring at the floor. Arsen almost felt bad for him. He didn't know when or how, but Ever had won Levi over and then some. He was borderline obsessed. He might be worried if Ever showed anything but brotherly affection towards Levi. But he never did. He only saw Arsen.

"We go in shock and awe style, catch them off guard, and start shooting immediately," Jericho said. "Target acquired. Target eliminated. No second-guessing. No hesitation. We know they're armed. And stupid. You'll have vests thanks to Atticus, but that's not going to protect your head."

"But…I thought we needed to make this look like a cartel killing?" Nico asked.

"That's our job," Asa said. "You drop 'em, we'll ugly 'em up. Make 'em look real gruesome for the crime scene photos. Don't you worry."

Ever stared at Asa hard. "You really like what you do, huh?"

Arsen's stomach churned. Some small part of him worried that, after what they'd done to Cherry yesterday and what they planned on doing to others in only a few hours, this was too much for Ever. He was too soft, too sweet. He wasn't meant for a world of blood and guts. Maybe he'd leave now that he'd seen who Arsen really was.

"It's my passion," Asa teased, not even a little ashamed.

Felix rolled his eyes, looking at his husband. "Can you shut him up before he scares the baby?"

But before Avi could even think to say anything, Ever sighed. "I wish I had a passion," he said wistfully, blushing when the others laughed. "What?"

Arsen's heart swelled. Ever was a constant surprise, as sweet and pure and angelic as the day he'd found him, but he was also somewhat feral, prone to biting, swearing, and was horny almost around the clock. It was like Arsen had cooked him up in a lab. He was perfect.

"You're just very cute, *besenok*," Arsen assured him, giving all of them a glare that told them not to laugh at his boyfriend, even if Arsen kind of wanted to laugh, too.

Ever put so much pressure on himself to go from captive to productive member of society, as if that was an easy thing for any of them to do, much less him. When this was finally settled, Arsen was going to sit down with Ever and Jericho and make a plan for Ever's future. It was clear he wouldn't feel settled until he was working towards some kind of goal, even if Arsen thought his only goal should be healing. Maybe a plan was what he needed to start that process?

"You have your whole life to figure that out," Jericho promised. "In the meantime, let's get back to the plan. Thomas thinks you guys taking out the cops is too much heat"—a bunch of groans sounded, but Jericho shut them up with a single arched brow—"on such short notice. He's sending Adam and whichever Mulvaney is free to take them out as we speak. They have the money and the resources to make it look like they were never there. Besides, it's easier to divide and conquer."

"I hope they send August," Seven said. "Imagine what he'd do to those bodies…and he won't even wait until they're dead."

"To be fair, we're only waiting until they're dead so you guys can play, too," Avi said, then looked at Ever. "I think chipmunk has had enough of the blood and guts for now."

"He won't be there so it doesn't matter," Arsen said.

Ever's gaze snapped to his. "What? No way. I'm going."

Arsen's mouth fell open, and he stared at Ever for a full thirty seconds before he realized he wasn't verbalizing any of the words bouncing around in his head. He couldn't help it, though. His heart hammered against his ribcage hard enough to steal his breath. "Absolutely not. There are too many things that can go wrong. You could get shot, you could get taken again. No. No way. I won't allow it."

Nico snickered. "You won't allow it? Okay."

Ever's eyes went wide, and, for a split second, Arsen thought he might cry. Then Felix was behind him on the couch, running sharp nails through his hair. "You don't have to listen to him, gumdrop. He's not the boss of you."

Ever's eyelids flickered as he arched into the touch, practically purring like a cat. He really was touch-starved. Good thing because his friends clearly had no fucking boundaries. Besides, none of that was the point. "I'm not saying I'm your…boss. I'm saying I can't think straight if I have to worry about where you are the whole time? Please, just…sit this one out."

Felix's petting wasn't enough to keep Ever from glaring at him, chin thrust forward, arms crossing. "No. I'm going." His voice wobbled slightly. "I-I need to see for myself."

"Wasn't Cherry enough?" Arsen begged, feeling sick.

How was he supposed to concentrate knowing Ever was in danger? This wasn't fair. It would be like trying to do this with one of his arms tied behind his back.

"Okay, enough," Jericho said. "Ever, you can come, but you wait where we put you. Atticus will keep you company. Once they're all dead"—he looked at Asa and Avi in turn—"but *before* we start carving up bodies, you can bring Ever in so he can see for himself."

Ever frowned then shook his head. "I don't care about them. I never want to see them again. I care about the people locked in that shipping container. Do you know how bad it probably is in there? No bathroom. No ventilation. No blankets or heat. They might not even have food or water. They don't know what happened, or why they're there, or if anyone is coming to save them. I just…I just need to see for myself that they're all okay. That they're all…alive."

All eyes went to Arsen. How was he supposed to argue with that? He wasn't a fucking monster. "Fine. But you have to stay with Atticus. Promise?"

Ever nodded.

Jericho looked at Ever. "I can't have Arsen distracted or he'll be a liability. Got it?"

Ever nodded. "Yeah, okay."

"Good," Atticus said. "We leave soon. Everyone start getting ready."

There was a pause, then—

"Why are there so many blankets here?" Seven muttered, looking around at the assortment stuffed in baskets and thrown over the sofa and chairs.

"Yeah, do you guys get cold a lot or something?" Nico asked.

Atticus turned red, looking to his husband like he was asking for help. When Jericho just smirked at him, he said, "I hired a decorator. She was…clearly a fan of the look. Neither of us cared enough to change it."

"Maybe she just noticed you're pale enough to burn indoors and wanted you to be able to cover up at the first touch of the sun's rays," Avi said.

Atticus glowered at his brothers. "Nobody fucking likes you."

Nico elbowed Asa. "I like you, man. I think you're hilarious."

"Aw, thanks, I think you're neat, too."

"Traitor," Atticus muttered. "You're all traitors."

Jericho chuckled. "Enough chit-chat. Let's do this."

Everyone grumbled but nodded. "Yeah, yeah."

The sun was just starting to peek over the horizon when they parked their cars about a mile down the road from their destination at a place that rented tiny fishing cabins. The air was slightly chilled, a low layer of fog making their job harder. Arsen kept Ever in front of him the whole way, holding onto his arm with his free hand, keeping him upright as he stumbled over roots and knotted vines.

When they found the cabin, they stayed hidden, hunkered down behind the trees while Jericho scanned the place with binoculars. "It's quiet. Not even a guard on duty. Morons."

He put the binoculars back and pulled out a strange contraption, pointing it at the side of the house.

"What is that?" Arsen asked quietly.

"Think of it like x-ray vision," Atticus said. "It can tell us where they are in the house by their heat signature."

"Man, you guys have the best toys," Levi muttered, then yawned loud enough for his jaw to snap.

It was true. Whenever they involved the Mulvaneys in their jobs, they always came with Kevlar vests, weapons not even available on the market, and toys that looked like something straight out of a spy movie. It was helpful but also somewhat intimidating.

Arsen held Ever against him, resting his chin on his head. Ever was tense, his eyes locked on the only thing he cared about. The shipping container was barely visible from their current location, but it was clearly the one Cherry mentioned. It looked more like a storage unit or a shed, but the locks were so big Arsen could observe them without effort even at that distance.

They'd brought bolt cutters for that reason. Atticus had insisted, saying the last time they'd done a rescue mission like this there'd been a struggle to find a way to unlock the door without hurting anybody. Ever held the bolt cutters in a death grip, like he was taking his one job very seriously.

Arsen's mouth was dry, his adrenaline through the roof. These large-scale jobs were always way more intense than taking out a single bad guy…or woman. There was so much room for something—anything—to go wrong. And now, he had Ever.

"They're all in there," Jericho said. "There are three bodies lying prone in one room at the back. Bedroom, most likely. Another two bodies with a lesser heat signature, also prone. Chances are we got another bedroom. There are two sitting up in the front room and several on the floor. If they weren't all glowing hot, I'd say someone beat us to it with how still they are."

"You're going in two teams. Felix, Seven, Nico, and Avi take the back, Arsen, Lake, and Asa take the front with me. Head on a fucking swivel. We make no mistakes. Comms check."

They all checked to make sure they could be heard by the device in their ears, then parted into their own groups. Arsen didn't want to leave Ever there, so close to the action, even though he knew he was out of the line of fire. He turned him around and gave him a hard kiss, then pulled ear plugs from his pocket, handing them to Ever, who frowned at them.

"The gunfire will be loud. They go in your ears," Atticus supplied.

Oh, right. How would Ever know that? Arsen shook his head, then helped Ever put the plugs in, then took his cat headphones from his bag and gently placed them over his ears. "Please, be safe, *besenok*."

Ever nodded, then cupped his face, pulling him down for a much longer kiss. "Hurry back, Senya."

A shiver of lust rolled over him. Now was most definitely not the time, but hearing Ever call him that was still a novelty, still excited him. He hoped that never went away.

"Ready?" Jericho asked. They all nodded, weapons at the ready. "We go on my mark."

Arsen, Jericho, Asa, and Lake jogged quietly across the brown and dying lawn. In Jericho's hands was a SWAT-issued battering ram—identical to the one Avi carried around the back. There was no way the door would stand up against that.

The sound of gravel crunching under their boots sounded as loud as the gunfire that was about to ensue. He could only hope they were all too liquor-soaked to hear them coming.

Once they were gathered at the front door, he glanced back at Ever, who looked so small beside Atticus. He was doing this for him.

"We breach on three," Jericho whispered into the mic.

"Uh…" Avi said.

"Yeah?" Jericho said in a harsh whisper.

"Like one, two, and then we breach on three, or one, two, three, then go?"

There were snickers of laughter in Arsen's ears, but it did nothing to quell the turmoil. He just wanted this over with.

"I said *on* three not *after* three," Jericho said, irritated.

"Just checking, jeez," came Avi's own grumble.

"One."

Arsen raised his gun, taking a deep breath and letting it out, then cracking his neck.

"Two."

A wave of perfect calmness swept over him as he narrowed his focus down to the single task at hand.

"Three."

The battering rams hit the door in sync, creating a bomb-like boom as the wood splintered in protest. Jericho kicked the ruined door in just as the first shot rang out from the back. Arsen leveled his gun at a man scrambling for the weapon tucked in his belt and pulled the trigger, a perfect hole forming in his left temple as blood spattered on the wall and he collapsed in a heap.

It was a slaughter. Totally unfair in every conceivable way. Arsen aimed and fired, aimed and fired, watching with some satisfaction as each body hit the floor.

"Save some for the rest of us," Asa muttered in the mic as he took out two men in rapid succession.

It was all happening so fast but not in Arsen's head. Whenever he was in these situations, it was like time slowed down to give him an advantage, even though he knew it was simply the body's response to stress.

Asa pulled a vicious knife from his belt. It looked like something out of a horror movie. "You want a picture for the boy first or are we good?"

Arsen's stomach churned. "Do what you have to do, man."

Asa's laugh was chilling as he grabbed a man by the hair, taking the knife across his neck in one smooth motion.

Arsen watched the man's skin part before turning away. There was a sick, squelching sound but Arsen couldn't bring himself to look.

"Fuck!" Lake shouted, sounding pissed. "That fucker shot me."

"You let them get the jump on you?"

"Seven shot me."

"You literally jumped in front of my gun, bro. You shot yourself."

"How bad is it?" Jericho asked.

"It's bleeding pretty bad. It might have hit an artery."

"Fuck!" Jericho shouted. "We need you, Freckles."

Arsen's eyes went wide. "We can't leave Ever out there alone."

"You want him in here? With this?"

Arsen looked at the horror show Asa was creating in the living room. "God, no."

"He'll be fine. In about fifteen minutes, you can take him to open that shipping container and be the hero."

Atticus busted through the door. "Where is he?"

"Back room," Seven called. "It's his right thigh."

TWENTY-FOUR

EVER

EVER COULD HEAR NOTHING BUT the sound of his own labored breathing. It sounded like he'd run a marathon, even though he was only sitting there, waiting for the others to finish slaughtering people in his name. A tiny giggle escaped him, drawing Atticus's attention away from his granola bar.

Ever stifled the next laugh threatening to bubble up from some place deep inside him. Why was he laughing? None of this was funny. People were dying. Ever should care about that. He should feel something. Did it make him a bad person that he didn't?

He was just numb. That perfect, lovely numbness he usually only got from trauma. But this didn't feel traumatic. It was...exhilarating. His heart was pounding, and his breath sounded like rushing water in his ears.

Maybe this was why people jumped out of airplanes or climbed mountains without ropes. Maybe it wasn't trauma that caused the numbness but the adrenaline that came from the danger? Even with his earplugs and headphones, as soon as the first shot was fired, his stomach clenched. It sounded muffled, like he was hearing it from underwater, but he heard it nonetheless.

The gunfire sounded like fireworks. The ones he'd seen kids playing with that made a cracking sound when you lit one end. Then they would just...*pop, pop, pop*. Then silence.

Ever looked at Atticus, who seemed unfazed. Until he didn't. He spoke, but not to Ever. To someone in the house talking to him from that little button in his ear. The world was a strange place, and Ever didn't think he'd ever fully understand the technology available, but if it helped keep Arsen safe, he was grateful for it.

Atticus gently removed Ever's headphones. "Stay here. Don't move. Lake is hurt. I need to go help."

He didn't give Ever any time to process that information, just started to run across the lawn with his backpack in hand. Ever pulled the earplugs free, grateful for the almost eerie silence that followed. Until he realized it wasn't silent.

At first, he thought it was an animal—this high-pitched sort of keening wail, like it was injured. Ever frowned, moving towards the sound without thought, making sure he stayed behind the cover of the treeline. The closer he got, the louder the sound grew, until it dawned on him that it wasn't an animal at all, but a baby. A human baby, crying hysterically.

Ever looked back to the house, then at the shipping container where the sound came from. There was a baby in there. An actual baby. There was no more gunfire. It had to be safe to open the doors. What if that baby was alone? No. Cherry had said there were two women and other children in there. He couldn't leave them in there.

He took a deep breath, then let it out slowly, before marching across the lawn to the container, lining up the bolt cutters against the lock and squeezing. Nothing happened. He tried again. And again. But he wasn't strong enough.

The people inside heard him attempting to open the doors. They were banging on the metal sides, speaking in a language Ever didn't understand. A knot formed in his throat, tears pricking his eyes as he tried and failed again and again.

"What have we here?"

Ever froze, trying to see who was behind him. The man made it easy, taking a step to his side so he could place the barrel of his gun directly against Ever's temple. He wore a dirty black t-shirt and baggy ripped jeans. He had three teardrops beneath his left eye. He smelled sour.

"I'm guessing you're with them?" he asked.

Ever couldn't speak. He vaguely noted the bolt cutters in his hand falling to the ground and the racket they made when they bounced off the metal side to land at his feet.

"Yeah," Ever said, his mouth a desert.

"Good, then you can come with me and maybe I'll make it out of this alive." He gave a gruff laugh. "Probably can't say the same for you."

Ever couldn't move. He wanted to, but he was frozen in place, aware of nothing but the barrel of the gun cold against his sweaty temple. Arsen was going to be so mad at him.

"I—"

"Ever!"

Arsen. The man swung his gun in Arsen's direction, clearly intent on firing. Ever cried out, then grabbed for the man's arm. But it was too late. His head just…exploded. Not really, but that was what it felt like. Bits of blood and bone hit Ever's face as the man beside him dropped. He stood there, trembling so hard his teeth were clacking together.

"Ever? Ever? Can you hear me?"

Ever could hear him, but it was hard over the ringing in his ears. "There's a baby in there," he whispered.

"What?" Arsen said, gripping his shoulders and turning him around. "Are you hurt? Did he hurt you? This isn't your blood, is it?"

"There's a baby in there," he said again, this time more frantically, trying to shake Arsen off him to grab the bolt cutters. When Arsen fought him, he made a growling sound, wrenching himself from his grasp.

He tried to pick them up, but his hands wouldn't cooperate. It was like his brain was giving the wrong signals. He gave up on the bolt cutters and just started clawing and pulling at the lock until Arsen was physically dragging him away.

He fought with everything he had, but he was no match for Arsen. But Arsen wasn't alone. Jericho was there. And Seven. Jericho grabbed the bolt cutters, cutting through the lock in one clean motion.

They moved out of the way, swinging the doors wide but staying behind them in case there was another threat within. When nothing happened, Arsen peeked around the door, gun raised. He dropped it almost immediately.

Ever ducked under his arm, stopping short. There weren't just two women but four, all filthy and in various states of undress. They were young, some maybe even younger than Ever. One was breastfeeding a baby that looked to be no more than a few months old. The one he'd heard crying.

Jericho held up his hands, holstering his weapon, as they all cowered against the back, shielding the children behind them. Once more, Ever tried not to cry. They were protecting them even if it killed them. Seven was still scanning the perimeter, gun at the ready.

"You can come out now," Arsen said.

"They don't speak English," Ever said.

"I do."

A tiny little body wiggled between the women's legs, dodging them as they tried to grab him. He was small. Like a toddler. He was filthy, but he seemed surprisingly chipper given the circumstances.

"You do?" Jericho asked. "Is one of those ladies your mommy?"

He shook his head. "No mommy. Brother." He pointed to a small boy with brown hair and brown eyes cowering in the back, eerily quiet. "We stay with Ms. Tracy, but she gave us to bad men for the med-cine."

Jericho flinched, but then hid it behind a smile. "Oh. Well, you don't have to go back to Ms. Tracy," Jericho assured him, gathering him into his arms. "How old are you?"

The little boy held up four fingers.

"You're four? You talk like a grown up," Jericho gushed.

The women moved forward, one of them picking up

the boy at the back. As Arsen helped each of them out of the container, they looked around, blinking like they were standing in the noonday sun and not the early morning. How long had they been in there?

The woman handed the frail boy to Arsen and said something none of them understood. Jericho attempted to speak to her in Cantonese, but she frowned at him in confusion.

"Shit," Jericho muttered.

The others made their way across the lawn—all but Lake and Nico. Atticus reached into his backpack and pulled out more granola bars and water. The boy in Jericho's arms snatched it, took a big bite, but then immediately broke it in half for the little boy in Arsen's arms. "Brother's hungry," he said.

"We gotta get them out of here," Seven said. "I know the exchange wasn't until this afternoon, but I don't want to wait around to see if a bunch of Sons of Anarchy wannabes are punctual. What do we do with them?"

"My father has a friend in social services," Atticus said. "She's going to meet us at the rest stop just before Bennington. We'll give them over there. She'll make sure to keep our names out of it."

"This is yucky," the little boy said even as he took another bite.

They must be so hungry.

Jericho laughed. "I think so, too. How about we stop and get you something to eat on the way?"

"Jericho…" Atticus said his name like a warning.

"Come on, Freckles. They're hungry. A trip to McDonald's in BFE nowhere isn't going to mess with the plan."

"Yeah, okay," Atticus said, giving in easily.

Arsen handed him the toddler in his arms. "Here you go. Good luck. The rest of us are heading home."

"Lake is heading to a private clinic," Atticus said. "I'll drop you a pin. He's gonna be there for a while. That wound is bad."

Arsen gave a single nod.

Ever wanted to protest, but Arsen was already dragging him away. He looked back over at the women, who were following Jericho and Atticus at a slower pace than Arsen's hurried one.

"Why are you dragging me?" Arsen didn't answer, just kept tugging, leaving Ever no choice but to let him. "Hello? Why aren't you talking to me?"

Arsen turned on him abruptly, causing Ever to come up short or plow directly into his chest. Arsen gripped his shoulders hard. "You could have died. You could have fucking died. That man had a gun to your head. What were you thinking?"

"I-I heard a baby crying," Ever said quietly.

Arsen's face crumpled, and he dragged him into his arms. "You... If anything had happened to you, I would be ruined. Do you hear me? I will never get over it."

Ever's tears soaked Arsen's shirt. "I had to do something. They were crying so hard. I thought maybe it was alone."

"Your soft heart could have gotten you killed," Arsen said against his ear.

"I just wanted to save somebody," Ever said.

"You did," Arsen shot back, voice raw. "You saved *me*. You saved me the day I found you, and if I lose you, I will never be okay. I know you have a big heart, and you want to help the world, but please, let me be selfish with you. I can't stand the thought…" He trailed off. "Please, *besenok*. Can I just be selfish with you? I will give you your happily ever after. I promise. Can you just let me do that? Can you just let me love you and keep you safe?"

Ever could barely speak past the lump in his throat. His happily ever after.

"Yeah," he whispered against Arsen's shoulder. "You can do that."

"Thank you," Arsen breathed against his cheek, like he'd granted him some gift.

"Can we go to the bookstore?" Ever asked suddenly.

Arsen pulled back. "What?"

"I—" Ever blushed. "All my books got rained on in the fire."

"I was professing my undying love and devotion and you're thinking about books?" Arsen asked, sounding more amused than angry.

"You said happily ever after, which made me think of books, which made me remember my books are all damaged. You said you'd give me my happy ending. My happy ending has books."

Arsen laughed. "Okay, *besenok*. Once we get home and get some sleep, I'll take you to get books."

"And to the diner?" Ever asked, giving him big eyes.

"Your happily ever after includes diner food as well?"

Ever nodded. "And dessert."

"Are you trying to take advantage of me in my weakened emotional state?"

Ever grinned. "Is it working…Senya?"

"You really are a little demon. Yes, it's working. Let's go home."

Home. Ever had a home. Well, he would have a home with Arsen, wherever they ended up. Hopefully back in the apartment over the garage, but if not, somewhere else. Arsen was his home. Arsen was his happily ever after.

EPILOGUE

ARSEN

ARSEN ENTERED THE APARTMENT JUST as Ever's malicious cackle cut through the space. He smiled. His *besenok* was wreaking havoc online, no doubt. He glanced at the clock on the wall, a fancy piece with little mirrors in the shape of a star that Ever insisted they buy the last time they were at Walmart. That and an ugly daisy mat that kept you from slipping in the shower. Arsen had argued that the small space was what kept him from slipping, but Ever had looked him dead in the eye and placed it in the cart.

Arsen lost every fight and he couldn't be happier about it. Between the money they made streaming and his paycheck from the shop, he could afford to keep Ever in books and ugly daisy mats for life. And he intended to do just that.

He had a good thirty minutes before Ever's stream ended, so he headed to the bathroom to wash off the dust and grime of the day. Once he stripped down, he stepped under the scalding hot water, letting himself enjoy the way it beat against his muscles before grabbing the heavy soap he used to scrub the oil from his skin.

He took extra care this time. Once Ever's stream ended, they could go have dinner. It was their only free night this week. Ever had remedial math classes on Monday, Wednesday, and Friday, and he worked at the bookstore on Tuesday, Thursday, and Saturday. Arsen had hoped to have Sunday together, but Jericho had sweet-talked Ever into watching the boys for them so he and Atticus could have a date night.

Arsen grabbed the coconut-scented shampoo then scrubbed his hair. He still couldn't believe Jericho and Atticus had taken the boys from the container. Jericho had been heartbroken when they'd made the handoff to the social worker and the little boy had screamed and sobbed for him until he'd thrown up. After two days, the social worker had called and said the boy was barely eating and wouldn't speak at all.

Atticus hated seeing Jericho so upset and had agreed to take the boys on a temporary basis until they could find a permanent home for them. But that idea only lasted roughly three days before Atticus was eating his words.

Maybe psychopaths really were narcissists because the boy from the cargo container—the older one—once he was cleaned up, they found he had red hair and freckles just like Atticus. And, almost by magic, Atticus seemed to forget he hated kids.

The adoption was quick and quiet, and they waited a few months before announcing to the world that they had adopted not one but two toddlers: Jett and Jagger. That was what they'd named them. Well, renamed them. At four and three years old, they were already a handful, and Jericho couldn't get enough of their chaos.

Neither could Ever. He was obsessed with them. It made sense. They liked all the same things. Bubbles. Coloring. Games. Candy. Books. So many books. Whenever they were together, it was hard to say who was having a better time—Ever or the kids. Jericho was grateful to Ever for always making time for them, but Ever didn't think of it as work. To him, they were family.

It made Arsen think about the future, about someday having kids of their own. Eventually. Ever had plans. He wanted to get his GED so he could go to college and become a social worker. Arsen worried it would just break his heart, but he was determined, and when Ever was determined, there was no stopping him. Arsen had learned that the hard way.

He was so lost in his thoughts that he never heard the bathroom door open and close—just felt the shower curtain shift a split second before Ever slid in behind him. Arsen smiled as hands came around his waist, Ever's lips pressing between his shoulder blades in an open-mouthed kiss.

"Hi," Arsen said, rubbing his hands over Ever's.

Ever's teeth sank into his shoulder blade, then he licked over the marks. "Hi."

Arsen frowned. "Are you done streaming already?"

"Mm," Ever said, sliding his hands down to trace Arsen's hip bones, then his belly.

"Did you win?" he asked with a smile.

Ever scoffed. "I never win. I'm terrible. That's why people

tune in. They like watching me die."

Arsen shuffled his feet until he was facing Ever in the tight space. "Now, that's not true. They just like how cute you are when you're running and screaming."

"How is that any better?" Ever asked, sounding only half interested in the conversation.

"Well—" Arsen started, but then Ever's tongue teased over one hard nipple, his fingers toying with the other. "What are you doing, *besenok*?"

"What does it look like?" he asked, dropping a hand to stroke Arsen's semi-hard cock, making a happy noise as he hardened under his attention.

Arsen worked himself into Ever's loose fist. "It looks like you're trying to seduce me. I thought you wanted to go out to dinner."

"We live in the city. There's always someplace open," he assured him.

Ever wasn't wrong, but there was only one place expecting them at a specific time. But Ever didn't know that. He opened his mouth to find a gentle way to say they could do this later, but then Ever went for his other nipple. It was his weakness and Ever knew it, especially with the tight squeeze of his hand stroking him.

"I know, but you never let me take you anywhere nice," Arsen reminded him.

Ever's steely gaze found his. "Are you saying you don't want me to jerk you off in the shower?" he asked, disgruntled.

Shit. Ever had ended the live thirty minutes early. They had time. "If you ever hear me say no to you giving me any kind of sexual favor, take me to a hospital because I'm clearly unwell," he teased.

Ever gave him his puppy eyes and pooched lip. "That's better."

Arsen groaned, pushing Ever back against the tile, tilting his head up so he could kiss him like he wanted, tongue thrusting between his lips, hoping it was enough of an apology.

For a few moments, they contented themselves with kissing, hands sliding over wet, soapy skin. But soon, Ever was whining into his mouth, rubbing himself against Arsen, trying to get some much-needed friction.

Arsen's hands slid around Ever's ass without breaking the kiss, lifting him up. Ever's arms and legs went around him, and he moaned as their cocks aligned and Arsen thrust against him. "This seems dangerous," Ever whispered into his mouth.

Arsen grinned, then licked the water from Ever's chin and jaw. "I thought you liked danger. You said it made you all tingly."

Ever snorted. "I like zip-lining and when they let me hold that baby tiger at the zoo," Ever said, breath catching as Arsen picked up the pace. "Breaking my neck because we were rubbing off on each other in the shower is just embarrassing."

Arsen wheezed out a laugh, even though his muscles were burning. Despite the casual conversation, Arsen was already hurtling towards his orgasm every time their hips met. "Don't worry, we have your ugly grippy mat."

Ever looked down at the shower floor, smirking at the daisy mat beneath their feet. "And you said ten dollars was too much for it."

"Mm," he said. "I did. I told you you're smarter than me. I lack your vision."

After that, they fell silent, just enjoying the feel of each other, the taste of each other, the slick slide of their bodies moving together. But soon, Ever was restless, making frantic little noises against Arsen's lips.

"Faster. Fuck. I'm already so close. I've been wanting you all day," Ever said, burying his face against Arsen's neck.

That was news to Arsen. If he'd known that he would have taken an extended lunch break. He braced Ever's back against the wall, sliding a hand down to slip between his cheeks, rubbing a finger over his hole. Ever moaned long and low. "Yeah, that's perfect. Fuck. Fuck. Fuck."

Even now, he only swore during sex. And it was still so hot.

Ever reached between them, taking both their cocks in his hand and stroking them with purpose. Fuck. He knew just how to touch him. He always knew just what Arsen needed. "I'm gonna come."

"Do it," Ever said breathlessly, eyes locked on his hand as it worked them both.

Arsen groaned, his release spilling over Ever's fist. He continued to work them both until Arsen was wincing. Just when it got to be too much, Ever cried out, his cum mixing with Arsen's as he shuddered.

After a moment, Arsen gently set Ever on his feet, then

moved him to the front of the shower, quickly washing his hair and body. The water was barely lukewarm, which meant they had maybe three minutes before it was an ice bath. They finished just in time.

Arsen wrapped Ever in a towel and then himself. He sat Ever on the counter while he blow dried his hair, then let Ever dry his. This was their sacred routine. Every night, they showered then brushed their teeth and did their skin care. It was silly, but it was something they'd done every night since Ever had held his hair back for him to wash his face.

Dr. Jones said having a routine was important, and it seemed to keep Ever's nightmares and panic attacks to a minimum. He only had therapy once a month now unless something triggered him, but he seemed past the worst of it.

Arsen still had the occasional nightmare about his father. He was almost positive they would never go away entirely, though some small part of him hoped perhaps his father's inevitable death might take his bad dreams with him.

But probably not.

"Where do you want to go, *besenok*?" Arsen asked, already knowing the answer.

Ever fixed him with a look that told him they both knew the answer. "You know where I want to go," Ever replied, pulling a sweater over his head.

Arsen laughed. "Again?"

Ever flounced onto the bed to put his socks on. "I love it there."

"Oh, I know," Arsen teased. "It has your two favorite things. Food and books."

"Please? Please?" Ever said, clasping his hands together.

Arsen rolled his eyes. "Do I ever say no to you?"

Ever grinned. "Nope."

Arsen checked the time once more before they headed out the door, keys in hand. They were right on time and Ever seemed none the wiser. Arsen fought the urge to gloat. Noah had said he'd figure it out immediately. But Arsen knew Ever never cared about his own needs.

Out on the street, they walked a short distance to where Arsen's car was parked. Two girls leaned against the wall outside of a dive bar blaring hard rock loud enough to hear it behind the closed door.

"Hey, Arsen," one girl cooed.

"No," Ever said to the girl, leveling a hard stare at her until she looked away, rolling her eyes like she wasn't terrified of him.

Arsen laughed. Ever was relentless. Even knowing Arsen had no interest in women didn't stop him from terrorizing any girl who so much as looked his way.

"You're such a monster," Arsen teased as they reached the car.

His car. Arsen's baby. His '69 dusk blue Chevy Impala. The car he'd dreamed about since the moment he laid eyes on it.

"How am I the monster? They're the ones who try to hit on you when I'm standing right there. I just remind them you're taken. I only use force when necessary."

He opened Ever's door, letting him slip inside before jogging around to the driver's side. It had taken months to restore. Jericho had gifted it to him for his birthday. Well, what was left of it. It had been in terrible shape, barely more than the frame. But Jericho had also agreed to buy whatever parts Arsen had needed and had spent weekends helping him restore it.

He turned over the engine, smiling as it roared to life and purred. He patted the steering wheel.

"I swear you love this car more than me," Ever said.

Arsen caught Ever's gaze, his face lit by the street light above shining through the windshield. "I don't love anything more than you," Arsen said without hesitation, taking Ever's hand and kissing it.

Ever melted, giving him a sappy look. "You can't just say that stuff."

"Sure, I can."

They drove hand in hand in comfortable silence for the short drive to the restaurant, Ever's leg bouncing faster the closer they got. He really did love the place. Noah had discovered it after he and Adam had been invited to the opening, and Ever had practically swooned the first time he'd taken him.

They rolled up to a brick building with black awning and wooden double doors.

The valet jogged up to them, opening Arsen's door. "Hey, Arsen."

They were there a lot.

Arsen tossed him the keys. "Hey, Jared."

Jared winked at him and something unknotted in Arsen. Everything was still going to plan. He took Ever's hand, opening the door to a warm room with soft amber lighting. Book Bar wasn't just a bar but a restaurant and bookstore of sorts. The walls were dotted with nooks filled to the brim with books of all kinds. First editions, trade paperbacks, trashy dime store books from seventy years ago. Each booth or table sat in an alcove surrounded by books.

"Ever. Arsen."

They turned to find the owner, Joe, rushing towards them. It was a family-owned business and they doted on Ever like he was actually a member of their family. Ever likely expected him to lead them to his favorite booth in the back, but, instead, he kept going through the restaurant to the atrium, a glass-encased room filled with books and greenery and dozens of tables.

For the first time, Ever looked confused. "Why are we out here?"

"Just for a change of pace?" Arsen hedged, toying with a menu they didn't need.

Ever's legs slotted with his under the table. "You're being weird. Why are you being weird? You're not gonna propose are you? If you propose to me and I'm wearing this ugly sweater in pictures, I will never forgive you."

Arsen smiled. "I'm not proposing." *Yet.* Arsen would propose there one day. Not now, because Ever had a plan. And they were still so young. But someday, after Ever graduated, he would bring him here and get down on one knee and finally make good on his promise to give him his last name.

Ever seemed temporarily appeased. "What are you

thinking about?" Ever asked, taking his hand.

"You."

"What about me?"

"Just wondering if you're ever going to remember your own birthday?"

Ever stopped short. "What?"

Arsen laughed. "Today's your birthday, remember? You picked it."

Ever stopped short, then grabbed his cell phone, looking at the date. "Oh. Yeah, I guess it is."

Before Arsen could say anything else, the doors burst open, their friends and family pouring in, shouting, "Happy birthday!"

Ever's mouth fell open. "What's this?"

Felix and Zane both kissed a cheek, Felix saying, "It's your birthday party, gumdrop."

"Oh…"

"Yeah, oh." Zane laughed.

Ever watched, mouth slack, as the staff brought out tray after tray of food, setting it all up on banquet tables. Gifts were piled on a separate table.

"Hungry, *besenok*?" Arsen asked.

Ever nodded, still looking at their friends, who were laughing and chatting, waiting their turn to wish him a happy birthday. Everyone was there. All his friends—their friends—had come to show Ever he was loved.

Arsen felt a little guilty when he saw Ever's overwhelmed expression. Still, he got up to make him a plate, watching as Ever finally stood and walked to where Levi and Nico stood off to the side. Arsen smiled. Of course, he went straight to them. They were his emotional support humans. Arsen didn't know when they'd stopped being his friends and started being Ever's friends, but he wasn't mad about it.

They spent the next few hours eating and laughing. Joe had not only made Ever a huge cake but had also set up a candy buffet with all of his favorite treats. Ever opened gift after gift, his face a mixture of happiness and maybe a little confusion. It wasn't that he wasn't used to this kind of attention, but it was his very first birthday.

As the night wore down, Ever found him, slipping his arms around him and putting his head on his chest. "Whatcha thinking?" he asked.

Arsen smiled, tightening his arms around him. "Just wondering how you're enjoying your happily ever after, I guess."

"You give me a million happily ever afters every day, including this one."

Arsen's chest tightened. "Yeah?"

"Yep," Ever said. "But you're my favorite one."

DEAR READER,

THANK YOU SO MUCH for reading *Paladin*, Book 1 in Jericho's Boys, my Necessary Evils spin-off series. I hope you loved reading this book as much as I loved writing it. Look for book two in the series, *Rogue*, coming soon, as well as *The Bone Collector*, Book 1 in my other Necessary Evils spin-off series, The Watch.

If you've read my books before, you know I worked as a psych RN for many years and often refer to some of the horrors I saw there. *Paladin* was no exception but, this time, the mental health crisis wasn't just Ever's but my own. As Ever slogged his way through therapy, I was as well, doing my best to get through my own past trauma. Neither Ever nor I have quite gotten there yet, but we're trying. Maybe that's why it's my longest romance to date at just under 90,000 words. While all my books are personal to me, this one might be the most personal, so I hope you enjoy it and maybe can relate just a little.

The situations depicted in *Paladin* are fictional, but anybody living in the US right now knows human trafficking is a real and growing problem in this country, so I will continue to talk about it.

As always, thank you so much for loving my boys and my books. I'm blown away by your support and super grateful you were willing to go along for this ride with me.

If you guys are really loving the books, please consider joining my Facebook reader group, **ONLEY'S OUBLIETTE**, and signing up for my newsletter on my website so you can stay up to date on freebies, release dates, teasers, and more. You can also always hit me up on my social media and find all my links at **FANS.LINK/ONLEYJAMES**. You can find me literally everywhere so say hi. I love talking to readers.

Finally, if you did love this book, (or even if you didn't. Eek!) it would be amazing if you could take a minute to review it. Reviews are like gold for authors.

Thank you again for reading.

ABOUT THE AUTHOR

ONLEY JAMES lives in North Carolina with her daughter, her daughter-in-law, son-in-law, and a menagerie of animals, both good and evil. James splits her time between writing m/m romance and mainlining dangerous levels of caffeine and attempting to maintain her ever-slipping sanity.

When not at her desk, you can find her whining about how much writing she has to do while avoiding said writing by binge-watching unhealthy amounts of television and doom scrolling on social media. She loves true crime documentaries, anti-heroes, and writing kinky, snarky books about morally gray men who fall in love with other men.

Find her online at:
WWW.ONLEYJAMES.COM